Warren Chase

The Life-Line of the Lone One

Or, Autobiography of the World's Child

Warren Chase

The Life-Line of the Lone One
Or, Autobiography of the World's Child

ISBN/EAN: 9783337119843

Printed in Europe, USA, Canada, Australia, Japan

Cover: Foto ©Raphael Reischuk / pixelio.de

More available books at **www.hansebooks.com**

Love One

THE

LIFE-LINE OF THE LONE ONE;

OR,

AUTOBIOGRAPHY

OF

THE WORLD'S CHILD.

BY THE AUTHOR.

"Honor and shame from no condition rise ;
Act well your part ; there all the honor lies."

THIRD EDITION.

BOSTON:
PUBLISHED BY BELA MARSH, 14 BROMFIELD ST.
NEW YORK: S. T. MUNSON.
1861.

PREFACE.

This little volume — a true and literal history of the struggles of an ardent and ambitious mind to rise from a dishonorable birth, and the lowest condition of poverty and New England slavery — is published more for a guide and advice to those who live in the humble walks of life, and for a rebuke on the tyrannical and malignant spirit of arrogant and selfish individuals and societies, who ever attempt to trample upon and despise such reformers as attempt to rise, by individual effort, to distinction or fame, than for the book market, or for the pecuniary reward it may bring the author. The name is only left in obscurity to those who are unacquainted with the subject of the narrative; and to such it is of no value. The subject of the narrative has passed to a plane of reconciliation and harmony, in which he feels only a spirit of forgiveness for those whose consciences have already punished them for their physical abuse, or moral and religious misrepresentations, slanders, and falsehoods, or their political curses. In every relation and condition of life he is now beyond their shafts, and hence is in a condition to forgive. As the persecuted Jesus, when the malignity of his enemies had done its worst, and he was about to triumph in the personal demonstration of his own theory, could afford to forgive Peter and Judas, and say of those who took his life, " Father, forgive them: for they know not

what they do;" so the Lone One has often exclaimed of
those who attempted to crucify his reputation, and
destroy his efforts to make others happy, "They are
forgiven: for they know not what they do."

"Speak gently to the erring one,
   For, O! ye may not know
The untold weight of suffering
   That bows his spirit low.

"A kind and gentle word, perchance,
   May call all back to him, —
The pleasant dreams of early youth,
   Ere the light of life was dim.

"Harsh words may be the only ones
   His ear hath ever heard ;
Then like an angel's loving voice
   Will sound your gentle word.

"In joyous hours, with friends around,
   Rich with the love they give,
You hear of wicked deeds, and say,
   He is not fit to live.

"But only think, if yours had been,
   Like his, a cheerless life,
Your soul, perchance, might then have been,
   Like his, as full of strife.

"There's seldom found a heart so hard
   But love may enter in ;
And love hath ever magic power
   To chase away all sin.

"Then spare not gentle words, that bring
   The erring unto God,
To learn that life is beautiful,
   When spent in doing good."

LIFE-LINE OF THE LONE ONE.

CHAPTER I.

FIRST DECADE OF THE LONE ONE.

The Unwelcome Birth. — The Unhappy Childhood. — The Untimely Deaths. - The Uncharitable Bondage. — The Unmerciful Treatment.

SECTION I.

THE IMPERFECT LINEAGE.

NOT long after the Pilgrim Fathers made their homes on the rocky and bleak coast of Massachusetts, a vessel from the European side of the ocean landed, among her passengers, from the "sea-girt isle," three brothers, who brought to this country the name which has since gained many a niche in the records of our country's local and general history, and which may now be seen permanently or temporarily posted in many business villages of the nation, but which I shall dispense with, as too common for my narrative. The history of these three brothers, and of several generations of their descendants, is robed in a mantle of obscurity, and cannot now be easily unwrapped and spread before their descendants, even by those who seek through it a fortune of dollars. Most that is well known is, that they had Abraham's blessing, to increase and multiply. It is deeply to be regretted that there are not more and better words on the hard old granite and marble tomb-stones of New England, bearing to us more of the history of the each one each bears the name of. But our Christian style of epitaphing brings us little knowledge, except the name of the person whose body lies under the stone. Had the sextons placed over the graves permanent records of the three great events which constitute the important part of many lives, — birth, marriage, and death, — it would often aid the searcher after lineage, when the human posts with memory-marks had all been swept away by the merciless besom of time. Our generation has a better chance of leaving individual records on the blank pages in the grave-yard of Jewish history furnished us by the Bible societies ; which records may be of more value to coming generations than the printed pages, when the march of science has carried away the idolatry and superstition of this age, and the centuries have removed the tall steeples and stingy creeds of the nineteenth Christian century.

But we must still grope among the tomb-records, to renew the search after the lineage of the Lone One. We find the records of both grave-yards very imperfect, from which we can only glean sufficient to make out the following : In the third, fourth, or fifth generation of these three brothers, among the descendants of the one of them who bore the singular cognomen of Aquila, was a family of eight children — four sons and four daughters. The younger of the four sons joined a small group of hardy pioneers, who had procured a title to a piece of God's earth (from some regular descendant of the original owner, as is supposed by the land reformers, who assert that God never gave any "fee simple" title-deeds, but only heirships), then far up in the wild regions of New Hampshire, on a small stream now called Suncook. Near the middle of the eighteenth century this little group began to fell the tall old pines and sorry-looking hemlocks, and let down the sunlight and dews upon the soil and rocks (mostly rocks) of this little spot of their heavenly Father's earth ; or rather on their own spot, for they had bought a few acres of surface running inward to a point at the centre of the globe, but not outward, for the atmosphere and sunlight were still owned by the Father, and free for the use of all his children. They arranged the trees across the rattling Suncook, and, the river being dammed and heaped up, its waters, in their wrath, plunged, foaming in madness, over the obstacle, such as no red man had ever placed in their way; or, forced through the narrow aperture, for many years turned a clattering old mill-wheel, to make boards for the settlers; or, twirling the circular and poised rock, cracked the corn for the lesser grinders of the bipeds. Long ago the mill was "torn away, and a factory dark and high looms like a tower" beside the stream. How changed the place in a century! And what is a century in the midst of eternal time? Not even as a drop in the ocean. **The** red man and his fur-clad quadruped companions are gone [where?]; and civilized man, with his domesticated animals and labor-saving **machinery,** his cottage homes, his noisy shops, and busy stores, has **taken** their **place,** and driven them, not *to,* but *beyond,* the wall. Wonder often seized the red man, as he watched his white Cain-like brothers fell the trees, remove the rocks, till the soil, build warmer wigwams, and plant more " **heap of** corn ; " but he passed in wonder away, stupefied in soul, and poisoned in **body, by the** rum and tobacco of God's whiter Christian children. Now the spires **of** the Puritan's descendants point upward in place of the red man's forest spires, from which, two centuries ago, the prayers and praises of man and beast were sounded to the sky in simple strains of nature's music, as acceptable to God as the best harmonies of our time. **Now** the slender fingers of the factory-girl guide the cotton thread, through whirling machinery, into webs of sheeting, to wrap the more tender forms of the white mother's babes of **a** Christian **land ; but it** is not certain that these babes or mothers **live purer lives,** or give more pure devotion to God, than did the fur-clad mothers and naked babes of the forest-homes ; and certain it is that the belief in **a** future life entertained by the red man of the forest was far more natural, more rational, more honorable to God, and more desirable to man, than that of the Christian which has supplanted it.

Soon after a shanty was prepared by this descendant of Aquila wide enough for two, the loved one, selected from the daughters of a neighboring settlement, came to share its hardships with the occupant. Not a score of moons had been reported, new or old, ere the pair had to make room for a third, a darling boy, whose origin was between them; the first white face of male child born in the settlement, and of course it would have a place and name. Simon (not Simon Peter) was the cognomen by which this shanty boy was designated from his fellows. When peopling the settlement by births was fairly begun, it was not carried on slowly in the several homes, but especially in this one. The family record was soon filled up; for Simon's name was followed by eleven more, marking, as milestones, the line **of** domestic life, nearly in biennial periods. Seven received female names, rights, and duties, and five male names, rights, and duties. The eldest, born when the trials and hardships of life were most severe, was of course the brightest and smartest, although the parents were less developed and matured than at the birth of Joseph (for they had **a J**oseph). Two of the dozen went early and young to reside on the other side of Jordan, **" to join a** choir of juvenile singers in the land of spirits." Four more have since followed them, at various times, and six were still lingering here in the autumn of 1855, timeworn humanity-marks of the last century, and of **the** generation which has been mainly transplanted into the other life. The old pioneer parents, too, whose hold on life enabled them to stay almost a century on earth, and live more than half a century in wedded life, have joined those, who, according to the new theory of spirit-spheres, are living in **families and** societies of harmonious and congenial *life* in the land of the *dead*. 'T is a beautiful thought, whether true or not, for the lone pilgrim here, that, at the end of life's journey, he or she shall lay the **" staff** and sandals down " **for the** wreath and robe of a brighter and happier home, and join there, in happy life, the " loved ones gone before."

We have now done nearly all we can to register the genealogy of the Lone One, and will here leave the ancestors, all except the first-born of the sons of the new settlement. Of him we have more to say, for, in matured life, he became the father of the Lone One by a mother fully ripened into womanhood; the last child of each, and the only child of the twain. This Simon-son, of the Pittsfield town, has now no tomb-stone monument to mark where his body lies, and no epitaph inscribed to record his religious belief, or pious character; but only the memory-marks made, during his life, on those around him which have not faded. His parents, and brothers, and sisters, all accorded to him the qualification of *good* and *smart;* but his early life had not the advantage of schools, and books, and sermons, and lectures, as the youth of our time have. Hard work by day-light, and rude plays by fire-light, occupied his youth, and the former did not cease when manhood came. Those still living who knew him say he was physically and mentally more than a common man, and morally not less, but religiously at zero. Many of his trite sayings, and some of his doings, still linger around the memories of those who knew him half a century ago.

Such were the father and the paternal lineage of the Lone One, which, with one more brief notice in its proper place, must be left to the fast-fading shadows of memory; for lineal descents are difficult to trace, and not very reliable when written. When forty years had worn away upon the records, these were nearly all the links the Lone One could find in the chain to connect him, through his sire, with the Puritan Fathers. The great fortune said to be waiting some heir in name and line had never arrested his attention, for he was not registered in the records of lineal descent, but dwelt alone, and away from all kindred of name and descent from Aquila. It is doubtful whether, if he had died before this record was published, or before the days of modern spiritualism, he could have received a Christian burial, with head to the west, to meet at the resurrection of the bodies, the Saviour, who is to come from the east, when the trump of the angel shall call up the dead and decayed forms from the earth. But he has already outlived most of the follies, superstitions, and prejudices, of the Christians, and expects at death to find a home with the *spirits*, if not with the Christians, of the other world, and not so cold and unwelcome a reception as he found in this world.

Section II.

THE MOTHER AND CHILD.

" Silently, strangely, the darkness
  Has fallen upon thy way,
And the hands of no earthly morning
  For thee shall open the day.

" And yet in a world of sunshine
  Thou *seemest* to dwell **the** while ;
For the light of thy soul looks on us
  In the light of thy beautiful smile.

" And much for that one **affliction**
  Shall this recompense **atone**—
On the path of thine earthly journey
  Thou shalt not walk alone.

" For when human love shall leave thee,
  Thy wanderings almost done,
Then the hands of invisible angels
  Shall softly lead thee on.

" And their arms shall be round about thee,
  Till thy feet through that gate have trod
Standing dark at the end of the pathway
  Which leads **from the world to** God.

" And then what an over-payment
  For the night of thy mortal ills,
Shall come with the light of that morning
  That breaks o'er eternity's hills ! "

ON the fifth day of the first month of the eighteen **hundred**
and thirteen, at the opening of the morning light upon the snow-clad
hills and vales of New England, a poor, lonely, and sorry mother,
with a newly-born **and** unwelcome babe, might have been seen in
an old, shattered, and oft-deserted house, through which the winter
winds and New England snow-storms played almost unobstructed ;
a house long since gone to " dust **and ashes**," leaving only the
hole in the ground to mark the spot where its frame once protect-

ed, as well as society then did, the entrance of the Lone One on his earthly pilgrimage. Few marks of a modern New England home were to be seen there, except the bright eye of the sorry mother, and the quiet face of the babe, sleeping in innocence and ignorance both of its "totally depraved nature" and totally deprived condition (especially of the comforts of life). The mother's eye grew dim and weak as it dropped its tears fresh-wrung, from the heart, while she pondered on the fate of herself and child. What would become of them she knew not. Her hands, so used to toil for her support, were now confined to a new task, to which maternal love alone called her, and which returned a reward only in the satisfaction to her heart, but which would neither feed nor clothe herself and babe. A few — only a few — persons were willing to be known as the friends of this poor mother and babe; but probably as many as were willing to be seen and known to be friends of the mother and child in a stable in Bethlehem, once on a time. The few did call to see the mother and child, but they were mostly from that class of persons whose entire wealth is in charity, sympathy, and love, and who, however much disposed, were unable to relieve the wants of the sufferers. Death would indeed have been a welcome visitor then and there, if willing to take both to his home ; and far more welcome to the child, could he have seen the path of life before him. Thus dark and gloomy, and sad, hopeless, and loveless, uncalled for, a curse, not a blessing, was the earthly dawning of the Lone One's life. Well might that saddened mother say, with a sweet sister of song, on a bank of the Ohio,*

> " For me, in all life's desert sand,
>   No well is made, no tent is spread ;
> No father's nor a brother's hand
>   Is laid with blessing on my head.
>
> "The radiance of my mortal star
>   Is crossed with signs of woe to me,
> And all my thoughts and wishes are
>   Sad wanderers toward eternity.

* Alice Cary.

> " Stricken, riven, helplessly apart
>   From all that blessed the path I trod,
>   O, tempt me, tempt me not, my heart,
>   To arraign the goodness of my God !
>
> " For suffering hath been made sublime,
>   And souls that lived and died alone
>   Have left an echo for all time,
>   As they went wailing to the throne.
>
> " There have been moments when I dared
>   Believe life's mystery a breath,
>   And deem Faith's beauteous bosom bared
>   To the betraying arms of Death.
>
> " For the immortal life but mocks
>   The soul that feels its ruin dire,
>   And like a tortured demon rocks
>   Upon the cradling waves of fire.
>
> " To mine is pressed no loving lip,
>   Around me twines no helping arm;
>   And, like a frail dismasted ship,
>   I blindly drift before the storm.''

This was the mother and child. Nobody owned the mother, for no priest had bade her obey and serve any man; and hence no one man was bound to feed and clothe her. She owned herself and child; and we never heard that she attributed its origin to a spirit, or to spirits, or spiritual influence of any kind, although she was a Christian woman. Whether she repented the hasty and imprudent bestowal of her love on that Simon-son of Nathaniel, from an overflowing heart, we cannot say; but that she deeply deplored her sad fate is but too well known, however much she may now rejoice over its results. Few had pity for her. Some had scorn; more had contempt; but the angels smiled on her; and when the heart of man cast her out, the heart of God took her in. But Simon, O, Simon! where art thou ? What screen can hide thee from her suffering ?

When the nation's second war with England sent its notes echoing among the granite hills of New Hampshire, it called to the field and the ocean many brave hearts from among her hardy sons. Among them was Simon, the son of Nathaniel, who speedily released himself from home and relatives, and sought associates in the camp, with the frontier army, on the Canada side of New England. His restless soul and troubled mind sought and found food and interest in the army for a brief period, until the terrible battle of Plattsburgh, after which the army record contained, among the names of the wounded and died, this same Simon, thus shortening the journey of life, and abruptly terminating the path to fame and glory, by a precipice and a plunge in oblivion's stream. Here ends all the Lone One could glean in 1855 of a father's history. In his ripened years, he was never much inclined to search among the tombs for relics, while living subjects of more interest were ever around him. At this infancy period of life, which we have now introduced, dark clouds with heavy storms hung lowering over his horizon; and this burst and crash in a father's death was distant and faint, compared with many others that follow; but fate would have its fixed course. In riper years, he often wondered why God (if there were a God) had sent him here without consulting his choice to come and be thus born, and also whether he could be accountable for involuntary life and actions resulting therefrom; but none could answer or tell why God had done thus, by special or by general laws. Some power had certainly, without consulting the will of either, sent the child into earthly consciousness and the father out. The eager, ardent, restless spirit of the father (but not a spirit of wrangling) had been transmitted to the child, to mark him, in the babe, the boy, and the man, through life. Here our history leaves the father for the more minute detail of life and character by the numerous relatives, while we follow the Life-Line of the mother and boy. The babe would not die, although many wished it would, to relieve the mother from a burthen, and them from deeds of charity they felt so unable to perform. It lived and grew, and the mother loved it, perhaps the more, for the hard fate which had befallen her. She sometimes thought, perhaps,

> " Heaven her nuptials did record,
> Though man did deem her love abhorred ; "

and that her babe might yet live to bless and love her and others, and be useful in life, if she could only raise him to manhood. But joyless poverty in a hard country! — O, who can describe its trials! — its withering blasts, its pinching wants, its trampled and despised condition? Then add to it the disgrace of being a mother without the sacred mantle of legal marriage, and you can scarcely imagine the depths of a mother's woe forty years ago. Marriage might, indeed, have screened the mother from public scorn; but how much guilt, and of what nature, attached to the child, society did never define. But it long despised him. When the rude cold winds reached their icy fingers for the heart-strings of her babe, and the rattling boards, nor tattered garments, could save him, then the mother folded him to her bosom, and fed and warmed from her scantily-supplied body, and bade the cold and hunger take her with her babe, or leave both together. She was a mother worthy a better fate, who might have filled, with honor and love, a stately mansion, had fortune favored her with one, instead of a hovel. It was, indeed, a hard task to supply by her labor the wants of both, for few would hire her with her boy. Susan did not name her boy for either family, nor borrow a name from either record of ancestors, but selected a name left on the scroll of fame by one who fell at the battle of Bunker's Hill, where the tall monument marks the spot of conflict and death ; and that name he is still known by, as much as by the sire-name. But a name of one beloved by thousands did not bring even friends to the Lone One, for now the

> " —— years pressed hard upon him,
> And his living friends were few ;
> And from out the sombre future
> Troubles drifted into view."

Never yet did a child start on the pathway to fame, even in New England, with harder prospects, and through a darker and colder social atmosphere, than this unblessed babe; and yet his eyes sparkled with gladness, and his heart leaped with joy, at each kind look, loving smile, or gentle word, of mother or friend. He had not yet learned that the world around him was full of scorn, contempt, neglect, and slander, for his sensitive soul to meet and overcome with its own love and devotion, which alone could overcome such obstacles to happiness. The meagre pittance which Susan could obtain for unwearying industry enabled her to feed and clothe herself and babe. It was no doubt a blessing to her to have the screen over coming events sufficient to obscure all vision of the terrible fate that awaited her and her boy; else she would have earnestly prayed (for she did pray) that the cup might pass undrained by each or either. How oft, in riper years, have the eye and smile of the Lone One rested on a mother and child in a home of poverty, while the mind has turned back to his own mother and his childhood, and wondered if here, as there, love alone constituted the wealth of mother and child! Tears and sympathy never have, and never can, abandon the heart once schooled in the experience of the Lone One; nor can it ever fail to appreciate, reciprocate, and feel, the genial love of kindred souls.

Four times our latitude felt the freezing winds and drifting snows of a winter solstice; cold without, and cold within; cold the forms, and colder the hearts, around the tender germ in earthly mould, born, out of time and out of place, of a mother, but not of a wife. The father had gone to Paradise, with Jesus and the thief; but the child was not taught to speak of his father, even the Father in heaven; and although he saw other children with fathers to accept and instruct them, yet he knew not that he had a father, living or dead, till many years after the transition of Simon. The mother enjoyed tolerable health; the heart only was diseased; and whose heart would not be, in such a world, and under such trials, — a widow in fact, but not in law? The messenger from the "Kingdom of Ponemah" had already started after her; and the car of death was moving toward earth, to bear her to the "Islands of the Blessed;" but she knew it not; for still the earthly form swayed to the will obedient, still "the magic car moved on." Avon's bard has truly said, "Misfortunes never come single;" and the Song of Hiawatha truly sings, in lines of Longfellow measure,

> "So disasters come not singly;
> But, as if they watched and waited,
> Scanning one another's motions,
> When the first descends, the others
> Follow, follow, gathering flockwise
> Round their victim, sick and wounded,
> First a shadow, then a sorrow,
> Till the air is dark with anguish."

But there is no hardest fate, no deepest woe in the trial-lives of wandering souls. Superlatives are meaningless. Comparatives alone are appropriate. Every hard trial has a harder, every sad time a sadder, and every dark day a darker; so of the bright, the beautiful, the good, and the happy, with a superlative only in the Perfect, the Infinite, the Omniscient. The child, or boy (for at this age he was both or either), was deposited with a Quaker family on the mountain, while the mother went to watch by the bedside of a relative, where the camp-fires of life were slowly expiring, little suspecting the angel of death was reaching for her to go first to the "Land of the Hereafter," and welcome there the dying one, and leave here her lonely babe to buffet the storms alone. She retired from the sick bed late one night, and lay her wearied body on its couch for repose, and quietly arose into the regions of eternal dream; for, ere she awoke she died, — died without a struggle, apparently without the motion of a muscle, for the quiet face wore still its genial smile. In the morning they found the pale, cold form at rest; but the spirit had been called, and obeyed the summons, — taken passage with the messenger to the sphere where the angels bid her welcome to their home. But she could not stay quietly there, for her boy was lingering and struggling in the wrangling world below; and she asked and obtained permission to return, and guard him for a few years, to aid his feeble soul in its trial-hours and combats with a world of scorn and contempt. The Infidel laughed at the idea of her being a spirit, and the Christian ridiculed the idea of a spirit coming to earthly friends; but both were ignorant and in error; for she was a spirit, and did come back from her happy home, to fill a mission to earth and to the lonely child. The physician said she died by a nightmare. She says she died by a disease of the heart. No matter; she was dead to the world of touch and sight, to the outer sense and earthly form, and only alive to herself and the spiritual senses of others; and the Lone One now inherited his name and organization, and nothing more. No wonder the neighbors said they sometimes saw her form, pale and shadowy, sitting on the bier which stood long over her grave, in the orchard where they laid her body to rest near its kindred! No wonder the timid and superstitious said they heard her voice moaning in the breeze, as it whistled through the orchard, answering to the wind, which "sat in the pines, and gave groan for groan!" No wonder the whip-poor-will flew directly from the house to the grave, and from the grave to the house, and sang mournfully his sad song at each end of his short journey! No wonder all who knew her asked each of each, "What will become of her boy?" Few, very few, in that day, knew that our parents dead were living still, our spirit-guides. Her blessing came in the lines of the angel, F. S. Osgood:

LABOR.

Pause not to dream of the future before us;
Pause not to weep the wild cares that come o'er us;
Hark, how Creation's deep, musical chorus,
   Unintermitting, goes up into heaven!
Never the ocean-wave falters in flowing;
Never the little seed stops in its growing;
More and more richly the rose-heart keeps glowing,
   'Till from its nourishing stem it is riven.

" Labor is worship ! " the robin is singing ;
" Labor is worship ! " **the wild** bee is ringing ;
Listen ! that eloquent **whisper** upspringing
   Speaks to thy soul from out Nature's great heart !
From **the** dark cloud flows the life-giving shower ;
From the rough sod **blows** the soft-breathing flower ;
From the small insect, the rich coral bower ;
   Only man, in the plan, shrinks from his part.

Labor is life !   'T is the still water faileth;
Idleness ever despaireth, bewaileth ;
Keep the watch wound, for the dark **rust** assaileth ;
   Flowers droop and die **in the stillness of** noon.
Labor is glory ! — the flying cloud lightens ;
Only the waving wing changes and brightens ;
Idle hearts only **the dark future frightens ;**
   Play the sweet keys, wouldst thou keep them in tune '

Labor **is rest from** the sorrows that greet us, —
Rest from all petty vexations that meet us, —
Rest from sin-promptings that ever entreat us, —
   Rest from world-sirens that lure **us to ill.**
Work, **and pure** slumbers **shall wait** on thy pillow ;
Work — **thou** shalt ride **over Care's** coming billow ;
Lie not down wearied 'neath Woe's weeping willow !
   Work with a stout heart and resolute will !

Droop not, though shame, **sin, and** anguish, are round thee ;
Bravely fling off **the cold chain** that hath bound thee !
Look to yon pure heaven smiling beyond thee !
   Rest not content in thy darkness, a clod !
Work for some good, be it ever so slowly ;
Cherish some flower, be it ever so lowly ;
Labor !   All labor is noble and holy !
   Let thy great deeds be thy prayer to thy God !

SECTION III.

SUFFERING.

The first half of the first decade in earth-life was now by the
Lone One counted in years.   Both parents (if he had two) were
gone up out of their bodies, and he was left alone in his, — fath-
erless, motherless, penniless, friendless, worthless, useless, and

deathless. The last, and indeed, only, warm heart that beat for him was cold and still. The last and only face that smiled for him could smile no more. No hand to sustain, no arm to support, no voice in kindness to direct, could he expect more, for now he was the world's child. Its cold selfish heart beat only for gold and glory, of which the child had none. The tears often stole down the cheek as the heart uttered its grief, while in child-like innocence he wildly asked, "Where is my mother?"—"Your mother is dead," came, coldly, stupidly, back the answer. —"What have they done with her?"—"Put her in the ground."—"Cruel, wicked men!" exclaimed the boy. — "O, no; God took her away." — "Did God kill my mother?" wildly asked the child. — "Only took her away." — "O, cruel, cruel God! bring me back my mother; for the world has no friend for me when she is gone!" But they laughed at the child, whose innocent and ignorant heart condemned God for taking away his mother, whom he needed so much and God so little; for now he felt himself fully to be the "poor outcast of creation," "no more to hear a kindly word, or grasp a kindly hand."

In obedience to the statute of New Hampshire, each town at its annual meeting selects three men who are overseers of the poor, and whose duty it is to provide homes for those who have none, and no means of support. Of course the world's child became their ward at the death of his mother. In the town was a citizen farmer, whose name we will call David, not because he slew Goliah, or Uriah, but because he was known by that name at the time. He was a trader in cattle, and sheep, and swine; not well organized for a happy life, and badly educated in social and spiritual affairs. This citizen applied to the authorities for the boy, whom he had attempted in vain to obtain from the mother, for he saw in him a machine capable of doing much hard work, and releasing his own children from many tasks. He readily obtained the boy, and the bond was signed which sold the world's child into bondage for sixteen long years to one of the most cruel and cold-hearted masters. The bond required schooling each winter; and at the expiration of the time, when twenty-one years of life should render the boy a man capable of selling himself, two suits of clothes, and a hundred dollars in money, were to be his compensation for services. He was transferred from the mountain to the home of David, but never to the affections. Even the children were taught to manifest superiority over him, — he was with, but not of them. Not one spark of sympathy or love could be afforded him, for he was the child of nobody in this world. Many a time a sore back, or a bruised body, evinced the physical superiority and heartless cruelty of David; often for trifling offences unavoidable to the boy; the marks of frost and exposure on the extremities of his body remained for years, and the effects of hard labor, sadly unproportioned to his strength, remained still at the end of the fourth decade. True, the old jockey would sometimes come to visit his son David, and pat the boy on the head, and say " my son," — words which he never heard from other lips addressed to him, and at which his heart would leap with joy; and he thought, if David would only say those words, how he would try to be good. The effects of this severe treatment can only be entirely removed when he changes his home for that of his mother, or other spirit-friends. The summers came, and the winters came, and toil, toil, toil, was his portion. Not school, nor play. True, an old spelling-book said, " All work and no play makes Jack a dull boy." If so, he must have been a " dull boy." A poet says " work is worship." If so, the Lone One was indeed a " devout child;" and yet the Christian creeds would have consigned him to hell, as the fashionable circles of society already had done for this life. Heavily, and slowly, the years rolled away, bringing to his childhood only misery and grief. There was no " under-ground railroad" to take him to freedom; and no freedom for him to be taken into, except in the far-distant, and to him mystic, number, twenty-one. Why that should be the age for freedom, he knew not; but so it was written, and he was the victim. Why that three-seven number should be a key to unlock manhood in a boy was, and still is, a mystery to the Lone One. Gladly would he have

escaped from this bondage to his mother, in " silent sleep," or
" spirit-land," or heaven, or hell, or anywhere where she could
meet him, and once more embrace him, and call **him** her child.
But large **caution,** and a naturally timid heart, prevented him
from self-destruction, even years after the point of time registered
here. Thus rolled away the last half of the first decade, and
brought the age of ten, to which he longingly looked **as a time**
when he should **be** almost a man; but, alas, how disappointed was
the boy! — he was still a stinted lad. Sorrow, too deep, too keen,
to be impressed here, bore down the childish glee and youthful
impulses of his **heart.** Reasoning superficially, one would say
this treatment followed so long in this period of life would crush
out every spark **of** love and sympathy from his tender and childish heart, and that **he** would **be hardened for** crime, and
driven in madness to wage war on the race; but it **was not so.**
Deeply seated in his very soul was an ardent yearning for love
and sympathy, that no cruelty could extinguish; **it was ready at
the** first warm ray of love **to** spring into life and growth. He
had felt, although he **had** not **read, that** " Whom **the heart of**
man casts out, straightway the heart of God takes in."

Five long years with a mother's love and nothing else, and five
longer ones without even that, — for a God, said to be a " God **of**
love," had taken her away, and left the boy without any **consola-**
tion, — save in the future, and **in** freedom at twenty-one; when
the new year and **fine** days **brought a birth-day dream, from the**
poet.

> " He dreamed that in another sphere
> 　He had the cycles **run ;**
> Ten million million centuries,
> 　**Yet life had but begun.**

> " Earth on her **way was** moving still,
> 　The moon wore **still her** light,
> The planets **wheeled** their stated **round,**
> 　The unfading sun was bright.

> " And many a universe he saw,
>   Ranged in the boundless space,
>   Around the Almighty's central throne,
>   That saw their tireless race.
>
> " But yet he sought this little earth,
>   The scene of life's first years,
>   Where first he knew of joy or grief,
>   Of loves, and hopes, and fears.
>
> " Earth had become a paradise ;
>   No more was strife or wrong,
>   Or poverty or fell disease,
>   That it had known so long.
>
> " No more o'er virtue vice arose,
>   Or worst above the best ;
>   All shared the gifts of God alike,
>   And all alike were blessed."

Thus closed the first ten years of life in sorrowful bondage, condemned, despised, scorned, abused, only because he had entered the world, (not voluntarily) ; not because he had abused it or sinned, but because God had (as the Christian said) sent him here with a nature totally depraved, and forced him through a totally depraved channel, in the estimation of society, without his consent. Whether he was here to expiate the sins of a former life, or as a missionary, or only for development and growth, could not at this period of existence be determined.

> " There is no wind but soweth seeds
>   Of a more true and open life,
>   Which burst, unlooked-for, in high-souled deeds,
>   With wayside beauty rife."

CHAPTER II.

SECOND DECADE OF THE WORLD'S CHILD.

The Ragged Orphan. — The Fugitive Slave not delivered up. — The Change of Homes. — The Commencement of Education. — Good and Bad mixed. — Winding into Manhood.

SECTION I.

FUGITIVE.

ON the cold, stormy morning of January 5, 1823, the boy awoke from his "sweet dream of peace," and found himself still a boy in condition and stature, in the worst form of limited slavery, such as New England retained after she had freed her colored slaves. Within her limits slavery had not then ceased, although she had received the applause of some philanthropists, and even many years after, barbarism could be found; for an old man was imprisoned sixty days, in Boston, for publishing in his own paper the fact that he did not believe in their orthodox God. Selling orphans and imprisoning infidels were sufficient works of cruelty to moderate her zeal on the subject of oppression, — or ought to have been, at least, until her own hands were clean. True, it did not palliate the crimes of others; but trying to get the mote from our brother's eye, with a beam in our own, was appropriately condemned by One long ago. The second decade opened with a renewal of the gloomy pilgrimage of his earthly journey, ragged and dirty, despised and dejected. The great pendulum of time made its monthly crossings, and at each swing groaned "no hope," — no hope in this life, nor of heaven beyond. He had now begun to sin, although he could not read; and was on the broad road to hell for sinning against God, of whom he only knew what the swearers and boys told him ; for he had neither time or clothes that would allow of his going to hear what the preacher could tell about God and the devil ; and, if he had, in his unsophisticated nature, it is doubtful which he would have chosen for a master ; for he still supposed God killed his mother. New England had her churches, her schools, her social and family circles, her high life and her low life. The latter alone could he endure (not enjoy) ; the songs of joy and mirth went booming up from the groups of boys and girls at their merry plays, but the Lone One had no share in them.

> " Without, in tatters, the world's poor child
> Sobbeth alone his grief, his pain ;
> No one heareth him, no one heedeth him.
> But winter, his friend, with his cold, tight hand,
> Grasps his form, whispering huskily,
> What dost thou in a Christian land ? "

David had already begun to make encroachments on the title-deeds of his neighbors, adding at least one farm to his own, and was reaching after others, when, for reasons not to be mentioned here, his affairs became neglected, his business left at loose ends, and he began to go down-hill, as the neighbors said. Then every one was ready to give him a push or kick, which only made him more cross and cruel to those under his control. Domestic troubles, too, and unkind treatment of his wife, made her not less severe and cruel to the world's child. She, however, was never as severe as David — being by nature a woman, and a mother, in marriage. She seldom used the rod, but only used her tongue for a weapon ; which, although severe to the sensitive heart of the boy, did not lacerate the body and soul both, as the treatment of David did. Prosperity and adversity are neighbors, and their dominions border on each other. The sun crosses the line at the vernal equinox, and lets winter into summer through spring, and again at the autumnal equinox lets summer glide through the autumn into winter. So our lives often are changed by crossing a line, and we glide into prosperity or adversity, after nearing each day or week the margin; then turn again, as David has, since he crossed over Jordan, and went to the world, but not to the home, of the mother of the orphaned boy. David usually kept his own counsel, and consulted himself only, on business matters. For reasons best known to himself, he rented the rocky farm and old homestead, and moved to a small manufacturing village on the Lamprey River, to make money by keeping boarders. In this new home the almost constant presence of boarders or other persons rendered it more difficult for David to treat the boy as badly as he had done on the farm ; for he had some shame, as most persons have, and did not like to have people see him abuse the little urchin. New, and more, acquaintances were now formed by the Lone One, and all, especially the boys, had much sympathy for him ; for they knew he was not treated well and could not read, for the schooling contract was not fulfilled to the letter, but another kind of schooling substituted for that designated in the bond. He heard stories of runaway boys, and boys going to sea, &c., and his mind dwelt much, both day and night, on the subject, until he was fully resolved to try his luck for freedom, by running away. But where to go, and how to introduce himself, penniless, friendless, ragged, and unlettered, was still a source of great perplexity, and one on which he could form no plan, and did not. He ventured to consult some of his more intimate boy-companions, and they advised him to go to the ocean and get on a vessel, and " go to sea," as the safest mode of escape. But how to get there without a penny ; for, although he was fourteen years old, he had never possessed money in his life, except once a few cents to spend at a training, and scarcely knew the value of common coins, except what the boys had taught him for amusement, or from charity ; for they had both for him. Seven years more of such servitude was too much for endurance, and almost any change preferable ; and he resolved to embrace the first favorable opportunity, and flee from bondage and the " wrath to come."

About the middle of the first decade, the transition of the

mother and the sale into bondage made a great change in the condition of the Lone One, and now approached the middle of the second decade, with another important event in embryo. The fourteenth birth-day had passed over in the winter, and spring had come round with a May-day and flowers, and yet no opportunity for escape offered itself to the captive, until near the middle of May, when David left home for the old homestead on one Saturday, intending to return on Monday. The day set apart for the preachers to labor and the lay members to cease work had dawned beautifully on that spot of earth where the Lone One slept and mused, feeling the sentiment of Gertrude Ladd, as expressed in these beautiful lines:

> "Alone, I murmur, as I gaze upon the darkened past,
> Alone I 've wandered on my weary way,
> While dangers thick and fast
> Have gathered round me day by day,
> My happiness to blast.
>
> " Alone, alone I sigh, as in the future drear
> I turn my weary, wandering eye,
> And hope some friendly voice to hear,
> Some cheering beacon to descry,
> My soul to cheer.
>
> " Alone no more I 'll murmur, for I see
> Far in the future dark a glimmering light,
> Which seems to beckon me
> Unto a region beautiful and bright,
> Where day reigns ever, clouded ne'er by night —
> Alone no more I 'll be.''

When the noon had passed, and the still pleasant day was declining, three boys parted company two or three miles from their homes: two returning, and one going on from home — if, indeed, it was a home he left. They have never met again, and the one has never returned; for he "ran away," so they said From a poor old friendless man, once acquainted with the mother of the Lone One, who labored sometimes for David, the boy had heard of a distant connection of his mother, who lived in poverty about seven miles from the boarding-house; and he had learned the direction to her house, or shanty. When the sun sank in the west, and tinged with its beautiful rays the skirt of clouds on the horizon's verge, the world's child was nearing the poverty home of the widow and the old-maid daughter, which made up the family of these relatives. He had three small crackers in his pocket, and nothing more of any kind; barefoot, old chip hat on his head, cotton shirt (clean, for it was Sabbath), tow-cloth pants, and short coat, made up his dress, and his all. A body and a sensitive heart were there; for, although ten long years of cruelty and pain had worn upon the youthful frame, yet the poet's words were true, who saith,

> "You may break, you may ruin, the vase, if you will,
> But the scent of the roses will hang round it still."

He reached and entered the poverty home, so like the one where he once lived with a mother, with one treasure, — only one — the currency of heaven. Love, only love was to be found, of all the comforts of life; but that is a treasure. They met him not with scorn, for

> "Scorn is for devils; soft compassion lies
> In angel hearts, and beams from angel eyes;"

and by this rule two angels met him here, and shed around his lonely heart the balmy influence of love once more, — but only a fitful gleam, to brighten for a moment the pathway of life, then let it sink again to loneliness and gloom; but it was all they could do. They shared with him the homely meal at night and morn, and divided for him the scanty bed-clothes, and heard, with tears of sorrow and pity, the story of his woes; but could not offer protection or relief; for, in that hard, cold place, it was barely possible for them to sustain life in themselves by the strictest economy and industry. When the morning was come it was necessary for them to part, for the first and last time; and, however painful, it was

their duty to give the best advice they could, for this, and the
sympathy of loving hearts, was all they had to spare. They did
not know his mother was with him. He did not know it; for his,
and their, spiritual senses were not opened sufficiently to recognize
the presence of spirits. But she was with him, and guiding his
course by an unseen influence. They advised him to return, and
excuse himself as well as he could for his visit to them, and await
a better opportunity to escape; for they could conceive of no
means of escape, and no prospect of assistance or of a home for
him elsewhere. A hearty good-by and God bless you parted
the three, and he started in the direction of his master's residence,
making slow steps, and with a sad heart. Soon as he was out
of sight of the house, an impression, strong and irresistible,
induced him to get over the fence and wander away from the
road, and turn his steps again to the eastward, and *from* the home
of David; and some unseen power, for many years of unknown
origin to him, kept him out of sight from the road, until the man in
pursuit of him on horseback from David's home had passed on to
the bridge at Durham, and returned, unable to see or hear of such
a boy as he was seeking. After this man in pursuit of the
fugitive had returned (although unknown to the boy, for he did not
expect to be pursued until David returned), he again, near noon,
entered the road near a bridge and ship-yard in Durham, and
crossed the bridge. The men stopped their work and looked at
the boy, the same one inquired after a short time before, by
the man on horseback, and described as a runaway; but they
did not arrest nor molest him, and he passed on, turning unconsciously to the left, and taking the road which led to his native
town. Hastening on, but he knew not where; a cracker served for
a dinner; for he did not dare to enter a house and ask for food,
lest he should be questioned and detected as a fugitive, not from
justice, but from servitude. When the sun was again in the west,
and the curtain of day lowering down to the western horizon, and
his limbs were already weary, and his stomach stayed by one
small cracker, he recognized a tavern in Northwood, a town ad-

joining his native Pittsfield, and thus for the first time discovered that he was on the road leading to his old home. Scarcely had he passed the place, when a new difficulty arose in his mind. David was to return this day from his old place, and might he not meet him, and with another terrible beating be returned to **servitude**, and watched so as to prevent another escape? In the **very** midst of these fears a team appeared on a hill before him, and he recognized the horses and driver. It was David, truly. **Not a** moment was there to spare. No house, or barn, or grove, **was near** enough to screen him; but David did not know of his escape, and of course was not on the lookout, and, beside, was busy in conversation with a passenger. Over the stone wall, and curled down behind it, was the runaway boy as the master passed unsuspectingly by, in the heat and glow of earnest conversation, and the trembling boy now returned to the road and his journey. That great danger had passed, and become another evidence that

> " We see but half the causes of our deeds,
> Seeking them wholly in the outer life,
> And heedless of the encircling spirit-world,
> Which, though unseen, is felt, and sows in us
> All germs of pure and world-wide purposes."

When the sun was gone down, and it was yet light, he was on old Catamount Mountain, from which he could see the spires **of** those buildings erected to save the souls in his own native town, and where, of course, he ought to have his soul saved, if he could not his body. But there was poor chance for either to be saved in him; for he was the world's child, and the town was his guardian — not the church, for the church turned his mother out for becoming a mother, as Mary of old did, without their or the magistrate's permission; but God soon after took her into heaven, as he did Mary. Down the long and winding road of the mountain-side to the village, as the daylight passed away circle by circle, he moved weary and sad, hungry and dejected, in a Christian land, with a spirit for a guide, unbeknown to him or others. The mother and

child entered the village late in eve, when the lamps were
gone out in the parlor, and the smoke-fires covered up ; when
Somnus had spread his net over the village. Where to go, on
whom to call, was the next great question. He had no friends in
the village. **About two** miles to the eastward was the grave of
his mother, and some remnants of her paternal home, and its *poor*
but **kind** inmates ; but it was night, and a dark wood of pine and
hemlock was **by the** way on each side **of** the road part of the
distance, and the boy dare not go over the road in the night. **A
still** greater obstacle was the grave-yard which lay by the road-
side, skirted by a wood on one side, and church on another. By
this he certainly could not pass in the night ; for he had heard
marvellous stories of ghosts, and something of a Holy Ghost which
dwelt in the ghostly church, and he dreaded and feared them all,
both the Holy and unholy. These obstacles were insurmountable ;
therefore he retired to the tavern barn-yard to take lodgings with
the cattle, for **they did** not have to pay money, and he had none
to pay. Sometimes he crept on their backs, and sometimes he
drove them up, and took the warm spot of ground till it was cold ;
and thus he spent the long, cold May night in the tavern-yard
with the cattle, sleeping on the ground till awakened by the cold
several times. At length morning came, and the ghosts retired
from their night-watch over the graves, and the imaginary bears
to their forest dens nowhere, and the boy again started, his bare feet
on the ground white with frost, (nothing new for him), and by exercise soon warmed his chilled body, rendered feeble with the exercise
and hunger of twenty-four hours. He reached the old home of his
grandmother, who was still alive, but just on the verge of the other
life which comes next after this. He was soon warmed and fed,
and the neighboring women called in to council with those of the
household upon what should be done. A little incident occurred
here which made a deep impression on the boy's mind. He had
found in the road, the day before his arrival, a pair of long stock-
ings, done up as is usual for packing in a valise, and had brought
them with him to this home. He heard the women express a fear

that he had stolen them. To be suspected of stealing was too
much for his sensitive soul, and he went off and wept alone, sorry
that he must live in such a suspicious world, or world of rogues
on the constant lookout for rogues, and of honest people full of
suspicion.

The council of women decided to take the boy to the **selectmen**
of the town, and **send** the best pleader among them to make a plea
for his release **from the bondage, and to induce them to try and**
find him another home. The best pleader was a lady, — **not a con-**
nection, but a sympathizing friend ; and she went with the boy to
the trio **who** were in session next day after the arrival of the
fugitive. They were aware of the cruel treatment by David, and
that the boy had not been sent to school according to the agreement; and also that David had failed, and was not likely to be able
to pay the one hundred dollars at the end of six more years.
Hence the cause did not need the skill and pleading **powers of**
Mrs. R., for they at once resolved that the boy should not be sent
back to bondage in that place. When this announcement was
made one glad heart leaped with joy. One bound of joyous feeling, too strong to utter, filled his soul to overflowing ; and a burst
of tears gave them the thanks his lips could not speak, and proved
the sensitive soul was not all callous or frozen ; yet it could scarcely
prove that Tupper was wrong in this sentiment,

" Scratch the green rind of a sapling, or wantonly twist it in the soil,
   The scarred and crooked oak will tell of thee for centuries to come."

Section II.

EMANCIPATED.

One of the three, whose Christian name was Nathaniel, readily
offered the boy a home at his own house ; for he at once felt the
warm and deep gratitude gushing from his soul at the prospect of
release from the tyrant. The Lone One never saw David again ;
for when he came after the fugitive he soon learned that the
authorities had agreed to protect the boy, and returned to reflect

on his treatment. A few years after, he passed over the cold Jordan stream, and judged himself " according to the deeds done in the body ;" passed sentence, and went away to work out a happier condition, which he has long since attained.

> " Human life is as the Chian wine,
> Flavored into him who drinketh it."

And

> " In the perfect circle of creation, not an atom could be spared,
> From earth's magnetic zone, to the bindweed round a hawthorn."

That night the boy slept at a new home, — a home where he was treated as one of the family, with a kindness he felt but could not respond to, save by feelings and tears which were almost constant, now the crushed heart collected and expressed its native and instinctive fragrance. It was no task to labor now, for he was fed, clothed, and treated kindly by all the family; but how utterly unfit he was for such company, having been for ten long years treated as a dog, never admitted into company, except to skulk and sneak as a dog in a corner, eating on soiled dishes the fragments left at meal-times by the family, or boarders, and only allowed to speak in answer to questions to the head of the family. How truly the family of Nathaniel proved the truth of the poet's words —

> " The very flowers that bend and meet
> In sweetening others grow more sweet ! "

for they did truly sweeten the bitter life-draught of sorrow which the Lone One was compelled to accept with life. God or nature did reward this family ; for, twenty years after the Lone One left the town, he returned, and found Nathaniel, ripened in years, going in peace, happy, to his spirit home ; the wife already gone over, and the children all grown up in health and plenty, educated and happy. But the Lone One was not needed at this home, which was only offered him temporarily ; and, after a few months, moved to the old homestead of Nathaniel's wife, where her two old-bachelor brothers carried on the large farm, and hired,

instead of marrying, housekeepers. Here the orphaned boy found
a happy home, and kind treatment from Samuel and John and their
housekeepers. He was no more abused, and his soul continued
to swell with gratitude and with love and kindness to other beings.

" For love through love increaseth, and hate begetteth hate."

Summer and autumn passed, — the first happy ones to the lone
heart since the days of his mother, — but when winter came a new
trouble arose. He must go to school; a fine large schoolhouse
was near, and a long school-term, with many scholars, and he a
boy of fifteen, and could not even read. How could his sensitive
soul bear the laugh and scorn of the boys and girls of his age who
were advanced in their studies? But when the school began he
appeared and took his place with the least and youngest class in
the school, to learn to read ; the butt for jokes, and object of ridicule and scorn of the school, but not of the teacher, for his sympathy was called out, and he aided the ardent and sensitive
spirit in its struggles. The progress was rapid, and did not stop
until, at the fourth winter, he was the best and furthest-advanced
scholar in the school. Then the jokes and ridicule turned to
admiration. The whole power of the soul was called into action,
and it soon made up for lost years by renewed energies. Two
years the boy lived with this happy family of Universalists, and
they were real and true Christians, if, indeed, Christians were the
good and charitable people of earth ; for no cross word was ever
spoken to the boy by them, and his heart began to grow into sympathy with the world, for he found, at length, that all were not
like David. At the end of two years he entered into a contract
with a family whose farm adjoined that of the bachelors, lying at
the foot of the hill, where the large old two-stories house is still
standing, with many other marks of the industry of one of the best
families of the town. There he lived till the number of years
required by law made him a man, with civil and political rights, like
other men. Earned and received the one hundred dollars and two
suits of clothes, such as were named in the bond of David. Re-

ceived the schooling and the best of care for his health of body,
and always kind treatment and a good home. He was ever one
of the family, and treated as one, but was the only young person
in the family, which consisted of Bracket and his wife, his father
Moses and wife, and two maiden sisters of Bracket ; all of whom
were gone over to the other home, when he returned, twenty years
after he left them, and in the old homestead was a second wife of
Bracket, a widow, with her two bright boys, overjoyed to see one
of whom they had so often heard the family and neighbors speak.
Bracket and his mother had, by the advice of some physician
ignorant of human nature and the nature of tobacco, been advised
to smoke, and were inveterate smokers; and the Lone One, who
wished to imitate and copy the acts of good men, here learned the
filthy, contaminating, and expensive habit of smoking, and followed
it for near fifteen years, until his mind reached a degree of development that could not longer tolerate the nuisance. Many marks of
the four years' residence and labor on this farm by the orphan boy
are yet visible, and many marks of books and facts obtained there
are still bright in his memory ; for a younger brother of Bracket,
then in college and at law, lent or gave to the Lone One many
books which he needed and was not able to buy, and thus assisted
him in his education.

At this home terminated the second decade. Still lonely and
desolate in soul was the world's child. But cruelty to him had
ceased, and kindness, and care of his body and its wants, were now
secured ; yet life was desolate, dreary, and almost aimless, for
what could he do to erase the stigma of his birth, and evade the
" sleet of scorn," the scorching flame of contempt, the vulgar disgust, of those who were better born. No matter whether it was
God or the Devil who was author of the causes that brought about
the event ; the boy alone was now left to bear the stigma, for it
could not be forgotten nor forgiven while one was living to bear
it. How could he overcome it ? How could he become respectable ? How obtain friends, wealth, fame ?

Much he needed books and instruction on physiology, as all

children do in the second decade of life ; **but at** that time works, on that subject, most required of all, were prohibited by a squeamishness in public opinion, and as **much** excluded as metaphysical works were by religious teachers.　True, the boy did not have his mind filled with superstition and fanaticism.　**He was not taught** to call Moses the meekest man nor Solomon the wisest that ever lived, nor David a man after God's own heart ; but most of the books which he found in the town library, or elsewhere, were saturated with the insipid, or poisonous, doctrines of theology, and even the school-books had been revised and corrected or originally written by theologians, and filled with absurdities mixed with the truths **of** science, and it was difficult for a youthful mind to sort out and reject all the sophistry of an educated clergy.　Yet his mind was too much in accord with nature to admit many of these impositions on her beauty and harmony, and too much in love with **nature to** admit such absurd imputations on her character as modern theology taught.　Thus he grew more **and** more in love with science and her conclusions, and came fully to the conclusion that the truth was to be found in the following lines :

> " 'T will be all the same in a hundred **years** ! —
> What a spell-word to conjure **up smiles** and tears !
> **O, how oft do I** muse, **'mid the** thoughtless and gay,
> On the marvellous truth that these words convey !
> And can it be so ? — must the valiant and free
> Have their tenure **of life on** this frail **decree** ?
> Are the trophies **they 've** reared, **and the glories they 've won,**
> **Only castles** of frost-work **confronting the sun** ?
> And must all that 's as **joyous and brilliant to view**
> **As a mid-summer dream be as perishing, too** ?
> Then have pity, **ye proud ones** ! — be gentle, ye great !
> O, remember **how mercy beseemeth your** state ;
> For **the rust that** consumeth **the sword** of the brave
> Is eating the chain of the manacled slave,
> And the conqueror's frowns and his victim's tears
> Will be all the same in a hundred years !

> " 'T will **be** all the same in a hundred years ! —
> **What a** spell-word to conjure up smiles and tears !

How dark are your fortunes, ye sons of the soil,
Whose heirloom is sorrow, **whose** birthright is toil !
Yet **envy not those** who have glory and gold,
By **the** sweat of the poor, and the blood of the bold ;
For 't is coming, howe'er they may flaunt in their pride,
The day when they 'll moulder to dust by your side.
Death uniteth the children of toil and of sloth,
And the democrat reptiles carouse upon both ;
For Time, **as** he speeds on **his** viewless wings,
Disenables and withers **all earthly** things ;
And the knight's **white plume, and** the shepherd's crook,
And the minstrel's **pipe,** and the scholar's book,
And the emperor's crown, and the Cossack's spears,
Will be dust alike in a hundred years !

" 'T will be all the same in a hundred years !—
O, most magical fountain of smiles and tears !
To think that our hopes, like the flowers of June,
Which we love so much, should be lost so soon !
Then what meaneth the chase after phantom joys,
Or the breaking of human hearts for toys,
Or the veteran's pride in his crafty schemes,
Or the passions of youth for its darling dreams,
Or the aiming at ends that we never can span,
Or the deadly aversion of man for man? —
What availeth it all — O, ye sages, say ! —
Or the miser's joy in his brilliant **clay,**
Or the lover's zeal for his matchless **prize—**
The enchanting maid with the **starry eyes—**
Or the feverish conflict of hopes **and fears,**
If 't is all the same in a hundred years ? "

But it was long years **after that he** *felt* **the truth of the closing**
stanzas of the poem.

" Ah ! 't is not the same in a hundred years,
How clear soever the case appears ;
For know ye not, that beyond the grave,
Far, far beyond, where the cedars wave
On the Syrian mountains, or where the stars
Come glittering forth in their golden cars,
There bloometh a land of perennial bliss,
Where we smile to think of the tears in this?

And the pilgrim reaching that radiant shore
Has the thought of death in his heart no more,
But layeth his staff and sandals down,
For the victor's palm and the monarch's crown.
And the mother meets, in that tranquil sphere,
The delightful child she had wept for here ;
And we quaff of the same immortal cup,
While the orphan smiles, and the slave looks up.
So be glad, my heart, and forget thy tears,
For 't is NOT the same in a hundred years ! ''
4

CHAPTER III.

THIRD DECADE OF THE LONE ONE.

Boyhood changed to Manhood. — Education. — Scepticism for Religion. —
Love and Separation. — Long Journey. — Sickness. — Marriage. — Poverty.
— Struggles for Life in the West.

Section I.

MANHOOD.

THE kind-hearted Bracket, who graduated and smoked the
orphan into manhood, fulfilled every agreement, and even more in
kindness; and, some months before the expiration of the service-
time, the school-months enabled the boy to enter the academy at
Gilmanton Corners, to obtain such educational aid as could not be
furnished him in the district-school where, five years before, he
commenced to learn in the lowest class, the object of ridicule for
the school. The hill-foot home was to be his home no more. It
was visited by him soon after, at the death and burial of the wife
of Bracket, who had been kind to him, and ever attentive to his
wants. Her suffering was great, and almost a double affliction
to the family; for she left them at a period when more fortunate
circumstances might have doubled the joys of life to her and
Bracket. It was the beginning of Death's encroachments on the
family circle, which only ceased when it had taken all, and the
father of Bracket last. The new wife and two boys were introduced before the messenger took Bracket. In the spring of 1855
the Lone One halted an hour, to cast a hasty glance over the
farm, on which many a stone was resting where his hand had
placed it, and trees were growing where he had planted them.

The lovely boys and lonely mother welcomed **him** as one of the family of **the old** homestead. Sadly and sorrowing, he turned away, and wished not to turn back the pages of his history nor theirs, but felt more inclined to say, "'Fly swiftly **on, ye** wheels **of time,**' and carry me over **to their present home.**" The Life-Line, which had now run through its boyhood, was about to **enter** manhood, and run in a broader and deeper channel. **The sub-**stantial traits **of** character **were already** formed for life, and ever after bore him above the grosser vices of civilization, — dissipation, profanity, vulgarity, and licentiousness. Even in riper years, when in the fascinating circles of social and political life, where others around him were led astray, he was ever firm to the first principles of character, and by them was enabled to become a guide and counsellor for others, and **often, in** public and private, to lecture for temperance and morality, purity **and reform.** New emotions, new impulses, new desires, new attractions, had arisen in the mind and heart of the Lone One; and he saw the world around him as he had never seen it before. Comparing his own sad fate with other young men, he wept bitter tears of sorrow for his existence, with powers and capacities for which he had no use, which could neither be used for his own or others' happiness. Then the wheel of fortune turned to him its historic page; and the record called his attention to the fact that nearly every son of noble lineage, placed by wealth, family, and ancestry, high up the ladder of life, to begin a self-sustaining career above its poverty base, fell to the bottom, and, if such ever arose again, did it by individual effort, and through trials and struggles; while most of those who were ever ascending, and nearest the summit, arose from the very foot of society, and **by** unwearying effort overcame obstacles which at times seemed insurmountable. Then the muses, ever his friends who could reach his sensitive heart with the spirit of song, let into his soul, in substance, the sentiment of the beautiful poem of Mackay:

> " Were the lonely acorn never bound
> In the rude, cold grasp of the rotting ground ;

LIFE-LINE OF THE LONE ONE.

Did the rigid frost never harden up
The mould above its bursting cup ;
Were it never soaked in the rain and hail,
Or chilled by the breath of the wintry gale, —
It would not sprout in the sunshine free,
Or give the promise of a tree ;
It would not spread to the summer air
Its lengthening boughs and branches fair,
To form a bower, where, in starry nights,
Young love might dream unknown delights ;
Or stand in the woods, among its peers,
Fed by the dews of a thousand years.

Were never the dull, unseemly ore
Dragged from the depths where it slept of yore ;
Were it never cast into searching flame,
To be purged of impurity and shame ;
Were it never molten 'mid burning brands,
Or bruised and beaten by stalwart hands, —
It would never be known as a thing of worth ;
It would never emerge to a noble birth ;
It would never be formed into mystic rings,
To fetter Love's erratic wings ;
It would never shine amid priceless gems
On the girth of imperial diadems,
Nor become to the world a power and pride
Cherished, adored, and deified.

So thou, O man of a noble soul,
Starting in view of a glorious goal,
Wert thou never exposed to the blasts forlorn,
The storms of sorrow, the sleet of scorn ;
Wert thou never refined, in pitiless fire,
From the dross of thy sloth and mean desire ;
Wert thou never taught to feel and know
That the truest love has its roots in woe, —
Thou wouldst never unriddle the complex plan,
Or reach half way to the perfect man ;
Thou wouldst never attain the tranquil height
Where wisdom purifies the sight,
And God unfolds to the humblest gaze
The bliss and beauty of his ways.''

The quiet and industrious farmers of New England, who count the annual round of seasons by seed-time and harvest, have a dialect peculiar to their section of the inhabited world, as every other people has. Mixed in it are many meaningless words, and many good ones badly accented, and often inappropriately applied; and these, early acquired, are often retained by her citizens through life, and carried to other regions, where they sound badly to those not accustomed to them, but who use others equally or more absurd. **Some of these were retained by** the Lone One through his school days, and through years of residence in the West, and often called out expressions of ridicule from egotistic critics, who knew how to swear by rule, and eat tobacco by the pound, — expressions that touched keenly his sensitive feelings. "He murders the king's English," meaning really their own English, which was often more defective than his. Even these were, however, turned to good account, in enabling him to correct many erroneous modes of expression. Profane language he never used, for he did not go much to religious meetings to learn **it**; nor did he believe it more proper for a preacher to take God's name in vain, or abuse the devil, than for others to do so.

The body and brain had now attained their forms and proportions, and exhibited a body five feet nine inches long, round shoulders, and stout, muscular form, with nervous-bilious temperament; ardent and active, keen and very sensitive; with a brain above average, large, but not *very* large; sharp and active organs; largest organs, firmness and caution, — next, causality and perceptives; with benevolence large, social organs large, and destructiveness least; time and tune, small; marvellousness small, and hope large; eventuality small, **and** intuition very large; veneration full, and conscientiousness even; language large, ideality and sublimity full. These gave the general and tone of feeling, and leading traits of character; and as he was not accountable for his organization, it is yet to be determined how far he could **be** accountable for his character, which resulted from it. The texture of brain and nerve were extremely fine, and gave tone and keenness to his feelings. His large caution, small self-esteem, and sensitive nerves, made him extremely timid in early life, and until a knowledge of phrenology and his own brain enabled him to overcome it. When he entered the academy, among all strangers, with book-knowledge mostly acquired alone, evenings and Sundays, this timidity was felt, and often extremely embarrassing, of which one instance may serve to illustrate : On committing his first piece for declamation, and standing before the school to speak it, not one **word** could he utter, — a full-grown man, before the students, laughed at by the whole school ! For such an ambitious and timid soul, this was no joke to him. It was not long, however, before he could occupy his time and place in uttering his own thoughts in public, instead of attempting to repeat those of others. He was soon marked as one of the best and most active and ambitious students of the school. This led to the inquiry who he was, and who and where his parents and family, and soon brought down the contempt and scorn of jealous rivals on his sensitive soul ; for they despised and were ashamed **of one** who had no legal right to be born, although forced into **earth-life** involuntarily. But he found sympathy and some warm friends among the students, and no partiality in the teachers, even though he was an Infidel in a school under theological control. He was ever punctual, and obedient **to** every rule. Here he formed **an** acquaintance with several students whose views were similar to his own ; and here he found works of Infidel authors, as they were called, which he found to contain more reason, and more charity, than any religious books he had ever read. **Here** he became confirmed in **his** religious scepticism. The common **branches** of education were reviewed, and some proficiency made in Latin, when he left this school, to attend one commenced in his native town, where his history was better known, and where he deserved, at least, more sympathy. **Here** the period of study was short ; for all **the funds** acquired **by** hard labor ever since the death of his mother were nearly exhausted, and would not allow him to continue long in an academy. It was with deep regret that he left the school; for his soul had caught a glimpse of the beauties of science, and began to taste the sweet waters of literature, and he yearned for a feast from those fountains, but yearned in vain, for Poverty had set her seal on him. In that day it was far more difficult than in this for a poor boy to acquire an education. Theology offered to open the doors, and educate him into the ministry, if he would get religion; but his soul abhorred hypocrisy and deception; and he did not believe their doctrines were true, and would not pretend it, although he was aware that many students in theological charity believed as little as he did, and only accepted it to obtain an education, and an easy way to obtain a livelihood. Such a course he spurned, and chose rather a crust and freedom of thought with an honest heart. He could discover no opening to an education for him without sacrificing his honesty and integrity of character; and without a thorough scientific or classical education the path to the highest hill-tops of society was indeed a rugged one; but History turned down to him her scroll of fame, and pointed out this road:

> " If thou wouldst win a lasting fame,
> If thou the immortal wreath wouldst claim,
> And make the future bless thy name,
> Begin thy perilous career;
> Keep high thy heart, thy conscience clear,
> And walk thy way without a fear;
> And if thou hast a voice within
> That ever whispers, ' Work and win,'
> **And keeps thy soul** from sloth and sin;
> If thou canst plan a noble deed,
> And never flag till it succeed,
> Though in the strife thy heart shouldst bleed:
> If thou canst struggle day and night,
> And, in the envious world's despite,
> Still keep thy cynosure in sight;
> If thou canst bear the rich man's scorn,
> Nor curse the day that thou wert born
> To feed on husks, and he on corn;
> If thou canst dine upon a crust,

> And still hold on with patient trust,
> Nor pine that Fortune is unjust ;
> If thou canst see with tranquil breast
> The **knave or** fool in purple drest,
> Whilst thou must walk in tattered vest ;
> If thou canst rise ere break of day,
> **And** toil and moil till evening gray
> At thankless work for scanty pay ;
> If in thy progress to renown
> Thou canst endure the scoff and frown
> Of those who strive to put thee down ;
> If thou canst bear the averted face,
> The gibe and treacherous embrace
> Of those who run the self-same race ;
> If thou in darkest days canst find
> An inner brightness in thy mind
> To reconcile thee to thy kind ; —
> Whatever obstacle control,
> Thine hour will come, — go on, true soul !
> Thou 'lt win the prize, thou 'lt reach the goal
> If not, *what matter ?* — Tried by fire,
> **And purified from** low desire,
> Thy *spirit* **shall but soar the** higher.
> **Content and** hope thy heart shall buoy,
> **And man's** neglect shall ne'er destroy
> **The** inward peace, the secret joy."

He accepted the **offer and** left **the school,** yielding **desire to**
necessity, and **started on the road to fame, as** marked out by the
poet, although **he often met those** to whom the other lines of the
same poem were **more appropriate.**

> " Pause e'er thou **tempt** the hard career ;
> Thou 'lt find the conflict too severe,
> And heart will break, and brain will sear.
> Content thee with an humbler lot ;
> **Go** plough thy field, go build thy cot,
> **Nor sigh** that thou must be forgot."

Buried in clouds, far, far away, was the " tip-top house " where
fame had her sentinel-guarded citadel ; but thither he was bound

even though it might take centuries to obtain a niche in it, unless he should cease to exist ere he reached it; but this he feared would be his fate at death.

Full of hopes and fears, — about equally mixed, — he started for Boston in search of fortune, loitered about her streets a few days, too timid to ask often for employment, and too bashful to make his wants and situation known to those who could have aided him. His mind, however, was active, gathering shells of knowledge for a cabinet. Surprised at the close proximity of extreme wealth and extreme poverty, he wondered if both were necessary for the existence of each, and finally concluded that extreme wealth could only exist by extreme poverty, as some must be robbed if others possessed *their* wealth. Then he asked the Christian why God allowed a portion of his children to be robbed by others, and the Christian said it was a mystery. But he thought it ought to be revealed in order for us to be reconciled to it, and set his mind to work out the mystery which God would not reveal to his worshippers, and found the cause in an aristocratic monopoly, and unjustifiable worldly selfishness; but he soon saw the truth of Shelley's lines, —

> " There needeth not the hell that bigots frame
> * To punish those who err ; earth itself
> Contains the evil and the cure."

Finding no business, he went to Brookline, a few miles from Boston, and engaged to work on a farm that was all a garden, — or a garden that was large enough for a farm, — labored a few weeks, and was taken sick with pleurisy. The physician told him to leave the coast, as the sea-breezes were bad for him to take. Then he nearly drained his little purse to reach again his native town, and be laughed at by the boys, if not the girls ; but the latter did not as often grate his feelings with rudeness or ridicule as the former.

The younger brother of Bracket had married and opened a law-office in the village of his native town, and was post-master and partner in a store of goods. To him the Lone One engaged, to tend store and office, and boarded in the neat little home of Moses the lawyer, where the happy life of Moses and Abby, and the kind and loving heart of Mary, the sister of Abby, made social life attractive, almost fascinating, to the lone heart of the orphan. Not many months was he in this house before he found his heart involuntarily leaning toward Mary ; for she was beautiful and lovely, externally and internally ; both body and mind were attractive.   How could such a being fail to call out the love of an ardent soul, which was more than full ?   For a time he yielded to the delightful emotions of a pure attraction, and spent some happy hours in her society ; but she was his superior in years and experience, and soon began to check the wild hopes and youthful fancies of his soul, and turned his feelings to, and through, his intellect.   Then he reflected on his condition in poverty and disgrace ; but she had too noble a soul to despise him for his birth ; but to live in poverty and dependence was too severe a trial for her delicate frame, reared in tenderness and wealth, in a seaport town, as it was.   The soul of the Lone One had been too much awakened to remain and endure the presence of one he loved so devotedly, and early in the spring of '35 he collected his little earnings, and called on his old friends to give a farewell parting to each, and last, but not least, a final sitting with Mary. Those who know need not be told, and those who do not, cannot understand, the feelings which this parting produced ; for now, if not before, he knew she loved him, and he long before knew he loved her ; and the chord must be broken, never more to be united. They parted, never met again, nor exchanged one word by correspondence. She was married not many years after to a friend of his, who was often called by the same name, — for his middle name was the same as the first of the Lone One, — and lived a few years with him, and then went home to live with the angels, where more congenial society for her refined soul could be enjoyed. The tie must break, but he felt what Shakspeare wrote, — "A fiend as dear as thee might bear my soul to hell," or Moore, in

> " O, grief beyond all other griefs ! when fate
> First leaves the young heart lone and desolate
> In the wide world, without that tie
> For which it loved to live or feared to die.
> Lorn as the hung-up lute, which ne'er hath spoken
> Since the sad day its master-chord was broken.''

It is not probable that the heart of the Lone One will ever, in this life, drop this subject ; but we will drop it here, and ask thee, reader, if thee was ever in New Hampshire in an election-storm, or town-meeting-time? If not, I shall not attempt to describe that either, for only those who have been " out in it " can know how it blows, and beats, and makes the stout hearts bend as reeds before " Mudgekeewis." One of these annual monsoons passed over New Hampshire a few days before the Lone One left, and he was out in it, trying, with others, to elect his democratic friend, Moses, to the legislature. They failed this time, but afterward it became easy to elect him even to Congress, and the U. S. Senate, where he lived and died, many years after, with democratic honors, but not many others. The Lone One soon learned that Democracy was more a name to elect *persons* with, than a principle ; and that nearly all political strife was personal, and only personal. The boys, old and young, great and small, in that state, think it requires a great man to hold a seat in the legislature, and that to be elected is a great honor ; but those who obtain it usually find it of little worth, except to lengthen the name by a prefix of Hon., but seldom makes a man honorable. Society is a three-fold structure, corresponding to our houses, with the social relations for the basis, or foundation, cemented with love in marriage, — when there is any in it, — and with the political relations for the frame, finished and braced with officers, and with the covering, or third part, of religion, nailed with rusty preachers, or bright and new ones, and sometimes painted with creeds, red with the fire of a pit, or black with eternal doom, or white with universal salvation, or yellow with hope, etc. The three are all essential to man, and hence we must not repudiate even politics ; for society would fall without them. Perhaps we can improve the old mode of framing and raising, but cannot dispense with it. Morality is an ingredient, or should be, in society, and in each part; and is what the finish is to the house, or texture to the body and brain of man. It is rather scarce in our day in either department, especially in politics, but may be cultivated even there.

The heart of the Lone One was already yearning for the love and sympathy of a happy home and social life, and his ambitious mind was aspiring to and for political action, and his religious nature was already feasting on Rationalism, the best religion he could find in that country. The Boston *Investigator* was his religious paper and guide, and one of the best for a young mind; for it teaches a reader to think, and develops intellect, which, in riper years, will be able to discover its errors.

Section II.

FLED.

The last days and sad hours spent in his native town at length passed by, and the tears ceased for a time to drop from the eyes of the *few* whose swollen hearts pressed them out. The coach came rattling up to the door, and the passenger entered, bound for the West, over hill, and vale, and river, and mountain, — green as name, or April, could make them, towards the old Dutch city of Albany. In his memory, well stored away, as in a picture-gallery, were faces and forms to be recalled in the far-distant land; and hills, and valleys, and houses, with scenes of sorrow and joy, all arranged in order for examination and review; sundered ties, and broken strings, arrows from hearts, and lutes without strings.

> " Where'er a human heart doth wear
> Joy's myrtle-wreath or Sorrow's gyves,
> Where'er a human spirit strives
> After a life more true and fair,
> There is the true man's birth-place grant,
> His is a world-wide faderland."

The Albany city was duly reached by the "post coach " from the Green Mountain state, and every familiar face was left behind by the Lone One, — all save the likenesses as they were taken in joy or sorrow on the memory-plate. Here he soon found the water-path westward, and "ticketed through " to the west end of the Clinton Ditch, and had **a quiet** week or more on canal-boat in reaching Buffalo. O, what a crowd, and city, and bustle, and confusion! No chance here for a raw Yankee, who had no money to speculate on. Therefore he took a steamboat passage as far as steamboats run to **the west,** and landed with a crowd of passengers at Detroit. Here, too, was crowd, and bustle, and still poorer chance for a Yankee. Here he found a schooner loading for Green Bay, and tried to get a passage, but his money was too short; he **was** therefore compelled to stop, but was now far from every relative and old friend, and **ready to** make **new friends.** After seeking business about the city for a **few** days, **he took** passage on **the little** boat, and landed **on the River Raisin, at Monroe,** and there sought a quiet family to **board with, and sought** work, of almost any kind, to pay it. After entirely exhausting **his money, he at** length found a place and wages in the variety store **of the "red-coat** man," whose fun and mirth and jolly soul did the heart of the Lone One good every day; for he **was** a ' heap " of fun, running over upon all around him, and **as** full **of** business as he was of fun. He had now found employment **and** rest for his anxious mind, and sat down to write the history **of his** journey, of which the eight **days on canal** reads somewhat in this wise: " Quartered in the cabin, well filled with emigrants westward bound — occupied with passing events, **and** events that were passing — on deck gazing at the moon, stars, **or** ' lower things ' — the mountain tops, ' low bridge,' **or** ragged rocks. Sitting in the cabin, early or late, chatting with a red-haired passenger, less in years than himself, and of the other sex, trying to forget the past. But this one was a 'Mary, also, and too often recalled one he would, but could not, forget. Sleeping in the cosey berth, as the horses towed him along the ' raging canal.'

5

At length the locks were lifted, the flats passed, death by mos
quitos escaped, — the long level shortened, the red-haired girl
landed, and Buffalo in sight. "What was next to be done, was next
to be planned." The Yankee boy was now in the far West; for Michigan was then Michigan Territory, and full of speculators and land-
hunters, and the best school to study the speculating side of
humanity that the nation offered to a student. The honest heart
of the Lone One was often shocked at the stories of immigrants
and emigrants, — for both were in Detroit, — some reporting
land covered with rattle-snakes sufficient to fence with picket
fences into ten-acre lots, and others saying it was almost a garden
of Eden, full of fruits and flowers; some cursing and shaking
with ague : one the effect of exposure and bad food and drink, and
the other of tobacco and bad habits. Never was there a deeper-
seated home-sickness than had now possession of the Lone One;
and, although he had left no home, and had none to return to,
yet,

" O, never can there be to man an earth
So green, or sky so pure, or stranger hearth
So welcome, and so warm and bright,
As where his boyhood's years fled by ! "

The Lone One was now fully resolved to once more return to
his rocky native state, which was also the native state of the red-
coat man, as soon as his wages would enable him to do so. The
River Raisin is wide, rapid, shallow, and beautiful, at this place.
For many years the banks had been settled and cultivated by the
Canadian French, who were quietly smoking the domestic tobacco, and eating their cabbages and sturgeon, before the Yankees
started a city and smoked out the old settlers, or bought them out
by, or with, whiskey and cheat. The new settlers were often mo-
lested by ague and fever, and occasionally by cholera ; and some
were driven back East, and some over Jordan, by these enemies to
quiet and speculation. During this season the Toledo war raged
in all its violence, and Monroe was the head-quarters for the
armies of Michigan and mosquitos. Those who have never read

the history of this war need not look for it here ; for our narrative will only admit **of a** few allusions to important facts, such as the whole number killed in the war was, *one* horse, and all the hens, and **turkeys,** and bees, and most of the pigs, between Monroe and Toledo, and an equal or greater number in Ohio, by the Buckeye army.   The Lone One was sent for, but could not go, for his soul abhorred wars, and this ridiculous farce more than any other. The red-coat **man did go,** but only for fun, with a red coat and tin gun, to make **joke-music** for the crowd ; for he could do it.

> " O ! who would fight, and march, and countermarch,
> Be shot **for** sixpence in a battle-field,
> And shovelled up into a bloody trench,
> Where no one knows — and all for fame ?
> Not I ! "

There was an end **to this war, although no** historian has ever recorded **it,** and this **narrative does not** contain it ; for the Lone **One did** not **have hold at either end nor middle.   The bush** end **was,** however, supposed **to be** among **the tax-payers some years after peace** was restored, not declared, **for it never was** declared. **Once** only **had the Orphan** been made to **follow a man in** " cap and feathers," with a gun **on** his shoulder, **at a** training, and that at sixteen ; and this he resolved should be the sum of his military experience, even if **it** cost imprisonment ; for both conscience and reason rebelled **against the farce** of training, and the cruelties of war.   Governor **Lucas, of Ohio, and** Governor Stevens T. **Mason,** of Michigan, were **the two great powers who** won the immortal honors in **this war, which has been equalled only once in our** country, in the " War of the Gauges," **the seat of which** was at Erie, Pennsylvania, through **which the Lone One** also passed with about the **same** dangers and glories **as in the other,** though somewhat later in the history of the **wars of Ohio,** These wars were like the Chian wine, " flavored unto him who drinketh it," but had not much pleasant flavor to others, and even to them who **drank, like** other wine, **they** caused a severe hair-pulling **afterward.**

Section III.

NEAR JORDAN.

The summer-greens, which constituted the principal fruit and shade-tree vegetation of the region round about Monroe, were fading into autumn-brown, or had already cast off their foliage, to scud in the winds, under "bare poles," during winter, when the Lone One began to count up his wages, and feel that he could once more return to the land of his childhood and hardships ere the close of navigation; for, after the lake and canal boats stopped running, there would be no chance till spring should again unlock the ice-bound shores; but "there is a power that shapes us to our ends," and lays the lines of human life that lead us to our goals. Down came the blow of fate's great hammer, and a fever, hot and cold, wrapped the body of the Lone One alternately in a cold and hot "pack," till he sauk, sank, sank, to the struggle with life and death, and with the old catholic physician, who had not much interest, but some anxiety, in the pending fate. Now came a time when he needed not only care and attention, but love and sympathy; for his excitable soul could only be holden to earth and to his body by the magnetic power of a kindred soul; and this he found and received from the sister of the red-coat man, with whom he boarded. She was mated, and lived pleasantly, without wealth or luxury, and furnished a quiet home for her brother and his clerks. Now, for the first time, the Lone One discovered the affectionate nature, the kind heart, the loving soul, of the sister; for she saved him, when the doctor could not, by the magnetic power of her ardent soul. Slowly the recuperative energies of his body revived and renewed his hold on life; and, with the aid from others, he recovered, late in autumn, sufficient strength to get back to the store, and shake with ague, and burn with fever, on each alternate day, for a few weeks, until he learned the nature of this loathsome disease, which of all diseases of our Western States plays upon our hopes and fears most carelessly, and ever leaves us more discouraged at each turn of its chill-tide. Gloomy, indeed, was the prospect ; his wages were used up, and he was in debt for " medicine and attendance," and winter had come, and, worse still, the ague had come, to hold him down from a recovery of health and strength. Sorry and sad was the heart of the orphan in this gloom of prospects ; but the pleasant smile and kind words of the sister and her husband (for he was a kind man) often touched and encouraged him, and the jokes and fun of the red-coat brother would sometimes almost make a pious man laugh, or a Quaker forget his gravity. Thus he lived into winter, outgrew the ague, and again engaged, at low wages, once more to try and pay the debts, and procure means to return to New Hampshire. Those, and those only, who have taken a course of ague and fever, can realize how it makes a live person feel. How it provokes one to wish the " Old Nick " would take hold and shake the body to pieces at once. How it makes one hate to live in it, and feel too mean to die with it. This is probably the reason so few **do die with it.** When the spring of '36 came, and one year's experience in the West was summed up, it read about thus : No money gained ; hard battle with chill fever, and acclimated by ague ; lived through one war ; found one affectionate woman, with a heart and soul worthy a better country and society ; but, like every person with whom he had found true charity, or real sympathy of soul (except Mary), she was not a professor of religion. Thus his experience continued to prove that professed Christians were not better than others, if as good ; confirming what infidel writers had written on this subject, and more firmly convincing him that religion was only a shell, covering a rotten system of creeds and pretences.

. When the May roses began to blossom, the restless and unhappy spirit resolved to make one more effort to better his condition and obtain money to return, of which he had not enough, and feared he never should have, when the demands of sickness and raiment were taken from his earnings. A prospect of higher wages induced him to start south, even in that unfavorable season of year, which would really endanger his life. The boat took him to

5*

Cleveland, and the stage to Beaver, Pennsylvania, and a river boat to Cincinnati, where, with some letters of introduction, he sought employment, but in vain. Diffident, even timid, and almost entirely unacquainted with western business life, he failed, as nineteen in every twenty would under such circumstances, to find employment, and made one more move, to Louisville, Kentucky. Fed at a hotel, and engaged an old man in an intelligence office to get him a place. The old man gave him good advice, and much caution against the vices which ruin so many young men in the South and West. Although it was not needed by the orphan, it was kindly received and duly appreciated, while what he needed more for his money was never obtained. Somebody always stepped in before him, and the old man's fair prospects and encouraging promises all ended in disappointment, and so did all other efforts, until the Lone One, almost distracted with his condition, entirely friendless, nearly penniless, and too sensitive to make his condition known, and accept some service to pay his board, finally resolved to return, but how, he could not devise. His trunk, with his all, scanty as it was, he could not carry, and did not think he could part with his books and few remaining clothes, and take the foot-path to Monroe. He found he could pay his bill at the hotel, and a deck fare on a boat to Portsmouth, where a canal from Cleveland lets down its boats to the Ohio. This was soon resolved upon, and he was moving up the river moneyless and supperless, with no prospects of a change in his favor by which he could go further, or get food and lodging; but he had looked hunger in the face before, and once almost stared him out of countenance, and thought he could do it again rather than beg. To work he was willing, but to beg he was not, for he had health and strength, and in such a country as ours these ought always to supply our wants, but they often fail. He reached Portsmouth, and found a boat ready to start for Cleveland on the canal; and on board he went and engaged a passage with board, and thus procured food, for his body was now suffering for want of its aliment. The next great question was how to pay. It was a great relief to find he was not required to pay in advance. There were several passengers on board, and he brought out some of his school-books, and tried in vain to sell some of them. That was " no go; " had they been novels, or trash of the yellow-cover stripe, no doubt he would have been more successful. What next? He had no clothes worth offering or to spare, but he tried next to sell his best coat; but it was an " old coat," and would not bring any money. One or two offered to *swap* with him **for** *boot*, **so** he could have a better one. **No** relief; and the day passed, and early bedtime found him weeping in his berth. Sleepless through the night he lay, turning in body and mind, reviewing himself and all his past life, and wondering what sin he had committed to merit this punishment. Almost resolved to go out and fall in the canal, and try to escape from the miserable existence which his parents or God had forced upon him. But his soul shuddered at the thought of self-murder, as it ever had at every species of crime. How could he believe there was a God? or, if there was, **that** *It* was **a good** God? Especially, if it was God who killed his mother and now **allowed** her poor orphan child to suffer in this way, certainly he could not be good. Perhaps he was offended because the boy did not pray for, and supplicate favors and aid ; but he never knew an instance of God feeding a hungry person by being asked to do so in prayer, and he had no confidence to ask God for money to pay his passage. He would have been ashamed to ask a fellow-mortal, and more so to ask God. There was no hope for help in **that** direction, nor could he see any in any other. The long sleepless night at length came to an end, and he was early up to meet the faces of all strangers, as the day before ; but, when they crept out of their berths, behold, one familiar face came out ; a young man whom he had **seen** at Monroe had come on board in the night at some landing-place, and crawled, unobserved by the sleepless orphan, into a berth. Had he seen him, he might have slept some, or, at least, found a new subject for reflection. The next difficulty was how to approach the young man with his case, and try to obtain relief; for his acquaintance was very limited, being barely sufficient for recognition. The Lone One lost no time in securing such items as would free his mind from doubts and fears. First he learned that the young man was bound for Monroe; this produced a thrill of joy which only those who know the importance of such little circumstances at times of trial, and whose souls are keen and sensitive, can know. A wave of joy ran over the nerves of the orphan at this news. After much ceremony, many delays, and several unsuccessful attempts, like a timid lover at question-popping time, he at last succeeded in asking for money enough to pay his fare to Monroe on the canal and lake boats, and promised to repay it on arrival, for he was sure he could borrow it there. His heart leaped for joy, and the tears filled his eyes, until he was ashamed of his weakness, when the almost stranger took out his money, and handed him all he asked for, and offered more if he needed it. The confidence and kindness of this young man touched a tender chord in his feelings, that had seldom been vibrated in the music of life; the mournful notes were silenced, and hope beamed on his countenance once more. Until we sink into deep distress and suffering we can never know how much joy some little favor, at particular times, can afford us; then we duly appreciate kindness, and learn important lessons for life, and often learn how to make others happy. It was not long after our sorry orphan had reached Monroe, and borrowed the money of a clerk in the store of the red-coat man, and repaid it to the passenger with more thankfulness than he could express in words, that he found out that this young man, who was intelligent, moral, honest, and consistent, in his life and actions, was, in the estimation of the Christians. a notorious infidel, and the son of infidel parents, — that the family never attended church, nor paid the preacher. This made another item in the experience of the Lone One.

A few friends seemed glad at his return, but none welcomed him more cordially than the sister and her husband. He soon procured employment as clerk in the post-office, and began once more to try the up-hill of life in a journey after money; for he found himself in a world of mostly Yahoos, where

> " Gold is the god the Yahoos adore ;
>   There no man 's criminal unless he 's poor."

There are said to be times, in the history of men, when the boy
sows his wild oats ; being a sort of reckless time for scattering
moral, and all other qualities of actions broad-cast. This may be
as applicable to states, territories, and communities, as to persons.
Michigan was sowing her wild oats in the years which were running through the great year-glass when these incidents occurred,
the most prolific crop of which came up and were harvested in
wild-cat notes some time after. The population consisted mainly
of land speculators and fortune-seekers, which pursuits in themselves would not make persons bad ; but the constant commotion,
fluctuating prospects, and varied vicissitudes, of those times, brought
out to the surface, as a warm pack does the measles, the worst
features in the population. Michigan was then a hard state, or
territory, for it is not yet certain when she became a state ; for
this was a year of two governments, or one, or none ; and the
people could not determine which, neither can history. Only a
few months of quiet business in this department, and another
change of occupation, although he had heard it said " a rolling
stone gathers no moss." Shrewd business men in Michigan, who
watched the passing events, knew that breakers were ahead, and
the red-coat man was of that kind ; and when the autumn
glided into winter a new firm occupied the old store, and tried
to sell the remnants of everything ; for the old variety-shop
contained all sorts of traps, from ox-yokes to little pills of
Nux put up in homœopathic bottles. One of the new firm soon
sold to the Lone One. Poor as he was, his credit was good, because his habits were good, and his word reliable ; but at this
time such credit did not prove an advantage, for it gave, in the
change, promises of better days, and brought darker and harder
trials than ever before, in consequence of changes which had their
origin in this misstep in business. He had not learned the necessity, every young man without pecuniary means was under, of

securing first some money before he assumes debts and liabilities
or social responsibilities requiring money in greater or less abundance. But he was now in a fair way to learn it by experience,
which would doubtless make a deep and lasting impression. The
young merchants were not elated, but resolved on the strictest
economy and close application to business, which in ordinary
times would have enabled them to sustain themselves even without the capital, as they had long credit and low interest, neither
of which were common in that country at that time. The desire
to return East had expired, burned itself out, and the Lone One
now resolved to make the West his future home ; and, indeed, he
might as well, for Mary was married, or engaged to be soon, and
he had no relatives, east or west, who felt any interest in his
whereabouts, save as they did in other persons who were not akin ;
or rather only two or three females, who could not aid him, except
by sympathy. Of these was one fair-haired cousin, whose sympathy he could not receive, because in him it produced love in
return, which she could not receive ; and he had now resolved to
break every tie to New Hampshire in his feelings, and harden all
but his conscience for western life. That he never could harden,
for it was master over him, although it might have been a creature of education, as some people say it is. His home was with
the kind sister of the red-coat man, for certainly he would never
board at any other place while she would feed him at her table,
where kind words were only in correspondence with the neatness
and order and excellent selections of food and dishes. She was a
native of New Hampshire, and had an attractive old homestead
there, and many kind friends, and relatives almost without number ;
and in this autumn of '36 she repaired thither for a visit, leaving
the Lone One to take care of the house and girls, &c. Of this
visit it may be said " thereby hangs a tale" which requires a
rest ; so we will stop over here.

> " Hands of invisible spirits touch the strings
>   Of that invisible instrument, the soul,
>   And play the prelude of our fate."

SECTION IV.

ANOTHER LINE.

> " I saw two clouds at morning
>   Tinged by the rising sun ;
>   And in the **dawn they floated on,**
>   And mingled into **one ;**
>   I thought that morning cloud was blest,
>   It moved so **sweetly** to the west.

> " I saw two **summer** currents
>   Flow smoothly to their meeting,
>   And join their course with silent force,
>   In peace each other greeting ;
>   Calm was their course through banks of green,
>   While dimpling eddies played between.

> " **Such be your gentle motion,**
>   **Till life's last pulse shall beat !**
>   Like summer's **beam and summer's stream,**
>   Float on, in joy, to meet
>   In calmer sea, where storms shall cease —
>   In purer sky, where all is peace."

On the west side of the Granite State is a small district called
Sullivan County. Two hundred years ago it was a dense forest
of evergreens, with subsoil rich in granite boulders and sand. Now
it comprises some of the best farms in the state, and several beautiful villages, with long rows of summer-green shade-trees, fine
gardens, capacious dwellings, and plenty of churches and school-
houses. On one of these farms, high up on the hill-side, lived
Enoch and Betsey, and reared a family **of boys** and girls by
unceasing toil and rigid economy; for **only** by such could a
family live on **such** a farm, and improve it, until, like this one, it
became a valuable old homestead. Many, many years ago there
lived in England a man whose occupation was thatching, and they
called him John, or William the Thatcher. He took to himself a
wife, and they had little thatchers. These grew up, and did like-
wise. The friends dropped *the*, and thus, like many other family

names, began the Thatcher family, which has branched out and multiplied exceedingly ; one line of which ran so close to the house of Enoch, that the farms and families joined, and the kindred currents of blood connected the families as the brooks did the farms. Hand in hand, and side by side, the two families struggled through years, with rocks too vast for " Ajax' throw," and snow-drifts deep enough for an Esquimaux den such as Dr. Kane describes in his Arctic expedition. The father of Enoch had nearly worn out his body on the farm before he transferred it to his son and Betsey, and quietly resigned his body and deaconship to rest, after a long life of toil. Then his spirit went home to its heaven of kindred souls, for he was a good man. Enoch was a man of industry, economy, and practical piety, but was never entangled in the meshes of a church creed. He trusted God to judge him by his life, without a priest to plead for him as a member of a church ; and, as we learn from the spirit-world, to which he moved in ripened years and extreme old age, he found as warm a welcome and good friends there as those who spent much of life in building churches and supporting preachers, and progresses much faster there than the creed-bound souls. Betsey, who was closely linked to the Thatcher family, but not in name, was more closely entwined in the religion of a church, and securely locked in the Baptist fold of close communion notoriety ; but she was one of the best of New England's wives and mothers, and a conscientious and exemplary Christian, and would have been as sure of heaven (if there is a heaven for the good), if there had never been a church in the nation, as she is with all her church connections. She still lingers at the old homestead, familiar with its growth and changes through more than half a century. Enoch and Betsey reared to man and womanhood two sons and three daughters, and let several others drop into the arms of angels, to be reared under the guidance and direction of spirits in the other country, where so many little children go to get their education, and growth, and religion ; whether under more favora-ble circumstances than in this is not certainly known, but by many believed to be so. The elder son served out his time on the homestead farm, with much sickness arising from the bite of a mad fox; then married a religious wife of excellent disposition, and with her, settled in the vicinity of his native home, travelled some, and traded more, till he had a homestead of his own, **and** with his mate reared a large family of sons and daughters. The sons, with much business talent and well adapted to speculation in the West, repaired thither to get rich, but with no religious tendencies, and little mental, intellectual, or spiritual development, in or for other departments of life. The daughters grew to a goodly stature in body and mind, and would have been fine specimens of Yankee girls, had not the natural powers and elasticity of their minds been cramped by the theology of the school where they completed their education, and by the still more narrow creed and discipline of the church at home, into which they were pressed. The father stemmed the current of superstition until about the middle of life, when he was caught by an epidemic revival and locked in the Baptist fold, and, with a zeal and devotion worthy a better cause, lost his labor in his efforts to convert sinners. **But** he is still stout for the fight; has on the whole armor of the church, and is zealously aiding to roll on the sectarian car over "Jordan's hard road to travel on." The other son was the red-coat man of the River Raisin, whose peculiar genius led him early from home, to roam and speculate, and get rich two or three times in life, and to get into, and out of, religion, and almost everything else, several times. His narrative-path, on land and sea, high and low, up and down, to his present home, on the west shore of Lake Erie, at his own little village, where a large house, full of wife and babies, is the home of all who come to it, would be highly interesting; for he was always an interesting man. But we have no room for it here; we have already "switched off" our narrative too often to allow other trains to pass; and fear, if we do not keep the main track where we have the right of way, we may be behind time at our dépôt.

The eldest daughter married out of the name, and carried the homestead to another line of heirships; but for quiet domestic life, few daughters of the mountain did better, or as well, as Sally. Few happier homes could be found than she had, and made for her parents and friends. One only child, a daughter, was the offspring of this union. In childhood, the pet; in girlhood, the favorite of every acquaintance. In '55 a stranger found her at the old homestead with a beautiful little pet daughter swinging in a basket in the old red kitchen, the wife of a man who did not change her paternal name, a returned Californian, with as noble and generous a heart as ever beat in a visitor to that land of the sunset. "What a homestead!" exclaimed the visitor. "What a pet with its mother, and grandmother, and great-grandmother, father and grandfather, at home!" all in health and comfort. This eldest daughter and her husband joined church with the mother, but like her never allowed their religion to destroy their humanity, or kindness to all of God's children. They never attempted to force their creed upon others, nor to fight their way to heaven; but left the fighting for others, of more belligerent dispositions.

The second daughter was the kind sister into whose care our wanderer fell in the time of his sickness, and whose charity and good qualities of soul were always a sure guaranty of heaven in the other life, without a religious creed; and hence she needed and received none. She married in the West. Two boys were the offspring of the union, when a consumption seized her husband, and soon freed his spirit from its earthly tenement, and her from his efforts to obtain the means of support and education for their children; but she struggled on in the West against fearful odds, for a time, then returned to her native town, and there, by the industry and economy learned of her mother, with much skill and ingenuity aided her boys into manhood, ever maintaining that kind spirit and warmth of soul which were hers in days of prosperity. The other daughter was the last and youngest of the family, but not least in importance, especially in this narrative. She was the pet of both father and mother, and early pressed into the church to be saved; for at that time there was little hope of the other children being saved through the church, and certainly one of the family ought to go with their excellent **and** dear mother, and it was an evidence of kindness, if nothing **more, in** her to **join** church with the mother. Of religion at that time **she** knew very little, especially of the subtle creeds of the orthodox church. She was educated for **a teacher, and had some experi-** ence in training the young ideas **to** shoot **like buds into blossom,** when, in the autumn of '36, the sister from the West returned for **a short visit** to the mountain home of her childhood.

After much effort at persuasion the parents and eldest sister consented to the proposed visit of the youngest sister to Michigan, with a promise of return with spring. Thus arranged, when the husband came for his mate, and the one husband and two sisters started for the western home, from which very few girls ever return to New England without being first married. Pleasantly they jolted and glided over road, and canal, and lake, and safely landed at Monroe, where the guest was soon introduced to the friends and visitors, among whom was, **of** course, the Lone One; for this was the most like a home of any he found. Only a few weeks, and the industrious Yankee girl was found teaching a school some miles in the country; but Saturday nights she **was** found at her sister's, usually by the aid of one who boarded there; and, although the horse and buggy hire was greater than amount received for teaching, yet economy was never a consideration in love affairs, and one pocket paid, while the other received, the **sums.** Is it possible the orphan is contemplating marriage, with no home and no means to purchase one? Few friends, and none to help him to a home; and that to a beautiful girl, with precarious health, just arrived from the East, **and yet** to be acclimated, by sickness and trials, to the western climate, — he an infidel, she a Christian?

" The dream that wishing boyhood knows
Is but a bright beguiling spell,
Which only lives while passion glows .

But when this early flush declines,
" When the heart's vivid morning fleets,
You know not then how close it twines
  Round the first kindred soul it meets."

Moore.

" No one is so accursed by fate,
  No one so utterly desolate,
  But some heart, though unknown,
  Responds unto his own, —
  Responds, as if with unseen wings
  An angel touched its quivering strings,
  And whispers, in its song,
  Where hast thou strayed so long?"

Longfellow.

Thus it was; but the lonely heart of the orphan had borne its burdens of grief and sorrow long enough alone. Why should not some sympathizing spirit share with him the trials and griefs? The only question now was, Who shall it be? Who will volunteer for a campaign, in which hardships are most painful and soul-trying, but for which there awaits a pension and country's blessing, at last? Who will enlist and accept the commission? She accepted, and received the following commission ·

" When the day of life is dreary,
  And when gloom thy course enshrouds ;
When thy step is faint and weary,
  And thy spirits dark with clouds,
Steadfast still in thy well-doing,
  Let thy soul forget the past;
Steadfast still the right pursuing,
  Doubt not joy shall come at last.

" Striving still, and onward pressing,
  Seek not future years to know,
But deserve the wished-for blessing, —
  It shall come, though it be slow ;
Never **tiring, upward gazing,**
  Let thy fears aside be cast,
And thy trials tempting, bearing,
  Doubt not joy shall come at last.

> " Keep not then thy mind regretting;
>   Seek the good, spurn evil's thrall ;
> Though thy foes thy path besetting,
>   Thou shalt triumph o'er them all ;
> Though each year but bring thee sadness,
>   And thy youth be fleeting fast,
> There 'll be time enough for gladness, —
>   Doubt not joy shall come at last."

But a marriage ! **O, the thoughts of a marriage !** None but the ardent and impassioned youth can ever know the feelings, — the doubts, the fears, the excited curiosity, the dreams, the mys-tery, which hang over an appproaching event of this nature, to the young, the unqualified, the untutored mind, as these, and most others, were at their first experiment in social and domestic bondage.   How often these dreams of bliss unspeakable — these anticipations of joy beyond measure — prove only dreams, or fancy sketches, that fade like the mirage, or burst like the bubble when touched by real life !   How often does this happiest and most sacred institution of social life, under our present system of legal control and restraint, become only a wheel of persecution, and misery, and suffering, that soon crushes the weaker of the twain to an untimely death, to make way for another, often to follow !   How futile the attempt to legalize, regulate, and control the affections by statute, and make uncongenial beings love each other, because in the wild passions of uneducated youth they made **a sad mistake, and,** as many do by such mistakes, made each other miserable, instead of happy.   When will the institutions of men be founded on nature, and contribute to our happiness, instead of breaking **us,** bone after bone, **on the wheel of an** inquisition ?

Competent observers of the social relations of our time suppose there are about one couple in fifty who are spiritually and physi-cally married, — whose souls are united, and bodies harmonized to each other ; and about one third of the others are fraternally mar-ried, and live in a sort of business relation, quietly, and often happily, to all outward appearance ; some feeling a kindred bond of sympathy, bordering on love. The rest are in sunshine and showers mixed, or cat and dog life, barking and snapping much of the time when the neighbors are not in sight or hearing. It is almost a certain sacrifice **of happiness,** health, or life, for a delicate, sensitive and refined girl, with a pure body, to be united in marriage to a man with a body polluted with tobacco, pork, and strong drink, **and** hardened by physical exercise so as to endure those poisons. **Too** many victims are ready **to testify to** this assertion to need other proof, and yet how seldom they caution the young, and warn others to avoid their terrible experience !

Do not be hasty, reader, in judging the fate of these two streams from the mountains of the Granite State, which are hereafter to be united in one name and life, and move on in one channel to the ocean of spirit-life. For in your haste you may not judge aright. Wait and read, then inquire of each ; for from each you may learn the experience that at least will be an advice, if you need it. There are narrows and shoals, rocks and quicksands, islands and windings, in nearly every stream of life with double channel, and the experience of pilots is not to be despised **by the young.** Sugar River empties into, and is lost in the Connecticut. So this mountain lass from its banks lost a part of her name in that of the stranger, and took passage in the turbulent Life-Line **of** the Lone One, somewhat in this wise : On the 5th day of the year 1837, being the twenty-fourth natal day of the orphan, the sun sank slowly in the western haze of a winter sky, and the day faded from sight, leaving a long evening before bedtime. The Lone One was still only one ; had no relative in the West, had seen none since he left the East, and scarcely expected to ever more see one from that region ; for most of them were too poor to come so far. He was early this evening at the house of his kind friend. The younger sister was also present. She had numbered a score or more of the birth-day mile-stones, which are so conspicuous in our youth, and so much neglected in age. The parlor fire was burning brightly, the lamps were trimmed, the furniture tastily arranged ; **the** red-coat man also came early in,

and was amusing the company with jokes, when a gentle rap at
the door brought silence in the parlor. Slowly the doors were
opened, and in came a dark-robed priest, from the Episcopal fort
of devotion and defence. He was merry and sociable, and soon
restored mirth in the circle; but the orphan and the younger
sister of the red-coat man were absent. Still the laugh and joke
went round, until suddenly opened a door, and slowly, but majestically came in the Lone One, curiously robed in Quaker drab,
and the sister in wedding white, accompanied by a youth and lass,
who arranged themselves on either side, as the four placed themselves before the priest, who now began to look grave and solemn,
as if some terrible event was about to befall the company. The
company remained seated, only the·two who stood beside the pair,
to catch them in case of fainting or falling by the awful ceremony about to be performed. The mystic words fell slow and
sure from the *sacred* lips of the "man of God," who bade these
two to eat and sleep, to bed and board, to live and love, to command and obey, to support and serve, to hold and bear one name,
to the end of life's journey on earth; but they bound no further;
for the wise priest said, in his heaven, where his Saviour lived,
there was *no marrying nor giving in marriage.* Ah, false man!
why work against thy prayers? When thou prayest daily for
that kingdom to come on earth in which there is no marrying,
how shall it come while thy works are against thy prayers? But
great are the mysteries of thy ways, O priesthood of earth! They
did not faint or fall on receiving the awful bond by which the
priest said God put two beings together so that no man should
dare to put them asunder. If God did do it, then the priest did
not; and if God did not, then the priest surely did not; and
hence his act was useless either way, except as a license to society
to call them man and wife; for the priest said they might be called
so, for *he* made them so. The solemn part of the scene was short;
and soon the kiss, the laugh, the joke, the cake, and — last, but
not least — the wine, went round; and all, even the solemn priest,
partook, and became merry.

Slowly the company departed or retired; and the wonderful and fearful bed-time came for the twain who had never known such lodgings before, and never can again. Somehow, there is something mysteriously undefinable in the first month of a young married couple who have ever been diffident and reserved, and have known nothing of the relations of social or sexual life, save what a lying and gossipping world has told them. We shall not follow them to the chamber, nor through the sleepless hours, but leave curiosity on its tiptoe, with such caution as might be given by the saddened and paling countenance, and the tear-wet pillows, which have marked the early experience of many wedded pairs. Happiness! Shall we call this a change for happiness, — such a change as brought, for both, new trials and troubles, but especially severe ones for the one who had left her quiet mountain home, her name, and her liberty, and agreed to love, serve, and obey? No person with equal capacity ever tried harder to submit to fate, and be happy in an uncongenial condition of new and strange life, than did this fair girl in her new relation of wife. But the countenance paled, the form emaciated, the cough increased; but still the smile ever welcomed the husband, and no complaint was uttered, save the occasional hint that an early death was approaching. Is this a solitary experience? If so, it is not worth relating. If not, it hath other testimonies, and the cause should be sought and found; and if it was the pork, tobacco, and coffee, used by one only of the twain, others should be warned to avoid, and the young be cautioned against, their baneful effects. His soul could still be heard to murmur, in its sadness:

> "Though the day of my destiny's over,
>   And the star of my fate hath declined,
> Thy soft heart refused to discover
>   The faults which so many could find.
> Though thy soul with my grief was acquainted,
>   It shrunk not to share it with me;
> And the love which my spirit hath painted
>   It never hath found but in thee."

And hers :

> " No ! let the eagle change his plume,
> The leaf its hue, the flower its bloom ;
> But ties around this heart once spun —
> They cannot, will not, be undone."

> " But the mistletoe clings to the oak, not in part,
> But with leaves closely round it ; the root in its heart
> Exists but to clasp it, — imbibe the same dew, —
> Or to fall with its loved oak, and perish there, too."

SECTION V.

ANOTHER LIFE.

The female side of the two-in-one prayed, and the answer came :

> " Ask what thou wilt," said a fairy voice,
> " Ask what thou wilt of me ;
> Of all on earth thou canst have thy choice,
> On the land, or on the sea.
> I have the power rich gifts to bestow,
> And what thou wilt I 'll grant :
> But only *once*, I would have thee know,
> Can I supply thy want."

> Then I sat down, and pondered long
> On what the gift should be
> Which the fairy voice had kindly said
> Should be given but once to me.
> I will not ask that wealth or fame
> Should a worthless chaplet twine
> Around my brow, or adorn my name,
> Nor that beauty should be mine ;

> For these are transient as the dew
> Before the burning sun,
> And fade as quickly from the view
> Ere morning is begun.
> " In none of these," my heart replied,
> " Would the height of happiness be ;
> True love and a happy home," I cried,
> " Is all that I ask of thee."

The fairy wrote, " 'T is granted." But, O, the distance to it,
and the terrible path that was to be travelled, over rocks and
quicksands, quagmires and dismal swamps, in heats of sun, and
storms of icy rain, more than this narrative can record, or the heart
can ever recall and relate ! But we will follow her through the
years to the happy home of destiny and declining years, if we
can, (leaving out many of the sorest trials of domestic life), in a
new country, through deep poverty, poor health, and a sick heart.
The masculine side of the two-in-one prayed, and the answer came
also to him ; but the prayers were not one :

> " O, I envy those
> Whose hearts on hearts as faithful can repose ;
> Who never feel the void, the wandering thought,
> That sighs o'er visions such as mine hath wrought."

Then the impulsed answer came, with slow promise :

> " He who would be the tongue of this wide land
>   Must string his harp with chords of sturdy iron,
> And strike it with a toil-embrowned hand.
>   Such, such is he for whom the world is waiting
> To sing the beatings of its mighty heart ;
>   Too long hath it been patient with the grating
> Of scrannel-pipes, and heard it misnamed Art."

But thou shalt ever move

> " With a high and holy purpose,
>   Doing all thou find'st to do,
> Seeking ever man's upraising,
>   With the highest end in view.
>
> " Undepressed by seeming failure,
>   Unelated by success,
> Heights attained revealing higher —
>   Onward, upward, ever press.
>
> " Slowly moves the march of ages,
>   Slowly grows the forest king ;
> Slowly to perfection cometh
>   Every great and glorious thing.

> " Broadest streams from narrowest sources ;
>   Noblest trees from meanest seeds ;
>   Mighty ends from small beginnings ;
>   From lowly promise lofty deeds.
>
> " Acorns which the winds have scattered
>   Future navies may provide ;
>   Thoughts at midnight whispered lowly
>   Prove a people's future guide.
>
> " Such the law enforced by nature
>   Since the earth her course began ;
>   Such to thee she searcheth daily,
>   *Eager, ardent, restless* man.
>
> " Never hasting, never resting ;
>   Glad in peace, and calm in strife ;
>   Quietly thyself preparing
>   To perform thy part in life.
>
> " Earnest, hopeful, and unswerving,
>   Weary though thou art, and faint,
>   Ne'er despair, — there 's God above thee,
>   Listing ever to thy plaint.
>
> " Stumbleth he who runneth fast ;
>   Dieth he who standeth still ;
>   Nor by haste nor rest can ever
>   Man his destiny fulfil.''

The letter from the Baptist church in New Hampshire, which she brought with her, never reached its destination in another church ; for she adopted the more rational religion of her husband readily, and ever after, slowly but finally, sought a heaven and home with him for the other life, as she had chosen one with him in this. The Lone One now had a hired home, such as his low circumstances would allow ; **was** settled, not as a preacher, although he did sometimes *preach*, when opportunity offered, not because he was ordained, or licensed to preach, but because the spirit moved him to it, and he had the right by double baptism ;

for he was often baptized by the Holy Ghost, or good spirits, and he had once been baptized by water; not by human hands, but by God, somewhat in this wise: When quite a boy, he went alone on a cloudy day to a meadow, in a wood, quite secluded from road and farm, to angle for trout and pickerel, in a small stream which followed its snaky path through the meadow. It was on one of those cold, ocean-storm days so common on the coast of New England in May and June. When he reached the edge of the pine and hemlock forest bordering the meadow, the tall grass was very wet, and it began to rain steadily. Like the bathing maid in the Summer of Thomson's Seasons, he cast a searching glance around for man and beast, — for he was extremely bashful. Satisfied that none but he and God were present, — and before God he was not ashamed, — he carefully laid away every article of covering in a hollow log, where they would keep dry, and entered the meadow naked as he entered the world. Then and there God baptized him from the clouds for half a day or more. The witnesses were angels and crows, and the record made in heaven and his memory, and the manner was both by sprinkling and immersion, and he received it both in fear and trembling; for he feared some man or beast might come that way, and trembled with cold. Caught the fish, and probably a cold, and returned late, and quite dry for one whom God had just baptized with five hours' sprinkling, and an immersion in the brook. He always considered afterward, if baptism was a saving ordinance, that this was sufficient for him; as the ceremony was performed by the head of nature's church, and witnessed and recorded by angels. The other baptism was also of God, through nature, — for God was the author and father of his nature, — which had endowed him with both desire and capacity to preach, or rather to talk in public.

Persons who resided in the Western States and figured in business life in '37 and '38 have not forgotten, and will not soon forget, the convulsions of commerce and trade at that time; the suspension of banks, and failure of business men, both great and small. The scarcity of money, and entire want of confidence in all

western traders and speculators, induced the Lone One to close up
his small business, discontinue his auction and commission sales,
return his assortment of infidel books, — which had been kept
conspicuously on the shelf for sale, — to the owners and publish-
ers, — the Mattsells, of New York, — to pack up such goods as he
believed would be needed, or would sell readily, and could be
spared from the store, and send them by and with a friend to
Wisconsin, the land which he had selected as his future home,
and to which he had resolved to remove early in the spring of
'38, if the health of his wife would permit; for he could not now
think of going without her, although it might have been better for
both if he had gone, and prepared a home to receive them before
moving her. Neither the fourth volume of the Great Harmonia
nor Esoteric Anthropology had been published, nor had any other
book fallen into their hands which contained the instruction, so
necessary for new beginners in domestic life, which these, and
some of Fowler's works contain.

Late in the fall of '37 the business was all closed up, sold out,
and transferred, and the little family ready to move. But in the
mean time other changes had transpired, which must be noted
here.

The bachelor red-coat man had become a husband, and by the
aid of the Lone One had surveyed a village plot, ten miles from
Monroe, named it for his native town, moved to it, and commenced building a western city in a place where commerce —
which alone builds cities — never required one. At this new home
the husband and wife had resolved to spend the winter, with the
brother and wife; but there was one more whose interests and
welfare were to be consulted. Early in the autumn the skill of
an experienced physician was required at the home of the Lone
One; and, could an experienced mother have seen the pale face,
the often almost strangled and convulsed condition, by coughing,
of the wife, and other causes, she would not have wondered,
more than the physician did, that three pounds of boy were
hurried into outer life two months before the proper time, and,

breathing feebly, gave signs of life, which the skilful physician
said could by no possible means be saved and reared to manhood.
But he was not infallible; for, although the "*little thing*" did
not grow for several weeks, and often stopped breathing to
all appearance, yet the renewal of breath from the mother, and
stimulants, with a warm bath, renewed and continued life, till
the form began slowly to grow, which did not entirely stop until
it reached a stature nearly equal to that of the father, and
somewhat like it in form, with a mind capable of extending
further, and better adapted to life. They gave him the name of
a great and distinguished poet, but one whose mantle of mental and physical blindness they hoped would never fall on him.
Slowly the form of the mother recovered partially, but not fully,
from this premature sickness, and dragged out a miserable existence,
in great anxiety and constant care of this pet, at the new home of
the brother, during the long, cold winter of '37 and '38. The
brother and wife were kind, and all tried to make her as comfortable as circumstances would allow; but they expected the spring
would carry both mother and child to the grave-yard. But both
survived, and the mother is now reaping the reward for her
trials and care in the kind and dutiful attention of one of the best
of sons, and an excellent scholar, both in science and life. The
science of married life is a great and important science, but few have
published to the world, for the benefit of others, their experiments
or experience in it. If they would,— and especially those who con-
stitutionally break down, and send to untimely graves two or three
partners and more children, — it might be more useful to young
people than the thousands of religious tracts and foolish novels that
flood the markets of literature.

One yearly mile-stone on the journey of united life had now
been passed, and the experience of the journey deeply recorded
on each heart. Both had now realized what most persons realize
as the ultimate of courtship. The deep soul-yearnings of the
Lone One, who eagerly and ardently and constantly yearned for
love and fondness in such abundance as would bring up the want

of long years of dearth and coldness, through which he had lived, could only be met and satisfied by the deepest, strongest, and most ardent and devoted soul, in a fully-developed body and mind. The tender object of his love and care had ever been — as the youngest child of a large family — nursed with fondness, and loved and petted, without being taught to express the soul's deepest emotions in return. She had never been scathed in the fiery furnace of trial and trouble, which has ever developed and purified the soul of man or woman, and called out the inner life, with all its force and energy. With a feeble body and strong mental system; large brain, coarser and more uniform in texture, and slower in action than the other, but capable of great intensity of feeling when aroused. With a scrofulous consumption on the lungs, and the duties and burdens of a wife and mother in poverty pressing upon her mind and body, she bore her burden without complaint, but in misery and sorrow; for it was plainly written on her pallid countenance that the reality of married life, under such circumstances, was not the beautiful realization of the fairy dreams of girlhood, or the heaven of romance which novelists so often picture in the union of lovers. The constant labor of the husband supplied the immediate wants, but made little progress toward securing the more permanent comforts of domestic life. The snow-storms of winter were drifting around the border of Erie. The mother was watching and nursing, day and night, the pet at the new and rude home of the brother; the husband was some distance up the river, in the forest, tending, with his former partner in the store — who was also a young husband, and poor — a saw-mill which they had leased, and in which they were, by constant hard labor, making lumber quite fast, and piling it up near the mill, on the hill-side, to save the labor of carrying it far away. Late one Saturday night, in the midst of a cold and windy snow-storm, the mill suddenly stopped by some break or obstruction in the wheel under the high water. It was a cold and difficult work to uncap the wheel and remove the obstruction in the cold water, dark night, and exhausted condition of their bodies, and they "raked up" their fire, and, as they supposed, made all safe, and started for their homes. No family was living in sight of the mill; and only Thor, with his winds, was left to guard the mill in the absence of the occupants.

Next morning, near ten o'clock, a Frenchman came to inform the partners that God had let the winds blow the fire about the mill, and it had all burned down, and the large pile of lumber had rolled in and shared the same fate. This " providential occurrence" had taken place on the Sabbath day, when the occupants of the mill were resting according to command; but when the winds, and snows, and fires, would not stop to rest, showing that God did not rest on that day, in this age, if he ever did. The loss of rent, lumber, and labor, was a severe one for both the partners, but did not change the determination of the Lone One to start early in the spring for Wisconsin, where he hoped to be able to secure a home, by industry and economy, in a few years. The smouldering fire-ruins of the old mill went out, and the day brightened into a clear, calm, and beautiful evening, and the Lone One was again with the mother and babe. How pleasant, how calm, how happy, how full of joy and love, is a truly wedded life, where body and spirit and mind are united by God's harmonic law of true marriage, which ever binds two — *only two* — souls in one life, in which the will of each is the desire of both, and the desire of each is ever in harmony with the interest of the other. 'T is a beautiful picture, which cannot be too highly wrought, but which is seldom realized in what we call marriage. Only enough instances to prove it true are to be found; but the immortal Keats says:

> " Love in a hut, with water and a crust,
> Is — Love forgive us ! — cinders, ashes, dust ! "

And Rogers, that

> " Through the wide world, he only is alone
> Who lives not for another."

And Froude, that

> " Love is not in our power, —
>   **Nay,** what seems stranger, is not in our choice ;
>   **We** only love where fate ordains we should,
>   And, blindly fond, oft slight superior merit."

This little family had no home, and faint, indeed, was the glimmering hope of soon obtaining one. The restless and ambitious, but unsatisfied, soul of the husband had yielded to the earnest wish of the wife to **seek** first a home, after obtaining which, perhaps, all other desirable things might be added, as to those who seek first, and find, the kingdom of heaven, which, according to the latest interpretation, is the sphere of spirit-life. Early in spring the little group of three, **two of them** almost helpless, started on the watery path, by schooner, round the rivers and lakes, to a spot called Southport, on the west shore of Lake Michigan, where a company, promising the Lone One employment, had partly purchased a tract of land for purposes of speculation. Three long weeks, — sick all the time, — they were tossed, and drifted, and floated, and blown, on the waters ; and, passing, in a gale of wind, the Southport landing, they were at last unshipped, in persons and effects, in Chicago, to have their few effects nearly destroyed in being again shipped on another schooner, with another freight and passage bill to pay. After four more days of beating against wind and fate, they at last were landed on the sand-beach of destination, with a few dollars of good money, and a few of " wild-cat " and " red-dog," which only served to deceive them with illusive hopes of purchasing necessaries. A few articles for housekeeping were brought along, and those were nearly ruined in the journey, as the health of the three seemed to be. They had been often told, by the kind Captain M'Niff, **of the** Barker, that they would certainly have to deposit the babe in the lake, or bury it on shore, and that the mother's chance was but little better for life. But they all landed alive, and never was a heart gladder to set foot on shore than was that of the Lone One, even though in poverty and among strangers. Twenty dollars of the small amount with which he started had been kindly loaned to him by an infidel

and the path pursued to the point of destination. A corn-planter, on the prairie, directed the traveller to the claim he inquired for, but informed him his friend had gone from home, and might not return till the morrow. He sought the ten-by-twelve shanty, and soon unfastened its door, took possession, and diligently searched for food. Bread he could not find; but maple-sugar, and honey, and part of a ham of pork, he found; and the beautiful brook, which played along its narrow channel by the door, was lined with cowslips. Soon he had the tea-kettle (the only article he could find that was suitable) full of the stems and flowers, boiling, over a renewed fire, in the rude fireplace. The boiled ham, salted greens, and honey-comb, made him the best dinner and supper he had eaten for many years. It was a beautiful day, and a beautiful place, such as only those who have been reared at hard work, among rocks, and stumps, and hills, and swamps, can appreciate; and only those whose souls are inspired by the beauties of nature, and her wild-flowers, and magnificent landscapes, can enjoy.

When he had enjoyed all his tired body would allow, and the curtain of night had dropped down over the scene, he cradled in the bunk or berth that was roped up on the side of the shanty, about six feet long by two feet wide, in which were some parts of a bed. The tired body and worried mind were both soon wrapped in repose; and the " ocean of dreams without a sound " was not disturbed until long after the sun had begun shining on the beautiful prairie, awakening its songsters, foliage, and flowers. Suddenly the door opened; and, aroused, the Lone One opened his eyes 'to meet the face of his old friend, whose astonishment and curiosity could not be satisfied till long after the cake was baked, and meat cooked, and tea made, and the breakfast despatched. Sad news soon spread its terrible shade over the Lone One, as he learned that the vessel on which their goods were shipped had been wrecked, and his goods all lost. What next? Dark, darker, darkest prospect, what next? Surely it is true that misfortunes seldom come single; but once it was so, — when the Lone One was born. The claim-and-shanty Prince was somewhat the senior of the orphan. His female partner for life had left him in Vermont, and gone off with some other person to some other place, — they called it dying; and as she left her body a corpse, they buried that, and never inquired after her more. The daughters were scattered out to live; and the old man, poor and lonely, **had** wandered westward, where, at Monroe, he made the acquaintance of the Lone One; and they soon felt the truth of the old adage, "A fellow-feeling makes us wondrous kind." But he made his fortune in this claim, and ripened his years in wealth, but declined in loneliness, for his life was marked with troubles for which he was not accountable. His kind heart prompted him to offer all he could of assistance. He proposed to get an ox-team, to bring the family and effects to the prairie, and to this little shanty, and there make a common home, until they could do better. But the Lone One could not consent to bring the feeble mother and child to such a place and condition, and in such a manner. He declined the kind offer, and, with a sad heart, paced slowly back the winding way to the partner's quarters, to sadden the heart of the mother with the news of their loss, and to gladden the face of the child, who had no care about it. He informed the fat old householder (he could not be called a landlord, for he owned no land, and was anything but a lord) that he could not pay the board charges more than a week without some means of obtaining money to do it with, and received, in return, notice to leave, as he must have the room for those who could pay. After much effort, he obtained a single room on the upper floor of an unfinished house; hired an old cook-stove for one dollar per month; and, with the few articles they had brought with them, they tried to "keep house;" scraped up **all** the pocket-pieces of coin and little savings, and purchased a barrel of flour and a few indispensables; placed the bed on the floor, in one corner of the room, the stove in another corner, and the flour-barrel in another; and the *two* chairs and table brought with them, with the bureau, — a gift of the red-coat brother, — made up the furniture of the large room. Almost the only consolation of the establishment was the barrel

of flour, which they hoped would last until some way should be
opened to get more; but hopes are often vain, and " the way of
the transgressor is hard; " and they had transgressed in getting
married before their time, and again in having a child, doubly
premature; and they had also found the Bible told a lie when it
said the sin of ignorance was winked at. They found it was punished as severely as any. With this condition for a home, he sal-
lied forth in search of employment, and occasionally, but seldom,
found a short job for which he could obtain some kind of pay, but
never money, and seldom anything to feed his family; but, as he
needed almost everything, any kind of pay was acceptable, and
any kind of food desirable. When he could obtain labor, he could
get eight or ten York shillings per day in something at the owner's prices; but bread and butter, and all such necessaries, were
cash articles, and at prices something in this line : Flour went up
during the season from ten to sixteen dollars per barrel, butter to
fifty cents per pound, potatoes to one dollar and fifty cents per
bushel, and other articles in proportion. One day in the month
for stove-rent, and five more for room-rent, and Sundays to get up
wood, used up each their share of time; and time was his only
estate. **Only a** small portion of the remainder could he find employment with any kind of pay. These were the trial-days of life,
most severe of all in his experience, because others depended on
him. **What to do, or** how to avoid starvation-corners, which he
saw they were approaching at the end of the flour-barrel, **he knew
not.** He wrote one or **two** letters to old acquaintances, soliciting
aid, and one to the magistrate with whom he had left **store accounts** amounting to two or three hundred dollars. From him he
received answer that enough could not be collected to pay costs,
so terribly severe were the monetary affairs. This was the last he
ever inquired after the accounts. **From the** other friends he never
heard, and probably it was well; for twenty-five cents postage was
more than **he could** afford to pay for a letter, and that was the
price of postage.

There was one other hope on which they depended some. They

had brought with them an assortment of garden-seeds. He had
procured a piece of ground, highly recommended by its owner, and
labored days and nights, and Sundays, when no pay-labor could be
obtained, and planted the seeds and watched them spring **up, and**
waited with much anxiety the signs of food from that source. But
"storm after storm hangs dark o'er the way." Late in June
came excessive rains and cold winds, and every plant of his garden, except the weeds, was drowned or destroyed; and this carried more sorrow to the lone heart. Reader, do you think he had
reason to thank God for life, and ask his blessing on every meal,
and to believe him a God of love, with especial care of his children? Or, was he one of the adversary's children? If so, he
should pray to the devil, for he certainly ought **to** serve and obey
his parent, if any being, until his powers were equal to the
parent; then he should be free. But not free to serve his devil-
father's worst enemy. A life of sorrow, toil, poverty, and trouble,
seemed now before him; yet, with untiring energy, he devoted
himself to the duty of supporting those dependent on him. If he
had been the wicked man which sectarian Christians said he was,
and many of them would have made him to be, if they could, he
might have run away, and left his dependent wife and child; but
the wicked world could not make him wicked, with all its persecu-
tions, for his soul was "above, while in, the world." Now he
needed the angel's voice which whispered to the poet:

> "Hope on ! How oft the darkest night
>   Precedes the fairest day !
> O, guard thy soul from Sorrow's blight !
> Clouds may obscure the Day-god's light,
> But he will shine again as bright
>   When they have passed away.
>
> "Hope on ! Though Disappointment's wing
>   Above thy path may soar, —
> Though Slander drive her rankling sting, —
> Though Malice all her venom bring, —
> Though festering darts detraction fling, —
>   Still must the storm pass o'er.

> "If slave to Poverty thou art,
>   Bear bravely with thy lot ;
> Though keen her galling chains may **smart,**
> Strive still to rend their links apart !
> Hope on ! for the despairing heart
>   God surely loveth not.
>
> "Hope on, hope on, though drear and dark
>   Thy future may appear !
> The sailor in his storm-tossed bark
> **Still** guides the helm, and hopes to mark,
> Amid the gloom, some beacon-spark
>   His dangerous way to cheer.
>
> "Though wealth take wings, or friends forsake,
>   Be not by grief oppressed ;
> Stern winter binds with ice the lake,
> But genial spring its bonds shall break.
> Hope on !   A firmer purpose take,
>   And leave to God the rest.''

We have been more particular in this part of our narrative, because the Lone One was nearing, and now about to pass, the perihelion of his life-orbit, in which he and his family were nearly consumed by the devouring elements of conflict and antagonism which make up the life of competition in civilization. How deeply little incidents stamp themselves on the memory-canvas when they occur in the trial-hours of life ! The long and heated days of July were slowly passing. **The** flour was fast lowering in the barrel, being almost the only food. The search for labor was often in vain, and, when found, was only of the hardest kind, with poorest pay, as is the custom in our Christian society, where even religion **is** inverted.

Again the tightening cords of oppression were to be twisted, and the house-owner notified the tenant to vacate the room, for he was to open a tavern in a few days, and should need the rooms. After much effort and long searching, he obtained a claim-shanty from a Canada land speculator, who, with little money and much skill, had secured a claim-title to a portion of what is now the

city of Kenosha, which finally changed his condition from poverty
to riches, and became a complete stumbling-block to the development of his only son. This claim-shanty, for which the Lone
One was to pay one day's labor each week as rent, had a hole in
the ground for a foundation and cellar, and one room about twelve
feet square, with one window and one door, and a rude ladder
for stairs to lead up to the chamber with its loose floor, and a roof
so near that your head was ever in danger of contact with the
projecting nails.

A few loads on the wheelbarrow completed the moving of all
but the stove. This the wealthy owner could not afford to let at
one dollar per month any longer, for it would then sell for near
twenty dollars; but the Devil provides for his infidel children, in
such trials, about as well as God does for his Christians, and the
stove-place was supplied by one which was purchased of a keen,
speculating trader, who agreed to take hay for the pay; and as
the United States had plenty of grass near by the village, the
cautious child of poverty dared to promise the pay, for the United
States owed him for fighting service of his father.

He had fairly settled in his new residence, and paid several
weeks' rent, always boarding himself (for in those times board was
an essential item in all contracts for laborers, and the laborers
seldom got a meal from the employers), when the flour-barrel was
empty, and the stove-owner called for his pay to the amount of
twenty-five dollars, which could not be paid by less than twenty
or twenty-five days' labor in good hay-making weather. Reader,
what would you have done? — Pray? — what for? — to whom? —
would he answer? — how? True, he could collect some kinds
of food to prevent starving, if his time was at his own disposal;
but now five or six weeks *must* be devoted to paying for the stove.
But, "*What shall we eat?*" said a female voice. — "Let's take
account of stock," replied the Lone One. — "Where shall we begin?" said the woman of tears to the man of sorrows. — "With
the beans." — "Enough for three or four meals." — "Salt." —
"Half a peck." — "Good supply, that. Let's ask a blessing

over it," said he, trying to cheer up her heart. — " O, don't be too
sacrilegious ! Maybe some Christian will help us, if you don't scare
them off." — " *Christian !* I should like to see *one*, this side of
the land where no Christians thirst for gold." — " Well, what
next ? " — " Tea." — " The tea, and coffee, and sugar, which we
brought with us, are all nearly out, — may last two weeks. But
we cannot have any more milk of K.'s folks; so *your* coffee will
not be very palatable. Spices and such things we have some, but
no use for them. There is pork enough for *you* three or four
meals, and rice enough for *Bob* about a week, and that 's all."

She had not eaten meat nor drank coffee for some years, and
never did after she began to *live* this narrative, and this was one
cause of social inharmony. Physically she was his superior in
purity and refinement, her body being above that excited and irritable condition in which his was kept by coffee, pork, and tobacco ;
for, like all who use tobacco, he could manage to keep a supply
of the filthy weed, however poorly he lived. Smoking he thought
did help to drown trouble, but little did he think it only helped to
make it. " What can I eat ? If I eat Bob's rice, it will not last
us but two or three days, and then he 'll starve, for you know he
cannot eat anything but bread and rice." Potatoes had been one
dollar and fifty cents per bushel, and had not found their way
often into this family. " Well, that 's all ; now what shall we do ? "
" Flour is sixteen dollars per barrel, and they will not sell less than
a barrel ; and if they would, we have *no* money, and I could not
get a pound of flour nor a dollar of money for labor, and I must
get up the hay for that stove, now, or give up the stove." — " Well,
if we have nothing to cook, we shall not want the stove long."

His labor had already supplied him with haying-tools and a
small note of ten or twelve dollars, against a good man, payable
in produce after harvest. This he vainly tried to exchange for
flour or meal, and finally for other food ; but all efforts failed, till
he went to the debtor and told him his situation, and asked advice.
The man was his friend, and sympathized with him ; he was himself poor, but had a good claim, and improvements, and a fair

prospect of competence, if not of wealth. He had a field of potatoes planted early, and quite forward, and he gave the Lone One permission to use them as soon as they would answer to dig and measure, as he wanted them, and pay the market price, on the note. On examining them, he found they were about half grown, and would answer to eat with salt (not butter, for butter was a luxury for the few).

"Another streak of good ruck," said he, as he landed the peck of half-grown potatoes on the floor. "You see Providence always provides for us. Ought we not to thank Providence now?"—"Perhaps we ought; it might be worse with us than it is; very likely some people suffer more than we do."—"Well, then, I suppose they have more reason to be thankful; but I wish I was Providence a little while. I'd make everybody happy, and have one jubilee of joy and thanksgiving; but this Christian Providence seems to have no pity for the poor and suffering part of our race."—"We shall not starve, shall we? But I know these will make me sick, and I dare not give them to Bob to eat, for you know we have eat nothing but bread so long, and this hot weather I fear we shall all be sick."—"No, we shall not be sick; that terrible time we had on the lakes will save us this year from more sickness."—"Well, maybe so, but I will save the rice for Bob, and give him potatoes once or twice a day."—"Salt them well, and we can all stand it till some change betters our condition; then we will thank Providence, or anybody else that helps us."—"You'll forget it, then; for you never think much about Providence, except when we are in trouble."—"That is the time I need his help, if ever; for 'a friend in need is a friend indeed,' and certainly we are in need, and now I should like to see some of the kindness the Christians tell so much about."—"But that only comes to Christians."—"O, I thought He was no respecter of persons. I cannot be a Christian, but I might be a hypocrite, and pretend it; but I could not cheat Providence, I suppose, and I guess that is the reason He neglects so many who pretend to be Christians."—"Well, I don't view these things as I used to, but

I know mother would think we were dreadful wicked, and that God would not bless us in our sins."—"Would she think Him angry?"—"Perhaps so, but she is honest in her belief."—"Of course, but that does not make it true. Well, if he is angry at me, I cannot help it. I guess he will not strike me dead; and, if he does, I do not care, if he will only take care of you and Bob."—"Don't talk so; let's go to sleep."

The bed, the stove, the table, and two chairs, with a stool or two for themselves, when they had visitors, made up the furniture, with a packing-box made into a cupboard. The last effort to obtain flour had failed, by reporting honestly his condition, and offering any property he possessed (except his wife, for the law, or priest, made him have property in her), and any amount of labor, or money when he could obtain it. He only received in reply, "Our flour is sold on commission, and only by the barrel, sir; we can't accommodate you." Day after day, week after week, the morning and evening meals were made up for the family of the new potatoes boiled and well salted, and sometimes accompanied by little turnips, greens, &c. The same article was carried to the hay-field for his dinner, to which he walked near three miles to his daily toil, and returned at night weary and lonely, but encouraged, for he was paying for the stove, and should soon own it; and with this bright prospect he tried to encourage his wife, and she tried to enjoy it with him. But poverty was a severe trial for her, and this her first trial, but not his first.

Many will say he should have avoided this. So he should. But, "only think if yours had been like his, a cheerless life," how could you have known the dangerous way to steer better than he did? But the severest and most touching trial of poverty had now arrived and taken lodgings with the Lone One. "Behold me—I am Famine." The rice was exhausted, and the potatoes did make the feeble child sick, and his pale and quivering lip, accompanied by the imploring look of a keen bright eye full of tears, morning and evening, would entreatingly beg of the father, "papa,—cake, cake!" as the significant finger would point to the cupboard. The salt and potatoes, forced down by hunger, gave him a summer complaint, and his appetite rebelled against the only food his parents had to give him. The tears of the parents could not explain to the child why he could not have bread; but the mother's heart, under the constant and imploring entreaty of her child, gave up the last spark of pride for the time, and she went to the claim-owner and begged for the child bread. And another kind lady, the feeble but beloved wife of another claim-holder, learned the condition of this child, and (she loved children, but had none) she sent it a little milk almost every day; and still another lady, of the house where they had lived, had .sympathy (and needed it too almost as much as this poor mother), and sent a little flour and butter, and thus they, or rather the boy, was a charity student in a civilized world of experience.

The weeks passed by, the potatoes grew better, the stove was paid for, and they rejoiced over the acquisition of this necessary article. Haying-time lasted till late in autumn, and the Lone One cut more than fifty tons of hay, which, after paying for the stove, the rest was used to obtain other articles of necessity or use, and usually brought him about one and a half or two dollars per ton on the meadow when ready to load on wagons. He could usually put up a ton in a good fair day, and walk to and from the meadow owned by God, of whom United States was the agent in possession, with a kind of squatter-claim agent under him; and they managed, I believe, at last, to cheat God entirely out of the title, and got full ownership themselves, without a title from Him. Before haying was over the harvesting began. Grain yielded well, and flour was reduced in price and plenty, and the family were supplied a good share of the time with bread for labor or other exchange. But money was still almost out of the market. This life-trial was borne by the wife and mother with a patience and fortitude well worthy her New England ancestry, which proved that the stories of her grandmother's trials and hardships had not been told her in vain. She did not spend her time murmuring or fault-finding, but patiently waited and labored for a better condition, seeking and sometimes finding some light work she could perform for others when she had none for her own family. The Lone One had been schooled in poverty, and of course could bear it; for he had himself cried to a poor mother for bread and cake when her scanty pay could not furnish it, and when so few among those abundantly able would employ a woman who had a child to feed. The cough and disease seemed to relax their hold on the wife, in this hard trial, as they did in several others. She seemed to beat the waves of misfortune with increasing force. Every dark cloud must pass along; every darker night must yield to dawn; each tightening grip of poverty or hunger must relax, and let the sufferer feed at last on earthly, or celestial food. These were the days when small favors were thankfully received; and a few such were recorded then, not soon to be forgotten; and perhaps such trials are to some extent necessary to enable us to fully appreciate the kindnesses of life.

> " . . . In youth's unclouded morn,
> We gaze on friendship as a graceful flower,
> And win it for our pleasure or our pride ;
> But when the stern realities of life
> Do clip the wings of fancy, and cold storms
> Rack the worn cordage of the heart, it breathes
> A healing essence, and a strengthening charm,
> **Next to the** hope of heaven."

> " For when the power of imparting joy
> Is equal to the will, the human soul
> Requires no other heaven."

Section VI.

ANOTHER TURN.

Did you hear " old Satan, that arch traitor who rules the burning lake," say, " Turn the spit, Jack," and give the Lone One another change? Did you ever read the story about his chat with God, which occurred on the occasion of one of his visits to the kingdom with the saints, about one servant of God, called

Job, and what followed? That accounts for the introduction of boils and whirlwinds, if not for all other evils that afflict us " to this day."   You will find it in the Jewish classics. October browned the autumn leaves, and the frosts changed the greens of the earth to brown; the prairie-fires were pipe-lighted on many of the rolls of the rolling prairies. The hole in the earth under the shanty of the Lone One was well filled with potatoes, and turnips, and cabbage, and pumpkins, and the garret had corn and dried pumpkin. The poor family were congratulating themselves on the prospect of wintering without starving, when, on a cold November morning, the stern old Cannuck owner came in and told them he was sorry to disturb them, but he had sold the shanty to a man from Chicago, who had gone after his family, and would be there in a week to take possession, and they must be out of the way.   O, how little those families who have homes of their own know of this terrible infliction — being turned out of homes, with no money to hire others, and no others to hire, both of which evils were now realized. Reader, did you ever disturb a little animal with its winter supply of food, and rob it of all its dependence? If you have, an experience like this would prevent you from ever doing it again; and by it you may learn why the Lone One ever after, if not before, had such a sacred regard for the homes of the poor, both of man and beast.

> " Man was born into the world poor, naked, and bare ;
> And his progress all through it is trouble and care ;
> And his exit from out it is no one knows where ;
> But, if well he does here, 't will be well with him there ;
> And no more could I tell you by preaching a **year.**"

No other wigwam could be found unoccupied in all the region round about, and the family, whom poverty had made friendless, were compelled to engage board at the house where they once occupied a room. The little store of eatables was sold for enough to pay for three or four weeks' board ; and there, in prospect, was again the end of the fortune-rope. For the best season of labor was at a close, and nearly all the settlers lived during winter, and most of them the whole year round, by speculating on lots, and prospects, and on one another. In this the victim of poverty could not engage; for he was too cautious to even purchase on long credit a claim to one or more lots in the village, which he might safely have done, had he known the prospects of the place. "Another streak of good luck!" exclaimed he to his mate, as he came in, one day. "I have turned pedagogue, and engaged to teach the village school, for which I shall receive enough to pay our board." This was secured by the aid of the landlord, who no doubt found interest and charity combined. The first schools in a newly-settled country are usually the rudest and worst to teach; not requiring in teachers much education, but much patience, and more mental discipline, self-control, and power to control others. In this school the preceding teachers had allowed the larger boys to govern themselves, and mostly the school also; but the new teacher determined to have order and discipline such as he had been accustomed to see in New England, and he began with the largest and most unruly, who were not accustomed to being controlled at home or in school, and of course rebelled at this authority, entered complaints that he was too strict, did not pray in school, nor make them read in the Bible. The ready tongues of two or three pious mothers and their unruly boys soon made a commotion; and although the trustees sustained him, and wished him to continue, he declined and left the school, rather than have two or three large boys who needed most the school taken out by their pious mothers. This was the first and last time he ever found himself opposed by females, and even some of these became afterwards his warm friends, when he had gained the public title of Ladies' Advocate; for he was organically and instinctively a "ladies' man," and became more and more so as his life opened and ripened, and in riper years so much so as to excite the jealousy and envy of many sensual and selfish minds, and array them against him as enemies, because the ladies loved or esteemed him more than themselves.

The snow-storms had sprinkled the frozen flakes over the prairies. Thirty-eight was in his dotage; had made his will, and was about to depart to the region of the " home-wind," and be succeeded by his next of kin in numerical order. All day, with rifle, had the Lone One wandered o'er hill and valley, in pursuit of deer, with only tracks for game, when cold and hunger and approaching night bade him return home. It was far away. Snows were troublesome to his weary limbs, the mercury was falling, and darkness stealing over the earth, as drowsiness was over his brain; but caution was aroused, and informed the intellect that it was the signal of death. Pauguk was looking at him, but he was not ready to go to the " Islands of the Blessed," and leave a widow and orphan destitute, and among strangers. By extraordinary efforts, by rubbing his face and limbs with snow, he at length did succeed in reaching home, where the warm room soon brought fainting and intense suffering, from which, by the aid of brandy and friction mixed, he at last recovered, and then realized more fully the near approach he had made to " death's door." The experience of that day lasted until he left the school of hunters, which occurred a few years after, when his soul had become too sensitive to murder such animals as are usually killed for game; and then he was glad his history had never been stained by the murder of a single deer, although the blood of much other game cried from the ground against him, as Abel's did against Cain.

In the midst of the holidays the stove and scanty furniture were loaded on a wagon, and, with their legal owner, carted about three miles from the village, into the thick wood, and landed in an old, dirty log-house, near a saw-mill with a broken dam. The team returned, and left the owner to watch all night with the goods and the ghosts of the departed former occupants. The rats, probably supperless as the intruder, seemed anxious to pry into the new furniture, and had to be often silenced by the voice or tread of the watcher. He had no lights, and the teamster could not stay to assist in putting up the stove. It was one of those long nights that seem almost endless, when we are hungry, cold, sleepless, and alone, in the dark.   Even the rats were better than no company, especially when " a fellow-feeling makes us wondrous kind." Next day the team returned with the rest of the family, and the old-bachelor partner, and a supply of provisions advanced to the partners on a job of cutting saw-logs for the mill, which they were to repair and run on shares, when it should thaw out. As this home was the centre of some important events in the life-history, and the birth-place of an only daughter, now grown to womanhood and a classical scholar, I should like to present the reader a picture of it ; but my book must go into market without pictures. It was made of logs, and capacious, with only one good thing about it — a good roof. It had two windows, but needed none for light or air, until after the partners thawed the mud and plastered the cracks on the outside. The floor was easily taken up at any time, to recover the tongs, and spoons, and feet, which Bob often dropped through it ; and also to drive out the rats, which for a time disputed possession of the basement. The chamber was made to sleep in, or on ; and if you wished to keep the occupants up there, you could easily take the ladder down. The bachelor partner was a joiner, and the house was soon " fixed up," and housekeeping under way.

The house stood on an elevated ground, and overlooked the mill and pond, — when there was one, — with a garden and small meadow in the rear, where the woods had been driven back. A small clearing on the rich bottom-land below was also used for garden and corn. On these grounds, the garden, allowed with the tenement, furnished abundant pay for the labor bestowed on it by the Lone One for the two seasons he resided there. Day after day the bachelor, and he who ought to have been one, started early, carried dinner, and returned late, as they cut and counted saw-logs ; but it paid well, for they could earn near three dollars per day, and, as they shared equally in expenses, they could save near one dollar per day each. But the job was short, and soon came warm days, and work on the mill, etc.

" Shall we damn the dam to-day ? " said the Frenchman, Louis, who, with Peter, boarded at the house several weeks while they chopped cord-wood, except when Peter eat coon-meat for break-fast, and went up a tree to sleep.

"Yes, damn the dam!" said the bachelor, as breach after breach was made and repaired, and the mill running about one day in four or six. A few weeks were sufficient to satisfy the bachelor, for he had no pets to cry for bread, and he proposed to take his share of the pay for chopping, and "put out;" and so he did, and that was the last and least they saw of him, for he went to the prairie-land of Indiana, took a wife, and engaged in raising babies. Louis and Peter also departed for their Canada home; the stream dried up, and the never-lasting dam staid, when the water was gone, as they fixed it.

During the little jobs of sawing he secured in his share some lum-ber for a small house, and bargained for a lot in the village, — about half an acre of land, — and agreed to pay in lumber. The good man of whom he purchased lengthened out the time for payment, and only asked for promises, and interest yearly, till it could be paid. The summer crowded along, and the Lone One often trav-elled two or three miles to do his day's work, and back at night, to the home where the mate was passing terrible days of trial and suffering, watched and aided by an excellent little French woman, who had moved into a small frame-house near by the log one, and owned by the mill-owners also, but which the Lone One was too poor to obtain with the mill; for the greater our necessities, the less favored we are. The long, hot days had not all passed, when the physician had to be called, and the maid hired, and the baby cried. Another unwelcome intruder, to be fed and clothed from the scanty fare. O, the ignorance of poor, and rich, hus-bands and wives, in this bigoted Christian land! It is deplora-ble! Not half, or even one fourth, of the babes are distributed where they are needed and desired; and yet enlightened Christians are continually prating about God's mysterious providences in such matters, as if God had more to do with it than we have, when the parties are priest-tied. Several works recently pub-

lished by H. C. Wright, T. L. Nichols, A. J. Davis, Fowlers, etc.,
will do more to remove suffering, and enlighten minds on the most
important subject of this life, than all the religious books of the last
half-century; and every family too poor to purchase any book should
apply for a Bible to the Society, and exchange it for Davis's fourth
volume of Harmonia, or H. C. Wright on marriage and parentage.
If there could be a society formed to supply these and other
works of a kindred nature to every family, and especially every
newly-married couple, it would do thrice the good of any Bible
Society, and the beneficial effects would be at once felt and lasting.   But we must return to the cabin — not to live, " thank the
stars."

The mother slowly recovered, the child was well, and the poor
little sickly boy — O, reader ! could you once have a look at, or
picture of, that family, and this object of pity !   " There," said
she, " I hope now we are done raisin' babies." The fall winds and
rains came, and the mill did run some, but the dam run more, and
trial after trial came backing down, until one of the owners really
believed it was bewitched ; but he was pious, and afterward became a preacher, so he had a right to believe in witches. Winter
came slowly along, and the garden crops, and day wages, and the
little lumber, all economically appropriated, enabled the poor family to live until spring brought the fish in the stream, and more
water and work on the dam.   In the deep cold winter the feeble
boy came near a change of homes, one severe cold night, which
greatly cooled after bedtime.   He was bedded, as usual, on his
sacking creek, on the opposite side of the room from his parents,
with perhaps two or three thicknesses of quilt under and over
him.   Toward morning, one or both the parents were awakened by
some unseen, unheard agency, and directed to the noiseless boy.
The father was soon by the boy.   He was cold, and not a warm
spot in the clothes where he lay, nor on his body, save about the
vitals.   He was instantly transferred to the other bed, and after a
long time became warm, and awakened ; but there was never a
doubt in the parents' minds that he would have been borne away

in the sleep to the land, or world, of dead children, but for the agency that awakened them. One notice of this kind was sufficient for the blended life-line of the family. Thirty-nine went noiselessly out, and Forty — of hard cider notoriety — came noiselessly into power. At the cabin the *hard* could be found, but not any cider. Wisconsin was a minor, and had no vote; she raised no cider, and had no need to import any. They survived the frosts and sufferings of the winter, and came out, as usual, "spring poor." It was probably the poverty and hard times that kept the wife alive; for she was too poor to die, and they were too poor to have a funeral, and fate designed they should each of them have one, and a meeting of real friends, not a few, on such occasions. One principle of philosophy always bore her up, namely, "All that is, is for the best."

Again, in the spring of Forty, the snows and rains run both mill and dam, but, by often working eighteen hours out of each day, he had sawed lumber enough to fence his lot, and sufficient for a small house, of such kinds as grew in that forest where there were no pines or hemlocks, and had paid nearly half the price of the lot. Every such little success encouraged him to renewed action. Again the garden was planted and flourished, and again work for wages on the dam, and elsewhere, supplied the family scantily with food and clothes; for by this time even the wedding clothes were worn out, with nearly all of the good supply brought with them.

The elder sister, with her consumptive husband, had by that time arrived from Michigan, and also a box of goods from the mother of the sister, whose liberality was fully equal to her ability. At the close of the fall term, the Lone One resolved to leave the mill and cabin, and seek some other home. Half-way to the village was a pious Methodist farmer, for whom he often labored, and who was scrupulously honest, for he believed in hell, and in his religion, and feared both God and the devil. The old man lived and raised his large family in a log cabin, but had a large farm and plenty of provision. He had put up a wagon-

house, with large doors in the cold end, that faced the home of
the west wind. This he proposed to patch with boards on the outside, and with papers inside, put up a ladder for stairs, and take
them in as tenants, till they could do better. So they did, and
did better as soon as possible, but not till a year had been spent
there as a home, in, not quite the hog-pen, but wagon-house. It
was while they lived in this house that the family reared, fattened,
and slaughtered the one, and *the only one* hog they ever did or
ever will feed or own.

This was not the only event of importance that occurred at the
wagon-house station, for here in '41, about two years after the
birth of the daughter, God, or somebody else, sent along the
doctor, and, probably by mistake, left a boy at the wagon-house;
but this fine boy was such an improvement on the other that she
was not very sorry, for everybody praised this boy, but did not
consider the other worth praising. This summer a schooner bore
the Lone One down the lake into Green Bay, and to the Escanaba
River, where for two months he made pine boards, and returned with
his fifty dollars wages, and with it paid for his lot, and received the
first title he ever had to a spot on his Heavenly Father's earth,
where he could set his foot in his own right. His hopes were now
high with the prospect of a home for his wife and babes, and as
many more as God should please to send; for they came without prayers or solicitation to this, as they do to most poor homes.
But, not yet, said a silent voice. "Turn the spit, Jack."

> " Pain's **furnace** heat within me quivers,
> God's breath upon the flame doth blow,
> And all my heart in anguish shivers,
> And trembles at the fiery glow ;
> And yet I whisper, As God will,
> **And in** his hottest fire hold still.
>
> " **He** comes and lays my heart, all heated,
> On the hard anvil, minded so
> Into his own fair shape to beat it,
> With his great hammer, blow on blow ;

> And yet I whisper, As God will,
> And at his heaviest blows hold still !
>
> " Why should I murmur ? — for the sorrow
> Thus only longer-lived will be ;
> Its end may come, and will to-morrow,
> When God has done his work in me ;
> So I say, trusting, As God will,
> And, trusting to the end, hold still.''

Two physicians in **constant** attendance, — seven of the nine-
family in the log cabin of **the** Methodist sick ; the wife-
mother given up by the family as the victim of death, and, with
terrible groans and screams of fear, and repulsion of the change,
which need not have taken place but for *fate* and friends, she
crosses over to the other shore, and the others are pronounced safe ;
for death had gone with his unwilling Methodist victim, amid
groans and shouts of the preacher, enough to disgust the savages.

But let us turn to the wagon-house, for the doctors also called
in there every day. A raging fever held the body of the infidel
husband fast to the couch, and the same terrible gripe was also on
the elder boy, and the younger boy shook daily with ague, and
cried piteously to the feeble mother and little two-years-old sister.
All were in one room, and that a wagon-house, in the autumn of
the year. The preacher did not come in,— he was not invited; but
the doctors said the boys were safe, but the father's case very
doubtful. On the day of the funeral, the husband of the body
(for he was never the husband of her spirit, for he had a wife
before and after her) said there was no hope of the Lone One
ever recovering, **and** obtained from the **physician** an approval of
his opinion ; and the echo soon reached, **in the** wife's whisper and
tear, the heart of the sick man, and **he** well knew the desire of
his friend for **a** death-bed conversion, as better than **none.**
Calmly, and almost smilingly, he whispered, " No, I shall **not
die;** but, if I should, I do not want any howling priest, nor any
of that kind of religion which makes death so terrible."—" I hope
you will **not** die such a terrible death as she did ;" and she was

one of the best women they had ever met, and beloved by all who knew her. — "No, I can die as quietly as I could go to sleep, if my time has come, and my work is done ; but it is not, and I cannot go."   Now, at the very time when most needed, came the kind sister whose magnetic powers had once saved him from death ; and a few hours of her magnetic influence, unconsciously bestowed on him, carried him beyond danger, and astonished even the doctors, who could not tell what, or which, of their medicines had thus wonderfully saved his life; but surely it was not the calomel, for that, by his request, had been left out, by his agreeing to run the risk of recovery by other remedies.   The son was soon well, but slowly the father recovered strength enough to shake with ague each alternate day, and hear the friends anticipate an all-winter business of it.   What a prospect for winter !   It seemed impossible to keep all the babies from freezing, in that wagon-house, through the approaching winter.   True, the lumber for a little house was already on his lot in the village; but he had no means to procure other articles and labor for the house, and was even now in debt for provisions, for now he had a little credit at the stores, and had been obliged to use it for flour, &c.   Then there were the physicians to be paid.   One thing was sure — if he could not work during the winter, both the lumber and lot would have to go, and thus all the struggles of near four years to secure a home would be in vain, and his future prospects darker than those of the past.   Thus had these prospects been changed by the sickness — or the fever — which seems a terrible scourge to the poor, but sometimes a blessing to the rich, and perhaps to all.

> " The cloud which bursts with thunder
> Slakes our thirsty souls with rain ;
> The blow most dreaded falls to break
> From off our limbs a chain ;
> And wrongs of man to man but make
> The love of God more plain;
> As through the shadowy lens of even
> The eye looks farthest into heaven,

> On gleams of star, and depths of blue,
> The glowing sunshine never knew."

With a resolution worthy a better fate, he went to the village, hired his board with a family who had once been poor, but could now afford to trust him, where the good living, and the medicine selected by himself, with constant labor on his house, soon restored him to health. The house, about sixteen by twenty-six, one room high, was, by the aid of the old farmer a few days, up, enclosed, shingled, and floored, and with a little more store credit, lathed, plastered (all of which he did himself), and ready to move in; and the farmer's team soon brought them to their new home, all but a cow, which, amid the trials of saw-mill life, had been purchased, and came with far more rejoicing to the family than either baby. This they left to winter, but not to sell, for well he knew the long, even years', trial he made to obtain one, which he at last secured for lumber. They were now moved into their own house. "Suppose we sing Sweet Home," said the Lone One. — "Sing! — we can never have singing in our family, for you learned in a saw-mill, and I in a prayer-meeting, and both are about alike." — "Well, we are out of flour, and that last you got is not paid for, and they won't trust you again, will they?" — "And out of almost everything else, except a house; but . . . . this is *our* house, and lot." — "Yes, and I am so glad, I feel as if I never want to move again." — "And we can have such a large garden here, I guess we can live." But another evil was upon them; in plastering the house, for want of a glove, he had worn his fingers on the joints, and, by the aid of lime, the sores had become extremely bad, — so bad he could not use his hand, and for weeks was laid entirely up from labor, when they needed so much the pay, and when the creditors were in constant fear of losing the little money he owed them; but he had a home, and this served to sustain him under all afflictions.

Through all these trials, he had never learned to drink, to swear, to gamble, nor to cheat; perhaps he did lie some — most people do; but on this and all subjects he was strictly conscientious, but very infidel, for the Boston *Investigator* furnished his mental Sunday food through nearly all his trial-days; and she liked its beautiful poetry, and interesting prose, **nearly as** well as he did. They were now once more close neighbors to the elder sister, who was also in a little shanty of their own, and poor, for the husband was sick with consumption, and, with their **two** boys, they were trying to breast the **waves** of competitive life.

A **mild winter of 1841** and 42 was slowly wearing off; the hand **recovered slowly, and** the Lone One found labor, often **several miles from home;** and, since the exorbitant rents were closed, **the debts were worn slowly off. The** lot had been **fenced, and** ploughed, **before the house was** built, and was ready for a garden **soon as** spring **should** clear **off** the snow. One subject was still **in** mystery: why God **had not sent these babes** to some **of the fine homes** of the rich, **where such "blessings" were desired, for** the pious always affirmed **that** "God giveth **and** taketh away." **Certainly, if** they **had a** choice themselves, or were "free agents," **they would enter such** homes, and not crowd on to the poor in such **profusion. Yet no** family could have **a more** tender care and **watchfulness than** these parents over the germs intrusted **to them. To the ignorant,** God ever deals in mysteries ; to the **enlightened, *never*.** Spring and summer of 1842, labored in gardens, on farms, **on the streets, in** the woods, or anywhere where labor **could** be found, **and pay obtained, and** thus fed **and** clothed the family, with the **aid of the milk of one** cow, and also during the season obtained **lumber, and built** a small barn, and supplied it with hay **for** the cow; bought **an** old log school-house, where he had once tried to teach, and **tore it** down, built a wood-house, and secured **some** comforts around their little home; had a good garden on the **new land;** where only the Indian had dug before; and when '42 **was about to** leave his Santa Claus tokens, the cellar and spare room **in the** little home were well supplied for winter. "Guess we shall not be turned out this fall," said the laborer. — "Hope we never shall move again, I do like this little home so," came the answer back. When **the** year went out, it also put out the third decade of the Lone One, and his effects summed up in, a wife and three babies, in a little seven by nine house, on about half an acre of his Father's earth, which, by several years' hard labor, he had at length obtained a title to, from those who had purchased, as he **had,** from an original robber, or thief, — for, as God had never sold it, of course those who did stole the title, or robbed God, and his weaker children.

> " **A** billion of acres of unsold land
>   Are lying in grievous dearth ;
>   And millions of men in the image of God
>   Are starving all over the earth !
>   O, tell me, ye sons of America,
>   How much men's lives are worth !
>
> " Ten hundred millions of acres good,
>   **That never knew spade or plough ;**
>   And a million of souls in our goodly land
>   Are pining in want, I trow,
>   And orphans are crying for bread this day,
>   And widows in misery bow !
>
> " To whom do these acres of land belong ?
>   And why do they thriftless lie ?
>   And why is the widow's lament unheard,
>   And stifled the orphans' cry ?
>   And why are storehouse and prison full,
>   And the gallows-tree high ?
>
> " Those millions of acres belong to man !
>   And his claim is — that he needs !
>   And his title is signed by the hand of God —
>   Our God, who the raven feeds;
>   And the starving soul of each famishing man
>   **At** the throne of justice pleads.
>
> " Ye may not heed it, ye haughty men,
>   Whose hearts as rocks are cold ;
>   But the time shall come when the fiat of God
>   In the thunder shall be told !
>   For the voice of the great I Am hath said
>   That the ' land shall not be sold ' ''

Thirty years of struggles with disgrace and poverty had now been worn off, and, although he had obtained a little spot of earth, to eat and sleep on, and to house his family on, yet he plainly saw that the whole system of land monopoly was robbery, and the greatest of all curses in the system of civil and political economy adopted by civilized nations. He had also given some attention to the study of phrenology, called to it at first by the abuse and ridicule which priests and religious papers heaped upon it; for he had ever found them abusing the world's best reforms and reformers, and so it proved in this. He had already become an active participant, and the " Ladies Advocate," in the lyceum, and ever the opponent of theology, and the defender of new and unpopular truth. For, since he was what Christians termed an infidel, he could afford to defend what they condemned, until it should triumph, or be beaten.

January 5, 1843. — Let us take account of stock : One tolerably healthy man, working out by the day, with a good prospect of following it through life. One poor, sickly wife, the mother of three children; far more willing than able to do the work of the family. One sickly boy, near five and a half years of age, with poor promise of usefulness. One healthy and petulant girl, of three and a half years. One healthy boy, of one and a half years. A little cabin for the family, and one larger for the cow. Good supply of garden vegetables, and not much else, to live on. Was he not well paid for living and laboring as he had, for thirty years, in his heavenly Father's vineyard? " Truly, God is the God of the poor," said a Christian. — " Guess he is," said the Lone One; " but he pays them, I suppose, in heaven." — " If they are Christians," replied the saint. — " And if not, does he cheat them out of their pay?" asked the sceptic. — " If not Christians, he sends them to hell." — " Poor place that for his children!"

CHAPTER IV.

FOURTH DECADE OF THE **LONE ONE**.

Death. — Birth. — Death. — New Field of Mental Search after Spirits. — Change
of Homes and Life. — Entered the School of Socialists, and reached the Graduating Class. — Entered the School of Politics, and graduated. — Entered the
School of Affectional Development, and graduated with Honors, alias Slanders. — Entered the Class of Teachers, and graduated a Preacher.

SECTION I.

THE LONE ONE AT HOME.

" BROTHER, art thou poor and lowly,
    Toiling, moiling, day by day —
Journeying painfully and slowly
    On thy dark and desert way?
Pause not, though the proud ones frown ;
Faint not, fear not, — live them down !

" Though to vice thou dost not pander,
    Though to virtue thou dost kneel,
Yet thou shalt escape not slander ;
    Guile and lie thy soul must feel —
Jest of witling, curse of clown ; —
Heed not either, — live them down !

" Hate may wield her scourges horrid,
    Malice may thy woes deride,
Scorn may bind with thorns thy forehead,
    Envy's spear may pierce thy side ;
So through **cross shall** come the crown :
Fear not foemen, — live them down ! "

> " Strive on ! the ocean ne'er was crossed
>   　Repining on the shore ;
> 　　　*　　　*　　　*　　　*　　　*
>
>   Strive **on**, 't is cowardly to shrink
>   When dangers rise around ;
> 　　*　　　*　　　*　　　*　　　*
>
>   Bright names are on the roll of fame —
> 　*　　　*　　　*　　　*　　　*
>
>   And these were lighted 'mid the gloom
>   　Of low obscurity,
>   Struggling through years of pain, and toil,
>   　And joyless poverty."
> 　　*　　　*　　　*　　　*　　　*

Elegant tombstones are erected only to preserve the memory of
the rich.　The poor do not need them, for they have their reward
in the other life, if the Lazarus and Dives story is true as an example, or if Jesus' blessing **reaches them.**　It is probably best that
riches should be displayed over the graves of those who possessed
them, as they will not mark any distinction in the next life.　So
of books, and especially biographies and lineage lines.　They are
mainly written of and for — but not by — the rich.　The lines and
lineage of poor people are of little account ; but this narrative
will be an exception, and no doubt excepted, in the list of supplies, for it is only the history of a poor man, not trying to get
rich, but trying to get a home, and then a deserved reputation,
in spite of scorn and envy.　If we follow the line of life of this
family, I trust the record may be as useful as a tombstone over
the grave of one who has gone to another world to live, and left
his accumulations here.

Forty-three entered the throne of time in the winter, and held
a cold grip for months, but at length began to soften, as the seasons were turning their varied phases.　So the world of mind was
in commotion, and constantly crowding individuals over the ups
and downs of life.　At this time the " Millerite excitement " was
having its run in **the West as** well as East, and the deep snows, or
prairie-fires, the eclipse, **or the** whirlwind, were alike seized as an

evidence that *He* was coming. Always betraying the deplorable ignorance of the very superstitious. A religious revival had converted most of the inhabitants of the village, and many of them, by their own acknowledgments, needed it, and some as often as once a year. The sceptic was compelled to admit a use in religion, as it made some bad men acknowledge their sins, and thus warn those not to trust them who knew such conversions did not change the real character of the convert. Some of his neighbors were caught in the revival meshes, and some in the Millerite storm; but he moved calmly through each, saying to one class, you will know better when you get sober; and to the other, you prove it clearly from the Bible, but the Bible is not reliable, and this will show you it is not. And it did open the eyes of a few; but the blind priests threw dust in the eyes of most of them, so they did not see the real truth, although they saw the world jog on as usual.

Scarcely had the spring of '43 unlocked the casket, and distributed the jewels of winter, when an entire stranger came to the little obscure home, more unwelcome than the one who brought the babies. It was a messenger from the "Islands of the Blessed," after one of the boys; and for a few days it was uncertain which he would take, or whether both, or neither. But he finally called the younger, but had put his finger on the elder, and left him almost breathless; and it was long before the father could catch from the low whisper the word *salt*, as the same boy that shed tears when he could not obtain bread for tears struggled with every gasp for breath, and dropped its tear again in grief, that it could not make an anxious father or mother understand the word salt. He was dying for salt, but the tear answered in the father's eye, as he at last caught the word, and only dared let him touch, with the tip of his tongue, the lump of salt, from which moment he began to recover.

The stranger had gone, but he had taken the mother's darling, the noble boy, whom everybody praised. Reader, do you think it was God who sent that child to the wagon-house, and then took it

from the little home ere it had either said or sung its mission here ?
The doctor could not save it, and perhaps he thought they had
enough without it. It broke a chord in the heart of the Lone One,
and started a search, and *research*, which never ended until he ascertained whether that child had ceased to be conscious ; and when
he found it had not, he did not stop until he ascertained its condition, and heard from his own darling boy the story of his new
life, and friends, and home. But the body — what would such
religious sceptics do with it ? No priest or deacon was called, and
no sermon preached to save its soul. Their only fear was that it
had no conscious soul. By the assistance of a few friends the
body was put under the soil, in the burying-ground, and an apple-
tree planted on the top of the grave, and a crib fence placed
around to protect the tree. The grave was often visited by the
parents during their stay, and has been often visited by the father
since. There, no doubt, lies yet the body, never to be resurrected ;
and there grows the apple-tree, yielding its fruit. But the boy,
now grown to a fine youth, with another body, often visits both
father and mother, and they both know the fact, and him. The
mother has often been made to feel, by his presence, that

> " An angel came to me, one night,
>   With glorious beauty clothed,
> And with sweet words of hope and joy
>   My way-worn spirit soothed.
>
> " He fanned my cheek and burning brow,
>   And cooled my fevered brain,
> And with his own deep music-voice
>   Sang many a loving strain.
>
> " ' O, mine is not the power,' he said,
>   ' To fit thy heart for heaven ;
> The gift to purify thy soul
>   Unto thyself is given.'
>
> " I turned, the angel-guest to ask
>   What could the vision mean ;
> He **only** smiled, then flew away ;
>   I woke — 't was but a dream."

But, O, it has not proved a dream; for soon she, too, will "leave the shell below," to join the happy throng who wait her there, and who have watched her through her night of trials and pilgrimage below. Work by day, and watch by night; pay the doctor, but not the priest! O, foolish man, why not stop the doctor, and stop smoking, and leave the coffee in the store, and the meat in the market. Then, perhaps, you might feast, instead of fasting on spiritual food all the time. But he did not know it. He had begun his studies in phrenology and mesmerism, and was making progress and practical use, as far as his time would allow; which was not much, for he was street commissioner and road master for the town and village, and had plenty of work for himself and others on the roads, and constructing a bridge, all the summer and fall of '43. This was his work six days in seven, and in his garden and house on the seventh; for he had not yet become a preacher. He collected or returned all the road-taxes of the town, for the land had been purchased, and the titles were now secure, and the property taxable, and the village fast growing to be a city, which it accomplished about ten years after, though rather a diminutive one. It does not grow much since. However, it is Kenosha, and nothing else, and has a selfhood among the cities. Occasionally he had sold goods at auction, as he had often done in Monroe, and this brought a call from Chicago. Two months he sold goods for Stanton & Russell, one of whom not long after went to "Ponemah," from the kingdom of "Wabasso," in one of Frémont's excursions in the snow-drifts, and the other is "nobody knows where." He had also rented a spot of ground on the street, between two stores that were near neighbors, and roofed it over, and had a store to use or rent, and tried to make it pay for itself; which it nearly did in the end, although **the** zealous anti-slavery man who furnished the materials shaved him with a two-edged instrument — high prices and great usury. But that is customary in all trades with the poor. The rich will not stand the shave, and how could a man get rich unless he could shave somebody?

I think I hear the reader say, about here, "I wish you would

hurry up this life-line; I want to get at the marvellous part of
the story." You might as well stop here, if that is what you are
after; for there is nothing marvellous about it, except the two
ends of the story, and the knot that ties them together. All the
rest is " commonplace," and such as you have seen. But it is a
hard-twisted line, and has been twisted from both ends at once;
perhaps yours has not. It is not a rope of sand, either, for it will
not break between the ends. Perhaps you wish it would, but I
do not wish so; therefore we will go on, after a dessert.

> " . . . . Those who greedily pursue
> Things wonderful instead of true,
> That in their speculations choose
> To make discoveries strange news,
> And natural history a gazette
> Of tales stupendous and far-fetched,
> Hold no truth worthy to be known
> That is not huge and overgrown;
> In vain strive nature to suborn,
> And for their pains are paid with scorn."

In the summer-time of '43, the inside history is also worthy to
be recorded here; for the Lord or the doctor had again visited
the little home of one room in-doors, and one out-doors, and left
another baby-boy, which several causes had hurried into this
sphere both in embryo and in birth before its time. It had
sparkling bright eyes, but none praised its body. The seven-
months boy was approaching seven years, and doing well; but the
eight-months boy, of course, could not stay here, for all the
women said so, and therefore it only staid about eight months in
the outer world, and began to be interesting and attractive, when
the one who had gone to the other home came after him, accompanied by a sister of his mother and several others, and they took
him away **to rear and** educate in their new home. They laid its
body beside the **other** under the tree, and returned sorrowing to
the little home. **But** the poor, feeble mother — O, what a trial
was her life! In the sexual blending of natures, in the mutual

affinity of desires, in the congenial attractions of souls, in the mingling soul-sympathies of a love-life, in the deep, ardent emotions of a united heart-beat, the twain had never been one. The weaker form and milder nature of the wife and mother had ever been the greater sufferer. The hasty and abruptly-broken courtship, which had been cut off ere it had ripened, had not been cultivated and preserved as it ever must be, before or after marriage, to secure happiness in conjugal life. Indeed, it is not certain that any but a life of courtship, in or out of marriage union, ever can be a life of mutual happiness for man and woman. It *is* certain that those who are most happy in married life court each other very much as before marriage; and it is also certain that the life of the Lone One and his mate became a happy life when they renewed and continued their courtship, and not before. True, courtship, in or out of wedlock, would be somewhat different, but should never be so different as to prevent either from absolute control of person, nor should marriage ever give one party the right to dictate to the other, or compel, even by entreaty, any social or sexual relations not mutually desirable. How much misery might be saved, and how many homes now miserable might be made happy, by observing this rule of life! This pair learned it, but late, later yet; and after years of suffering and sorrow, such as many others experience, but seldom write or relate, but hide from all but those who can read the history written in the countenances of all persons who have any to be written in or on. The time has come when a sensualist cannot hide his character without hiding his face and shape of head and neck; nor can his victim, if he have one, hide her sufferings without hiding herself; and close observation proves there are a few cases, and only a few, where the female is in the ascendant, and the man the victim; but they are so few as to be scarcely worth noticing.

Now we will let this domestic current run alone a while, since two babies have gone over, and two are trying to live here, and the mother is extremely feeble, and the friends all

say she cannot live long with such a weak and emaciated form.
Few, very few families can be found where there are less jars or
discord, before or behind the curtain, than were felt in this little
group of sufferers from hereditary and educational defects, and
social ills they knew not how to cure. Patiently she toiled
through these years of suffering, annoyed by a constant cough,
which sometimes gave her not one hour's rest for weeks, and
other trials of child-bearing in deep poverty ; but all these were
developing in her a soul-sensitiveness which will ultimately carry
her to the group who have come out of great tribulation. The
trials were not all on one side, nor were the sufferings all on one
side ; but his " eager ardent " mind had a wider range for exer-
cise than the one who was confined at home by poverty, sickness,
and babies.

> " A little longer, but a little longer,   .
> And earth, with all its griefs, its joys, its cares,
> Its beauty and depravity, its burdens for
> The pent-up, struggling soul, its aspirations
> **For** a holier clime ; its jarring passions,
> And its ' gushing sympathies ' (for even such
> Are found upon its rugged way), its loving hearts,
> And vile, unhallowed ones, and all it has
> Of beautiful and good, and bright and pure,
> And the dark stains upon its loveliness,
> Shall pass away."

> " Then let us meeker bear its burdens,
> Struggle on more patiently amid its sorrows,
> Enjoy with purer, more heartfelt delight,
> Its blessings, and, with eyes upturned to heaven,
> And hearts longing more earnestly for its
> Enduring joys, await ' the change of spheres.' "

When '44, the eventful year, began, some of the long evenings
were spent by **the Lone** One with a small group of honest and earnest
students of Mesmerism, who held regular meetings for experiment
and investigation. A paper called the *Magnet*, edited by La Roy
Sunderland, gave them most of their directions for management,

until their own experiments became interesting and finally useful, especially to the Lone One, for he did not leave this lead until he discovered the existence and condition of his boy in the spirit-world, and of many others; for, unexpectedly to him, it led directly to this knowledge, and those who dared to follow it far enough have found it to extend into and connect with the sphere of spirit-life most beautifully, in independent clairvoyance. **It** was through this channel that the Lone One entered the new condition of life, and became possessed of the, to him, all important knowledge of another life, and of the immediate and sometimes intimate connection of the two spheres. And by this, too, he learned that his mother was still in existence, and had, through many years of trial and hardship, watched over and guided him as well as she could, though not as well as she would have been glad to do, if possessed of more power. During these investigations, some of the works of Swedenborg fell into his way, and aided him much in forming a philosophy; for they were the first religious books he ever read that united religion with philosophy and science, and therefore were the only rational ones to him. But these references run along over several years, during which other very important living currents in the life-line were running their race also.

At this time the country was being much agitated by the discussion of Fourier's principles of association, and the zeal with which the *New York Tribune* and several other papers defended the science of new social relations, and the reörganization of society; and the glowing prospects of several societies already commenced — as they were portrayed by enthusiastic believers, who lived in, or visited them, — brought the subject before the lyceum of the little village, in which the sufferer from competition and social ills was a conspicuous member. He soon found enough to enlist him in its favor. Its vast economies, its equitable distributions, its harmony of groups and series, its attractive industry, its advantages for schools, meetings, parties, and social festivities, all seemed to make its theory invulnerable to attack, except from

the false and abominable doctrine of total depravity, which he
never did admit, and which he believed to constitute blasphemy,
if such crime existed. The Lone One entered ardently and earnestly into this new system, and sought all the information he
could obtain of its principles and results. Then came the taunt
from the opponents to him and others, "Why not practise it, if
you believe it the best way to live?" and they answered, We
will. It is singular how little incidents sometimes turn the channel of life. The home partner of the Lone One did not hear these
discussions in the lyceum and everywhere, and hence did not
become a convert to the doctrines, nor in love with the theory;
but she had ever been the *silent* partner, and acquiesced in all his
plans for life, or only gently remonstrated, and then gave up, as
she thought a true wife ought to do. In the spring of '44 an
organization was formed, and some old fogies placed at its head
to give it dignity. But the Lone One, who was really the mental
motive-power of the organization, but who had no dignity, and
very little money to add to it, was made vice-president, and of
course, in the absence of the chief officer, had to act as president, and this was in all business meetings and matters. They
had printed articles of agreement, which constituted an organization in all but the law. Had stock shares of twenty-five dollars
each, on which, by offers of great usury, they raised several hundred dollars, and employed one Ebenezer Childs, of Green Bay, —
a man long a resident of northern Wisconsin, and familiar with the
country and the Indians, — to select for them a location, with
land and water privileges. Sent with him three men, good
judges of land, to accept or reject such location as he should point
out to them. After about twelve days' search in a delightful
country, and in the most favorable spring of many years, they
at length returned, laden with the burdens, as those of old from
Canaan; but the committee, like that of the Jews, never went
there to live. They had selected a tract of government land in
Township Sixteen, North, Range Fourteen, East, ten miles from
the Neenah, and on a small stream that tumbled over cliffs of

lime-rock, and emptied into Green Lake three miles below the
falls and the location.   Next the money was collected and sent to
enter the land ; but, as the association, which had now assumed
the name of Wisconsin Phalanx, was not a legal body, therefore
it could not hold land-titles.   The treasurer had given bonds,
which, in law, ran from somebody to nobody.   One good friend
to the Lone One and the enterprise, a young lawyer, was aware
of this, and kept the leading mind informed on it.   It was now
evident that several prominent characters had only lent dignity
and character to the movement, and never intended to lend other
aid, and that the treasurer was of this character, and, like most
men, of doubtful honesty when beyond the reach of law ; but the
assembled officers had no other alternative for themselves or him,
and therefore resolved to let him enter the land in his own name,
and hold it till an act of incorporation could be obtained for the
society, and then transfer it to the soulless being which the law
should create.   But the treasurer had paid in no part of the
money, and by the resolve was not to send out all that was in his
hands.   The vice-president was made the business agent, to
receive eight hundred dollars, and see to the entries ; leaving about
one hundred dollars in the treasury, which never came out, for
reasons.   The lots were selected, and the money sent to Green Bay
by a merchant of that place, and the duplicates obtained as the
vice-president directed ; but they were not in the name of the enraged treasurer.   They came in the name of a quiet citizen of the
village, of irreproachable character, and far too honorable to
defraud any person, and one in whom everybody had confidence
who knew him.   This was a bold move for the Lone One, but
such as the necessity demanded, as was fully proven afterward.
He excused the assumption of power when it was necessary, by
the fact that the wife of the treasurer lived in another state,
and that his home, if he had any, was there also.   The commotion this would have caused was not felt by most of the interested persons ; for while this was being transacted they had collected teams, and cows, and tools, and provisions, and tents, and

started, — nineteen men and one boy, with three horse-teams and several ox-teams, — "overland," to the land of promise, by the way of Watertown and the long prairie. They camped and marched, and marched and camped, and, after six days, met, at the house of the nearest settler, the Lone One, who had taken another route on foot, and alone, by the way of Milwaukie and Fond-du-lac, the latter being their post-office, twenty-five miles from the location, and the place where he received by mail the duplicates of land, which they were now to find and improve. This glad, Saterler Clark, neighbor, pointed them out the *trail*, — which means an Indian pony-road, and is very much like a snake's path in the mud. They camped at night where the city of Ripon now stands, on the north bank of the stream, near where the stone mill now stands; and on the morning of May 27 — to them ever memorable — they repaired to the valley below, on the beautiful plain surrounded by hills, like an amphitheatre, and one of the most beautiful spots nature has formed in Wisconsin, and then, on their own land, pitched their tents, stuck their stakes, dipped their spades, and laid the corner-stone of the town of Ceresco, as the Lone One called the place, and the post-office, which was soon established, in answer to the petition and his request, with their acting secretary, L. R., one of nature's — but not man's — noblemen, and a true-hearted reformer, as post-master.

The 27th of May was duly solemnized and celebrated, this, and for several succeeding years, as the landing of the pilgrims; but it is now all done, for other hands and motives guide the settlement. Yet it is pleasant to look back to the hours of joy, and hearts of quickened and joyous beat, that once assembled annually on that day, under banners, and listened to speeches and songs, and partook of the best the land could afford. But perhaps, reader, you were never out West; and if so, perhaps never saw the beautiful spot here referred to, and you may not be aware that Uncle Sam bought the lands between the Mississippi and Lake Michigan of those who never owned them; and, being himself the highest tribunal of authority in this world, could not have his

title tried ; therefore he proceeded, by well-paid deputies, to run
out these lands into townships of six miles square, and then to
subdivide them into sections of one mile square, and again into
quarters and quarter quarters, the last and least being forty
acres. And these were sold and conveyed, by a title that was in-
disputable in this world, whatever it may be in the next, where
there is other authority.

The south line of Wisconsin was the base line of this survey,
and sixteen townships north of this line was the range of Ceresco,
and fourteen east of a line near the great river, from which they
counted eastward, was the exact spot which brought it in the
north-west corner of Fond-du-lac county. But, as prejudice and
envy has since changed the beautiful name of Ceresco, both of
town and post-office, to Ripon, it is thus pointed out to the reader
by landmarks. At the time of this immigration there was no
settler in the township, and none in the one north, nor the one
east, nor the one south, but three or four in the one west, on the
beautiful border of Green Lake, which was a strip of timber
between the prairie and the water.

The long days were well filled **with** toil by the pioneer socialists, and the short nights were devoted to sleep on the ground,
under the tents. The Scotch sailor cooked for them in open air,
and they eat on rough boards, under the shade of a bower, when
it did not rain ; and when it did, they eat standing, to avoid **an**
excess of water on the body, and because they could shed rain
better in that position. They put in one hundred acres of wheat
on the prairie for the next season, and potatoes, and corn, etc.,
for the running season. On the morning of June 10th, the
ground was white with frost, and used up most of the corn, and
beans, and vines, which they had hurried up on the new sod, so
beautifully turned, where no rock nor root was in the way of
plough and spade. They also began to erect three dwellings,
twenty by thirty feet each, one and one half stories high, and
thirty feet apart, which were completed by winter, from oak-trees,
which furnished, without saw-mill, the frame, the clapboards, the

shingles, and the floors, and all except the stairs and upper floor, which were obtained at a saw-mill twenty-two miles distant, at Waupun. A saw-mill was also erected, and a dam; and on this, in the hardest work, and most exposed labor, could be found the Lone One, almost every day, never to be beaten at hard labor, nor outdone in devotion to what he believed true. It was late in winter **before the** saw-mill was in running order, and then the stream was frozen too much for use, and they had to winter once **without** many boards for man or beast. The hay, which was abundant, supplied the place of boards for shelter for beasts, and for beds for the families. In this excursion the families had been **left** behind, and some of them were as impatient for their new homes as the husbands were to have their wives with them; and ere the dwellings were enclosed, some families were already on **the** spot, brought by the horse-teams, which were kept constantly travelling from and to the old and new homes.

Toward fall the Lone One returned to his home, and found **the mate had improved in health,** and all were quite happy **in the little house.** He informed the quiet citizen, M. F., that he **was the legal owner of** all their lands in Ceresco, and that, in due time, **they should call on** him for a transfer to the real owners; and was assured that all was safe, and that the trust should be honorably fulfilled to the last. "O, dear!" said the sorry woman, "I am so fearful we shall not get a home of our own again, if we sell this and go up there!"—"I cannot think of always working out **by** the **day** to support my family, and there would be no other chance for me **here.** Our prospects are better there than here; **and** we shall have a home in the *domain* as long as we own a share of it, of course."—"Well, just as you say; but I don't feel **reconciled to it;** but, as you have to earn all we have, it is right **for you** to control it." He soon found a purchaser for the little home, at seven hundred dollars, by taking a horse and buggy, and other property in part, and cash and notes for the rest; and their effects were soon loaded on two wagons, and the wife and children in the buggy, and all on their way to the *no home for her,* called the *new* home, on the domain of the Wisconsin Phalanx. The first night found them at Burlington, where the elder sister, now a widow, was living; for her kind husband had at last shaken off the consumption and his body together, and gone to the hereafter to fit a better home for her. They could not take her and the boys along, as they would have been glad to do, for the new home was only new land as yet, and they were yet dwelling in the tents, but not in the "tents of wickedness," for they had no rum, or drunkenness, profanity, or licentiousness, and no lawing, doctoring, or Gospel-preaching, and, therefore, were nearly free from the wickedness of civilization. Through awful roads and rainy days they at last reached the hill-top, which overlooked the plain below, and were soon discovered by the eager watchers, for they all felt the necessity of the Lone One's presence, and willing feet brought happy faces and ready hands to meet and greet them, ere they reached the quarters allotted for them, which were one fourth of one floor in one of the dwellings, parted from the other three families by carpet and quilt partitions, and from the out-doors by the crooked oak clapboards, through which light and snow could easily find entrance. Here they placed one bed and a stove, and packed and piled the rest as best they could, and thus, somehow, eight families lived in that house through the winter, which, fortunately, was a mild one. They all eat at a common table in the basement of another house, where all the cooking and eating was done by, and for, the society. Well may you conjecture, reader, that she was unhappy, for she had not partaken of the excitement that brought others willingly here; but she did not scold nor complain much, but tried to bear it as well as her feeble body would admit.

> "She is content to stay, and smile, and suffer;
> For when the 'golden gates' unclose for her,
> She knows a spirit, that has waited long,
> Will clasp hers in a wordless welcoming;
> Making the very memory of tears
> A strange dream of the night we misname life!
> O! when the sad smile trembles on her lip,

In tenderness for other hearts that ache,
She would not barter hers — a sufferer's — boon
Of power to sympathize, for even the love
Most tearless, sinless, sorrowless, in heaven ! "

The history of the Wisconsin Phalanx would be interesting to many and useful to some, at least in disabusing the minds of those who never heard any good of it when it was alive. But we cannot give it a place here, save as it was connected inseparably with this Life-Line; for surely this line run directly through it, and formed the main artery of the body, without which it would have given several convulsive throes, and then been dead. When the families (about twenty) were all packed for winter-quarters, and the boys hunting fence-timber and saw-logs on Uncle Sam's land, then the Lone One started to secure a charter, or act of incorporation, for the society. The act had been carefully drawn up by him, and submitted to the members, and approved, and he was authorized to secure its passage with as few amendments as possible. With this view he visited several members of the territorial legislature, and submitted it to them, and secured the aid of some of them. While on this errand, and far from home, and they knew not where to send for him, a violent fever seized the wife and son, and both lay gasping for life in the rude corner they called home. Twenty miles distant was a skilful physician ; and a faithful friend, whose noble English heart ever beat in unison with the Lone One, made rapid strides till he reached the home of the doctor, and would not allow any delay till the doctor was by the bedside and heard her say, " My husband would not allow me to take calomel, nor will I consent to its use myself for either of us."— " Then I will do the best I can without it," said he ; and for eight days and nights he did not return to his home, nor leave them for many hours ; and on the ninth day the Lone One returned suddenly, unexpectedly, impelled by some interior force to him unknown. The physician said they were both out of danger, if attended with great care, as they had been by the ever-watchful friends. Forty dollars paid him, and ten more the coun-

sel-doctor, who had been called from Fond-du-lac; for tney all
expected *she* would die, and did not intend the husband should
attribute any neglect to them. Soon the boy was **up, and** the
mother gained fast under the magnetic influence of her husband,
and soon was out of danger, so he could leave for the capital **where
the** chosen committee to repair the laws of God and man **were**
assembled. He was soon **in the lobby,** closely watching **the fate**
of his bill, which did **not excite much opposition in the** Assembly,
but, **by** the aid of **his good friend, the doctor, from Fond-du-lac, who**
was a **member in seat,** was slowly **and properly** passed, **with** but
slight amendments. **It** then went **to the** Council, where he also
had some good friends, especially **the** one who held **the** titles **to
their** domain. But here the cormorants attacked it, **because** they
thought **it** a good subject to make capital on ; **and down** came the
giant *Argus*, which **was** *the* **paper** that watched **the interests of**
itself and party. **The Lone One** offered replies and defence, **and,**
although **a** politician of the same school and **party, the** *Argus* dare
not admit both sides, and *it* had decided the bill evil, and only **a cheat-**
ing scheme, and most especially a social heresy. But the Lone One
did reply **through the** whig paper, and through a daily democratic
sheet in Milwaukie, until the *Argus* was sorry it ever took up the
subject ; and long after was more sorry still, for it felt the effects
of the injury it had inflicted on innocent persons. But the owners
got rich out of the territory and state, and therefore could afford
to have sore consciences. Two lawyers, — one a democrat from the
west part of the territory, **who** fell through some years after,
because he kept bad company and bad **counsel ;** and **the** other a
whig, then **rude and** undeveloped, but **who afterward** became a
noble man, and the first and best chief justice in the state, — attacked
the bill ; the first to please the *Argus,* **and the** last more for sport
and fun than in earnest ; and it was **a hard** conflict for the law, so
essential at that time for the security **of** the settlers. But at last
the final vote let it through, and the rejoicing man in the lobby
was permitted to follow it to the executive rooms. " It will not
compromise my democracy to sign it, will it ? " said the smiling

Governor Tallmadge, as he pleasantly added his approval to the act, which enabled the Lone One to return to his anxious family and more anxious friends, who were waiting, in deep suspense, the fate of the charter. He soon reached home, and exceeding joy ran through the crowd as they heard the good news. "Now we are safe, for our property will be in our own hands."

Soon the deeds were executed, and all the property safely lodged in the corporation, which, although, like all such bodies, it had no soul, had a name, and that was the Wisconsin Phalanx. The officers were soon elected under the charter, and the "tempest-in-a-teapot" excitement, which lasted till it was done, all subsided, and the machine was a thing of life in the spring of '45, — breaking and ploughing its way in the new township like a "little giant." The neighbors, who had begun to locate in the vicinity, were greatly alarmed by it, and most of them were sure it would do mischief; for it had great power, they said, and would monopolize. They wished the cursed thing was dead. A few only saw no evil in it, but only a power for good. These "four-year-ites" furnished the material and news for prairie-yarns and gossip for all the region round about, and tended greatly to alleviate the trials of tedious labor and long patience in the new homes.

Summer of '45, the saw-mill was making boards; the "long home" was going up in sections, which continued to lengthen till twenty tenements, of twenty feet each, were joined together in two rows, with a hall between, all under one roof, with a ridiculous plan of a double-front house and hip roof, looking more like a rope-walk, or salt-works, than a house; but it was the best they could do, so the architect said, and so the workmen responded. By personal effort, and great struggle, and some jealousy, the Lone One did get his tenement finished in the winter, and moved into it, — the most capacious house he had ever occupied in Wisconsin; having one room twelve feet square and a bed-room below, and two bed-rooms above; no cellar, of course, for they lived a unitary life, which meant to eat at a common table and work a common farm. But the families all had separate homes to retire to after meals. A stone schoolhouse had been erected, and a school commenced, which **never** stopped, except for necessary vacations, till the society ran out its race; and then it left the children of the members qualified for teaching the other schools, and children **of** their own ages around them. The township was set off and **organ-ized, and** an election held on the domain for town officers; **and, as** there were only three **or** four other settlers, of course the officers were elected from **the** members **of the Phalanx.** The post-office also **was in their** hands, but they had to bring the mail from Fond-du-lac for the proceeds of the office; which they cheerfully did, at much expense, once a week, for their own and their neighbors' bene-fit. They felt the great advantages and economies of combined labor and living; but some were not satisfied with the unitary life, especially of houses, and sighed for the retirement of quiet meals in family circles, **as** of old. Others were greatly pleased with the unitary table. **Both** males **and** females **were about equally** divided on this subject; but the plan and buildings had been com-menced for the unitary living, and could not easily be changed now. The single men, of which there were quite a number, were very much opposed to a change. This apple of discord finally grew until it was of sufficient power to break up the society, with other feebler aids. In '46 the improvements were greatly extended, a grist-mill erected for their own use, and this had to **be** watched to keep the envious neighbors from burning it; and so strong was the prejudice because they would grind their own grain **in their own** mill, and would **not,** because they could **not,** grind for others. The jealousy increased as fast as their prosperity, and the Lone One saw that the only obstacle to success in social and coöperative life was the undeveloped and prejudiced condition of the people.

The widowed sister and her two boys had been moved to the new home. A payment obtained on the old home enabled the younger sister to leave her son and daughter with the elder; **and** now, nearly ten years after she had left her mountain home in New Hampshire, to think of a first and last visit to it. Soon all

was arranged, and she, feeble and emaciated, started, piloted by one
of the best of sea-captains, who was also on a visit to his old
home and family in Newburyport, where his wife, long accustomed
to being captain in his absence, had learned to manage so well
that she was captain when he was at home, and therefore, to be a
captain, the old gentleman chose to sail on the prairies of the
West, as he was too old to sail on the ocean. Safely they moved
down the lakes and " raging canal," and over the mountains, till
she reached her paternal home, where glad hearts welcomed her,
as they would not have dared to do if she had come from the
spirit-home, which she had so often neared, but never quite
reached. Rapidly her health improved, and the release from
cares, and home, and husband, enabled her to greatly recruit her
natural powers, and become quite fleshy by the time set for her
return in the spring of '47.

> " Is this the spot where once so well
> My taskless childhood loved to stray ? —
> Where now the sweet but nameless spell
> That lured mine idle step away ?
>
> " The charms which then my fancy fed
> In vain I now essay to find ;
> The spirit of the place is fled,
> And left its grosser part behind.
>
> " The rocks are not so quaint and gray,
> The leaves are not so fresh and green ;
> The brook, upon its noisy way,
> Is cheerless through the sylvan scene.
>
> " I am not raptured now to hear
> The warbled joys from every bough;
> The witching sky, so blue and clear,
> Is but a common prospect now.
>
> " 'T is I have changed ! for nature still
> To childhood's heart is just as dear,
> And forests, waters, field, and hill,
> Have music for its listening ear.

> " The dream of youth, which comes to all,
>   Has passed like morning's starry train;
> Sweet memory may its form recall,
>   But cannot give its power again.
>
> " The silvery streamlet of the glen,
>   Which loves and fairies hovered o'er,
> Has flowed into **the** haunts **of men,**
>   And lost its beauties evermore.''

Thus she sang and **mused** as the autumn closed its **work** of disrobing the trees, and winter drifted the high rocks under snow, and the April suns sent the white sleet foaming down the cliffs. Then she sighed **for** her pets and her distant home again, with all **its** perils and trials. She was accompanied, on her return, by a cousin who came West to visit a sister in the Sucker state, and who soon married there and engaged in **raising** Suckers, beside her sister. **They were met, on** their return, by **the** Lone One, **at Sheboygan, and** visited their old Southport home, then slowly **returned to their new, but to** her ever less happy, one, for not yet was she **imbued** with the principles of associative life. The Phalanx was **now** in **the** days of **its prosperity** ; increased **its lands** to near two thousand **acres, and** its stock to about thirty thousand dollars, and its families **to over thirty, and** members to about one hundred and fifty. Most of them ate at one table, **and worked** together on the domain. Had **a** good and successful **system of** rewards for labor, by which they were not troubled with **drones** — danced one evening in each week, or rather the dancers **did.** Our family, whose line runneth herein. never danced nor **sung ;** but the Lone One usually preached on the Sabbath, and practised all the **week.** He also kept the public well **informed of their success and prospects,** through the *Boston Investigator,* **the** *Phalanx,* **and** *Harbinger,* and later the *Univercælum,* for which he wrote **during its life.** The latter was almost worshipped at the domain,—at least, registered as the best of papers, — the little Pleasure Boat, of Capt. Hacker, too, sailed **out there. But we** must close this Phalanx history, and let it rest, for other lines require our record-pen. Capt. D. P. Mapes

11*

had settled in the town, and declared war against the Phalanx, although in sentiment he held opinions nearly the same as its leaders, especially on religion and politics ; but he was jealous of its power. He was a brave captain, but he could never make any headway in this opposition, but only served as an outside pressure to crowd them closer together, and prevent, for a time, the internal pressure from separating them. But at last the internal pressure overcame the external, and the Phalanx died of a lingering fever in its collapse. It was interred in its own burying-ground, by its own children, and the requiem sung by its own council, and its epitaph written by the Lone One, about as follows: Born in the spring of 1844, in Southport, Wis. ; nursed and educated by several teachers, but principally by the Ladies Advocate; married in 1845, by the Territorial Legislature, to the statutes of Wisconsin (the wife died when the territory became a state); certified by Gov. Tallmadge ; settled and lived in Town Sixteen, Range Fourteen, which it named Ceresco, in honor of Ceres, a corn-goddess, of which it was a worshipper; grew and flourished, and controlled the town for several years, until it "took sick," first of chills and fever, and finally of severe fever, which weakened its vital powers, until in 1850 it died, quietly and resignedly, having reigned six years triumphantly, and put all enemies under its feet, by its justice and honor. — Owned a large farm, which was divided among its children, greatly improving their estates, and leaving all but the Lone One better than it found them. — Had been a great stock and grain grower, raising in one season as high as ten thousand bushels of wheat. — Had one genius who did most of its preaching and law business, and others who attended to the sanitary department. — Never used intoxicating drinks, nor allowed them on its farm. — Never used profane language, nor allowed it, except by strangers.— Never had a lawsuit, nor legal counsel. — Had little sickness, and no religious revivals. — Never had a case of licentiousness, nor a complaint of immoral conduct. — Lived a strictly moral, honest, upright, and virtuous life, and yet was hated, despised, abused, slandered, lied about, and misrepresented, in all the country round about,— mostly by preachers. — **Kept** a school of its own all the time. — Took five **or six newspapers** to each family. — Stopped work on Sunday to **accommodate the** neighbors, and **rung** its bell for meetings — **But** they danced without **rum, or** vulgarisms and profanity. — They had meetings without prayers, and babies without doctors. — But it was prematurely born, and tried to live before its propei time, and, of course, must die and be born again. So it did, and here it lies.

The charter was amended so as to allow a closing up of the affairs, **and the books,** papers, and business, placed in **the** hands **of the Lone One;** and by him all **deeds and legal** papers were executed, and all the **business settled and closed,** leaving the books in the hands of **the still** living president of the dead Phalanx. The papers noticed its death, and **some rejoiced, and some were** sorry; but **many true friends** mourned throughout the land, and none more than some of its heirs. But not the Lone One; for he had seen the necessity for its death, and submitted to fate willingly. In the division and sale of the estate, he bought a portion of the fine large mansion, which had been erected, but not finished, and lots for a garden; and again, with his own hand, soon had a better house than ever before, and a fine garden; soon made up his loss, and was worth more than when he came to the domain, although he had expended much of the little sum he received for **the** old house in defending the system, by lectures and letters, etc. The burying-ground (six acres) and the bell still belong to the estate, and are to be heired by the last survivor of the domain.

DIRGE OF THE PHALANX.

What spot shall I choose for my long, last home,
When a wanderer on earth I shall cease to roam?
When the angel of death shall come sweeping by,
And his cold breath shall close my weary eye?
When above my heart lies the cold damp sod,
And my spirit returns to its maker, God?

O ! say, shall I lie by the ocean's side,
Where my grave will be surged by the briny tide?
Where the sea-gull screams, and the wild waves roar
As their fury breaks on the craggy shore?
Say, is that the place where my form shall rest,
When the winding-sheet is upon my breast ?

Or some drear spot in the church-yard share,
Without e'en a flower above me there,
Where alike are buried both friend and foe,
When the arrow of death has laid them low ? —
Not there, not there, would I wish to lie,
In the cold, cold grave, when I come to die.

But dig me a grave in the prairie land,
Far away, far away, from the ocean sand,
Where my friends may come, when their work is done,
And sing o'er my grave at the set of sun
The song whose music was wont to thrill
My heart e'er the pulse of life was still.

O ! there is the place I would wish to lie,
When the angel of death shall have sealed mine eye ;
And my friends, should ever they chance to roam
Near the spot I have chosen for my long home,
Let them kneel by my grave and breathe a prayer
For the friend who is sleeping in silence there.

It had no soul to be saved. One more feeble effort at associative advantages was made after the burial of the Phalanx, and during the settlement of the estate, by a few friends who joined the
Lone One in the enterprise. A large and commodious store was
erected, by shares, and the Protective Union plan adopted to supply it ; and thus an attempt made to purchase merchandise, and
market the products of their labor, by agency, and save the enor-
mous profits of merchants. This enterprise " started and run well
for a season," but a fever of somewhat different character from
that which proved fatal to the Phalanx seized its vitals, and it
cost so much to pay the doctor, that its friends abandoned it,
perhaps rather cruelly, but, as it seemed at the time, necessarily ;

and of course it died, and was buried, and its estate settled itself; but the store stands on its foundation still, a fading monument of premature birth, much resembling good principles in bad company. Now all the reformers of Ceresco joined, and sang one song, and parted. The song was written by one N. Brown, some time, and somewhere, and ran as follows :

> " My heart is sick, my soul is pained within,
>   To see this Babel-world so **rent with strife ;**
>   **To hear** its heartless shouts, its Babel-din,
>   **As** onward flow the feverish **streams of life :**
> There rush the worshippers of gold and pelf ;
> Here stand the human gods of pride and self.
>
> " Behold the struggle ! the mad, selfish rush
>   For shining baubles or a beggar's crust !
>   In vain, divines, ye try the tides to hush,
>   Though hearts are dead or bleeding in the dust :
> There kneels the nabob, drawling out a prayer;
> Here dies the o'er-worked victim in despair.
>
> " Like chaos-fragments strewn upon life's sea,
>   And hastening onward to an uncared shore, —
>   Whirling and dashing ever as they flee, —
>   Leaping and crashing 'mid the storm-king's roar,
> **Is the mad world of men.** Wrecked is the world
> By self and sense, to very chaos hurled.
>
> " Gold, give me gold, though dimmed with orphan's **tears !**
>   Fame, give me fame, though bought with human **gore !**
>   Away with heart and soul — away with fears ! —
>   **Gold,** gold, though here 's the grave, yet give me **more !**
> Shut up the book ; **talk** not of brotherhood ;
> Man lives **for** self, **not for** the common good.
>
> " For untold ages thus the world hath gone,
>   By self and sense in broken fragments riven,
>   Yet yearning still for a millennial dawn,
>   When this same world should be a type of heaven.
> Talk not of heaven, or of a golden age,
> While social ills in ceaseless battles rage.

> " Ten thousand temple-domes in grandeur rise
>   Where priestdom learned expounds the ' word of life,'
>   Where man is taught to live but for the skies,
>   And leave to Satan this mad world of strife ;
>   Where Sinai's flames assay the **soul to awe**,
>   And creed **is** worshipped as the **saving law** !

> " **The human mind by threats of heavenly wrath**
>   **Has long been** chained within **a narrow** sphere ;
>   Like **a poor blind** man groping for the path,
>   **Yet fearing** still that pitfalls **opened** near. —
>   **Thus man,** alas, choosing a moral **night,**
>   **Lest reason lead** him from the **creed's** dim light.

> " **The world is rich in musty lore and creeds** —
>   **In mysticism, and in temple show** —
>   In spirit-chains ; **but poor in brother** deeds
>   To the great **brotherhood of man** below.
>   The central truth designed the world to save
>   Is crushed by self to a dishonored grave ! "

This **was the last, and** these the only, experiments ever **made** by the Lone One at associative or coöperative life ; and these the **only societies,** public or private, to which he ever belonged ; and **they** died so young they did not destroy his heirship to the name **of Lone** One.

Section II.

POLITICS AND THE POLITICIAN.

We must now turn back to '47, and **fetch** up the lagging stream **in** this current of life-history. Wisconsin Territory began **to** scold about her rights, and demanded larger hoops for **her skirt, and** larger dresses for her form ; and, after considerable fretting, finally proved, by the number of her *soles* (not years), that **she** was old enough to leave the nursery, and be her own mistress. Uncle Sam was glad to get rid of the troublesome flirt, if she would cease squalling for wider skirts on the Illinois and Michigan sides, and, with that restriction, gave her permission to run at large, and dress herself.

The "unterrified democracy," who are always on the alert when offices are to be filled, sounded the tocsin, and called their local conventions, to double up in counties, and organize for action. The Lone One was born nothing, and almost nowhere; but he was educated into democracy, and heard the sound. He called the roll for democrats in the Phalanx; but a majority, including women, were whigs or nothing. However, there were enough democrats to hold a meeting, and send him to the county session, where a ticket for the campaign was to be put up, and those elected over the territory, to the number of about one hundred and twenty-five, were to assemble, and adopt a constitution, and submit it to the voters for acceptance. The whigs were not much later in action, and equally efficient; and, although less numerous in the territory, they were not less zealous. But Ceresco had no ambitious whig, and took no part in the caucus. Notwithstanding the strong prejudice against the Fourierites and the Phalanx, still the Lone One received the nomination as one of the three to represent Fond-du-lac county in the constitutional convention. The other two and their friends were, however, greatly concerned lest they should be defeated by his connection with the unpopular society. The day of election came, and the whigs of the Phalanx had resolved to nip the ambition of the aspiring democrat in the bud, and labored hard to prove it was not best for him to be elected, and did succeed in leaving him one or two votes behind his colleagues in the town. But in the county he was, to the surprise of all, so far ahead as to be the only one elected on the ticket; and, with the two whigs from the other ticket, he went to the capital at the time appointed, to make his début as a political actor on the stage, and inside the circle. The convention was a motley group, called from city and town, from prairie and grove, from forest and "deep-tangled wild-wood;" fat and lean, short and tall, bright and dull, keen and stupid, democrats and whigs, and some who could only register when they saw which was strongest — and that did not take long, for democracy was greatly in the ascendant. Some half a dozen saucy lawyers expected, and determined, to rule the convention, and make all the noise for their own glory. But they soon found some material that was not so easily whipped down, and among the most "unruly members" was the saucy tongue of that Fourierite, which he soon learned to use as freely and sarcastically as the best of them. But, as he ever used it to defend the weak, and those who needed defence against the arrogance and abuse of impudent demagogues, he of course made friends of such, and even commanded the respect of those who did not love him.

The capital was situated on a beautiful eminence between two lakes, at a place called Madison. The building was erected and enclosed with ten acres of the land, purchased of those who never owned it, by Uncle Sam, and of course given, as an outfit, to the daughter when she married the Union. A greater variety of "odd sticks" was probably never assembled since the "Council of Nice" than was now in session at this capital, to *make* a constitution for a still greater variety of people. The white-haired sage and beardless boy, the thinking sceptic and superstitious fanatic, the sober conservative and the fiery radical, the hunker wheel-horse and the prancing progressionist, those who pray and those who swear, those who preach and those who sleep, speculators and honest men, knaves and fools, — "all mingle, mingle, while you mingle may." It was a long session, and made great noise ; but, like the "mountain in labor" "a mouse was born." As the Lone One was a leader of the progressionists, and had much influence in securing such features in the instrument as rendered it too radical for the people, and partly caused its defeat, and as this was the first chance he had to record his political views on public records, it is proper to notice some of the leading principles he advanced and defended. His first blow was aimed at capital punishment. It met a good reception in the convention, and might have succeeded, but for the alarm raised by several lawyers and preachers, and the awakened Christians, who " would have sacrifice, and not mercy ; " and they voted him down as a matter of expediency. But he labelled them with somebody's poem.

> " How is it, when you doom to death
>   Some victim for his crimes,
> Accounting him not fit to live,
>   You still allow him time
> To make his peace with God for what
>   Yourselves will not forgive ;
> Presuming him, when fit to die,
>   **As not yet fit to live?**
>
> " **Now,** though he be **not fit to** live,
>   **Is he** prepared **to die** —
> Sent strangled from this world of woe
>   **Before his God on high?**
> You send unto his darkened soul
>   Repentance and the priest,
> And when reduced to penitence
>   You hang him like **a** beast.
>
> " How can you know just how much time
>   Your victim should **be** given
> For such repentance **as** shall send
>   **His** spirit pure to heaven?
> Supporters **of the** bloody code,
>   I pause for a reply
> How is it, if unfit to live,
>   A man is fit to die? "

His next attack was **upon the** qualification of **voters**; and he exposed the ridiculous position of those persons, or laws, which make color, or sex, a qualification to vote, or even age, **and** demanded an intellectual standard, or a taxation standard.   **Some** were amused, and some horrified, at the proposition to let women **and** " niggers " vote ; and almost all voted against the women, and all but fourteen against striking out color **as a** test ; by which he saw the men would sooner let the **negroes** have their rights than the women, and he was confirmed in what he before believed, that **the** slavery of women was deeper, and more lasting, than that of **negroes** in the hearts and prejudices of the people, and even often approved **and** sustained by woman herself.   How can she expect **the** " lords of creation " to give her her rights, when she does not ask for them? But he recorded his vote for the right, even if alone, and left it to await the "good time coming;" for well he knew all these principles must triumph, if the race continued to progress. Next came the right of married women to hold and control real estate. On this they had a great contest, but it succeeded, and was incorporated in the instrument, and was one of the principal features that caused its defeat, although the agitation brought the public mind up to it, and it became one of the early and permanent statutes of the state, and remains there "to this day." Next came his firm and uncompromising opposition to land monopoly, and in favor of limitation of titles to occupancy. But this was a vain effort; for the *supreme* law of the nation, to which, in that day, the people knew no "higher law," was in the way, and they could not disturb the absolute power of the government to give titles to the lands it had obtained of the Indians, who only borrowed it of God, and had no right to sell it. These principles could only find an expression in a limitation of leases, to prevent what will probably never again occur, the "anti-rent troubles" of the Rensellaer estates. He next planted himself against all military shows and parades, and endeavored to crowd the whole system out of use. But several old fogies were there who had no other honor, and could not afford to lose rank, and title, and honor, and they voted him down.

He was a democrat of the Jackson school on "banks and banking," and took the hard-money side with the hardest of the hards; and thus aided in adding this fatal dead weight to the instrument. He next planted himself against all laws for the collection of debts, and would have swept away the whole system of civil policy on this subject. It was not difficult to prove that the cost of collection was greater than the amount collected, in every state, and almost every county, of the nation, and that it would be better to tax the people with the debts than with the cost of collection. There was in the territory an old, thick-skulled hunker judge, — Miller, — who holds to this day a post of profit (but not honor to him), who was for some years greatly alarmed at this heresy and prospective innovation, and tried to make others, if not himself, believe it was unconstitutional. Whether he was so blind he did not see, as the simplest reasoner would, that if the state repealed its collecting laws, and enacted *none*, they would not be unconstitutional, is more than we can say of him. But more than this record proves that he was very much wanting in judgment and perception, although **he** had much dignity, and **a** " little learning," which Pope said was a " dangerous thing." Of course this measure could not succeed in this convention, and the Lone One did not expect it to ; but he wished to agitate the subject, and give promise of the future. There were many able advocates of this measure in the state, and among the early ones his old friend, who so safely held the titles, and so readily surrendered them.

These were not all, but some, of the principal radicalisms and wild vagaries that gave the Lone One notoriety in his first public mission. **He was ever found in his place,** and always had a word to say for every proposed extension of freedom and rights to all, and ever went for the largest liberty and broadest platform. **He** had already become quite an extensive writer; and during this session he often pictured for the press the scenes and persons, and gave many comic, **and some** ludicrous, descriptions of the prominent actors, the effects **of** which **were** felt long after, and proved it true that " **A** chiel 's amang ye takin' notes, an' faith he 'll prent 'em." Like all long things, **this** convention had its last **as well** as first end ; and all returned to their homes, **some to deny** and oppose **their work, and some to support it, and the Lone One of** the **latter** class ; **and both tongue and** pen **were** occupied in its defence ; **but it was no go. The voters laid it** out, and the terri- torial session assembled, **and** called another convention, of about seventy members, **to prepare another.** Most of the old members were slain in the conflict, **and did not** appear again at the capital **for some** years. **The Lone One was returned by his county as one of the two delegates, by a large and greatly increased majority over the other election, and met there five — only five — of the first delegation. He soon found this a more conservative, but far

more practical, body, and one in which he could exert more influence, and on which he could place more reliance, than the first.
He felt much more at home in this body than in the other; but he
had learned, by the result of the last election, the true position of
the people, and knew about what they would bear of reforms and
radical measures, and was not inclined to crowd reform measures
before the people were ripe for them, nor to insert in a constitution
what belonged exclusively to the statutes of a state. He soon
found his place, as the journal shows; the most active member of
the convention; in his seat every hour of the session; voting on
every question. This time he succeeded in leaving out the military code, and all militia laws. He secured the civil rights of all
persons as jurors and witnesses, whatever their views of God or
religion, and found many good friends to coöperate with him in
such sanitary provisions. They also inserted a provision designed
especially to prevent the legislature from employing chaplains, and
other useless appendages to its sessions; but the provision is dis
regarded. Capital punishment, homestead exemption, rights of
married women, collecting laws, and usury laws, &c., were all left
for the legislature to tamper with as the people would bear or
demand. The banking question, of which the Lone One was
chairman, was the worst and most difficult of all, after such a
hard defeat of the hards; and still the return of democrats showed
the politics had not changed. The subject was at last adjusted
somewhere between two extremes, and the short and business-like
session adjourned.

Is it strange, reader? — when the Lone One returned to the
tenement in the long home, from this convention, he found another
boy had been added to the family, — not one of those returned
who had gone away, but a new one; came from God, the pious
old women said; but he thought it came from its parents. Either
way, it was a pretty child, and they concluded to keep it. The
elder sister and her two boys drifted slowly over the way to her
eastern friends; and neither she nor others knew his regret at his
inability to assist and even support her; but he was poor yet, for

his expenses were exceeding his receipts each year, while the quiet laborers on the domain were gaining fast under his system of policy, with which he was satisfied. "But how are the honors in these two games of politics?" asked a friend. "Are you anything by honors?" — "Yes," he replied; "I am two by honors, and nothing by tricks." — "Then you do not play your hand well; better take me for a partner." — "No, **never**! I shall paddle my own canoe in every storm, and sink or swim, as fate will have it." — "Go your own way, then; I shall oppose you." This came from the colleague in the last convention who lived in the liquor-end of the county, and wished to attend **to** the drinkers, and get the Lone One to aid him with his temperance friends; and thus they could win by tricks in selfish games of political chess. But he was the Lone One in this, as in all else; never entered a league, nor joined any society but the Phalanx, and that promised now to be sufficient as a school of experience. The friends were glad to see him home, for they had many tangles to be straightened out as he each time returned; and some did work up a prejudice against him, because he possessed, and yielded to, ambition in political life. But it was a school in which it became necessary for him to graduate for future usefulness, although he did not then know it.

> Who make politics a trade, and struggle for the spoils,
> Had better take to spades, and shuffle in the soil.

Ye worker in the soil, tell me, if you can, where is the happy man? Statesman, politician, merchant, lawyer, doctor, preacher, Christian, pagan, heathen, tell me, if you can, where is the happy man? "Not I! **not 1**!" cries each and all; but Pope replies,

> "Man never is, but always *to be* blessed."

Heaven is in the future, happiness in the distance, and we are going to it, certainly. "Hope springs immortal in the human breast." A little longer, and yet a little longer.

The work of the second convention was readily accepted by the

people, although many thought the first constitution the better of
the two; but there were too many impatient office-seekers to longer
delay in starting the machinery of state. Provision was soon
made for an election, and the conventions assembled to set up the
candidates, to be shot at by friend and foe,— one shooting to kill, and
the other to save, **the** mark. The pen of the Lone One had started, not soon to stop; and he had already become a scribe of some
note, both far from, and near to, home; and his articles (not always over his own name) were often trite with satire, or keen with
acumen, or graphic in description, or prophetic for politicians, and
often had a marked and wide effect where the author was unknown.
The friends of the Lone One, after a long and hard contest, at
length secured his nomination for the state Senate, for the district
comprising Fond-du-lac and Winnebago counties, to which fell a
full term of two years; and at the canvass, again, to the surprise
of friends and foes, he was elected with an aggregate majority of
two hundred against his ticket in the district, and three Assembly-
men of the opposite party in the other branch, and every effort of
his former democratic colleague made in secret to defeat him.
But the Germans had caused the result, for they knew he was the
friend of human, and of equal, rights; and some of his letters,
without his knowledge, had been translated, and circulated among
them, and caused the result. This proved to be his graduating
class; for after this all other degrees were merely honorary.
When the roll was called, the Lone One was in his place in the
Senate of law-makers for the new state, better prepared than ever
before for public or private duties. For, some time before this, he
had quit the filthy habit of smoking, had abandoned forever the
use of swine's flesh, and, at that time, even all meats; and tea
and coffee, and other mixtures, were forbidden drinks. His gran-
ulated eyelids, which had annoyed him for ten years, soon recovered their healthy condition; his mind was calm; and his excitable, passional nature was quiet as a calm sea in a still atmosphere.
Thus he was prepared for duty. Other causes than political ones
had induced these changes, which will be given in due time.

At the assembling of the session, he met an old and intimate friend, whose political, religious, and social opinions corresponded with his own; and for the two sessions they occupied the same desk, and became the "David and Jonathan" of the Senate, usually, but not always, voting on the same side of questions. Among the first permanent laws secured was a homestead exemption, without a pecuniary limitation; thus securing a great principle, for which they had both been early advocates. The darling object of the Lone One, to repeal the usury laws, and let money seek its own market and value, like any other commodity, passed the Senate, but was lost in the House; but, at the next session, passed both, and remained the law two or three years, when the speculators again triumphed, and set up the usury "statute of limitations," as a screen for rogues, which was all it ever was in any state, allowing them to take transfers of property, to avoid the law. Of course the repeal of the collecting laws was introduced; but the lawyers dare not submit the question to the people, lest it should succeed, and the collecting business find an end. The death penalty could not be removed at this term; but, after three or four years' fight with the religious bigots who defended it, it was at last removed, and the state came up where she ought to have been before. The rights of married women to hold property, real and personal, were soon and early secured; and thus that principle, at first so odious, was secured, and the state not ruined by its adoption. Senators to Congress were elected, and pledged to "Land Reform;" and strong resolutions, drawn by the Lone One, were passed in favor of "free soil," in its true sense. Commissioners to revise the statutes were selected; and, by extraordinary effort, David and Jonathan secured the election of the Southport friend, who held the titles for the Phalanx, as one of them; for he was a good man and true, as well as capable. Some old laws were repealed, and some new ones enacted; and soon the business of the first, the summer session was closed.

The commissioners commenced their labor, and the members returned home to attend to elections, etc. Many questions and points of controversy arose in these sessions, in which it would be interesting to the politician to see the course and vote of this singular person; but, as our Line is for all sorts of readers, we must be brief in these sketches, for there is a longer line of another quality to follow. We must, however, say, he was ever true to the principles which had governed him through life, of equal rights, without distinction of sex or color, to life, liberty, and the pursuit of happiness. Some one asked him how he could take the oath; to which he replied, that he never did take an oath, and never should, but entered upon his duties as an officer, or juror, or witness, with an affirmation of the simplest nature allowed by law; and he did endeavor to dispense with all forms of oath in the state, and let the penalties attach to the falsehood or default, as they ever should. He sustained the constitution against the chaplains; but the profane and dissipated members, who needed some support, always succeeded in giving them a chance in, by the aid of a few honestly pious ones, who felt it a religious duty.

During this session the little daughter came very, very near a change of spheres, by a lung fever; and but for the magnetism of her physician, rather than his medicine, no doubt would have crossed the line. The pale babe, too, had its sick time, and the feeble mother had "heaps" of trouble and trial — almost enough to kill a well woman; but she lived, and so did the children, for God had concluded not to take away any more of them, and had also resolved not to send any more to that house.

Soon after his return, the tangles of the Phalanx, and the family, were picked out, and some progress made in straightening the political tangles of the county and state. But these were too extensive for one mind to arrange, although the poet hath said,

> "The steady Greeks old Illium won ;
> By trial all things may be done"

And another, that

> "A man's best things are nearest him, —
> Lie close about his feet ;

> It is the distant and the dim
> That we are sick to meet.''

In 1848 the national campaign called all the voters to the
defence of their respective candidates, and Lewis Cass was placed
before the democrats.   But the positions he occupied on some
questions of policy were widely at **variance** with those advocated
by the Lone **One or his senator-friend,** and **they** both rebelled
against **authority, and refused to support him** ;   and both took
bold and **open ground against his** election, covering their retreat
from **the democratic nomination by** the Buffalo platform, and the
support of **the foxy Van Buren,** who was really not as good a man
at heart **(as subsequent events** proved) **as even Cass;** but **it** was
principles, not **men, they** claimed.   This **closed a door which** was
already open for **the Lone** One to pass to Congress.   And no doubt
luckily for him ; **for it** was well for his spiritual development that
his political **ambition** was cut short at the end of **this** time.   For

> ——— '' Our feelings and our thoughts
> Tend ever on, and rest not in the present.''

> ——— '' In the human heart
> Two master-passions cannot coëxist.''

The second session, which followed close on the heels of the
first, was a very important session to the future welfare of the
young state ; for the whole code of its laws was remodelled by it,
principally by introductions from the commissioners.   The legal
ability displayed **by** the Lone One in the first **session** gave him in
the second a place on **the** judiciary committee of three, which, in
this revising **session, was** constantly taxed **with** complicated and
vexing questions ; **but** the benefit of **his rigid** system of diet — his
cool head and devoted **heart — were of** great use to him **and** his
colleagues, both of the committee **and the** Senate.   By his special
care and effort **the divorce** laws were greatly changed from the
report of the commissioners, and nearly as he wished them, but
not quite ; for he wished all cases arising under them entirely at

the discretion of the court, whether presented by one or both of the parties in contract. An observation of the civil contract which we call marriage, in its practical workings, had convinced him that it should be subject to general, and not special, laws regulating civil contracts, and treated and controlled as other contracts between contracting parties. But the facts are, that the law has never recognized woman as capable of doing a legal business — of binding or unbinding herself; and hence the special laws of marriage and divorce in all countries where they have laws and **marriages.** Of course we must trot in the beaten path where our **fathers** trotted, however **rough and** crooked the way!

At this session **he** early secured **the** repeal of the usury laws, and several other obstructions to prosperity; and it was generally admitted throughout the state that no member in the Senate did more business or had more influence than the Fourierite. But his most intimate friend, and almost always co-worker for reforms, was not wanting in effort, capacity, or devotion. The schools and **university of** the state were set in motion, and, in fact, all the important machinery of a new state **had** to be put in place and motion by these two sessions; and all persons who studied the **condition and** prospects of Wisconsin admitted the liberality and **advanced condition** of her constitution and laws, much of which was really the effect **of** action and influence exerted by the Lone One and his brother. During these four sessions which he had spent at the capitol **he** never drank even a single glass of any kind of liquor at a bar or counter, except lemonade or soda, nor met with a **single dinner or supper party,** except at ordinary meals; attended **no balls,** dances, or night **meetings** of any kind, and joined no **riding or** skating parties; but was always steady, constant, attentive **to business, and** ever in his place **in** session, or at his quiet and **retired private** boarding-house when out of session, or walking **with his friend the senator from Southport.** Among other labors of the session, he wrote and published a personal, mental, physical, political, present **and** prospective description of each senator and state officer. These likenesses ought to have been hung in the capitol, with the frame that contained their faces. His style and expression betrayed him as the author, and some were offended at the boldness with which he told the truth about them. But fretting would only serve to prove him correct, for he knew them well, having examined most of their heads; and, being well read in phrenology, physiology, and psychology, and fully posted in politics, he had advantages that no other possessed in that body, and he used them when he chose to do so. One thing puzzled them all (except the brother), and that was, who wrote the description of the writer. They thought it was too severe to be his own hand. But this only proved that they did not know him as he did them.

This was the graduating term of the Lone One. All his offices after this term were professorships. He certainly graduated with honors, for no man in the state was more popular with the people; and had he not left the great democratic party, which alone had power to bestow offices for the state, he could have received any office in the state. And even with his change to the new and weak party, he would soon have risen to place and power, had he not abandoned the field of political labor. But he had seen enough of political intrigues, traffic, toil, and tricks, and was fully resolved to leave the arena to gladiators. His labors closed at the capitol, and the affairs at home once more arranged, the prejudiced members of the Phalanx guessed he would stay at home now, as he belonged to a party that could not elect him to office.

In '49 he attended the conventions of the " Free-Soil " party — ever the champion of Land Reform especially; and, in the campaign of that fall, he received the nomination of his party for governor, and its vote, which brought him the **vote of** two large counties in the **south part** of the state, Racine and Wallworth, and gave him more than both his opponents in his own town, and left him, at the canvass, at the head of his ticket, in numbers as well as position. But this was honor minus profits and duties.

At the assembling of the session for '50, a necessary alteration in the charter of the Phalanx, to enable them to close their affairs, and settle their own estate, brought him again to the capitol,

when the farce of the lobby, so long kept up, of choosing a sove-
reign governor, called him to the place, and gave him a chance to
deliver a satirical message, which took the veil off some persons
and events, and pointed like a significant hand for some politicians a way to oblivion, or " salt river." Some idea of the effect
may be gained from the fact that a neighbor, to whom he gave the
manuscript, sold in three days copies, in pamphlet, to the amount
of one hundred dollars, in the capitol. He soon secured the
amendment to his charter, and returned home ; for he could never
be found long where he had no business, and his business was now
in settling the estate of the Phalanx. He prepared a new and
greatly abbreviated form of blank deed for his use, and, as notary
public, used them as long as he remained a citizen of Ceresco.
In '51 he was again called to the capital to defend the name of the
town against the proposed change to Ripon, which Captain Mapes
and others attempted, who had now started a whiskey, beer, and
tobacco village on the hill, and secured the services of a pettifogger
from one corner of the town to get up law-suits. But the Lone One
was chairman of the town board, and had most of the town officers
on the side of Ceresco for a name. They of course prevented the
change at **that** time, and for several years after. But the Ripon
village was very much opposed to its more steady and sober
neighbor in the valley, and kept up a constant strife, until the
speculating Ripon at last **outgrew** and conquered its rival. But
this was not till after the Lone One had ceased to make any
efforts to sustain the valley home, and begun to look out a home
elsewhere for his family. One more game, and we end this line
of history, which does not connect well with the first or last
chapter of the narrative.

Fifty-two came. Again the national tocsin sound, To arms, ye
politicians ! and the Lone One was registered as one of the vice-
presidents of the National Convention at Pittsburg, and one of its
speakers also. From thence he returned, received a nomination as
one of the electors **on** the Hale and Julian ticket, and again came
off with honors only ; for at the canvass the David and Jonathan

— for both were on it — found their names had led the ticket, although the preacher at Ceresco had stricken them off, because they were believers in spiritual life, from evidences which he did not possess.   This was the last game, and closed the political career of the Lone One.   On counting up, he found himself six by honors and nothing by tricks, and concluded he was not a good player, and had better abandon the game **forever.**

> " **Only in lowly places sleep**
>   **Life's** flowers of sweet perfume,
> And they who climb Fame's mountain **steep**
>   Must mourn their **own high** doom."

But,

>   . . . . . " Fortune at her will **bestows**
> On mortal works the appointed close ;
> And sometimes have the better men,
> Through guile of worse, supplanted been."

Like the father of **our country,** on one occasion, the Lone **One** was now between **the** two contending armies, and **received the** shots and abuse of both ; **and of** course it was a glorious place to die a political death, and be buried with honors.

Section III.

AFFECTIONAL DEVELOPMENT.

We cannot better introduce this section and subject than **by the** following beautiful unpublished gem, from the **pen of Mrs. F. O.** Hyzer, of Vermont, entitled Love :

> " That **impulse ris'ng in the** soul
>   Which needeth form or chain
> Its warm outgushings to control,
>   Which reason must restrain,
> Lest it should make defrauding claim,
> I would not clothe with Love's sweet name.

13

" I would not call that *Love* which could
  Be poisoned, marred, or stained ;
Which could **by** any wealth be bought,
  By **any** power be chained;
Which **could** not take unerring flight,
Guided by its own magnets **bright.**

" **O, no, thou** pearl-winged dove, **go forth!**
  I 'd scorn to check thy flight ;
Soar onward wheresoe'er thou **wilt,**
  Where'er thou wilt, alight;
I know thine own God-given powers
Will guide thee to celestial bowers.

" **Go forth in freedom,**—**seek no guide,**
  Save **that deep pulse** within,
Which swelleth like the ocean tide,
  Where thou hast found thy kin,
Then fill thy cup with bliss divine, —
Thou canst not drink what is not thine.

" **Trust thy attractions, and in turn**
  Attract whate'er thou wilt;
I know that in thy nature burns
  No flame of lust or guilt ;
Thou couldst fold up thy wings, and rest
Within the purest angel's breast.

" **When man can make the** new-born spring
  Withhold her fragrant breath,
Or the eternal spirit **bring**
  An offering **unto death,**
Then thy white wing may feel the chain
Which now **is** forged for thee in **vain.**

" **Go** forth ! Enraptured **I behold**
  Thee spread thy **snowy wing ;**
So will I love the fragrant dews
  Thou e'er dost from it fling. '
Go ! naught can bind thee, spirit-dove ; —
Wert **thou not** *free*, thou wert not Love."

The unfolding of the affections, in the ripened years of man or womanhood, is not often the gist of a novel, but it may form a part of a life-line, and it must certainly have a place in this; but, of all subjects to talk or write upon, the subject of the affections and the relation of the sexes is the most delicate and difficult. This arises mainly from the fact that few persons have any heart-love, or pure affection, but in its place have a passional and sexual love only; and such persons ever judge others by themselves, measure others by their own ritheous rule, and of course cannot appreciate the motives or feelings of those whose souls have been touched by a living coal from the altar of celestial and pure love. Much of this is owing to a want of proper respect for woman as woman, equal with man, both in, and out of, marriage. When she is properly educated, made more free and equal to man, she will become far less the object of lust, and more the companion and associate, and have a greater influence in elevating and refining the too often polluted and lustful partners, now so often the tyrants, instead of true husbands and fathers, as they should be. It was not until the tobacco, pork, and coffee, had been turned out of the diet, and the mind had been schooled in studies of physiology, and moral and mental science, that the Lone One began to discover his own position and condition, and the relation he bore to others, both of his household and the world. A new fountain of feeling burst forth within him, higher, holier, purer, and more devoted, than he ever felt or knew before. As it increased in power, it restrained the animal and passional impulses, and craved food congenial to its own nature, purely spiritual and affectional. How could the poor victim of poverty and disease, child-bearing and hard labor, with whom he had journeyed long, but whose advantages had been less favorable than his own, reach this condition as soon as he did, and respond to the demands of his ardent soul in its new requirements? Of course she could not, and did not, and the demand of his soul was, in this higher department of its nature, responded to by another, far more advanced than himself in the purest and holiest aspirations of the soul, and led onward and upward **by** her. But outwardly she **was** far more unhappily situated than himself. Between them ran a current of written correspondence for several years of as pure language and ideas as were ever expressed **in** written words; and never was there **a** purer, more reserved, chaste, and truly mental correspondence **carried on between two** mortals than between these **two. Seldom did** they see each **other,** and when they did meet their meeting was public, and **of the** most chaste and **reserved delicacy.** Any other would have disgusted **her or repulsed him. It has** ever been designed by the Lone **One to publish a volume of this** correspondence, and it has been preserved **for that** purpose; for it contains many gems of pure thought, **and** much philosophy of the present and future life, worthy an extensive reading. The change in him was not understood by the mate, and **of course** was attributed to **a** wrong cause, nor could he explain **it to her;** for her time and condition of appreciation had **not yet arrived.** Deep and terrible trials were yet awaiting her, **from which, in due** time, she **was to** come as one from great **tribulation, having her robes washed and** white in the trials of **martyrs to reform.** I am aware that **it** will be casting " pearls **before swine " to say** much of this holiest subject in all our nature, in **this book, or** elsewhere; but it is **due to** truth and justice in the **narrative to give the** causes of the highest and holiest development **of the moral,** social, and affectional nature in the subject of the narrative, **and** certainly **no** one cause contributed so much as the language **and** influence of this noble lady.

> " —— Met her when the bridal wreath
> Had long been withered from her brow ;
> When she had learned no love had breathed
> In the words of her marriage vow.
> Her heart unwon, her hand she gave
> **To** one who knew its value not, —
> **Buried** beneath a living grave
> **Love** which yet knew no happier lot ! "

Unfortunately, as it then seemed, — but fortunately, as it after-

ward proved,—on one occasion, after this **delicate** and refined correspondence had continued for years, — every word of which might be
published in connection, with the willing consent of both parties,—
one of her letters was opened, through mistake, at his home, **in** his
absence ; and, being left **on** the desk, by foul means was **stolen by**
some neighbor before **he** returned, or **ever saw it, and placed in**
the hands of a priest of **Beelzebub, who copied it to suit his pur-**
pose, **with as many interpolations as the Gospel of St. John has,**
and sent it floating around the country to prove this Infidel, Fourierite, and Spiritualist, was more **licentious** than himself, when his
own wife had been compelled by his brutal lusts **to flee** with her
babe to her own paternal home for protection. This furnished
him an ample subject **for slander and gossip, and kept the** public
inquiry from his own case for a while. **It was also a glorious**
event for the pettifogging doggery **lawyer of Ripon, who had a**
suffering victim with marks of his treatment that **pointed to the**
grave-yard, **and in whose power no decent female would be** safe,
unless guarded by others. **The garbled** copies **of** the **letter**
reached, probably, **near fifty in number, or perhaps more ; but it**
was never published, because that would show it was in and of the
most pure and chaste subject, and language. But allusions were
made to it in many slanderous newspaper articles, as started by
the pettifogger and preacher.

The great stories of the preacher, who was **prolific** in words,
soon led some persons to **seek out the female, and discover** that
nearly **the** whole of his stories **were lies.** But he was gone — he
had left his **sting, and fled, like the wasp.** His church and falsehoods fell with him. This pressure of public prejudice bore hard
on the inside of **the little home ;** for now *she* feared that her con-
jectures were **true, and that his real and true affections** had strayed
from his home. But, O, how **little did** she know of him in this
her trial-hour ! But when the sunlight burst upon her, as it did
soon after this, O, what a glorious morn of the purer and holier
day, which has ever since been brightening into its noon ! But
the Lone One was not alone in this trial-time ; for he had many

true and warm friends, who knew his life and motives were as far
above the licentious rabble as the sun above a glow-worm ; and
they obtained, as near as possible, a true copy of the original letter, and easily proved to the candid there was neither improper
nor unchaste language in it. But the circumstance came near
breaking the sensitive heart of the author, whose soul was as sinless as an angel in this and all her acts, and as far above the
brutes who abused her as the angels are above them

> " **A** whisper woke the air —
>   **A** soft, light tone, and low,
>   Yet barbed with shame and woe ;
> **Now might it only perish there,**
>   **Nor further go !**
>
> " Ah, me ! a quick and eager ear
>   Caught up the little meaning sound !
> Another voice has breathed it clear,
>   And so it wanders round
> From ear to lip, from lip to **ear,**
> Until it reached **a** gentle **heart,**
>   **And** that — **it** broke !
>
> " **It was the only** heart it found,
>   The only **heart 't** was meant to **find,**
>   When first **its** accents woke ;
>   **It reached that tender** heart at last,
>   And that — **it broke !**
>
> " **Low as it seemed to** *other* **ears,**
>   **It came a thunder-crash to** *hers* —
>   *　　*　　*　　*
>   'T is said a lovely humming-bird,
>   That **in a** fragrant **lily** lay,
>   And dreamed **the summer morn away,**
>   Was **killed by** but **a gun's** *report,*
>   Some **idle** boy had **fired** in sport —
>   **The very** sound a death-blow came ! "

This letter, magnified into scores, and even hundreds, by report,
also formed the basis for magnifying the pure and most valuable

correspondence he ever carried on with a mortal into a constant stream of letters from scores of women, which the vulgar and licentious were now sure he retained over the country, amounting to a concubinage nearly equal to that of the wise Solomon. But the stories **ran** till they ran themselves out, or broke of their **own** weight. But the correspondence **was continued for some years** after this, and until its mission to both hearts was completed. When it ended he was far more pure in soul and heart, and she **not less — (for she could not be** more) — than when it **begun ; and certainly he was never** less, but ever more, attached **and** devoted to his home and family, through all this growth and development of his higher affectional nature.

> " 'T is bitter to endure the wrong
>   Which evil hands and tongues commit,
> The bold encroachments of the strong,
>   The shafts of calumny and wit —
> The scornful bearing of the proud,
> The sneers and laughter of the crowd.
>
> " **And** harder **still it is to bear**
>   The censure **of the good** and wise,
> Who, ignorant **of what** you are,
>   Or branded by the slanderer's lies,
> Look coldly on, or pass you by
> In silence, with averted eye.
>
> " **But** when the friends in whom your trust
>   Was steadfast as the mountain rock
> **Fly, and are scattered** as the dust
>   Before misfortune's whirlwind shock,
> Nor love remains to cheer your fall —
> This is more terrible than all !
>
> " But even this, and these, — ay, more, —
>   Can be endured, and hope survive ;
> The noble spirit still may soar,
>   Although the body fails to thrive :
> Disease and want may wear the frame —
> Thank God ! the soul is still the same !

> "Hold up your head, thou man of grief !
> No longer to the tempest bend ;
> For soon or late must come relief —
> The coldest, darkest night will end.
> Hope in **the** true heart never dies ;
> **Trust on, the day-star** yet shall rise !
>
> "**Conscious of** purity and **worth,**
> **You** may with calm assurance wait
> **The** tardy recompense of earth ;
> **And, e'en** should justice come too late
> **To soothe the spirit's** homeward flight,
> **Heaven at last the** wrong shall right."

Through this correspondence his soul's highest and holiest affections were cultivated, expanded, **and** ripened, like the flowers of June under the glowing sunlight. **His** heart grew rich in fragrance and purity, and shed its influence on others ; thus rend r-ing himself still more and **more** an object of suspicion, jealousy, and gossip for the wicked and corrupt, who could see no motive for any man to converse **or correspond with** females except **a** lustful or licentious **one, as none other could** prompt such acts in themselves. **Little did they know how much he** pitied their condition, **and deplored** their depravity. But they could **not** be **lifted, except by long** years of " prayer and fasting," **from their** slavish and brutal **conditions.** Therefore he resolved to **labor in** the field where **more congenial** sunlight **shone** around the **homes ;** and for that purpose sought, **far and** near, the spot to **which he could** move his family, and **have a** society of congenial beings **where** his mate could unfold **her** higher and purer nature, which **was even** more elastic than his own, and more depressed than his **had been, but which** he knew would soon or late come up **to the** surface **of life.**

In **travelling he** found many friends, and usually the best of them among **the most** refined, and educated, and developed females. With **several of** these he carried on, more or less regularly, correspondence, until the accumulation would fill several large volumes; much of which, with changes, is still continued. The present wife of A. J. Davis was among **those** with whom he corresponded in her days of trial, and a purer **soul** than hers never uttered words through human lips; and she, with many **others** who could be named, can bear testimony to the nature and character **of his** letters, **and** they **ever will** when called upon **to do so.** No female voice ever charged him with wrong act or **motive** to herself, or **in her own knowledge; for all** the slanders **were** inverted **mirage,** groundless, without **facts,** and mainly rested **on** the fatal **letter.** No suit, civil or criminal, was ever commenced against him **on earth or in** heaven, neither here nor in the hereafter. He **had more** and warmer friends, and more bitter enemies, **than** any one in the state; and there was a reason for it, and that reason lay in his own nature and capacities of soul. When the "Uncle Tom's Cabin" for married women shall be written, as it surely will, the readers will find the Lone One was among the number whose sympathies, at least, were ever with the sufferers, and **not** for selfish but for beneficent purposes, as many already know; for many **a** sad heart can say, with one of his correspondents:

> "I had labored to make my garden fair,
> But the river of love was not flowing there,
> And the flowers I tilled had a poisonous breath,
> That fell on my heart like the dews of death;
> Still hope would toil on, **o'er** the deep lines of care,
> **And** the sadness so mournfully resting there
> Told plainly I struggled to conquer despair."

The political and associational history both close in this fourth decade; but the social, the affectional, and the **one** yet to be taken up, the spiritual, all run into the next, and no doubt far beyond this volume into the future, to "no one knows where," but surely to the hereafter. Up to the January of '53, where this chapter must end, the light of a glorious development of soul in its highest affections had not burst in upon the mate of the Lone One;

but, like the ice under March winds and suns, the crust was beginning to soften, and air-holes for the pent-up soul to breathe were
occasional, and plainly his rejoicing soul saw the signs of its
approaching summer-time. For well he knew the hardest ice
must yield to spring, and the darkest cloud pass over.

> "O, who the exquisite delights can tell,
>   The joy which mutual confidence imparts?
> Or who can paint the joy unspeakable
> Which links in tender bands two faithful hearts?"

> "The shaken tree grows faster at the root;
>   And love grows firmer for some blasts of doubt."

How few, very few, know, or rather feel, the true, and holy,
and pure affection for each other in married life that really
belongs to the conjugal condition of the soul! Most married parties live only domestically and sexually together, but affectionally
are utter strangers. Nor, indeed, can any person live in, or enjoy,
the holy and noble affection of which his nature is capable, while
love is merely sexual. Persons who do not love each other without the relation which marriage places them in to each other can
never do it in such relation. Most persons who have reached
the plane of spiritual development are happy in any relation of
life, provided they are not made the victims of lust, or the slaves
of brutal partners, who tyrannize over them and whose love is
only lust or ambition.

> "I have commingled with the throng,
>   In the wide world's ceaseless strife;
> Have listened to the endless song
>   That marks the onward course of life;
> Have heard the earnest words they spoke,
>   And conned their hidden object o'er,
> Till on my mind the light has broke,
> 'This it is, and nothing more.'"

> "No man caring for his brother,
>   Struggling after this world's pelf,

Each one trampling down the other,
  Each one striving for himself.

"Ay, I have stood within the hall
  Where beauty's triumphs are achieved,
Saw but two parties midst them all,
  And both deceiving and deceived ;
Have heard of Love's thrice-woven bond,
  And vows repeated o'er and o'er ;
But, searching for the light beyond,
  ' This it is, and nothing more : '
Each betraying one another,
  In the object they pursue ;
Each one caring for the other
  As it pleased them so to do.

"And if I sometimes stood apart
  From the thronging multitude,
And felt how welcome to my heart
  Were a lonely solitude ;
Asked my soul why this suggestion,
  And eager conned it o'er and o'er,
Found but one answer to my question,
  ' This it is, and nothing more : '
Each is some one else deceiving,
  In the world's tumultuous strife,
Those the greatest share achieving
  Who make deceit the aim of life ;
Each betraying one another,
  Be the object love or pelf ;
No one caring for the other,
  Each one striving for himself." ·

There were some pure, true, honest, and warm hearts in the valley of Ceresco, who ever shielded and sustained the sensitive spirit of the Lone One; and there were also other " vile, unhallowed ones," and it was not difficult to sort them by any rule, either by actions or mode of living, or by phrenological laws; for all these agreed, and told very much the same story. But a dark cloud was hanging over the place in '52 and '53, with drenching rain and beating hail; and the Lone One had already begun to seek other shelter, but had not found it, for the tender family still under his care. His government over his children had entirely changed; for now his authority was given only in love, and the often harsh and sometimes severe authority which the eldest had felt was now mild and pleasant, though strong and firm; and the elder boy, whose mind was now unfolded to an appreciation of these things, saw, and felt, and wondered at the change, but knew not the cause, yet knew well the effect. This eldest son was born September 1, 1837, and the youngest and last child God sent to the family on the second of February, 1848. Some old lady asked, one day, how they knew this was the last God would send; and they informed her that he left a note to that effect in the basket with the babe, when he brought it. Eleven years of such experience as this couple had, with five babies mixed in with poverty, disease, and misery, and the death of two of them, is plenty of that kind of experience, especially when a reform in the father would require him to coöperate with the mother in trying to eradicate the effects of the tobacco, coffee, and pork, from the nervous children, who must have inherited it, as all children do, more or less, in such cases, causing in them restless, irritable, and nervous dispositions and habits. Well he knew he had a work to do, and faithfully began the work of renovation in the children, both physical and mental *regeneration* and *reformation.*

It must be borne in mind that while these events were passing in the last half of·this decade, that the political line was running its race, and the important business of the Phalanx was also on his mind, and the Union Store, and his private affairs of business; and yet, as the diary showeth, the social and affectional development at this time, for himself and family, was the most important, and pressed most heavily on his mind and heart, and in the end brought the most reward; indeed, more than all other, except the line we have not yet taken up. In '50 the Lone One came very near forming a copartnership with his old friend, the senator, and starting, or purchasing, a paper at the county seat, and going, then and there, into new business. The friend had long been an editor, and was a printer by profession; and the Lone One was now quite an extensive writer, and for several varieties of papers, and found his letters read with much interest, as they **ever have** been since. He felt much the need of a classical education. **It** was well for him that the scheme failed in its incipiency, for a far more important mission awaited his development for its reception and demands.

The diary of the year 1850 showeth that the Lone One **was** President **of** the Annual Session of the National Industrial Congress, holden for that year at Chicago, in June; and that he made speeches there, and elsewhere, in which he, **as** he ever had, defended the rights of females to all and equal privileges with males. All these were only signs, to the conservative and lustful minds, of his licentiousness. But the greatest of all opposition came from his old and never-forgiving religious enemies, who were determined, at whatever cost of falsehood or slander, to destroy his influence, and they labored unceasingly to accomplish it; but in vain, as the sequel shows.

Sunday, June 14, 1850, the journal notices a lecture of his on woman's rights, before the Excelsior Church, in Southport; and others, on this and kindred subjects, in other places, all showing an affectional tendency and development. The mental capacity had now become so strong that it needed constant employment; and subjects were handled by him with skill **and power, both by speech and pen.** His manhood was fast unfolding itself. Westward from the valley home, about one mile, was a high and perpendicular limestone cliff, overlooking a large meadow, the lake, and much country below and beyond. **On this cliff** many Sabbaths, and some other days, were spent by the Lone One. It was often, and for years, the retreat and resort for reading and writing; and many a pencil-note was made on that beautiful and romantic retreat. It was not only the favorite retreat of the Lone One, but of many others. Skirted by a few shade-trees, which served

as a border to the prairie on one side, and towering above the
tops of the trees on the other. Several times the Lone One has
spent the stormy hours under the cliff, in spiritual development,
or deep meditation; and many a sunny hour on the top, under
shade of oak or linden. He courted solitude (but never married
her), when business would admit, and found her balmy shadow
and cooling shade refreshing to his soul.

> " Enthusiast ! dreamer ! such the names
>   Thine age bestows on thee,
>   For that great nature, going forth
>   In world-wide sympathy :
>   For the vision clear, the spirit brave,
>   The honest heart and warm,
>   And the voice which swells the battle-cry
>   For freedom and reform.
>
> " Yet for thy fearless manliness,
>   When weak time-servers throng, —
>   Thy chivalrous defence of right,
>   Thy bold rebuke of wrong, —
>   And for the flame of liberty,
>   Heaven-kindled in thy breast,
>   Which thou hast fed like sacred fire, —
>   A blessing on thee rest !
>
> " Tis said thy spirit knoweth not
>   Its times of calm and sleeping;
>   That ever are its restless thoughts
>   Like wild waves onward leaping.
>   Then may its flashing waters
>   Be tranquil nevermore, —
>   They are troubled by an angel,
>   Like the sacred pool of yore."

The subject of marriage he talked, wrote, and lectured upon,
boldly and fearlessly speaking his mind on the subject, as if it was
not too sacred for criticism. But this alarmed several classes of
persons. First, and most, those who had victims of tyranny and
lust, to whom they dared not have any rights or liberties extended,

because they could not make the victims of their cruelty love them; and if they lost legal control over their persons, they would rebel against the constant child-bearing and never-ceasing abuse of their bodies and souls. The second, and perhaps still more alarmed, but not as rabid, opponents to any reform in this department, were the religious bigots. But the Lone One contended that marriage should either be a civil contract or a religious rite, and in either case come under the general law of the department to which it belonged, and in no case give exclusive, or special, or superior rights to one party. That, if the husband owned the estate at the death of a wife, the wife should own it at the death of a husband. That, if the property of a wife was carried to a husband by the marriage, the husband's should follow the same law, and they should be joint and equal owners of all property and children while married, and both equitably divided at parting; and that, if either had superior right to children, it should be the wife and mother. That all contracts of this nature, entered into by mutual consent and agreement, should be subject to the power that created them; and of course they should have power to dissolve the contract, in the same manner they formed it, mutually, and by public record. Of course, these radical sentiments, the right of men and women to separate what God had joined in wedlock, and what he could only separate by death, alarmed the classes above named; and the anathemas of the religious, and the vulgar ribald trash of the pettifogger, and his rowdy legion, both fell, thick and fast, on the Lone One. He was branded, and stigmatized, and identified with every person, writer, or speaker, of offensive and obscene words or books; and heralded from "Dan to Beersheba" as an enemy to marriage, and all sacred institutions, by those whose hearts, if not homes, were full of "yellow-covered literature." But the Lone One knew the cost of defending such reforms, and took the job at the price, conscious of justice at the end of life, if not before. Well he knew there would be a day of judgment, and that God and pure spirits were both free, and both happy; so he should find himself in their mansion when this life was over, and the defenders of lust, and scorn, and envy, and jealousy, and those who took delight in them, would be bound in the hells of their own creation, with the effects of their own sins on themselves, for " their works do follow them."

> " There are flowers that ne'er shall wither,
>   Blossoms that shall ne'er decay :
> They are found beyond this planet,
>   In the realms of endless day.
> If you fain would taste these flowers,
> Blooming in immortal bowers—
>   Bear the Cross.

> " There are hopes that never crumble —
>   Lustrous hopes that ne'er shall die —
> Hopes that bud upon this fair earth,
>   But which ripen 'yond the sky.
> If these hopes, that ne'er shall perish,
> You desire to have and cherish —
>   Bear the Cross.

> " There are friends who live forever —
>   Friends whom Death hath sent before
> Through the dark and silent valley,
>   To a far sublimer shore.
> Would ye have these friends forever
> By your side, and leave them never—
>   Bear the Cross.

> " There are never-dying pleasures —
>   Pleasures sweet and holier far
> Than the bodiless enjoyments
>   Which around about us are.
> Do you wish to find these pleasures,
> These celestial, priceless treasures—
>   Bear the Cross.

> " There are bright and fadeless beauties,
>   Constellated by God's hand,
> Where the gentle waves of music
>   Flood with melody a land.

If you fain would see these beauties,
Never trifle with life's duties —
　　　　　Bear the Cross.

" There are never-clouded glories —
　Glories robed in holy awe ;
There are splendors that are grander
　Than **this world of ours e'er saw.**
Would **you, when your life-ties sever**
Gaze **upon these glories ever** —
　　　　　Bear the **Cross.**

" **There 's a life** which ne'er shall slumber —
　There are blisses blent with love ;
And, if you **be ever** faithful,
　You 'll **experience them above,**
Where, when cometh Death's **to-morrow,**
You shall, purged of every sorrow,
　　　　　Wear a Crown."

But there dawned to his heart a millennial day earlier, but not more surely, than **to** his mate. **Several years** after his emancipation, she, too, was free from " custom's heartless forms," and from the scorn-storm of jealousy, prejudice, and envy, and they met and **lived on** that plane of mutual love, mutual confidence, mutual purity, and mutual interest. **Then,** and only then, did life become **worth the cost.** Through all **the** previous years, they had been tenants, living in leased hearts, which were often full of vice **and** evil, from the hell of theology, or **the sleet-showers of scorn, or the** dazzling bewilderment of popularity and pride. **But now the home was in their** own affections, and they met congenial **and** equally developed souls ; **and with** such the seasons **of enjoyment** were of the holiest, and purest, and most heavenly of earth.

But this was a fearful condition to attain ; for whosoever has a **soul** developed to that condition that he or she is lovable, and beloved by the pure and good of earth and heaven, is sure to be **ranked as a** fiend of hell, and holy writ and doggery-slang will **both** be quoted to prove it. Whoever attains to a condition even approaching the love of Jesus, so far as to draw and attract others

14*

who need to be saved from lust and pollution, from slavery and tyranny, from degradation and defilement, is sure to have his or her reputation crucified in the market-places daily, and to be scourged with the basest tongues of slander that a self-styled Christian land can furnish. When his affections were expanded, and his soul developed to the sphere of harmony, and the angels came to minister to him, and those of earth nearest in condition to the angels were drawn to him, and became his friends and confidants — then was the time when every effort was put forth by the wicked to induce her who had struggled with him through the dark trials of physical suffering to desert him. Every effort of the pious, and polluted, neighbors combined to persuade her that he had abandoned her and was full of lust, as they really were themselves ; but they did not persuade, and their oft-renewed and extraordinary efforts tended, more than any one cause, to open her eyes. Slowly, but gradually, they opened, and she saw first the condition and objects of those around her ; then her own condition ; and then the light shone plainly on his — and, O ! what an earthly morning ! equalled only by the glory of an entrance into the other sphere ! Love supreme, heavenly, pure, such as her heart had never known before, filled her whole being, till, like a ruby cup, it overflowed, and filled her soul with joy and gladness immeasurable, unspeakable, and the boundless ocean has been flowing through her being ever since But what now ? Why, she drew around her, like the magnet, the objects attracted by her pure heart, and the pure loved her everywhere, as they did the Lone One ; and the vile cast her off, spewed her out as the whale did Jonah, as related in the fable ; but, like him, she landed safely on dry land, and the angels of both spheres came and ministered to her wants. She — they — found the good Samaritans ; and when the slanders were coming hottest and heaviest, there was not a family in the state, of which one or all were members of a church, that was as happy, as harmonious, as affectionate, as devoted, as the family of the Lone One ; nor is there "to this day," and when any Christian will present such a family we will engage to seek religion in that direction. Her overflowing soul drinks now from a source of joy and love, which affords her more happiness in one day than all the world ever afforded her before in years; and the two, with the three beloved **and loving** children, make a five-stranded chord to lash the liars **round** the **world, and** would do it effectually did they not take **shelter in** the churches, where lying for **the glory** of the church **is a pro-**tected virtue. He is no more **a Lone One; for his own home is** *the* happy home, and his family **a unit (and it was never less so than** most other families, **especially Christian** families), **and he is loved and beloved, as a brother, by** thousands in both **worlds,** because **his own love-nature** is ripened **and** developed to **its** manhood, and has been touched **by a coal from the** living fire **of the altar** of God, which is the throne of Love.

> "Ah! shouldst thou live but **once Love's sweets to prove,**
> Thou wilt not love to live, **unless thou live to love!**"

Section IV.

THE CHANGE OF BELIEF. — SPIRITUALISM. — MEDIUMSHIP. — TURNED
PREACHER.

> "**Imbued with the** seraphic fire,
>   To wake the music of the lyre —
>   **To** love, to know, and to aspire : —

> "Thou seest, in thy truthful dream,
>   All nature robed in light supreme,
>   And wouldst carol in the beam.

> "Happy — yet most unhappy still —
>   I dread to think what good and ill,
>   What joy and grief, thy heart **shall fill!**

> "Think, ere thou choose such high career,
>   If thou hast strength to persevere,
>   And scale the summit, cold and clear.

> "Great shall thy pleasure be, — thy soul
>   Shall chant with planets as they roll,
>   Made one with nature, part and whole.

" All shall be given to feed thy mind
  With love and pity for thy kind,
  And every sympathy refined.

" Thy words shall fill the mouths of men ;
  The written lightnings of thy pen
  Shall flash upon their wandering ken.

" **Reflect and weigh the** loss and gain ;
  All joy is counterpoised by pain,
  And nothing charms which we attain.

" **Who** loves the music of the spheres,
  And lives on earth, must close his ears
  To many voices which he hears.

" **'T is evermore the finest sense
  That feels the anguish most intense
  At daily outrage, gross and dense.**

" The greater joy, the keener grief ;
  Of nature's balances the chief
  She grants nor favor, nor relief.

" **And vain,** most vain, is youthful trust,
  For men are evermore unjust
  To their superior fellow-dust ;

" And ever turn malicious eyes
  On those whom most they idolize,
  And break their hearts with calumnies.

" Their slanders, like the tempest-stroke,
  May leave the cowslip-stem unbroke,
  But rend the branches of the oak.

" If genius live, 't is made a slave ;
  And if it die, the true and brave,
  Men pluck its heart out on its grave ;

" And then dissect it for the throng,
  And say, 'T was this, so weak, or strong,
  That poured such living strains of song.

" Each fault of genius is a crime,
  For cant or folly to beslime,
  Sent drifting on the stream of time

> " May all good angels keep thy heart
>   Pure to itself, and to thine art,
>   And shield it from the poison dart !—
>
> " And when **thou sittest on the height,**
>   **Thy life may be its own** delight,
>   **And cheer thee, in the** world's despite ' "

As has been before mentioned, the **Lone** One began in the winter of '43 and '44 to experimentally investigate the subject of Mesmerism. **With a steady, but sure,** march he progressed, as opportunity offered, for several **years,** to both study and experiment with this science, until the doubts which hung over the phenomenon of **death** and the existence beyond were all clearly and fully settled. The first point of importance, fully and positively established both by experiment and testimony, was the existence **of** a faculty of seeing without the use of bodily eyes, and unobstructed by distance or intervening objects. The origin and seat of this faculty was **a** subject of much speculation to one who did not admit the existence of a spiritual body, with faculties of its own, and powers of seeing independent of the bodily organs ; and finally compelled, with other evidences, the admission of an existence independent of physical or corporeal senses. But the utterly absurd idea of **an** immaterial existence, or of a being without form and locality, **was never for a** moment tolerated, however much dogmatical theology might assert or assume on the subject. When this point was fully gained, and the *seeing* faculty of clairvoyants had been established, and the laws which regulate it were sufficiently understood to enable him **to** know when it was reliable, then opened another arcana of "divine revelation." This sense, without the body as a medium (except to express it to others), and the others which were found to be equally acute and extended, and equally certain of existence, declared that and proved they could reach and realize the presence **and** existence of spirits who were really the very persons who once walked and talked with us, but whose bodies had been cast off forever, and whose conscious existence the Lone One ever had believed to end with death. Theology had taught him that this was the only *material* life, and that all beyond was immaterial; and he had therefore replied, It is immaterial what you teach, and immateriality and nothing are to me and philosophy synonymous terms.

But now, with new evidence, came a new theory also, and the spirits themselves declared that they were as really material as they were when they had earthly bodies, or bodies composed of the solids and liquids of earth, but that their present bodies were constituted of elemental matter, in as great variety as those of earth were ; and that these bodies, invisible and intangible to our bodies, because composed of such substances as were too rare for our sense, were to them as capable of expression for all emotional and passional life, and conscious existence, as those they had left. But here, again, came in the absurdities of theology, and they asked, What and where is God, Jesus, Heaven, the Judgment, Hell, and the King-Devil, &c.?— and the reply came back from these spirits, as it came back from mortals on the earth, We *know* nothing of these things, but we *believe*, &c. ; making as great a variety of opinion in that condition of life as in this, and just as little knowledge. Now the glorious truth of the other life began to gleam upon the mind of the Lone One ; first in the fitful glare of lightning's flash, or gentler lume of boreal light, until, at last, through all the faculties of his being the full glory of a real and *natural* spiritual sphere shone as brilliantly as a meridian sun through unclouded sky, and quickened all his powers into action, as the April sun does the sleeping vegetation. Here you read also one of the principal causes of the reformation in his diet and regimen, in life and affections, as related in preceding sections. The long-dormant energies of the soul, that felt this life a failure, and saw none beyond, — that felt mortality to be a " wheel of pain, at best,"— now had opened the volume of another life, or a continuation of this, where those who labor here shall see and feel their just reward. Now his energies were ready for action. First, the Phalanx was the result of this awakened energy. Then political efforts at reform, emancipation, and universal freedom and happiness; then commercial release of the masses from the bondage and slavery to monopolies. Then social and affectional freedom, and development to universal love and harmony. Then, and finally, spiritual freedom, growth, development, and illumination. The preacher, the reformer. In the winter of '45–6, the experiments of a company of investigators, in Cincinnati, **with** one or more clairvoyants, were closely followed **by the Lone One** and several **others at the** Phalanx-home, **and they** were also deeply interested **in** all they could learn of the wonderful powers **of A. J. Davis,** in New York and elsewhere. They learned, by occasional newspaper reports, of his delivering a series of lectures **in a** clairvóyant state, which were said to be rare and very remark**able** productions, but not fraught with marvellous stories, for such **to** the Lone One would have ended all interest **in them. But** these were said to be natural, or nature's revelations; and hence he became intensely interested in them, and with much impatience watched **every week for a** notice of the book, and no sooner received news of its publication than one dozen copies were ordered by express to Milwaukie, the end of the express line, by **the** secretary of the Phalanx, and **most** of them were read and re-read, **lent** and borrowed, sold and re-sold, until many minds were fed by these new truths, who could get no food from what Christians **call** God's revelations. The Lone One had now a firmer and more substantial basis for his lectures and strictures than ever before, and he boldly took up the defence of this book, — of its philosophy, in the main, and the truly divine manner of its revelations, — **and with** his senator-friend, who was also up to **the time in the philos**ophy. He ever had one or more copies with him at the capitol, to call out remarks and ridicule, and give him a chance to defend it, and compare it with Moses' revelation, &c. Although there were some theories and principles in this volume that he did not accept, **and** never has, yet the candor of the author, or authors, and the honest, unassuming style of the seer, gave the whole an irresistible recommendation to the mind of the Lone One. The vast amount of truth, with the natural, and rational, general systems of creation, of life, and of progression, and of harmony, was to his soul like a shower of rain to a parched and thirsting soil. He drank, and was filled. He spoke, and was heard. He recommended, and some read. But the author, A. J. D., became an object of great interest to the Lone One, and ever after he was among the first to read whatever bore his name, and to watch with intense interest every change in **his** eventful life. Some years after, he became a personal and intimate friend and colaborer in the field, scattering seed for the harvest-time. Sowing in corruption, to reap in incorruption. Sowing in the body, to reap in the spirit. Sowing in mortality, to reap in immortality. From '46 to '53 the Lone One was only occasionally heard, by lecture or by newspaper article, to defend the existence of spirits in our midst, with capacities to reach us with intelligence occasionally, as conditions would admit. His own mind being fully satisfied, he sometimes spoke or wrote. Chosen by a society of spirit-teachers, they had him under discipline and influence unbeknown to himself, of which the change **of** diet was a part, and the true development of the affections and loves was an essential qualification; and some years after their work on him had commenced, they related **to** him all they had been doing, and its objects, and **then** he discovered the cause of his abandoning every field of labor where worldly honor and distinction was before him, and success almost certain, and the reason why he had let every opportunity to acquire wealth escape **him,** even when he knew it was within his reach by honorable means. Now he saw why he *must* be poor and full of human love; for such must preach the true gospel of our age, as such did in the days of Jesus. It was necessary that Jesus should have nowhere to lay his head; and so it was of his disciples who went out to preach; and nearly so must it be with those who will, in our day, reach the hearts of the people, and kindle in them the living fire of love to God, by its expression to our fellow-beings. The pen-tracks of the Lone One can be found conveying his sentiments in the *Boston Investigator*, the *Phalanx*, the *Harbinger*, the *Univercœlum*, the *Spirit of the Age*, the

Young America, the *Landmark*, the *Spirit Messenger*, to the *Spiritual Telegraph*, and for some distance into its pages, and later in both eastern and western papers, with many local articles in local papers of the state in which he resided at the time. The **Patent** Office published from his pen, and the Crystal Palace, with its world's show-cases, registered him as one of the commissioners from a far-west state; but still, in all this, he was the Lone One, and the same orphaned and despised being, who fled from tyranny, and slept on the ground made warm by the bodies of cattle, with a guardian spirit-mother only for a friend and companion — she with little power, and much desire, to aid him. But now he had felt the touch of angel-hands upon his inner and outer being, and could read the past and present, and catch gleams of the future; and to his mother he would truly say :

> " I know thy form is ever hovering
>   In this gloom around me spread ;
> And I feel thy holy influence
>   In the daily path I tread.
> Thine 's the step so soft and mournful
>   Coming on each golden beam ;
> Thine 's the hand that gently pencils
>   Holy visions in my dream.
>
> " **Oft** in low and soothing whispers,
>   When my soul with grief is riven,
> Thou hast brought me golden beauties
>   Of thy far-off home in heaven.
> This that stills the throbbing, burning
>   Of this weary, aching heart,
> And unseals the crystal fountain
>   Whence the soothing tear-drops start.
>
> " Through the vale of gloomy shadows,
>   Be thou, loved one, ever nigh,
> And in thy low sweet accents tell me
>   Of thy home in yon blue sky !
> Pure, bright thoughts like dew-drops bring me,
>   Shadowings of that land so fair !
> That I may come, O ! ask our Father
>   Where thou, and love, and angels are ! "

15

The diary of the Lone One for the year 1850 closes by saying that during the year he had made many experiments, and examined carefully and critically the spirit-rapping and table-tipping phenomena, and become satisfied they were often caused by spirits, but very imperfect modes of conveyance for intelligence from the spirit-sphere to ours, with a fair prospect to become better and more reliable. The diaries of '50, '51, '52, also record lectures, at different places, on Phrenology, Physiology, Geology, Temperance, Land Reform, and other subjects. But never for pay, or as a business, until the autumn of '52, when most other business was dispensed with, and the dispensation of the new gospel absorbed his time, and he entered the field as a lecturer, mainly on spirit life and intercourse, and the philosophy of that life and our intercourse with it.

The life and business at this time, at home, was very much broken and distracted, for many reasons, most of which can be collected in this narrative. And now the ties to both home and business could, perhaps, for the first time in life, allow the Lone One to start on a pilgrimage to defend the most odious and unpopular doctrine of the day, and to meet and bear the abuse and scorn of the pulpit, the press, the bar-room, and the rabble, with all their bloated, or bombastic, or swaggering advocates. Every species of crime, including religious tyranny, was out on this new doctrine; and they did succeed in driving many timid hearts back to the shelter of public opinion, which could and did cover the most corrupt as well as many good and true hearts. But the Lone One owed nothing to public opinion. It had abused him in childhood as badly as it could, and had never ceased its abuse of him, although he had fully and plainly proved that he could control it, if he desired, and have its adulation and applause, if he would but fall down and worship. Nothing else was required of him; yet his soul could never "stoop to conquer," nor would it ever bow down to the image which any tyrant could set up. Boldly, fearlessly, he took his staff and travelled on, lecturing and to lecture, picking up here and there a few dimes, about equal to his expenses in amount, as the voluntary contributions of hearers or friends. Never disheartened **or discouraged, for he** had a sure promise of reward in the life to come for all **the good he** could do in the life already come. The philosophy of materiality and immortality, which he taught, rendered him and his doctrines **very** obnoxious to the orthodox defenders of the faith; and they **usually** opposed his meetings, and **used every** effort to prevent **the people** from listening **to the words of this infidel preacher.** The " houses **of God "** were almost as effectually shut against him as they **were** against Jesus **and John when they went out to preach.** I am aware that some persons, who **have been** accustomed **to idolizing** Jesus, will be shocked at our comparisons; but we **are unable to see** any impropriety in it ; for there were some **marked** correspondences **between** the two, especially in the heresies and blasphemies they both taught, and in the reception **of their** teachings by **the** people and the priests, and also in the genealogy, both being rather **im-**perfect beyond the mother; and, were we disposed to record **the** feats of healing, we might make **a** feeble correspondence there also. But these are of no account to us or to the Lone One, and only inserted to moderate the superstition, rather than to connect **the Lone** One by comparison to any distinguished personage of past or present time. The voices of his guardians were ever urging him on in his mission.

> " **Be** firm, be bold, be strong, be true,
>   And dare to stand alone ;
> Strive for the right, whate'er **you do,**
>   Though helpers there are none.
>
> " Nay, bend not to the swelling **surge**
>   Of public sneer and wrong ;
> 'T will bear thee on to ruin's verge,
>   With current wild and strong.
>
> " Stand for the right ! Though falsehood rail,
>   And proud lips coldly sneer,
> A poisoned arrow cannot wound
>   A conscience pure and clear.

> " Stand for the right ! and with clean hands
>   Exalt the truth on high ;
>   Thou 'lt find warm, sympathizing hearts
>   Among the passers by ;
>
> " **Men who have seen, and** thought, and felt,
>   **Yet could not boldly dare**
>   **The** battle's brunt, but **by thy** side
>   **Will** every danger share.
>
> " Stand for the right ! Proclaim it loud !
>   Thou 'lt find an answering tone
>   **In** honest hearts, and thou 'lt no more
>   **Be** doomed to stand alone."

Along the pathway of this development might be noticed many incidents of interest to the searcher after evidences of spirit-life; but it would be out of the line of our narrative to use up many pages for that purpose. But it must be borne in mind that the Lone One was originally, educationally, and reputationally, the most sceptical of all sceptics. Having no faith in immortality, he was not seeking for proof of the negative, but for evidence of the positive side of the question. He had become fully satisfied that the Christians could furnish no facts and no evidence for a reasoning, metaphysical, and scientific mind ; that their authority-evidence was not admissible as evidence at all ; that their theory was only theory, and **a belief** in it was no evidence of its truth. For well he knew that belief and doubt were twin-sisters, and never could be separated ; and that theory, without demonstration, could never claim more than belief—never knowledge. The very theory **of** another life, immaterial, and, of course, for that reason, **if** no other, beyond the power of manifestation, precluded the possibility of demonstration. He had, therefore, long since given up all hope of evidence from that source. Nor did he begin the search in mesmerism for the purpose of proving, or with the view or expectation to prove, the existence of spirits. He rather supposed it would more effectually confirm his unbelief. Step after step, he was led by facts, which are stubborn obstacles to a false theory, and strike hard as Ajax's rocks in an enemy's ranks. He had become fully satisfied and boldly defended the other life, and its intercourse with this through the systems which were susceptible **to clairvoyant condition,** before the alarm was sounded in the Christian tents at Hydeville and Rochester, by the raps **of the** then pious Fox family. He was not surprised, but overjoyed, when he became satisfied that the spirit-friends had found more ways **of** communicating to us a knowledge of their existence and presence; **and** he **was** not much surprised **to** find the churches and their **preachers** on the negative side, and opposing every form of demonstration **that could prove** continued existence; for he had long accused **them** of teaching their doctrines as a trade, and for a business, and not from a belief. And now he saw they were about to prove it so by opposing the only real and reliable evidence we can have of the continued existence of our friends after the body is cast **off.** Neither was he surprised when he saw the course they took after being compelled **to admit** the occurrence of the phenomena, and the intelligence **exhibited in them.** A theory which teaches that all invisible agencies around **us that** exhibit intelligence are from **one** of two sources, God or Devil, would, of course, attribute these **to** one or the other; and the God or Devil origin of each intelligent **communication** would, of course, be determined by its agreement **with the theory of the** judge who had a theory or doctrine as an **infallible standard of truth.** To the Catholic, if it defended Protestantism as superior to his church, of course it would be the Devil; to the Calvinist, if it sustained Unitarianism as superior to his creed, of **course it** would be the Devil; to the Methodist, if it upheld Universalism as superior to **his doctrine,** of course it would be **the Devil; to the Universalist, if** it denied the sacredness of the Bible, and the value of **his** preaching, it could not be attributed to the Devil, for this **church** is beyond the Devil-theory, and furnishes the singular phenomenon of a church without a **Devil, of which I think** many of them have seen the need in these **trying times,** with this most potent heresy. They are compelled to attribute it to electricity, to od-force, to deception, to anything

15*

but spirits. Not that; for, if that be the source of this intelligence, then we shall soon have a new set of preachers, and the old ones, who we supposed were above and out of our way, will be in the field again competing with the new. But to the infidel, who had no Devil or God playing with us by fallible intelligence, these phenomena became generally highly interesting, and brought to thousands of such minds the first ray of light from the hereafter, and the first point of evidence of continued existence.

Soon after the shout, and laugh, and ribald jest, of witling and clown, had gone over the country with the "Rochester Knockings" for a bait, the Lone One and a few eager souls formed a circle, and met weekly or oftener for more than six months, without a rap or signal of any kind from invisible spirits; and the Christians said, "Fools! you might know better!" But they retorted, "Fools! what do you go weekly for years to the church for, and never find God, nor any signs that there is a God, except those the infidel has in common with you, in nature?" After six months of perseverance, a new member of the circle was added as a visitor, casually, in the person of a young lady, a member of a Presbyterian church; when the raps came with her, and, for a few weeks, they were delighted by brief and imperfect messages from their spirit-friends. All over the clothes, and even on the hair of the Lone One, could be heard the tiny raps of the two little, over-joyed boys, whose bodies he had left in sorrow under the apple-tree; and soon, in stronger magnetic sound, came the glad beats of his mother, eager to make herself known by the new mode of communicating; for she had already done it by clairvoyance.

This medium was soon frightened out of her mediumship, or the use of it, by her religious superiors, who said it was the Devil, although she had the most incontrovertible evidence that her mother communicated to her, both when alone and in circles. But they told her it was surely the Devil pretending to be her mother, and getting the facts and knowledge from her mind, &c. "Poor, ignorant souls!" said the Lone One; "if you who are safely locked in the church, and faithful to every command of her and

God, are not protected and safe against the Devil without a priest
to guide you, then your religion is worthless, and mine is better;
for the Devil cannot, and does not, affect or disturb me."—"But
you are his child," they replied.—"Then I must serve my father.
And now let us compare lines. Bring out some son of a priest,
born forty years ago; run his Life-Line along by the side of mine;
and let us see how one of God's sons would compare with **one**
of the Devil's."—"O, horrible blasphemy! I do wish he had
left **this abuse of the** churches out of this book!" says the pious
reader. **But,** reader, it is only harsh to those who have idols.
The mother can bear to have you point out the faults and defects
of her neighbor's children, but not those of her own. Only the
virtues of them must be named to her. If we overlook the errors,
how shall we ever correct them? We have not attempted to screen
the Lone One from **the** blame that justly belonged to him. **We**
have only given him what belonged to him, — the credit of **hon-**
esty in belief and motive; and these ever prompted him, as any
one might know from the fact that his belief, boldly defended, was
always the unpopular one. One of the members of the six-
months' circle before referred **to** — an erratic, disordered, and
eccentric Scotchman, with domestic troubles and social inharmony
— became insane soon after, and, claiming to be controlled by
God, **or** Lambie, or the Devil, or all three, and more, cut up
strange, **but** usually harmless, capers about the village, until some
frightened **and** threatened citizens took him, chained, to jail, and
then **the horrors** of spiritualism were exposed. Insanity was its
effect, and **one** victim was already before the public, and was a
sure sign that thousands would follow. It was in vain that its
defenders pointed out other causes; **no** others would be received.
It was in vain they showed the hundreds of victims of religious
revivals; these had plenty of causes besides religion. But this,
and one or two they heard of in some unknown place, made it
sure this delusion was of the Devil. Now, more than ever, the
Lone One saw the necessity for bold and strong hearts to step into
the field, and defend the cause of truth, and the best facts the

world had ever discovered of another life, against the prejudice
and crushing power of the churches, which seemed as determined
to kill it out in its infancy as Herod and the priests were to kill
Jesus in his infancy. The friends, warned in a dream, seized the
young child, and fled into the Egypt of scepticism and Infidelity
(I use the term Infidel here in the sense the Christians do, — un-
believers in their doctrines), and there nursed it ; and it grew, in
spite of the Buffalo doctors, who were employed by the priest to
strangle it.

Next, Charles Beecher was employed to christen it with hot
water, or " hell-fire," that it might die ; but it was miraculously
preserved against this also, as it was against the poison emetics
of the doctors. Next, the speculators came, and offered great
prices for it as a slave to hunt up treasures, thieves, town-sites,
and corner-lots ; but it could not be bought, and they cursed it,
and said it would not pay ; it was worthless, a nuisance, and
ought to be killed ; and they engaged the services of a Dr. Richmond, of Ohio, and a sceptic — Rogers — of Boston ; and they
both shot at it, but their guns kicked them both over ; and when
they had recovered, like the Irishman, they saw the game laugh-
ing at them, and discovered that they had the wrong end of the
gun. Only one course seemed to be left to rid the country of
this terrible enemy to sanity and religion, and that was, to get
some president of a college to issue a " mandamus ; " and they
found a ready tool in a Mahan, who was willing to take the
chances ; and he filled up the instrument, but made a fatal mistake in the names, and sent his own religion to prison, and
" damned " himself " to everlasting fame." His college started
down a decline, and he went up " Salt River " soon after, and has
not been heard from since, except by those who have correspondence with that country. Several other distinguished citizens in-
jured themselves permanently or temporarily by throwing clubs at
this object of hatred to them, which often flew back and hit themselves, with more or less force, as they were hurled with more or
less fury and hate. By its side, and in its defence, stood some of

the noblest, purest, firmest, and truest hearts of the country and
the world.   Robert Owen and Dr. Ashburner, of the Old World,
came early to see the child, and "believed on him;" and, in this
country, Hon. J. W. Edmonds, N. P. Tailmadge, Senator Simmons,
J. R. Giddings, B. F. Wade, and a host of others from the side
of law and government, came **to** the **rescue;** and from **science**
came Professor Robert **Hare, Professor Mapes,** Professor Bu-
chanan, and **a host of** others from the medicine side of science;
and from **the theology side the Universalists and** Unitarians let up
a whole **delegation, and** some of the others a few of their best
specimens, **to** defend, in the days of its odium, the philosophy and
demonstration that is to convince the world of immortality. From
the ranks of the quiet reasoners and thinkers of the cities and
country a host **fell in** with the facts as fast as **they could** be presented to them.   **But** nearly every church was alarmed; **and the**
watchmen on the walls of Zion were sounding **the cry of "An**
enemy is coming! **Be up, and** ready **for battle! Put** on the
whole armor of **the** Gospel! **We will** lead you to the fight!
Come on! come on! Here is the old enemy, the Devil, in a new
dress! Be careful, **or he will** deceive **you!** Look **only** to us;
trust in the Lord; read the **Bible!** Do not look off the book, for
that light may dazzle **or bewilder** you!" The poor dupes were
thus **led captives into** darkness **by** thousands, who might have
seen the **light and known the glorious** truths of the new gospel,
and it would have set them **free.**

"There surely is some guiding power
Which rightly suffers wrong, —
Gives vice to bloom its little **hour,**
But virtue **late and long.**"

At the commencement of 1853 the fourth decade of the Lone
One terminated; and forty years had made their wrinkles on his
brow, whitened and curled his locks, and rather straightened than
bent his form. The last ten had done the work for his mind. He
was **now** emancipated from the bondage to cold and soulless scep-

ticism, and a full recipient of the glorious truths of spirit-life.
Freed from all political obligations and aspirations, he sought none
of its places, nor would he accept its offers. Free from the Phalanx trials, and all **partial** and isolated efforts to save a few souls,
and go with them through life and to heaven, his philanthropy was
now world-wide, and **his** home and "domain" the world, and all
men members **of the Phalanx.** He was **now** fully the cosmopolite, and his field of labor the world-home. True, his little **means,**
amounting perhaps **in** value to one thousand dollars, was in a little
house-and-garden home for his family, which he intended sacredly
to guard for them. But, other than this, his home and his busi-
ness, his time and his talents, were all now devoted **to** the spread
and dissemination of the new philosophy of spirit life **and inter-**
course. True, for some time after he **had** devoted himself **to this**
new business, the receipts did not sustain his economical family.
But he was not disheartened, but borrowed money of the state for
that purpose, with a hope that it would not sacrifice his little home,
and it did not ; for God always helps those who help themselves,
and " works in the working soul." Nearly all his old friends now
deserted him. A few only **of those** who were near in condition
of mind, and knew him best, stood by him **in** this last and best
consecration of himself to the last and most odious of all doctrines, — **a belief in spirits. Although this** itinerant labor did
not bring **dimes as a reward, it brought that** which to **him was**
equally valuable, — warm hearts, sympathy, open homes, **and** wel-
coming hands. These he often met, and they cheered him on his
way, and encouraged him to persevere, but not more effectually or
really than did the messages **from** the spirit-home which often
reached him, **with** the most cheering and encouraging **expressions**
of love and sympathy. For **a time, the** lonesome **and** grieving
mate was honestly and strongly prejudiced against this course, and
the doctrine he taught ; but it was only the sickness that precedes
the action **of the emetic which brings** up **the** superfluous bile ; so
this threw up and out, in time, the accumulations of the years in
error, with old Calvinism at the bottom ; all went over together,

and she became free and spiritually healthy. An entire change came over her day and night dreams. She saw, she heard; she felt, she realized, her change of heart; and she was a convert to the new philosophy, and thus added more happiness to the Life-Line of the Lone One than she ever had before; for now one heart, one life, one destiny, was theirs. Every cloud was removed; and they moved so sweetly toward the sunset of life, that they felt it was good for them that all this experience had been gained in this life, **where it properly belonged, but** which many will put over to the next. It was late, indeed, at forty, — sixteen years after marriage, — **to** renew and complete the court-ship which had been so suddenly interrupted, and lain so long neglected; but it is said by some to be " better late than never;" and well they knew that, with many, it was *never* renewed after marriage, and sadly deficient before. Ah! little do those whose lives are spent in **the** muddy pool of sensual and external life, or in the turbulent stream of contention and **strife, know of the** joys of harmonized and happy life, with the ascendency of the spiritual over the physical self in conjugal life; nor can they know until they reach it. Then, — O, what a payment for all the struggles to reach the summit! — what an *over*-payment for the night of life spent in tears and sorrows! Now his home was lonely without him, for a reason; and the pet daughter, joined by the mother, could *say*, but not sing :

> " Linger not long! Home is not home without thee ;
> Its dearest tokens do but make us mourn.
> O! let its memory, like a chain about thee,
> Gently compel and hasten thy return !

> " Linger not long! Though crowds should woo thy staying,
> Bethink thee, can the mirth of friends, though dear,
> Compensate for the grief thy long delaying
> Costs the sad hearts that sigh to have thee here?"

Now, when he came, the leaping hearts and joyous kiss were ever ready to meet him, and happiness, such as few ever realize in this life, was spread, like a "balm of thousand flowers," on all about this home. His friends felt it; but his enemies, with poison-tongue of slander, were only the more bitter, when every hope of making trouble in his family was lost, by her conversion to his belief, and the calm and happy life they had attained foiled all their efforts in that direction. The serpent was still biting at the file, although its teeth were often broken and loosened, while he moved steadily on his course, with the exclamation, often,

> "Not all they do, or say, can make
> My head, or tooth, or finger ache,
> Nor mar my form, nor scar my face,
> Nor put one feature out of place;
> Nor will ten thousand lies
> Make me less virtuous, learned, or wise.
> Their malice the best way to balk,
> Is quietly to let them talk."

Envy, malice, spite, and lies, were multiplied, and sent after him and before him, and the vigilant enemies of his teachings made every effort in their power to destroy his influence as a teacher of the Harmonial Philosophy. For well many of them knew the power of his mind, and the magnetism of his language, with truth for its weapon. To defeat, or retard, the spread of such doctrine, it was necessary, at whatever cost, to stop him from advocating it, or destroy his influence. But it was a failure. Every dart sent at him was caught on his shield, and, with a clear conscience and honest heart, boldly and fearlessly he moved on, though "branded by the slanderer's lies," till he lived them down; and when accusations reached him he smiled, and pitied those who aimed them at him, and asked those who received them as true to call for the execution of the law, or to bring him the person, and the testimony, and he would restore four-fold. This, of course, could never be done; for the cry of "wolf — wolf!" was not made because wolves were near, but only to alarm the sheep. He also boldly advocated the right of every married woman to an equal share and control of all property of the family, and to equal social, civil, religious, and political privileges, and to a divorce whenever she asked it, even without being obliged to reveal or make public the cause; for well he and many others knew there were thousands of suffering victims who dare not mention the causes of their misery, but who had ample cause, and good reason, for asking for divorce, with **sufficient** property to sustain them. These doctrines rendered him terribly obnoxious to a certain class **of sensualists and** petty tyrants; but they brought him the sympathy of thousands of martyrs, from their spirit-homes, and some still lingering here; and he knew, if the sufferers were his friends, **that** his cause was a righteous one, and he could afford to defend it, however unpopular, for he was by birth, education, and life, the legitimate attorney of **all** odious or unpopular truths and **rights.** Like the tree which brings the early and pleasant apples, **he had** been clubbed and pelted all his life, **and** grown stronger and more vigorous thereby.

> " Cheer up, cheer up ! Though life has days,
>   November days, I ween,
> When the lone heart wails like the wind,
>   And nothing bright is seen ;
> When smiles come faintly to the lips,
>   And eyes glance mournfully,
> And hope seems like a faded leaf
>   Just clinging to the tree ,
>
> " Yet smile — cheer up ! New hopes and **joys**
>   Within thy heart will spring,
> And He whose love is over all
>   A spirit-balm will bring.
> Cheer up, nor wear a clouded brow,
>   Thy home with gloom to fill ;
> Thank God for past and present good,
>   And brood not o'er the ill."

16

CHAPTER V.

FRACTIONAL DECADE.

The Cosmopolite. — **The** Harmonial Man, **the** Happy Family, and the New **Home.** — The Triumph of Justice.

SECTION I.

ETERNAL JUSTICE.

BY CHARLES MACKAY.

THE man is thought a knave or fool,
　Or bigot, plotting crime,
Who, for the advancement of his kind,
　Is wiser than his time.
For him the hemlock shall distil,
　For him the axe be bared ;
For him the gibbet shall be built,
　For **him the** stake prepared ;
Him shall the scorn and wrath of men
　Pursue with deadly aim ;
And malice, envy, spite, and lies,
　Shall desecrate his name.
But truth shall conquer at the last,
　For round and round we run,
And ever the right comes uppermost,
　And ever is justice done.

Pace through thy cell, old Socrates,
　Cheerily, to and fro !
Trust to the impulse of thy soul,
　And let the poison flow.

They may shatter to earth the lamp of clay
  That holds a light divine,
But they cannot quench the fire of thought
  By any such deadly wine ;
They cannot blot thy spoken words
  From the memory of man,
By all the poison ever was brewed
  Since time its course began.
To-day abhorred, to-morrow adored,
  So round and round we run,
And ever the truth comes uppermost,
  And ever is justice done.

Plod in thy cave, gray Anchorite !
  Be wiser than thy peers ;
Augment the range of human power,
  And trust to coming years.
They may call thee wizard, and monk accursed,
  And load thee with dispraise :
Thou wert born five hundred years too soon
  For the comfort of thy days.
But not too soon for human kind :
  Time hath reward in store,
And the demons of our sires become
  The saints that we adore.
The blind can see, the slave is lord ;
  So round and round we run,
And ever the wrong is proved to be wrong,
  And ever is justice done.

Keep, Galileo, to thy thought,
  And nerve thy soul to bear!
They may gloat o'er the senseless words **they wring**
  From the pangs of thy despair :
They may veil their eyes, but they cannot hide
  The sun's meridian glow ;
The heel of a priest may tread thee down,
  And a tyrant work thee woe ;
But never a truth has been destroyed :
  They may curse it and call it crime ;
Pervert and betray, or slander and slay
  Its teachers, for a time.

But the sunshine, aye, shall light the sky,
  As round and round we run,
And the truth shall ever come uppermost,
  And **justice** shall be done.

And live **there** *now* such men as these,
  With thoughts like the great of **old?**
Many have died in their misery,
  And left their thought untold ;
And many live, and are ranked as mad,
  And placed in the cold world's ban,
For sending their bright, far-seeing souls
  Three centuries in the **van.**
They toil in penury and grief,
  Unknown, if not maligned ;
Forlorn, forlorn, bearing the scorn
  Of the meanest of mankind.
But yet the world goes round and round,
  And the genial seasons run,
And ever the truth comes uppermost,
  And ever is justice done.

The remainder of this record will be mainly from the notes in **the Diary, or the** correspondence of the Cosmopolite, with foreign **items, inserted to finish or** furnish the apartment.

Jan. **5, 1853.** — **A** juror all day in court-room of **the** United States **district court** in Milwaukie, with the thick-skulled judge, of whom mention **is made in** this narrative, presiding, and **a** description **of whose character and capacity** was written at the time by this seer, and published **in one of** the city papers, and brought the approval and compliments of the ablest attorney in the city to its author. While the United States paid **for** his services at court, he had out his notices and lectured evenings, to small **but** respectable audiences in the city, on the philosophy of spirit **intercourse.** When court and the lectures were closed in the city, he journeyed westward, and stopped to lecture **in** several small villages, arousing much interest in, and opposition to, the **new** philosophy.

Jan. 20, '53. — Dines with the governor at the capital. Elected an officer of the State Agricultural Society, and declines an invitation to deliver the annual address. Lectures, by **invitation of** Assembly, in the Assembly Hall of **the** capitol to large and very intelligent audience, who seem highly pleased. Holds a conspicuous place in the Free-Soil State Convention, but declines all offices and honors. Writes **for** several papers sketches and criticisms. **Gave** several lectures in the court-house, and was confined for a week to house with rebellion among the nerves, and a severe battle in the forts of the mouth. But the soothing hand **of one dear** friend, whose soul sympathized with his philosophy, rendered misery bearable; but she had seen him in sickness and health, in joy and grief, and well she knew his life was above the rabble that abused him because he would not bend and endorse its falsehoods and follies.

Feb. 7. — Accepted renewal of commission as notary, which **he** had held for some years, because he executed most **of the deeds** and acknowledgments of the village when at home.

Feb. 13. — Sunday, holds a discussion in the Methodist church **of** the Ceresco Valley (for, since the dissolution of the Phalanx, one had been erected to save the fragments) with the most vulgar blackguard he ever knew to be clothed with priestly garments; but he conquered him by mildness and good-humor, and carried **the** audience against the priest, which **caused** the door of the church **to** be closed ever **after** against discussion of new or old truths.

Feb. 20. — Again at **the** capitol, endeavoring **to** secure the passage of a bill to incorporate and unite the villages of Ripon and Ceresco, under the name of Morena; but **he** left it, and it died before birth. He met several **warm** friends, among them his old senator-friend, who was now a member of the lower house, but still Hon. ———. A whirlpool **of** excitement was at this time about the capitol, caused by an effort to impeach a Judge Hubbel, charged with more crimes than Jesus or Robespierre; but the accusers were less successful in proving them, because they could not find the sinless man to cast the first stone, and he escaped with his judicial neck unbroken. Whether it deserved it or not, "deponent saith not." In this commotion the Cosmopolite had no share, and therefore he soon moved out of it.

Feb. 26. — In Janesville, put up bills himself, and lectured in the **evening to** small audience, in large hall. Poor subject, they said, but **good** speaker. "What a fool he is, to throw himself away on **that** ridiculous humbug!" Here he made the first **acquaintance with** the Higgins family, or the Columbians, a con-**cert-band** of brothers and sisters. The younger sister was then **recovering from a severe attack** of typhoid fever; in treating which, her physician had taken it from her, and died. She felt **the** magnetic healing power of the Lone One's system, and admired his Harmonial Philosophy; for this herself, and one sister, **two brothers,** and the father and mother, had already embraced and advocated. This enlightened, and developed, and happy family subsequently became his personal friends, and are **to this day** highly esteemed by him; for they, and especially the **parents, were** among the few who had been in and turned out of **the Calvinistic** church, and had their hearts purified and refined **in the refiner's fire of** persecution; and when he found them the **sunshine of the glorious** gospel of truth and deliverance fell **calmly on their souls. Two** sons, with happy homes of their own, are in **Chicago.** One has a **Mary, such** as God seldom blesses man **with in this life, and the other has** his cup of domestic joy overflowing. **Two other brothers are** also music-dealers in Peoria, Ill., and how or what **they have** for domestic music we cannot say, **but their** souls are tuned to exquisite strains of "**nature's harp-strings.**" The two sisters have also "tied up," **and, one southing and** the other **northing, have** no doubt found joy and **sorrow somewhat** mixed, **in this life, but** probably are more beloved and **happy than most** wedded hearts in the world's broad battle-field. **Their homes** cannot be other than homes of purity and love, for such their hearts ever were; and nature and education never qualified two females better than they did these for domestic happiness. The home of the parents is in Palmyra, Wis., where the Lone One occasionally has a happy day of rest. Thus the parted voices of the Columbians are uttering other music in new concerts; but each voice can yet sing the story of the Jordan road, and Judson can make you gaze after the " Old Mill by the hill-side where we used to go in the summer-time."

The following token from one of the family, received by the Lone One, at the close of a short visit at the old homestead, may serve as a specimen of their appreciation of him, and also as one like many others in the journeyings of after years.

" DEAR BROTHER: You are going now far away, on your angel-mission. The brief period you have been with us has indeed been precious to our hungry souls; it will ever be remembered with pleasure; and gratitude will swell our hearts in thinking of the kind words, and tender expressions of love and sympathy, that have flowed so spontaneously from your heart and lips. The heavenly sphere so truly yours attracts us, and we can **but** love to be with you, and regret your short stay with us. But you will not forget us, though absent; and, though other and dearer friends surround you, I know we shall be remembered in your prayers, and the expressions of your heart. We wish a thought once in a while from our brother, ... and if it would not tax too much on the time devoted to others, we should be glad to receive thoughts on scraps of paper. Now good-by! Heaven **will** ever bless one so good and worthy as thou art; and when the time comes will give to thee that lovely home so beautifully described to us by the dwellers there. That we may all meet in that happy home, is the prayer of thy sister and each of us." . . .

We might select from his margin scrap-book many specimens, from many authors, of purity and love, like the above, of a correspondence which, running through years, led the vulgar and licentious to believe he was continuing it from such motives only as could prompt them to correspond with females.

March 2. — Leaves Janesville; expenses six dollars more than receipts for lectures. Go to Beloit, and

Sunday, March 6. — Lecture in place of Universalist preacher, and in the evening lecture on marriage to a full house; good reception, but few spiritualists. Theological professors of the college keep the place in ignorance and darkness on this subject, by assuming to know all about what they know nothing about.

March 7. — Went to Rockton, and made the acquaintance of George Guthrie and Mrs. E. M. Guthrie and her mother and two sisters, all members of God's new church of Harmonialists. George was nearly unbodied by consumption, and he requested the Lone One to stay with him a few days, and point out the way through the valley of darkness to the sunny and flowery lands beyond. He did so, at the same time relieving his body from much pain; which body a few weeks after he left entirely, and in a new sphere commenced the work of preparing another home for Emily and their boy. Many months after his exodus from earth-life, he came to the Lone One through a medium, far away from his earthly home, and related much of his experience in the new life, as he promised to do when in his body. Not long after, the mother of Emily also, long a sufferer, made her escape from the body of pain, and met her companion, who was waiting her at the entrance of the spirit-home. Thus Emily and Elizabeth were unhoused; but Mary had still a home of her own, and a husband to supply it. Emily, whose soul had flowed out in poetry and prose that had interested and delighted many readers of the *New York Tribune* and other papers, had her heart wounded by the separation from George; and an attempt to supply his place by a subsequent marriage came near carrying her body to the grave, and proved how futile are all attempts to make commercial marriages happy. A few weeks only did she live in a miserable earthly union, when she broke the bond that would in a few more weeks have broken her thread of earth-life, and with her boy joined again her sister, a wiser and better spirit, for such trials ever develop, and often purify, the victims. These two sisters, now homeless, became itinerating preachers of the new gospel, and, for aught we know, are preaching " to this day." Wherever they are, they are messengers of heaven, and preaching for the Harmonial age, and struggling with a wicked world and its false societies, which ever pays its best teachers with persecution or death. A few words of extract from a letter from this noble soul may serve to show her true spirit, and its appreciation of the Lone One.

" *March*, '53. — We received your joyously-welcomed letter in due time. It came with soothing magnetic power to George, for which he was deeply grateful, as we all are. He has not been troubled with headache since you left ; yet he has often wished you were with us. . . . . But, to answer the question propounded in your very interesting note to the three sisters.

> . Ah, yes, we will strive **to meet with** you there,
> To dwell 'neath the Infinite Father's care,
> Where nature's laws are the guide of the soul,
> Liberty only our footsteps controls ;
> Where harmony lulls all strife to repose,
> Life with eternity only shall close ;
> The universe broad the field we explore,
> And spirits congenial are near evermore."

Not more than a dozen souls could be called out to lectures at that time in Rockton, who could understand, or who wished to understand, the Harmonial Philosophy.

March 11, '53. — At the beautiful home of Dr. George Haskell, in Rockford. The doctor's connection with the Baptist church had been already disturbed by sounds and sentiments from the spirit-world. By his aid, and the already harmonized and spiritualized family of Dr. Rudd, quite an interest was awakened in the young city, and eight or ten lectures were given to good audiences, and a permanent condition of inquiry and investigation started, that has not yet been preached down nor prayed down. Dr. Haskell, soon fully emancipated, became one of the boldest and ablest defenders of the new gospel in the West, both with tongue and pen ; and the powers of earth might as well attempt to

encase a singing-bird a second time in its shell, as to return him
to the little close-communion creed from which he has emerged.
At Dr. Rudd's the Lone One found, now and ever, one of his most
happy and congenial homes, to which he several times returned
with pleasure, to meet such spirits as he expected to meet on the
other side of Jordan.

March 23. — At Belvidere, at the house of Barney Smith, who
was a prominent target for the shooters who considered themselves
sharp enough to kill spirits with shots from the pulpit or bar-
room. Here he parted with Mr. and Mrs. Archer, who were
registered in heaven among his earliest and latest friends, as they
were to all persons whom man oppressed.

March 26. — At Elgin, at the house of a host embodied in the
person of N. E. Dagget, who had for years taken the wind out of
the sails of preachers, and been a stumbling-block to the churches;
and now he became the ablest " defender of the faith " in spiritualism in " all the region round about." They did have good
times, at the four-mile circle, on Sundays, in those days; but now
they seem as the days of " long ago."

April 4. — A course of lectures in Chicago; did not pay expenses: for the excitement created by Seth Paine and Ira B. Eddy
had *laid* the spirits, for a time, and the Lone One could not raise
them or the dead people, and of course he went out of the city
minus dollars and words. But he knew this gospel had to be
preached at somebody's expense.

April 8. — In Waukegan, but, alas! Seth Paine had been there,
and some persons, accustomed to magnifying trifles, told large
stories on small capital, and what was nobody's business was attended to by everybody, as usual, — a sort of change, for nobody
usually attends to everybody's business. They got up good meetings, in spite of slander; and the gospel went home with many
souls, and quickened them into life. This was one of the early-
lighted places, and has never let its lamp go out, but has rather
illuminated the whole city and county by its rays, shed in lectures,
and its papers. The Lone One met and left many good friends at

this place; but we cannot single out one or two, nor name all, and hence leave them with Ira Porter for selection.

April 15. — At the Kenosha, once the old Southport home, but now a dead place, with a few live friends in it, and the graves of his boys. The people would nearly all come to hear him lecture, if he would speak at, or on, some subject that they were not prejudiced against. But the Rochester knockings, and the communications of dead folks, could not be crammed into their heads, which were already overstocked with speculation and religion; but there were Sholes in the place (each one wrote the *we* for the *I*), and God never cased better spirits than were in these frames; but they were few and not far between, nor was it far from them to the kingdom of heaven. Their homes were always homes for Lone Ones from anywhere, and they always had a meeting when any one came along who could say a say for God or man.

April 21. — In the eve came off the closing lecture of the course, and a terrible storm shut out all but seven men, to whom a long discourse was given; for, the mayor being present, order was preserved, the fees collected, and they would have their pay for breaking the storm. Racine took a few lectures, and gave him a good visit in return. One of them, in Rev. A. C. Barry's church, went off at par; the rest were sold at a discount.

May 2. — The steamboat landed one passenger, certainly, at Milwaukie, and the Lone One had belted a district, and counted the cost, and weighed the profit. Here he had an acquaintance with one of God's children, in Dr. J. P. Greaves; and one of the children of science, in his skilful homœopathic partner. By the aid of Dr. G., whose pocket was short then, but afterwards greatly lengthened, the gospel had been spreading; — a hall was soon secured, and another course of lectures were scattered. At this visit he became acquainted with one of the most deplorable cases of manslaughter he ever knew; and, by expressing sympathy for the victim, he aroused the anger, and awakened the hatred, of the cruel tyrant; but he felt more than ever called upon to talk and write against domestic slavery, and tyranny, and the soulless cruelty of lust in wedlock, with a victim; and this, of course, aroused the ire, more than ever, of the petty tyrant. This poor victim, a delicate and sensitive, highly-nervous, and very affectionate lady, for near twenty years the slave to a man of coarse organization, full of lust, a tyrant in manners and actions, who had forced upon her unwilling body and mind maternity near a dozen times, and when she remonstrated, with decision, claiming control of her person, and the right to keep it pure, he became a madman, and in rage and jealousy joined the rabble in slandering the mother of his children, and accusing her of all manner of vices, which were charged to spiritualists, because with them she found sympathy and encouragement in her honesty and purity of life. Should the reader ever meet Dr. G., he or she can learn from him more of this heartless cruelty, and suffering victim. At this time he also became acquainted with a Mrs. P., one of nature's noble women, intellectual, refined, ambitious, and emotional. She had been unhappily mated, and, after many years of suffering, her legal husband left her to support their three children, and went to California; and when it was well ascertained that he had abandoned her entirely, she procured a divorce, and married one who loved her. This brought the condemnation, scorn, and disgust, of those who styled themselves the fashionable and popular circles of society. A few weeks after her marriage her new, and true, husband died, and she had no one to shield her from poverty and the scorn of the world. Of course it was not the duty of any Christian to aid or comfort her, for she had broken their sacred tie of legal marriage; and they not only let her suffer, but heaped slander on her with their scorn, that often sent the licentious to her to be repulsed **with** contempt; and, thus enraged, they would join the popu ar **cry,** and thus she had all against her except the few spiritualists who alone respected, appreciated, and sympathized with her; and here again, **as** in many instances, the pure and suffering victims of popular prejudice found their character and reputation connected with the persecuted spiritualists, even before they were believers in the philosophy. Soon after this, the father of her children died in California, leaving some property, which the scheming and designing enemies prevented from reaching the children, and left them all to suffer in extreme poverty, for aught I know, " to this day," relieved only slightly and occasionally by a kind old mother in England.

These were not all, but only a few, of the reasons why the Lone One was found in defence of the suffering victims of a perverted institution, which, like a bad government, oppresses those it should protect. He never did advocate its abolition, nor did he ever believe it could be dispensed with ; but he advocated those changes already alluded to, with a release of all the sufferers, without public scorn, as a consequence of freedom, as it now is, for woman. At this visit he also met (and it was the only time he ever did meet away from her home) the lady with whom he had so long corresponded, the author of the stolen letter. In passing through the city she saw a notice of his lectures, and called on him ; and they called on, and sympathized with, Mrs. P. ; when she returned, took the cars, and at the end of the iron track the stage, and was soon at her home, where she wrote the fatal letter, and referred to this meeting in it, which made the gist of the accusation, with the answer to some questions which he had asked her in a letter, in regard to her married and childless life. But the slanders connected with his sympathy for these suffering victims in Milwaukie were not less actively heralded, and the enemies thought surely now they could destroy his influence, and several chiefs in the army of slanderers were appointed ; but the staff-officers were the Methodist preacher, whom the better portion of his own church would not fellowship, and the Ripon pettifogger, who had atoned for his infidelity by his abuse of spiritualism, and afterwards still more effectually through a little seven-by-nine village paper which accidentally fell into his hands, and in which he echoed the abuse and slander of all humane efforts at reform and the amelioration of suffering that the church did not endorse ; and last, but not least, the Presbyterian deacon of the valley, who had a hard experience in early life in a state institution, but who now added

17

the dignity to the staff, an essential ingredient of which the others were deficient. During this stay he also met Miss Cora L. V. Scott and her mother. With the family he had a previous acquaintance, and had discovered the peculiar and remarkable **mediumship of** Cora and her remarkable organization of brain, when he first met her, at the age of thirteen, a little school-girl, at Lake Mills, Wisconsin. She performed some remarkable feats of mediumship **in** Milwaukie on this **and other** visits, **which, like** others of the kind, could only be denied, scouted, and ridiculed, **where** they were not known, and when the instruments were absent.

May 24. — Pleasant visit with H. **D.** Barron and his amiable lady, at Waukesha. **They were among** the first defenders of the **rappers in Hydeville and Auburn, N. Y., and, knowing the truth,** it had made them free.

June 5. — At Lake Mills he met Dr. Joslyn and several families, with one of the best and most successful circles he had ever met, in which Cora **L.** V. Scott was rapidly developing, and several others giving good tests of the presence of particular spirits. Here he gave several lectures to good audiences, as he **had at Genesee and other small towns.**

June 8. — **A** delegate **and** in attendance at the **capital, in a state convention,** making speeches, nominating candidates, etc., **and exerting as much** influence as ever, and even more; for his powers **of eloquence were enhanced by** spiritual aid, and his recent labors.

June 9. — Takes **part in the State** Temperance Convention, and makes speeches, **as he often had in that** cause; but he found too much of a sectarian and religiously-bigoted spirit pervading this movement for its own good or success, and he could not feel in harmony and full fellowship with **the** movement; for well he knew that whatever reform the **clergy** took hold of was thereby poisoned **to** death, for their kid **gloves soon** crowded off the hardened hands **of labor,** without which **there could** be no success.

June 11. — He reached his valley home, and soon found the effects of the lies based **on** the stolen letter before referred to

They knew his non-resistant and peace principles would not allow
him to prosecute them, and hence they took more liberties than
the law would justify, with only one cause, one reason, for their
abuse : — because he was a defender of spirits and spirit-intercourse.

> . . . . " Every age on him **who strays**
> From its broad and beaten **ways**
>   Pours its seven-fold vial.
> Happy he whose inward ear
> **Angel-whisperings can hear,**
>   **O'er the rabble's laughter ;**
> And, while hatred's fagots burn,
> Glimpses through the smoke discern
>   Of the good hereafter.
>
> " Knowing this, that never yet
> Share of truth was vainly set
>   In this world's wide fallow ;
> After hands shall sow the seed,
> After hands from hill and mead
>   Reap the harvest yellow.
>
> " Thus, with somewhat of the seer,
> Must the moral pioneer
>   From the future borrow ;
> Clothe the waste with dream of grain,
> And on the midnight sky of rain
>   Paint the golden morrow."

When **his** letter informed the delicate and noble soul of the lady
that her letter was stolen, and in the hands of the most wicked
and licentious of preachers, the news almost carried her to insanity or self-destruction ; for well she knew what use such heartless
and polluted wretches would make of her language uttered to one
in whom she had implicit confidence, and in whom she knew her
confidence was not misplaced ; and especially of such language as
he alone would understand correctly, because it was connected
with a long line of correspondence, and the words and sentences
much abbreviated — just what the guilty and suspicious would

need, to carry out their suspicions. The pedlers of gossip, by the aid of the priest and pettifogger, soon made a good story out of this letter, which story ran somewhat in this wise: That the Lone One, when absent from home, lived with the author of this letter, and had already raised two children by her, etc.; when, in truth, he had never seen her away from her home, except in the one instance referred to, and never at her home when her husband was absent; and she never was the mother of a child, and was a leading member of a church, and by all beloved and respected, and as worthy a member as any church possessed, and one whose life was, to all who knew her, above suspicion, and whose conscience was as void of offence in this intercourse as an angel's could be. But, when their own researches brought the truth of her situation to light, they at once changed the direction of the stories, and sent them on suspicion that there must be others, — at least to the number of five or six women, — in different places, with which he spent his time when absent from home; and although he was never absent a week without writing home, and often had his letters published, with name, and date, and public notices of his lectures, and address could be found at all times, yet all these facts were of no weight against the lies in the minds of the enemies of spiritualism; and, although there had never been a lisp of slander against him or his moral character before he became a spiritualist, yet now, at the age of forty, he had all at once become the most licentious of all men, and that, too, unaccompanied by any of the foods or drinks which cause or accompany such conditions in all others. And, although they could never find a victim of his, nor a bad character with whom he ever secretly associated, yet this was not a defence; for he was a spiritualist, and of course he was bad and licentious, for the priest said they all were, as he *knew* the Fox family were — they had been Methodists, and were turned out, while he remained in the fold. But, in truth, he knew nothing about them, nor the Lone One either, except that they believed in spirit-intercourse; and even that he could not have known, had they not been more honest than himself; for you could never judge of his belief by his words.

But all these slanders and falsehoods were no real or permanent injury to the Lone One, or his mate. To her they proved blessings in disguise; but on him they had little or no effect, for he moved steadily and calmly on his course, unruffled and unharmed. Some timid and wavering souls were sometimes prevented by them from attending his lectures; for the stories were sent far and near, wherever he was known to be travelling and lecturing, and wherever there was a priest or a Christian to send them to. This was all the effect he felt from them; and this fell on other heads, not his, for they often lost the benefit of his experience and observation, as given in his early lectures.

Sunday, June 19. — He lectured at the valley home, to large audiences, better than usual; for many enemies came to see how their lies had affected him, and found no change in him. The same calm, firm, consistent and energetic self-reliance and devotion to his subject. The wife was not yet developed, but the fever had turned, and she was rapidly growing into the calmness of the harmonial life. The enemies of her happiness and the harmony of her family renewed and strengthened their efforts to prevent this; but his influence and that of her spirit-friends soon overcame them. She had so long held herself aloof from the spiritualists, and considered them either as her enemies or deluded, that it was a hard trial for her to turn to them as friends. When she came to them she found them with open arms, welcoming and forgiving; and ever after found them her true and real friends, honest and confiding, and entirely unlike their enemies, whose selfish and jealous souls only tried to use her to accomplish their own ends, in destroying his influence. The notes in the diary at this time mention a strong internal pressure from the spirit-world to start again into the field of labor; for his restless and ever-active mind would not stay long at home without starting some business, and it might be such as would prevent him from doing the work his guardians designed him for; and hence the constant messages

17*

through mediums, and by impression, to start again ; and his only fear and reluctance arose from the pecuniary wants of his family, which he feared could not be supplied by lecturing.

June 26. — Lectured in Omro ; met good friends, had pleasant visit of several days, and found some good mediums. Among the first was Dr. McAllister, a man of science, skill, and reputation, and a bold defender of the truth of spirit-intercourse.

June 28. — Visited Dr. McNish, of Berlin, a man of science and skill, and much reading, who, being a bold and free inquirer after truth, had examined and found some truth in spiritualism, and more honesty and morality than in any phase of sectarian Christianity, and was therefore found in its defence. He had long been a personal friend of the Lone One, and ever defended him against the slanders and abuse of which he knew well the cause to be religious bigotry and sectarian hatred.

Sunday, July 3. — Lectures at the valley home, and the Methodist priest attends one lecture, and receives a good description of himself, as one of the opponents of reform and spiritual truth. He bears it, but never comes again, nor offers to reply, and soon after leaves the place.

July 4. — Makes a speech to the large assembly in the grove at Ripon, where he is much extolled by the highly-pleased audience ; and all, except a few jealous persons, who were ever afraid of his influence, knowing that he would always use it for the whole human family, and not for persons, or a party, or sect of any kind, because he was the World's Child, and now a Cosmopolite.

July 8. — At the magnificent home of Ex-Gov. Tallmadge, — not to get his signature to a charter, —-but the ex-governor had become a spiritualist, and the Lone One wished to know what had drawn him and his family over the walls of the Episcopal church ; and soon learned it was facts — incontrovertible facts — of spirit presence and intercourse. His heart was made glad by the accession of this noble soul and excellent family to the then little band of defenders of the most odious and unpopular truth. A pleasant day, fine circle, good manifestations, and the excellent visit, were soon over ; and he left with a promise from **the** ex-governor to lecture in Fond-du-lac, where no voice but that of the Lone One had been heard in public in defence of spirit-intercourse ; for he **had been** the ice-breaker for this truth in all that portion **of the state.**

Sunday, **10.** — Made temperance speech **in Presbyterian** church **at** Ripon, **and the** Methodist ranter **tried to** make **one also,** but **failed to do more than** disgust the audience, and confuse himself. **A** strong spiritual influence operated in the meeting, and bore **the** Lone One **in** triumph **over** sectarianism ; and they, seeing it, **let the** cause die immediately after, by closing the meet-**ing** and the church ; **for** it was not temperance **they** wished to subserve, but sectarianism.

At this period, in the rage of slander, it required all the philos-ophy and spirit-influence to prevent a legal **prosecution of the priest** for theft and slander ; but the milder counsel **of** Jesus' precepts and example prevailed, and he tried to forgive, but could not forget, those who knowingly and wilfully sent lies endorsed by themselves over all the country where he was known. But all this **time** a hidden blessing was lurking **in** the brambles and thorns that entangled and obstructed his pathway, — a fragrant rose for **his** spirit, that would shed its delights on his soul for ages ; for **by** these **slanders** he was **led** to examine more closely and minutely **the** family relations and conditions of society and the **sexes,** and **to** acquire knowledge which caused him ever after to **speak and write more boldly and** pointedly **on the sins of** domes-tic life ; **and this** separated some from him who had stood by him, to this time, but now he touched their idols also, and they left him, and angels came and ministered **unto** him ; and when they passed by on the other side, with the priest, the good Samaritan came with the oil and the wine, and the beast, and the purse, and his wants were supplied. He was let into a higher light and life by the angels, **as** he saw and felt more clearly the terrible evils of this, and dared to speak against them. But boldly he uttered

the sentiment, more recently so beautifully expressed through T.
J. Harris :

> " The man is ignorant of law who gives
> Being to offspring cursed before their birth
> With passions that destroy their future peace,
> **And make** the stately fabric of the soul
> A dungeon of impure depravities.
>
> " **The man** is ignorant of law who takes
> A forced reluctant wife unto his breast ;
> Whose inward soul another's spirit claims,
> Whose deepest heart expires in constant pain,
> Dying, and walking daily to new deaths.
> O, cursed ignorance ! that educates
> Maidens for public barter ; **that** first crowns
> With orange-blooms their brows, then turns the **key**
> Of wedlock, falsely called so by divines,
> To crush them in its infamous Bastile,
> Making the marriage-bed a rack, where they
> Must wed themselves — poor children — to despair,
> As to an iron giant, while the fire
> Of madness inundates the reeking brain.
>
>   *   *   *   *   *   *
>
> **Break thou that spell of ignorance** that makes
> Woman **the slave !**   **Redeem** her captive heart !
> Let marriage be the sacrament of soul,
> The deathless union of accordant minds,
> The blending of two perfect lives in one,
> Whose home shall be a paradise, whose bliss
> Chaste, fervent, lasting as an angel's love."

Now, more than ever before, he felt inspired with truth from
above, and felt it his duty to scatter the seed broadcast over as
much of the human world as he could reach, and let the seeds fall
as they would, in stony places, among thorns, by the wayside, or
in good soil. **He** prepared for his mission, but not with purse or
scrip, or two coats, nor staff, but empty-handed, and with empty
pockets. But first he summed up and published. in the *Oshkosh
Democrat*, the political condition and progress of the state, in an

article entitled "Signs of Progress;" and, having an excellent and highly-esteemed friend connected with that paper in C. J. Allen, — a young man of noble and generous but timid soul, — he continued to correspond for some time with that paper, until the religious opposition to the liberality of his sentiments induced the proprietors, **greatly to** their injury, to **request of** him **more** respect **for the** churches; and of course he gave them all the respect they could get, and sent his articles to other papers ever after.

July 19. — Visits and examines the academy at Ripon, which had now become Presbyterian, but in which his eldest son and the daughter were among the best students — prompt, faithful, **and** foremost in all but the religion; that they would not take, **and** were excused from attendance on church, but not on prayers. However, they did not learn to pray in that school.

July 20. — He set out on foot, and walked twelve miles to the home of a friend on the prairie; met several mediums, had a communication from George, and one from his mother, through a medium who was a member of the Methodist church. Next day he walked all day in the dust and extreme heat, and reached Dodge Centre, where he expected to find an old and prominent friend, Hon. H. Barber, who had recently discovered some of the truths of **spiritualism;** but the judge was absent, and the tired man laid up at the tavern, and soon went to the land of dreams, where **the** spirits refreshed his soul with an oblivion of the long walk and weary body. Next night the stage — for his limbs would not walk **again** — landed him at Watertown, where he found an **honest** and industrious mechanic (a Mr. Straw), whom the truth had made free and bold; and he found **a** home with him, while they made an effort to get up, and off, several lectures. But most of the people who felt any interest in another life had taken stock in some one of the churches, and obtained through-tickets of them for themselves, and cared little about others, unless to add their names also to their respective churches, and therefore the lectures were attended only by a few. It was very discouraging; but Mr. Straw, who was a good medium, saw and marked out much of the journey and its success, and named some of the places which the speaker would visit before his return ; and it all, and much more, was fulfilled. He was also designated as the tranquillizer, and directed to magnetize mediums, and circles for their development, and to produce in them a calm and quiet state of mind.

We have noted these little incidents about the home of the Lone One merely to show the condition at this particular time ; but shall no longer follow the winding path, but leap from point to point, as we notice a few of the more important events in his diary and travels.

July 29. — Lectures on temperance to large audience at Lake Mills ; found much interest in spiritualism ; good circle, some mediums, much excitement, and a slight tendency to insanity in one or two partially-developed mediums, owing mainly to the distracted minds of friends and enemies around them. He had already learned that when mediums are being developed rapidly there should always be the most quiet, congenial, and sympathetic minds, and none others, around them, to insure success, and avoid insanity. But people were mostly ignorant of this, and some even glad to have cases of insanity, to bring reproach on, or opposition to, the cause.

By various modes of travel, much of which was on foot, he made his way through Janesville and Beloit ; had a pleasant visit at Rockton, and brought up in Rockford, where the cause had steadily gained strength and force since his last visit. During this pleasant and profitable — spiritually and pecuniarily — visit, he made the acquaintance of a Mrs. Morrel, of Lawrence, Mass., who had been raised from an invalid of fifteen years to a tolerable degree of health by the spirits ; and, emancipated from church thraldom, made to speak many able and eloquent truths by spirits for the new gospel, which she continues to preach at and about her home, " to this day." In a circle with a few inquirers, with her for a medium, a clergyman inquired of the spirit the use and importance of prayer ; and the reply, purporting to come from Thomas Paine, was, "Prayer in your world is what staves and crutches are.   It is for the lame and sick ; the well do not need it."   The Lone One asked the priest if the answer was satisfactory, and he said, " Yes; but I think we are all sick and lame."   " Perhaps *you* Christians are," was the reply, and the end of the subject.

Sunday, Aug. 21. — Had a large and delightful meeting in a grove near Elgin, and many speakers, both in and out of trance, and happy time for all present.

Aug. 25. — Commenced a course of lectures in the Quaker meeting-house, at Battle Creek, Michigan. First visit to that place. Had good time and attention, and made the acquaintance of a noble soul, in Rev. J. P. Averill, who had grown out of his clerical garment, although it was of the most capacious, or universal salvation, pattern, yet it was too cramping for him to feel free in.   At this time he also visited the Bedford school, and the happy home of Reynolds Cornel, and the earnest and devoted soul of his son, Hiram Cornel, who had already sustained a school almost entirely at his own expense, for some years, when sectarianism, aristocracy, and bigotry, could neither get control nor stop it, although they had made every effort to do so, branding it as infidel, because the students were not taught to pray and read the Bible.   The Lone One was much pleased with these people **and their** efforts ; but did not at this time think of making it his future home, and went on his way, bidding them God speed **and good-by.**

At his lectures on Sunday there appeared an old Scotch Presbyterian clergyman, of the bull-dog look, with great head and body, short, thick neck, savage countenance, English make and manners, and took up the war-club, by a defence of the Bible and the church against the lectures and the lecturer ; but the hearers said that he got badly used up, and was ready in the evening to give up the contest ; but the lecturer and his friends would not allow it, and forced him to try to speak in defence of himself and his former positions, but it was only a broken apology.   Next day

he was gone, with his Bibles, which he pretended to be peddling as
an agent. It was afterwards ascertained that he had been sent for
because he was a savage blackguard, more impudent and tyrannical than any clergyman in the place; but he and they found there
were "blows to take, as well as blows to give," and those who were
in glass houses were not the ones to throw stones.

September 4. — Lectures in the Melodeon, in Cleveland, to
good audience. He had spoken before in this hall, when on his
way to, and returning from, the National Convention at Pittsburg,
in '52; but he found only a few truly devoted souls in Cleveland
at these early times, when it was a sacrifice of reputation and
character, in the popular circles of the city, to defend the truth
of spirit life and intercourse. But among the first and best mediums he found in Cleveland was a Mrs. P. M. Williamson (now
Mrs. Price, clairvoyant physician, &c.), and a Miss Jane Barnum,
of Rockport. She being an old acquaintance, through her he
received the most encouraging, cheering, consoling, and sympathizing communication he had ever received, and which proved
true in due time, so far as it was prophetic.

> "My heart is proof against all fear
> 　　Of what may chance in world like this;
> But tender words and looks appear
> 　　Like spirits from the realms of bliss.
>
> "They melt the heart hate cannot move;
> 　　They thaw the ice around it cast,
> **And purer feelings loosened rove**
> 　　Amid its dreams of love so vast."

September 7. — He reached the Carroll Springs, on the Kyan-
tone, near the line of the States of Pennsylvania and New York,
and found Dr. J. Mayhew, Dr. A. Underhill, Dr. Brown, Cora
L. V. Scott, and her father and mother, and many others, congre-
gated there, for some cause, as yet unknown to them, as to him,
or others. They had a pleasant visit, and several good circles;
he lectured several times in the vicinity; drank the sacred or *holy*
water of the spring, which, for a time, had such magic effect on

mediums, but none on him. In a few days bid them adieu, and made tracks eastward, but not until he had written, as he did regularly, all that was interesting in his travels. Lectured in Laoni and Fredonia, N. Y., and, in company with the Scott family, with Cora for a medium, held some good circles for communications. They visited a widow in Fredonia, whose husband had died a spiritualist in Wisconsin, and learned from her the **way** she silenced her Presbyterian mother and deacon brother, on the subject. They had persuaded her to return and reside with them in their ample home, and hoped to bring her again into the churchfold of *creed* (not Christ). When the proper time arrived, they asked her, mildly and pleasantly, if she had not felt it best to give up spiritualism, and return to the church. Her reply was, " Mother, you know I loved my husband, and he loved **me, and** we love each other still. Where he has gone, there I wish to go, be it heaven or hell, and I intend to live so as to accomplish that end ; and he lived and died a spiritualist, — so shall I." This was a clincher, and ended that subject finally, and at once. He also lectured in the transit-town of Dunkirk ; but a cargo of live hogs would then attract more people in Dunkirk than a legion of invisible spirits, however much evidence you could give of their **existence** and intelligence. Two or three families, like Lot's in Sodom, saved the place, no doubt, from going into the lake, or down the **road** to Gotham. There was a half-way house between Dunkirk and Fredonia, which had a *Hall* in it, in which spiritualism **had** done a work ; and a voice went out of this Hall every **day in** defence **of** spirits, and their rights to be heard in **our** world.

His next station was **in West Randolph, N. Y., where he** made the acquaintance of that devoted soul, **and** almost martyr to spiritualism, T. S. Sheldon, and several other good friends, and had a good time with circles and lectures. Here he made the acquaintance also of Mr. **and** Mrs. Love, — the latter, now **Mrs.** Mary F. Davis, — and, from the free expression of his views on marriage and kindred subjects, he soon had their confidence, and learned from them that they were legally married, but in no other

sense; that in the law and public opinion they were one, and in
every other sense and respect two. That they were only waiting a
chance to get a legal separation, without disgrace. He became well
acquainted, at this and a subsequent visit, with the restless and nervous condition of Mr. L., and the quiet, beautiful, genial, and harmonized soul of Mary, with a heart full and overflowing with love,
but which could only flow to one who in purity and devotion could
return a kindred element, which Mr. L. could not. He was familiar
with the trials and struggles of these two beings for freedom from **a**
galling bondage into which they had unwisely, but voluntarily,
entered, for which society would not forgive them. Her anxiety
at this time was wholly for Mr. L., that he might marry the lady
of his second choice; and his to accomplish it, and save their reputation, which, in New York, seemed impossible; and hence they
were advised to go West, where the laws were more liberal. **The**
clouds, with deep gloom and portentous forebodings, hung heavily
over her horizon at this time; and long after, she could see only
the stigma of the fashionable and popular, and no avenue to a
home or a living business in this world; and she looked over the
Jordan, and longed to go where slander and scorn could not reach
one who never did anything to merit it. But the Lone One
encouraged her as well as he could, and urged her to take the
field as a lecturer, and trust to the future, and, with confiding step,
walk boldly **to the struggle** with the wicked laws, confident of
purity, worth, and right. "When thou art sinking, give me thy
hand," said the Lone One, "and all my strength shall come to
thy aid, but walk in faith." It was interesting to the Lone One,
some years after, when the lying slanders of pulpit and press
accused A. J. Davis of causing all this trouble, and breaking up
this family, &c.,— when he knew all these facts and conditions to
exist while Mr. Davis was living quietly and happily with his first
wife, **personally** unknown to **Mrs. L.**, and having never heard of
her or her **legal husband.** **But this was as** near the truth as they
reported in his **own case,** and many others; and, as truth was not
their object when preaching or writing about spiritualists, of course

they would never correct their falsehoods when pointed out to them. If there was ever a being in this world who deserved happiness, or one who has found it, it is this same Mary F. Davis; and certainly there is one soul glad for her "sunny-side" of life. Had a "season of prayer," and poured out the gospel to a crowd in Cuba and Rushford, as he went on his winding way to Rochester, to see those early patriots, Isaac, and Amy, and Charles, and others.

September 30. — Mingled with a crowd at Syracuse, and found John O. Wattles, Gerrit Smith, S. J. May, Lucy Stone, Antoinette L. Brown, and many other true souls, and saw and heard them speak at the "Jerry Rescue" celebration; also Fred. Douglas, whom he had met before, but whose soul could not admit the light of spiritual freedom, as it had of political.

Sunday, October 2. — He delivered a funeral discourse in the City Hall of Syracuse. Strange preacher he must have been, who had no prayers over the dead. On the cars he met a friend who invited him to call and dine at Oneida, with the Perfectionists; and he did so, and found the first society of literal and practical Christians he had ever seen; indeed, he did not believe there were any Christians who tried to live the doctrine and precepts, but here he found a society who had abandoned homes, houses, and lands, making all things common, as Jesus and the disciples did, and even fulfilling the command to leave parents and children, husbands and wives, brothers and sisters, for Christ's sake, and trying to live and realize the condition of heaven, where Jesus said there was no marrying nor giving in marriage. So they had none, but live as the disciples and angels of God were said to live. It was indeed a rich treat to find, in this land of pretenders, a society of real disciples, who try to practise the precepts of Christ; but there they were, and there they are, with word and deed in harmony, trying to live so as to bring the kingdom on earth as it is in heaven, which so many have asked for in prayers, but never tried to practise. But, as the Lone One was neither a Christian nor a defender of that mode of life, nor a believer in it as the life in heaven, or proper for our time, and as he did not believe in abandoning family and companions for anybody's sake, and he believed in true marriage, both here and in heaven, now and forever, as the best, and most holy, and sacred, and happy life for man and spirit, therefore, of course, he had no attraction to these Christians, which could induce him to coöperate with them. But plainly he could see that in social life either they or the Shakers were the only true followers of Jesus, and his example and precepts.

Next day he was in New York city, and for many succeeding days in the Crystal Palace, on duty as commissioner, etc. The note in the diary says: Made the acquaintance of Dr. T. L. Nichols and Mrs. Mary Gove Nichols, but did not make anything else of them. The sphere of Mrs. N. was uncongenial, and his not attractive; but he could not but admire and respect them as bold and daring souls, who dared to tell society of its false and wicked acts, and take its scorn and contempt for pay. As such he viewed them, but as unharmonized souls in the struggles of life, with enemies within and without themselves; but the worst within, and the chief of the group egotism, as it appeared to him. Visited the North American Phalanx, at Red Bank, N. Y. How like old times, and how like a home, did their unitary table seem! But the seeds of a fatal disease were there, and they died soon after, and the mourners were numerous, and over the whole country; but, like most mourners, they could not save the life, nor resuscitate the corpse. So they epitaphed it; but, as we do not intend this for a Bible, nor a tomb-stone, we will not print the epitaph here. For the first time he now met that noble intellect, and very impressible early and able advocate, Hon. J. W. Edmonds, who had laid up his worldly fame for a martyr's crown, in the good cause. He found in him a true heart, and true friend to the new philosophy, and the most intellectual and influential advocate he had met with, and was highly pleased with his visit to his home. He also made the acquaintance of that more practical and matter-of-fact man, Charles Partridge, who was at that time pecuniarily the bulwark of printed spiritualism in the city, and also the brother, who had adopted somewhat of a sliding scale, but whom he, in the days of the *Univercœlum*, had ever registered as number one, William, — Fishbough, — he told this brother he believed him either entangled in one of Swedenborg's hells, or one of Bunyan's quagmires, but thought, with help, he might be extricated, but not until he let go his hold on the *sacred* handle of the Idol-Bible. He also spent an hour at breakfast with that great man, **who** sprang from **small beginning,** who is by those who hate him called the " fool of the nineteenth century," but who will prove by his *Tribune* that he is " nobody's fool." From this brief acquaintance the Lone One concluded he was number one in everything but honesty, and no doubt had once been so in that quality, **but** long and hard service in politics had worn it below threadbare, **and** thus it became leaky to other subjects. On the spiritual philosophy he evidently had one foot on **sea and one** on land, and was neither fish or fowl ; but on three other subjects he was firm as a rock, and **on two** of them firm in the wrong side, and on one, in the right — slavery, tariff, and marriage ; but on the latter he had been very much jaded by James, and Andrews, and others, and was **quite sore at** that time. He also met many other distinguished persons, and among them one he had long desired to meet, in S. B. Brittan. In him he found talent, refinement, and pride ; the **latter** an obstacle which would prevent him from doing for humanity what his uncommon ability would allow him to do if he could meet and mingle, heart and soul, with the world, as Jesus did, and **feel** its heart-beat, and respond to it ; but well the World's Child **knew** that a continued round of city luxuries, and city fashions and follies, had hampered and somewhat trammelled the noble and ardent soul, which was set like a diamond in this brain, and often shone with great brilliancy, in spite of the rubbish that surrounded it. He admired Mr. Brittan, but he *loved* J. K. Ingalls ; he felt free and easy in the dignity and manhood of J. W. Edmonds, but restless and watchful with Greely, as if it was not safe to take his eyes off him. He learned much in this visit to Gotham to confirm his previous opinions of the relations of city and country.

18*

A few minds in the commercial circles control the cities, and endeavor to control the country also. They control the business of the merchants, and bankers, and politics, and religion, of the rural districts, and regulate them by rules which they set up in the city. Some persons were unwilling that spiritualism should be an exception to this custom of our country. The Lone One saw this, but felt sure there **was** a disappointment **awaiting** all who **could set** themselves up, **with** or without an organization, as the **pivots or** centres for this movement. He left the city, resolved not **to labor** for the reputation and influence of any person or persons, but for the *cause* of the Harmonial Philosophy. Not for man-glory or man-power, but for humanity and the race; **and** although nothing was said on this subject, yet some persons felt and saw him and **his** object, and knew he would not aid them to centralize, nor labor for a central or city leadership; and hence, although he was one of the first lecturers in the field. and up to the autumn of '57 had given more lectures, and in more places, than any other person, on the subject of spirit-intercourse, and borne much persecution, made great pecuniary and personal sacrifices, yet the city papers and preachers seldom **mentioned** him, or gave notice **of** his labors, unless compelled to do it by his presence in **the** city. But this was what he wished, if his opinions were correct, that an effort at central control and leadership was made; for he could neither lead nor **be led, but** paddled his own canoe. His lone and independent mind could never be made to work in a harness, nor for any cause but that of God and man combined, so far as he knew it.

Oct. 13. — Stood high on **the** rock-cliff at Winstead, Ct. Lectured in the valley to large audiences of free minds. Wrote **a** brief note to A. J. Davis, at Hartford, to notify **him** of an intended visit. He had never been in Hartford, nor met Mr. **Davis, nor** Mrs. Mettler, and Mr. D. had some curiosity to try her psychometric powers on the stranger. He took the note to her, and, without any knowledge on her part, whether the writer was a man, woman or child, mortal or spirit, and of course without seeing a word of its contents, she said : "The writer of this is a person whose moral and intellectual faculties are most perfectly and fully developed. He is given to much thought. His intuitive or spiritual nature is always his guide and prompter. He possesses much acquired knowledge and true wisdom; venerates goodness and truth, let it proceed from what source it may. He is a true philosopher and philanthropist; has a mind that will conquer **all evil by its kind** and suasive manner. He is benevolent and kind, and his feelings universal. He cannot be sectarian, neither can he bear the shackles of sectarianism or tyranny. Freedom of speech and action is his motto. He is unmoved when the mind is once established. Has many original ideas, which are **easily** and happily expressed, and by that expression he is enabled **to do** much good to his fellow-beings. He is actuated in what he says and does by principle, and a great love for truth. **Firm and** steadfast, whatever is undertaken by him will be carried through with much energy and determination. He can exercise much self-control — endeavors to subdue the lower faculties, and bring them into subjection to the higher ones. He loves that kind of mirth and enjoyment that will harmonize and happify the soul. Is constant and ardent in his attachments, seeking ever to promote the happiness of all who surround him. He is cautious, but not timid. Deeply conscientious, and fond of the good opinions of men; he has considerable self-esteem, sufficient to give him a feeling of independence and self-control. He is *himself* — what nature intended he should be. He is exceedingly fond of family and friends; is constant and enduring under all trials of life. He is exceedingly fond of children, and pets, and everything beautiful in nature, — loves the wild-woods and their enchanting murmur, — loves woman for her virtues and intelligence. His principles are good, and his impulses truthful. His perceptive faculties are active, but the moral and spiritual nature predominates. He must be a person whose life is devoted to reforms, as his great motive seems to be the welfare and progress of the human race. I am quite sure he is a public speaker, and the ideas he would advance would **be** clear and lucid. His sphere is pleasing and agreeable."

Among the many tests of psychometry given through Mrs. Mettler, there are very few mistakes; and, indeed, it is yet to be ascertained there is one to be found among the hundreds of published cases. With suitable conditions, this art is fully reliable, and will in a few years be, with phrenology, the true guide to every person's true character, and enable us to put our trust ever in worthy persons, **and avoid the** unworthy and deceitful.

Oct. 19. — In Hartford, and welcomed at the magnificent home of Mr. Brown, and soon find the home and hearts of Mr. and Mrs. Mettler, and witness her remarkable powers of describing diseases, and prescribing for them; the most remarkable he had ever seen, as she was the most perfect medium **for this** faculty he had ever **met.** He now also met for the first time A. J. Davis, and found **in him the** happiest person he had ever found in this **world.** Although he was watching constantly by **the** couch of his dying companion, yet the sunshine of a harmonial and natural life was ever upon and filling his whole being. Without egotism or selfishness, he seemed to the **Lone One, who** had seen so much of human life, and been so long **a student of nature,** to be the first man he had ever met who had never been warped or twisted from a natural growth by the strife and conflicts of society. He took courage now, for, **with one** true man in the world, he felt sure there **was** hope for the race. He was more strongly drawn to this man than ever to any one before, and felt his heart beat more in unison than with any other; for he seemed to be wholly and fully devoted to the welfare of the race, and the cause of truth. He did not accept all of the philosophy that had been given the world through him; yet he accepted the man, and ever after loved him as a brother — in spirit — not in the flesh, for in the flesh he was not allowed to have a brother by the laws of his native state. A childlike honesty and playfulness, with the wit and acumen of well-disciplined minds, was about Mr. D.'s manners; the schoolboy and philosopher blended, the affections of a woman with the firmness of a stoic. One would hardly believe **these** extremes of character could blend, and yet they do and must in a true man.

As the history of this seer has recently been published in the " *Magic Staff*," those who desire can read it there ; and we will not comment more upon him, except to say that his companion passed to the other kingdom a few days after this interview, and left him leaning on his Magic Staff, gazing at the stars, and **talk**ing to the earth, until the voice of his second companion — the suffering victim of an unhappy marriage, before alluded to — reached him, and called him again to social and domestic life and relations. He was always happy, in sunshine or shade; for the angels watched over him, and he was their messenger. Among the interesting curiosities visited in Hartford was the Charter Oak, under the branches of which he was sheltered from a passing shower. And the sewing-silk manufactory of the Cheeney Brothers, at Manchester, where the sunshine of the Harmonial Philosophy had placed their establishment far in advance of others, where the old theology bears rule or ruin. His lectures were well attended in Hartford, and his visit made pleasant and agreeable.

Oct. 31. — In Boston for the first time since he moved to the West. Soon at the house of John M. Spear, that most singular, highly eccentric, and devotedly honest and philanthropic, of all mediums. The Lone One was greatly pleased with, and strongly attracted to, this man, and received through him the singular title of the " Elementizer," and a commission to do great things if he could, mentally and experimentally, with the elements. At this time some intelligence was directing, through this willing instrument, the erection of a peculiar machine in High Rock Tower, at the home of the Hutchinsons, in Lynn; and the Lone One was invited, **or** directed, to lend magnetic aid to the medium, and the machine, etc. For a few days he watched the process and progress of this intelligence. Fully satisfied that it was independent, in its existence and designs, of Mr. Spear, or any other person ; but he did not believe it a safe intelligence to direct the business affairs of this world, and yet he thought it *possible* that some discovery might be brought to light by such power, through the agency of mediums. The machine was at length completed at

great expense to somebody, and, as it did not start a perpetua.
motion, it was condemned by the edict of public opinion, and a
writ of scorn and contempt sent after it. The parents took it up
and fled into Egypt with it, and it still sojourns there, while the
parents have returned to build other and very different machines,
some more, and some equally successful. The second day of his
sojourn he was in the pinnacle of High Rock Tower, with J. M.
Spear and Mr. Hewet, and one more, when some intelligence
entranced Mr. Spear, and directed Mr. H. to "write what the
spirit saith to the wanderer." It then proceeded to describe the
World's Child as follows: "This man possesses, in an eminent
degree, several very important elements of character, which, when
combined, help to the formation of a very remarkable person.
First, This man is not what he is thought to be. Quite erroneous
judgments have been formed of him, insomuch that he has been
strongly condemned where he should have been highly approved.
He is thought to have a disregard for sacred things ; but this is
not true. He very highly regards sacred things ; but things
which some regard sacred do not appear to his mind to be
sacred. For instance, men and women regard the Bible as a
book sacred ; but this man does not so esteem the *book*. But he
opens it and examines critically its interiors, and perceives the
sacreds which are in the interiors. As it were, he does not
regard the outer covering of the nut, but picks, and picks, and
picks, until he extracts meats from the outer covering ; so he extracts the meats from the book, and they are sacred to him. But
he does not much care about the outside, if he can get the sacreds
of the book. Second, This man does not seem to care to talk
much about God. He does not much care whether there is a God
or not ; but he sees certain *laws* by which he discovers the universe is controlled. He hears the music which they make, and is
enraptured with the music ; but he does not concern himself
much about the maker. He is very peculiar in this respect.
Third, If there is any one thing which this man abhors more than
any other, it is dissimulation. He is a very rare specimen of

honest speech. He does not much care whether he is liked or disliked for this. Tell him he must not say a thing, and he replies, 'Who are you?' and he will say it all the stronger. This man is a thorough student, and that which he most studies is mind. He examines persons, and forms correct opinions of minds. He reads minds with great accuracy, and he does this by greatly unfolded intuitive faculties. Ordinarily he would not **be** considered a student; but he is a perpetual student of mind. **This** man calls forth large quantities of respect, because of strictest integrity. He never stoops to conquer; but he conquers because he refuses to stoop. Give him ample time, and he will entirely silence all opposers. He is a most adroit manager in the polemics. He plants himself on certain fixed principles, and no one can move him; and this is the secret of his polemical success. This man is also a great admirer of the beautiful as exhibited in *laws.* In a high sense, he is a student of law. While he is celebrated as a polemic, yet he knows not **of** bitterness. With greatest delight, when he had overcome his opponent, he would feed, clothe, and instruct him. This man has an important mission to perform, and that mission he will faithfully perform to the utmost of his ability."

This quaint delineation was one of many which the intelligences had given through Mr. Spear, and in which they usually were more correct than in mechanical constructions. While he was confined in his mediumship to healing, and reading character, and giving personal communications, he was very accurate and useful; but in his more recent labors he is not appreciated by many, if he is really in a useful work.

Among the acquaintances of this **visit were** Mr. and Mrs. A. E. Newton, two as genial and true **souls** as **God** had standing in cases in Boston; and Messrs. Seaver and Mendum, of the *Investigator,* which had, for so many years, furnished the religious dessert for his family reading. Met Mr. T. S. Sheldon **at** Mr. Spear's. Sleeping one night in the same room with Mr. Sheldon, he saw, for the first time in his life, a spirit bending over the bed, looking apparently at Mr. S. He carefully viewed the beautiful form, enraptured with the vision; and, on describing the form to Mr. Sheldon in the morning, he recognized his deceased wife, who often communicated to him. He was neither asleep nor in a trance, but saw, as he thought at the time, the light form in the dark room with his eyes. John S. Adams and Hattie were also among the good and true spirit-friends he found on this visit, and several others; but we must pass on to the end of the line. His lectures were well attended, and he was richly paid in the currency of heaven for this protracted visit. For many years he had desired to speak in the Melodeon of Boston, so long and so favorably known as the "stamping-ground" of reformers; and now the obtained wish gave little satisfaction, but the subject gave much. Mrs. Newton exceeded all vision-mediums he had ever met, and through her he received many of the most rich and highly-pleasing pictures of the future of himself and others, and of scenes in the hereafter of both spheres; but it was not always certain to which life they belonged.

Nov. 14. — He was at Manchester, N. H., and called on the family of Hon. M. Norris, who furnished the last home he ever enjoyed in New Hampshire before his emigration; but Mr. Norris was not at home, and Abby and her pets had all grown out of their early life and condition by the long line of democratic honors Mr. N. had received at Washington. For many years he had been compelled to condemn much of the political course of his old friend, and by that means had grown nearly out of their friendship; but he was glad to meet the little woman he had once known so well, and esteemed so highly. She was now the mother of a long line of children, and some in each sphere; but the dead ones were *dead* to her faculties, as was her husband also soon after. Returned to Boston, and doubled the visit over, and the last was better than the first. Hopedale, with a call on Rev. Adin Ballou, a pure soul, devoted to social reform and Christ, through the Bible; one of the best of men in all but his theology, and that is the mildest and best that the Bible, without, or placed above nature, can furnish.

He goes as far as the creed he has set up will allow, but dare not step one point over. He is not like a convict, with ball and chain, but like a martyr, tied to a stake, from which he cannot escape; and yet his honest heart is devoted, and would raise man to a far better and higher condition, if it could, than other sects will allow. His social efforts will, no doubt, die out soon after he does, as did those of Rapp.

Nov. 26. — In Springfield, Mass., and found a home with the "Lion of the tribe of Spiritualists," and in some respects found him rightly named. Had the most remarkable circle for performances on piano at Mr. Bangs', in which the instrument was believed by all present to be played without human hands, and often lifted from the floor, and the strings thrummed, etc.; but the room was dark, and of course they could not see what power did do it, but all believed it was spirits.

After doubling his visit at Hartford, also, December 2d he brought up in Troy, N. Y., where he met the most remarkable medium, of his kind, he had ever met, in P. B. Randolph. His peculiarity consisted in his being, when well controlled, the best and most profound speaker and reasoner he had ever met in his life, normal or abnormal, and **when** not controlled he was simple and rude. But he had a good-shaped and large brain, and of peculiar texture, but it was uncultivated. He also met here many new friends, among them one of the finest and most delicate and sensitive souls in a modest and diffident female, with a weak body and excellent mind, in Melinda Ball; a person who, with proper conditions, might be an ornament to the race, as she now is to her little circle. For some years he corresponded with her, to bring out her soul, and it unfolded like a rose in the sun and showers of June.

Her beautiful letters, and especially the poems, — several of which were published, — he still retains, as mementoes of a friendship that will be renewed in the life to come. He also had another battle and complete triumph over another Scotch Presbyterian priest at this place; and so completely conquered him as to get

19

an invitation to his house. Had a circle in the house of a Methodist priest, and good manifestations. Had a double hold on Troy — lengthened visit. Lectured at Ballston Spa **and Can**astota. At the latter place used a church, with preacher in attendance, etc. Next in the City Hall in Syracuse, but had small audience and cold time; which was more than made up at **LeRoy, where he** met the best of friends, and received the most pay he had received at any one place since he was in the field, which assisted to make up for the many small fees, and no fees, etc. Somehow, he got over the road to Cuba, Alleghany Co., N. Y., and there, in the night, the year 1853 died and was buried, and the successor was born there the same night; but **he did** not see it **born, for he was in the land of dreams, not being a Methodist watcher.**

Section II.

1854. — ITINERATING, AND PREACHING THE GOSPEL OF **LOVE AND** ETERNAL LIFE.

" There is a secret tie that **binds**
    Congenial minds together ;
A silent mingling **heart with heart,**
    Almost unknown to either.

" **And this sweet** influence may be felt
    When not a word is spoken,
And to the outward sense there seems
    To be no sign or token.

" Yes, those who ne'er had met before
    May meet and then be parted,
And, though no words may pass between,
    Feel they are kindred-hearted.

" And when such spirits meet and join
    In converse with each other,
How free the interchange of thought ! —
    No feelings there to smother.

> " It is not fashion's formal chat,
>   The inmost soul congealing ;
>   But the free, unbridled tongue
>   O'erflows the fount of feeling.

> " And though they part and sever wide,
>   As to an outward union,
>   Still they may often know and feel
>   A near and sweet communion.

> " They meet not with the bow and nod,
>   A cold and formal meeting ;
>   But 't is with open heart and hand,
>   A true and friendly greeting.

> " O, give to me a few such friends,
>   Who are with life contented,
>   **And, free from Custom's heartless forms,**
>   Our souls shall be cemented.

> " I care not whether rich or poor,
>   Of high estate or lowly,
>   If pure in heart and noble minds,
>   Of purpose high and holy."

New Year's day was cold and stormy, and at six in the morning the lecturer was in a sleigh with a friend, and they rode fourteen miles in the Alleghany winter, and, almost frozen, reached the warm fire of Mr. Houser, and the warm heart of Mrs. Houser, at Rushford, N. Y., and in good time **the** comfortable church **was** also warmed, and sounded with **the new** gospel-song. Mrs. H., with " Bloomer costume," bold and free, and with mind well stored, and intellect and affections well developed, was deaconed for that town ; and the wanderer returned with his friend to the Cuba home, where they were rejoicing yet, over the birth of the new year, and joined in the glee of Cora, Minna, Hattie, Dr. Brown, and others, till " New Year's " glided into the busy hum of ordinary life. Next day found the doctor and the three girls at La- oni, and the lecturer at Randolph, where again he met his friend

Sheldon, and the two unhappy and unluckily-mated *Loves*, and to them renewed his advice to go West, and part where the laws were more liberal. Mary had already begun to lecture on woman's rights and wrongs, and had good success; and on Sunday, June 8th, he spoke twice, and she in the evening, in the hall, to good audiences, and they seemed to be well appreciated. But very few then knew the condition of Mr. and Mrs. L., for they treated each other as brother and sister ought to do in public and private life; **and** this was so much more tender and affectionate than husbands and wives usually appear, that people often remarked, " How happy and loving Mr. and Mrs. L. are!" " What a happy couple!" etc.; because they were free in all but the legal bondage, and seeking the means to break that.

Monday morning Mr. L. handed her, with a parting kiss, into the full coach, where she found a seat by the side of the Lone One, and rode to Little Valley to meet her appointment; and he passed on to Cattaraugus to meet his, and this was the last time he ever saw Mr. L., or met her as Mrs. L. Soon after they repaired to Ohio, and parted, never more to meet except as acquaintances; for the law of Indiana decided, through its court, that she ought **and** should be a free woman, until she **should** again voluntarily bind herself. There was one other case among his friends, — on some accounts a far more trying one than this, — in Mrs. H. F. M. B., of Cleveland; but in that he did not feel at liberty to advise, because the parties were not agreed, and did not mutually consult him. At last that chain broke of its own accord, and let **one** of the noblest souls **out** of a social dungeon, to shine on society and speak of an experience of her own, and become a " Consuelo " to others and the country at large. His line of march soon brought him to Dr. Brown's, where were the three girls, Cora rapidly developing for her glorious and angelic mission, and the others — an aunt and cousin — with her for company. He stayed several days, and lectured in Laoni and Fredonia; but none but those who have seen the cesspools of gossip in commotion can believe the extent of suspicion, jealousy, gossip, slander, and falsehood, which

followed, and fell from the tongues of "priest and levite" on Dr.
B., and also on the lecturer, because he occasionally met these
and other female mediums. When the stolen letter story was
added to these, such was the jealousy that it was imprudent for
him to go into a house where there were more females than males,
or into a house where there were unmarried ladies, or ladies without their husbands, unless there were other men present to guard
them. This sensitiveness even affected some who called themselves
spiritualists, and some simpletons were afraid their wives would
leave them if they made the acquaintance of this reformer, when
they could find not a single case where he had advised a separation, except where it was mutually called for. But this current of
slander and falsehood did not affect his calm and happy soul. His
life and his home were happy, and he moved fearlessly on his journey
and mission, with a pure, and free, and happy heart. These slanders often gave him small audiences, when he should have had
large ones; and thus the enemies rejoiced, and felt well paid for
their trouble. To these and many other girls he was always like
a father and guardian, as they ever did and ever will bear testimony; and now, when the three here referred to are all married
and settled in life, they remember and esteem him as the best of
friends. But where are the slanderers? Only hatching some
new theme for gossip. Many a beautiful and encouraging message
he received through Cora from Mrs. Hemans, Frances Wright,
and others, on the occasions of these meetings with her; and his
soul was thus refreshed and watered from a fountain from which
few could, or would, drink.

January 19. — The girls went to Buffalo, where other friends
were prepared to receive and appreciate them; for Cora had already done much in that city to awaken in a few families the spirit
of inquiry after spirit-life, and Stephen Albo, Stephen Dudley,
Capt. Pratt, and others, were on hand to find homes and circles
for her. The lecturer went the other way, and brought up among
the pine stumps and trees of Columbus, Pa., where, at the home

of Judge Judson, he had a happy visit, and soon found good audiences in the church to listen to his gospel.

January 25. — He returned and commenced the first course of
lectures in Buffalo ever given in that city in favor of the new
philosophy; and had a good attendance in Townsend Hall, notwithstanding the celebrated " Buffalo doctors " had issued their
extinguisher in a pamphlet some time before, but which finally
extinguished their hopes of fame in all coming time. Buffalo
promised what she finally exhibited by the unwearying efforts of
S. Dudley, S. Albo, and others — a defence and support of the
new and most important discovery of the age. During this visit
he met the remarkable medium, Miss Sarah Brooks, through whom
such rich musical seances have since been given. She was at this
time just beginning to reach that development, and the guitar and
violin could be sounded slightly through her, as a medium, by
spirit-power.

February 1, he began his visit and lectures in Painesville,
Ohio. Had a good time, and a large audience. That indefatiga-
ble pioneer and defender of the faith, Joel Tiffany, had labored
much in that place, and many minds had received light and
reached freedom. His audiences here, as elsewhere, increased in
number and interest to the end of the course, which was given
Sunday eve, February 5 ; soon after which, he was again with
his old and true friends in Cleveland, where H. F. M. B. and
many others always welcomed him as a laborer in the field of
reform, on the side of human rights, and as one ever in the field,
browned by the sun and hardened by the toil, but fanned by
breezes from the spirit-world, and watered by the Ganymedes
with the nectar of heaven.

At Grafton he found a " fallow ground," and broke it up, and,
for a wonder, gave a course of lectures in an Episcopal church, to
large audiences. The truth he planted there was watered by
more than one " Apollos," and has never ceased to grow, although
there are a few tares among the wheat, and occasionally a defender
of the existence of a Devil may be seen there ; and, although they

have several churches, yet it is not probable they can collect more than one bundle of tares, at the harvest. But it is not yet sure whether the Methodist or Presbyterian band will hold them.

His next station was Ravenna, where the members of one church had been converted to spiritualism, and of course carried their church-house (and it was a good one) with them, for the new gospel, and always found in it a place for lecturers and preachers of " glad tidings of great joy to all people." Happy hearts, with listening ears, filled the church on Sunday, and he was happy and " filled with the spirit on the Lord's day." Next station was Middlebury, where an early friend of him and the cause, and a friend and admirer of Robert Owen, had recently moved from Cleveland, and prepared the way for the voice of the Lone One. Next station called was New Brighton, Pa., where the true man, Milo Townsend, and his happy wife, were happy to welcome the wanderers, and where he also found one of God's kind of homes at James Irwin's, where six daughters made the woods and " Alum Rocks" resound with glee, if not music. But the parents had quartered with the Quakers rather too long to give much music to the organizations of the girls. This family he ever remembered and loved as among the happiest and best of his friends; not rich in money, but rich in love to the pure and good.

About these days, and for some time before, Amelia Welby became a devoted friend and guardian spirit, and often visited him from her home; and ever, when through mediums she could do so, gave him words of heart-cheer, more sweet and affectionate than those of her beautiful poems, written while she dwelt in her body. Here he also made the acquaintance of the mother and brother and sister-in-law of Grace Greenwood, and found in them developed and harmonized souls, fully imbued with the spirit of the new gospel. Elma, the eldest of the Irwin daughters, he had met long before at the home of W. S. Courtney, in Pittsburg, and found her then with a soul ripened for angel-visits, and a mediumship worthy a brighter record on the historic page than it found ; for, soon after, the marriage tie consigned her to a quiet and happy obscurity and life.   But at this and one later visit she was at the home under the cliff of Alum Rocks, in the freedom of girlhood and buoyancy of youth, and the angels could use her and one other of the sisters to whisper to the listening ears of mortals.

Next, over the winding way to Columbus, Ohio, where only a few members of the legislature attended, with a few others, his course of lectures, which closed in time for the arrival of Judge Edmonds and Dr. Dexter, to meet their appointment for two lectures on the same subject. He had an interesting visit with the judge, who, for a social chat and short visit, in point of interest and information on this subject, is not excelled by any medium or spiritualist in the nation, as many persons can testify.

March 11. — In Cincinnati, lecturing successfully. Soon made the acquaintance of Caroline Brown, a noble and true woman, if the world has one, who was struggling, against fearful odds, to establish a character, reputation, and practice, as physician and surgeon, with her shingle hung out on the street-side, and her diploma in her office, in which the wise faculty, following the old Latin form, had declared *she* was a *true man*, etc. He also met the blind phrenologist, F. Bly, whose skilful hand, passed scientifically over his head, brought the expression that he must make a mark on the page of life that would be of value in coming time, if not in his day. During his short stay he became a warm and devoted friend of Caroline, whose bold and energetic character, blended with a most affectionate and loving heart, and a pure and noble mind, refined and developed by a thorough education and discipline, he almost worshipped as the model woman, or what he had ever contended woman should be; and a few letters in correspondence subsequently proved all he had believed of her. A defect in the nerves of her eyes, which was impairing her vision, seemed to yield to his magnetism, and furnished an excuse to her excellent female partner, who did not need one, for his frequent calls during his short stay in the city. At this visit he made many warm friends, and parted with them with mutual regrets and hopes of future meetings.

March 25. — Made his first visit to Richmond, Pa., where he awakened and renewed the interest in the new gospel, and made some warm and permanent friends for himself and the cause ; and this subsequently became one of the strongholds of the Harmonial Philosophy. Down the winding channel of the Ohio, and up the Mississippi, on steamboat, from Cincinnati to St. Louis, was not unpleasant, but the reverse, in all except the society and tobacco-stench, which on the river-boats is almost unendurable to one who has a body not saturated with the poison of the filthy weed.

April 1. — Lands in St. Louis, and homes with a Mr. Hedges, and an old constitutional-convention colleague in Judge Hyer, whose estimable lady was a medium. Mr. Hedges was one of the early and able advocates and experimenters in magnetism and spiritualism, since, extensively known as a business man of Cincinnati and Philadelphia. Met R. P. Ambler, the developed medium, and interesting and intelligent speaker, and an early editor of the *Spirit Messenger*. And John M. Spear had been sent by spirit-direction to the city, to ordain Mr. A., and for other purposes supposed by him to be of more importance. Mrs. E. J. French had also been directed there by spirits, from Pittsburg. Here the Lone One made the acquaintance of this remarkable woman, who had been a medium many years in the Methodist church, acceptable to them while she called it the power of God, or the "*Holy Ghost*." But when she found it was of ghosts who were not more holy than other human beings, and told the truth about it, then they cast her out, and said it was of the Devil. Her healing and other medium powers were remarkable and peculiar, as many have testified. He also made the acquaintance of that public and highly talented defender of woman's, and human, rights, Frances D. Gage, and registered her in his head and heart as one who was laboring here, for the reward hereafter, even though she had some doubts of that, or any reward, except in her consciousness of doing her duty. There was much spiritual power and influence in the city at this time, and the cause seemed highly prosperous.   At Alton he next found a warm reception, and gave several lectures, and then moved over the road to the prairie village of Bloomington, and quartered with an ex-clergyman, while he used a church to lecture in; and, April 28, reported progress at his old friend's, **N. E.** Dagget, of Elgin, where one of the best of families was always as glad to see him as if he were one of the houschold.   **At** this time a **church** door was opened for him, **and** he preached the new **gospel in the old** "shop."

May 1. — Dr. Haskell was reporting his progress in searching **for evidence, to the Lone One, in his** own elegant home **at** Rockford.   He had found evidence in abundance, and his heart was **full to** overflowing.   **Many warm** friends, in this beautiful city, welcomed him with heartfelt expressions that did his soul good; and he felt that he was valued, and determined, with renewed energy, to be worthy of all their friendship.   A delightful visit with the three sisters at Rockton, and the parting kiss was given to the prairie wind of Illinois, for that time.   And, by the 12th of May, he had reached the lake at his old Southport station, and stood by the apple-tree grave of his boys' bodies on the sandbank, amid the marble and granite slabs, which told both lies and truths of those who were both living and dead.   But the tree told no lies, and was a fit emblem of the *living* boys, whose epitaph it was.   Milwaukie heard his voice again, as he passed along to his valley home, where he arrived on the 19th, after an absence of ten months, during which time not one week had failed to bring one or more letters to his family from him, and, in small sums, all the money he had received, except that used for his expenses. Once more he was in the home with his happy family, and recounting the many incidents of travel to the wife and delighted children, and then examining their progress, which was not slow.

"Welcome home!" said the mate; "for

> ' I would not have a servile throng
>   Press round to bow the knee,
> But one light, free, and eager step
> Haste homeward unto me.

'I would not have a sumptuous couch
When pain had laid me low,
But one dear arm to fold my form,
One hand to press my brow.

'I would not have proud marble piled
Upon my lowly head,
But simple stone and grassy mound,
And one to weep me dead.

'I would, beloved, to thee and me
The priceless pearl be given,
That thy true heart may meet mine own,
And each love each, in heaven.' "

During his short *visit* at home, and the pleasant excursion of himself and wife up and down the Neenah, and to several new towns on its banks, he related much of the reception he had met with in his travels; told her of the excellent homes to which he was ever made a welcome guest, — of the warm greetings, the love and sympathy, he had received from both spheres; and how his soul was overpaid for its long, dark night of doubt, coldness, and death, through which it had passed; and how gloriously he had triumphed over the slanders and falsehoods of his enemies, leaving in them the stings of guilty consciences, and his forgiveness; how the demand for his services increased, and the bright hopes before him, — not of wealth, but of a happy reward in the life to come, and the love of kindred beings while here. These renewed her hope, inspired her with confidence, and cheered her on her way, which was now rapidly growing light and pleasant. He lectured several times at the valley hall, to audiences composed of most of the decent, intelligent, and respectable, of the vicinity. During these travels, and especially when at home, he wrote much for the press, and on various subjects, — among the rest a criticism on H. C. Wright's and T. L. Nichols' works on marriage, in which he did not wholly endorse either, but nearly that of H. C. Wright. Writing and speaking on this subject freely, and not endorsing or sustaining the popular errors and prejudices on one side, nor endorsing the theories on the other, of course brought him directly between the armies, where each shot at him, and tried to drive him to the other rank, but all in vain. As an old lady aptly remarked, they only shot him ahead in the path of right and duty, upward and outward, alone. Henry, however, and his friends, were not of the army that tried to hit him ; for they knew and appreciated his honesty, and his nearness to their teachings, and **so did many** individuals and **personal** friends of both armies ; but the officers of each army had ordered him killed. Still **he was** invulnerable.

June 29. — He delivered the funeral discourse of Isaac Lewis, an elderly and esteemed citizen of an adjoining town. Thus he was installed a preacher of the gospel of " life unto life."

July 4. — E. Daniels delivered an address, and the Lone One looked on, for the first time for several years, without feeling or taking a part ; for he had now separated himself entirely from politics and popular oratory, and become only a preacher of the gospel of reform and the future. Having visited and lectured at, and in the vicinity of, his home for near six weeks, on the 7th of July (the *lucky* Friday) he started again for a long journey of indefinite miles and months, and landed first night in a circle at Fond-du-lac. On Sunday he waked up the sleepers at Sheboygan Falls, and started a commotion that soon collected the means, and built a free church, neat and capacious, which he had subsequently the honor of first making a speech in, before it was finished. Met again the kind welcomes of his friends in Milwaukie, and escaped the curses of his enemies, and passed on to meet other good souls at Genesee and Palmyra ; and, on the 15th, parted with the Palmyra friends in Milwaukie, and closed one of the best and happiest visits of his life with those best and purest of friends, the Higgins family. Stopped at most stations where the spirits had a station-house, and especially at Waukegan, to examine that remarkable medium, Mrs. Seymour, who writes on her arm in raised letters, without touching it, and writes names, and other tests of individual spirits, in that way. Made the acquaintance of the

Baker family, — singers, — and of Peter Saxe, the better brother
of the poet. Short stay in Chicago; but switched at Battle
Creek and laid over, and visited again the Cornell home, and
became more attached and interested at each succeeding visit.
Did not yet resolve to make it a new home. Found friends at
several new stations, among them Bellevue, Albion, and Jackson;
and brought up at the tavern-home of that true friend of both
worlds, N. Stone, of Detroit.

August 13. — In Detroit large audiences attended, and were
pleased; but subsequently unfavorable circumstances and incom-
petent teachers dampened the ardor and slackened the speed here,
as in many other places, more than the enemies could. A terri-
ble crash and rattling of broken dishes near his head, on the
steamboat, in the dark night, on the river, started him next from
his sleep. He soon learned that a vessel had run her bow-pole
into the pantry, and waked up the passengers, some with screams
and fright, or prayers, or curses, according to their respective religious beliefs. But he soon "bedded down" again, for he had
paid fare to Cleveland, and was not so easily to be cheated out of
it; and in the morning he stood on the bank in the Cleveland city
overlooking the lake and its vessels, calm and happy as a sainted
judge. Had an excellent visit with many good friends, but his
lectures did not call large audiences. The cause lay quiet at that
time in the public mind. He was constantly learning of new cases
of misery and suffering from unhappy marriages; and constantly
his soul was called out in sympathy for these sufferers, and the
trials of martyrs. But he often asked, Where is the remedy, and
what is it? Knowledge of ourselves, and the laws of our being,
and relations to one another, seemed the only ones he could discover; and these seemed distant, and not easily reached by society
while it was running its mad career after wealth, fashion, religion,
and glory.

September was scattering its autumn shades when he visited
again that romantic spot, New Brighton, and the Alum Rocks,
and met the happy faces there. Again he found the happy face

of W. S. Courtney in Pittsburg, and turned the corner on New Brighton. Every traveller ought to visit this place once, and see where Grace Greenwood used to climb the rocks and paddle in the brooks, in the days of her girlhood, which gave her the noble body and excellent case for her expanded soul.

Sunday, September 24. — A. J. Davis lectured in the Melodeon in Cleveland morning and evening, and the Lone One **in the after-noon**; and certainly their philosophy harmonized, as their minds and feelings did. His former opinions of the honest and happy-hearted seer were confirmed, and he both loved and esteemed him, and ever **after** registered and reported him as the "happiest man that **lives.**" He coasted around the vicinity of Cleveland, and lectured almost constantly until October 10th. He brought up again at the office of Carrie, in Cincinnati, overjoyed to learn of her prosperity and success in her cherished art of healing, **in** which she had studied and struggled so long, and suffered so much. Large audiences, as usual, came to hear him in that city. He followed his subject and the calls to many places; but among the most attractive were Cincinnati and Richmond, and afterwards Dayton more than either.

October 26. — Met Mrs. Thomas, **the** preacher of the new gospel, at Middlebury, Ohio, and assisted her over some **of** the theological rocks that had been stumbling-blocks in the way of her progress. She ever after had more freedom. Also met one of God and Nature's *tall* specimens of human life, light, and beauty, whose gospel-mission has since commenced, and whose voice and actions have gone forth in battle "for freedom and reform." May God and the angels bless her noble soul, and impel her on her way, was and is his prayer for her! She deserves a better fate than circumstances have given her, but so do many who have harder **ones.** It seems, after all **the** speculating about "free agency," that we are creatures of circumstances; and how much we can do to make or modify circumstances with the aid of circumstances is not yet known. About this time the thread of correspondence, which had been spun out to near five **years'** length quite evenly, except the knot at the point of theft, was twisted off by a lady, supposed to be a mutual friend, for reasons probably known to **her,** and it was never after tied up; so the spools were laid away for future use; and if they are ever wove into a web, it will make a garment **that** will answer to wear to and into heaven; for it was pure as the robes of angels which cover their affections.

October. — Down the road he moves, with short stops in Buffalo, Rochester, Auburn, Syracuse, Utica, and Troy, to Springfield, Mass., and met there again good friends, and that feeble body and excellent medium for quiet, and pleasant, and reliable communications, Miss Angeline Munn, through whom many excellent messages have been given, that the public have read without knowing the gentle and obscure author. Met Lucy Stone at Hartford, and bade her farewell, as she was about to take a voyage in the sea of matrimony, from which her return was doubtful, and in which so many are totally lost, and others shipwrecked, a few of whom get back to shore. He hoped the silvery tones of her attractive voice would give a farewell address to the friends of freedom before she started, on the ship Ceremony, for *Blackwell's* Island; but she went off soon after, only registering her name at the station, without reserving the right to return when she pleased. Many loved her before, and not less after, she went to the nursery. Here he also met the woman whom he once found, a stranger, lying sick with a fever, of the typhoid species, and, taking her by the hand, bade the fever depart, and "straightway the fever left her" from that hour, and she arose and walked, but not until her emaciated body was recruited by **food.** Met also, for a second or third time, that beautiful little, Frank, medium, through whom Red Jacket calls the squaws and braves to their places, and gives them specimens of his wit and wisdom. Presented Mrs. Mettler with a lock of hair from the head of a sick lady in Ceresco, Wisconsin, and received a most accurate and critical description of all her conditions and relations, some of which were pitiable in the extreme, and beyond remedy while law and religion continue to make slaves, victims, and martyrs, to cruel

inharmonies in social life. Went to Poquonock ; found a church
with a two-story pulpit, pens for pews; and there preached the
new gospel in the old house, and it did not burst; and he left
with the best wishes of some good souls and a promise to return,
but left the time loose. So it is yet.

Went back to Springfield and met a New England Thanks-
giving-day, and found a great contrast between the table of
Mrs. Harrison, on that occasion, and the one he found at home
sixteen years before, in the days of salt and potatoes, eat with
tears for blessings. In this city he found a wolf, with a sheep's
coat on, trying to coax a lamb through the fence ; and he picked
up the willing lamb and took it to the station in Boston, and sent
it by express to its paternal home, among the mountains, where it
rested in safety till it went to sea. Found Boston and December,
and that indomitable worker for spiritualism, Dr. H. F. Gardner,
with his Fountain House for a spiritualist's home ; and there were
truly spirits at the house, but not the kind which make drunk
come, but those which make the raps and tips come ; and people
often came there to find that kind of spirits, but not to find the *evil*
spirits, which are usually bottled and headed, corked and decan-
tered, but for whose freedom the Lone One ever plead, asking that
the necks of the bottles might be wrung and twisted off, and the
heads of the casks broken, and the spirits allowed to *run* freely
away. The other kind always seemed to be free, and would not
always come at bidding, especially of wise savans and professional
dignitaries. More than one evening he was found sitting in Barnard's little spirit-room, where the drums did beat. the bells tinkle,
the trumpets sound, the tambourines. rattle, and the drumsticks
move about the room, all in the dark ; but he soon satisfied himself that an invisible power did perform many of the simple tricks,
— invisible of course in the dark, and he was satisfied it would be,
even in a lighted room, but it never was philosophically clear to
him why the room for such feats must be dark. The spirits *never*
gave a scientific reason, although they often attempted, and satisfied those who were ignorant of science and her laws. But these

and other experiments fully satisfied him that certain spirits required darkened rooms for particular performances. This seemed to have a connection with haunted houses, where the wonders usually occur in the night or dark — but why, is still an open question. Made the acquaintance of that bold defender of the truth, Theodore Parker, and loved to hear him send home the startling truths to the anxious minds that gathered in the Music Hall, each Sabbath morn. "Well," said the reverend, at the close of a sermon, "did I do your subject any injustice?" for he had been speaking of mediums and spiritualism. — "No, sir," said the Lone One, "only criticized it as I often do; but you have only reached the door of our temple, — would you not like to have it opened, and walk in, and view its beautiful decorations?" — "Certainly; I am always seeking for new truth. Come to my house and tell me what you have found." But the visit did not come off, for the two ends missed each other, and passed by the stopping-place. Heard the soft whisperings of angels through Hattie A. Adams, and the "Lily Wreath" of spirit-flowers fell from her hands on his brow in the beautiful visions more than once, as he heard the ever-smiling face of John S. relate how he penned and pranced the "Town and Country" for the market. But we have not time here to register all the good souls with whom he met and parted.

December 20. — In Portland, Me. Meets A. J. Davis, at the reformers' home of Lydia Dennet, and in the lecture-hall; for now the seer, too, is itinerant. It always did his soul good to meet Jackson, for then he knew God or nature had one specimen of a natural and true man — a man without a mask, inside and outside alike. Made arrangements for a course of lectures for himself, on his return, to follow Mr. Davis, and then ploughed on through the snow to the end of the rail. Almost froze in the sleigh-coach before he reached Bangor, although the passengers had the advantage of the heat of a newly-married couple, on a wedding trip to the eastern "jumping-off place." But they reached Bangor late in the eve, where he found warm friends and homes; but what became of the wedding-party was never known to him, for they were to go on at four next morn, and at six thermometer was near thirty degrees below zero , and whether it froze between them he never knew. He solicited a lock of their hair for their friends, but they would not send this token back to Vermont by him; for they had faith in God, and hoped he would preserve them, and let them return safe, and not frozen ; — perhaps he did. His old friend Melinda, of Troy, N. Y., was here, with a sister and brother-in-law, and they were a concert and made beautiful music at each lecture. The church was opened and ready, and a liberal public feeling gave him full audiences, and an interesting time. The Christmas-tree was harvested at the home where he rested; circles and happy visits used up the time, and closed the old year up; and, on the 31st of December, it sank quietly to its eternal rest, unless a resurrection-trump shall awake it, of which there is no promise. But the Hutchinson boys were there singing, and they sang its requiem, and the Lone One preached its funeral sermon. Ralph W. Emerson, whom the Lone One had never before met, said the comic and witty, acute and philosophical words for the old year, as it was about to die. The year thus closed, with a feast of fat things, in a deep snow-rich city, and happy homes, far down in the State of Maine, on the life and vision of the Cosmopolite.

> " The long dark night of the world is past ;
>   The day of humanity dawns at last ;
>   The veil is rent from the soul's calm eyes,
>   And prophets, and heroes, and seers, arise ;
>   Their words and deeds like the thunders go ;
>   Can ye stifle their voices ? — They answer, ' No ! ' "

> " We live in deeds, not years ; in thoughts, not breaths ;
>   In feelings, not in figures on a dial.
>   We should count time by heart-throbs : he most lives
>   Who thinks most, feels the noblest, acts the best ;
>   And he whose heart beats quickest lives the longest."

Section III.

1855. — ITINERATING. — INCIDENTS. — FRIENDS INCREASE.

ONE BY ONE.

One by one the sands are flowing,
One by one the moments fall ;
Some are coming, some are going, —
Do not strive to grasp them all !

One by one thy duties wait thee, —
Let thy whole strength go to each ;
Let no future dreams elate thee,
Learn thou first what these can teach.

One by one — bright gifts from Heaven —
Joys are sent thee here below ;
Take them readily when given,
Ready, **too,** to let them go.

One by one thy griefs shall meet thee, —
Do not fear an armed band ;
One will fade as others greet thee,
Shadows passing through the land.

Do not look at **life's** long sorrow ;
See how long each moment's pain ;
God will help thee for to-morrow,
Every day begin again.

Every hour that fleets so slowly
Has its task to do or bear ;
Luminous the crown and holy,
If thou set each gem with care.

Do not linger with regretting,
Or for passing hours despond ;
Nor, the daily toil forgetting,
Look too eagerly beyond.

> Hours are golden links, God's token,
>   Reaching Heaven, but one by one ;
> Take them, lest the chain be broken
>   Ere the pilgrimage be done.

The new year broke beautifully on **the life of** the Lone One in Bangor, and the day was spent visiting with the three Hutchinson brothers, **and Mr.** and **Mrs.** Shaw, with their sister, **the** Troy medium, writer, and singer, who had been so unceremoniously dismissed from teaching in Troy because the angels communicated to her beautiful messages of peace and love for those who needed such. The delightful and happy homes of General Hersey and Mr. McLaughlin both received and contributed to the holiday **joys,** and aided to wheel off the cold hours in pleasure and glad- **ness.** The day closed with a concert **and** crowd, and beautiful dreams took the Lone One late to other scenes. Next night he slept in Portland, at the home of N. Foster, where reformers find a welcome and **the** best of care ; but Mrs. F. had removed her " board and lodging **" to a** new home on the other side of **the** Styx, where she was expecting him, **as** soon as he completed his labor on **this side.** She was not so far away that they could not hear from her; for she often sent word, and assured her husband of her good health and happy life in the new home.

January 5. — **A letter** for a western paper commenced some- what in this **wise** : " My date reminds **me** that this day completes forty-two years that I have breathed the atmosphere of this earth, and boarded with its inhabitants. **I have** been fanned by its zephyrs, and chilled by its **boreas ; warmed** by its sunshine in summer-time, and bitten by its frosts of winter-time, both in body and spirit, from the world of matter and the world of mind around **me.** Much **of my life** has been a sad experience, full of **events** and vicissitudes **that may** one day make **up a** narrative for the curious. **My** attempt **at** life on earth was begun in the winter, in every sense **and** meaning of the word. In mid-winter, by the calendar, in the geographical winter of New Hampshire. In the abject poverty winter of society ; in the winter of social scorn and contempt, despised by the ignorant and vulgar. In the solitary winter of loneliness, with no brother, no sister, no father, and but a momentary visit from a mother; such was the winter of an ardent and sensitive soul. In the winter of intellect, too ; for by hard-earned coin I paid for the book-knowledge at school, and by toiling by day, and studying by night, for many years, I unfolded my intellect, and gradually melted away the snows of human prejudice. In a winter of religion, for even to the age of thirty no ray of hope for happiness, or even existence beyond this, to me, miserable life, enlivened one hour of toil and misery; hope sank in utter darkness, and scarcely could the light of God be seen through the snow-drifts which circumstances and society had heaped upon me. Twenty years ago I sought a home in the then far West; and there, after many years of toil and suffering, I have at last found the summer-time of life, and the sunshine of happiness, and my soul is full to overflowing."

The course of lectures were well attended in Portland, and a lively interest awakened in the city, which has never subsided; nor will it, until the city is "leavened." Returned to Boston, and homed at the Fountain House a few weeks, and missionaried about the country. Found Joseph Dow and lady in Woburn, with souls in them, and heard of others in the place, where a few attentive minds listened to his voice.

Jan. 14. — Lectured in Hartford, and had one of the most pleasant and happy visits with old friends there, and returned, passing Springfield. Came to Warren, and addressed a full house, and again in Ware met new friends and attentive listeners. Passed by and viewed the rocky home where Lucy Stone used to skip, and play, and work. But he did not call, for the bird had flown. Returned to Boston, and met Emma F. Jay, whose acquaintance he had before made at Troy, and who was now a remarkable medium. She, too, had in early life found a home in the same Southport village of Wisconsin, and sojourned also in the Battle Creek of Michigan, and schooled in the LaRoy seminary of New York. Orphaned out, and tossed about, slandered and scorned, for her mediumship, and defence of the truth. She had, by these means, attained, and deserved, a high place in the army of spiritualists. A well-deserved notoriety soon after took her over the ocean, with friends; but the spiritual atmosphere there would not hold her up, and she leaned on the social and intellectual arm of society. Made a visit of her mission, and returned to triumph more, and better, at home, as a messenger of the angels, till she landed on the island of domestic life, over the sea of matrimony, and homed at the old "stamping-ground," in the city of Kenosha, — once Southport.

Feeling lonely, one day, he stepped into a room where were a gentleman and his wife, both good mediums, and seated himself as a visitor, or friend. Soon the lady, with a sudden convulsed jerk of the body and arm, threw her work from her lap, and, in an entranced state, turned to him and said, "A beautiful white cloud hangs over you, with a richness of pure white too delightful for description. Slowly I see a small, delicate, and exquisitely moulded hand and arm project from the cloud! In the fingers is *one* bright red pink; — do you know its language?" — "Yes," he replied. "The arm reaches it to you, and, placing it in your lips, recedes. At a distance the cloud slowly opens, and I behold the features and form of one of the most lovely beings my spirit-eye hath ever beheld, and I hear her say, 'When thy wearying task is done, when thy earthly clouds are passed, when thy mission is performed, when thy wounded heart is healed, when thou layest thy body down, — then we will lead thee to our home, where thy soul shall mingle, one with mine, in pure, unclouded love.' Her smiling face and celestial form is again hid in the cloud, and it moves slowly away." The dark cloud was lifted off his feelings, and they were again buoyant and happy. Reader, who do you think did this? Was it a devil, or a bad woman? But some of you will ask who was the spirit. To him it was a vision of the future; not personal, on the part of the angel, but only representative. He knew too much of such visions to seek for names, or persons; for they are only given to represent conditions and times. The person represented in such visions may be in either world, known or unknown; and we are not often supplied with correct information of the persons represented, for usually it is not best for us to know.

Jan. 27. — Some excellent friends in Portsmouth, N. H., received a visit, and collected very large audiences, in the Temple, to listen to his lectures. The spirits were ringing door-bells, and making some other demonstrations in the town, that served to awaken an interest and inquiry. The social atmosphere was very pleasant at this station, and he lingered till his appointment at Kennebunk, Me., called him thither. Found friends and listeners numerous there, also, and filled the mission, and returned to meet his appointment at Natick, and lodge in the soul-refreshing home of his friend Hanchet, and shook once more the political hand of Senator Wilson, with whom he had been stationed on the platform at Pittsburg, in his day of political conventions. One of the most intelligent and appreciative audiences assembled to hear him in Natick, and long he remembered his pleasant visit, and the influences of the place.

Feb. 7. — Drifted in, by snow, at Essex, where a preacher had induced him to come and lecture, where a few good souls were ready for the gospel which he preached.

Feb. 11. — Attended to the sermon of Parker in morning, and spoke twice at the Melodeon to good audiences. A cloud hung over his soul about these days, for extraordinary efforts were made to destroy his influence by slander and falsehood, based on stories which were only valuable by transportation, but worth nothing at the places where they started. His loving nature and affectionate heart, which had been so crushed in early life, was now receiving its natural flow, and he was often found in conversation or correspondence with the best, and purest, and most intelligent ladies of his circle of acquaintance; and a letter or a visit from a lady unknown to the enemies, or jealous sensualists, was ample evidence, and testimony, that he was a "Free Lover." When this cloud passed away, it was the last that ever did, and probably the last that ever will, shade his soul, for he had drank deep of the

> * 　* 　"Pure and strengthening camomile,
> 　Whose crushed leaves ever show
> How the true and strong heart gathereth
> 　Fresh energy from woe."

It was truly a long time before his sensitive heart could be reconciled to the falsehoods of enemies and pretended friends; but at last he triumphed in that struggle, and felt the forgiving spirit of Jesus, who could as freely forgive Peter and Judas as he could those who crucified him. A point which Christians have seldom attained, but which the Harmonial Philosophy teaches, and A. J. Davis practises, as a disciple of nature.

Feb. 13. — Dropped a lecture in Lexington, not as famous as the battle, but may have hit some object. A second pleasant visit at Portsmouth. Heard Sally Holley try to unite Bible with anti-slavery. Vain effort to make it all read that way, while it reads both in defence, and condemnation, of every evil. A second visit to Portland, with better success than in first. Used up a week, and made new friends, and the increasing influence and constant labor in this cause made its enemies more bitter and vindictive than ever.

Returned to Boston to see February expire, and to part with a patient, whose system had received much benefit from magnetism, through his system. This patient is often referred to in the diary as Belle, and was a poor victim of disease, and medicine, with a fine and large brain, well balanced, and a nobleness of soul and character seldom equalled in one of only ordinary education. She had been totally blind for four years, from the age of sixteen to twenty, and during the time physicians had experimented on her nervous system, until they had nearly destroyed all its capacities for enjoyment; and when she ceased all medical remedies, she slowly and partially recovered her vision. The jealous friends and pious enemies both found good food for slander in his magnetizing this poor sick girl. But their fires went out when she got married to a distinguished business man, and left the circle of gossip, but never the feeling of gratitude to him.

March 2. — Visit the home of John M. Spear and daughter, in Melrose. Sophronia was an angel while here, and at that time, and now is with them in a more affectionate and happier home, as she testifies to the Lone **One, and many other friends, who** knew and loved her while here, and as her husband knew then, and still testifies; but the people abused her, as they **do all of** their best specimens of human-life purity.

Sunday, March 4. — Turned off three lectures in Lawrence, **to** large and intelligent audiences.

In Lawrence found a cousin in a happy home, with one of the **best** of husbands, and one little daughter. She was a daughter of Joseph, who had ever been the most sympathizing and kind of his relatives, and whose family had ever treated him as a relation. With this cousin he ever after sojourned when **in the city;** and now for the first time since he left **his** native town for **the West** he met with a relative. **She** had a story to tell, **a life-line to** follow. One of the best and most affectionate of girls, **she was** early married *by law*, and tried to live with a man who was **to** her anything but what a husband **should be, until her constitution was** nearly ruined, and at **last was forced to** leave him, and **be** unlocked by a decree of court; and, after some years of **struggle** and buffeting **the** world of scorn, she at length met her true mate, and unitedly and happily they wind **their** way along **the** married journey, happy in all **but** her poor health. Adding **this to** his cabinet of specimens of marriage unions, **he journeyed along,** wishing he had *all* the experiences **to record, that the law-makers** might see the picture, and be induced **to so change the law that it** would not be more honorable **to die or live in** misery, than to escape **from** such **pollution** and **adultery as** many live in, forced by law and public opinion united, **to crush their** victims.

Next point of note was Concord, N. H., **where** the lectures did not call out many hearers; but here **he** picked up a specimen for his cabinet of curiosities. In the old Chandler homestead he found John, with his unshaven face and head; of course, a singular man, and one of the odd sticks. Martha, with her pleasant face and contented look, and the fine-looking children. From them he learned the story of their marriage, which God or nature had cemented many years before, when they were young. They religiously repudiated marriage, but after an early and long acquaintance they believed they were mates. She had been much at the old homestead ; and one morning at breakfast, without any previous notice to his parents, or others, they both announced their intention to live together as much like married people as they pleased, and be as near one in life and labor as God had made them adapted to each other. When the surprise was over, then the rage of gossip began, and lasted for years, but gradually it died, for they ever lived true to each other, happy in and with each other ; and as God married them, of course no man has ever put them asunder ; and no earthly marriages have been more pleasant through the trials of life. They wandered to the West once after an association, at a time when John repudiated money. They returned, through many hardships, to the old homestead, which has recorded the years for more than a century, in Concord.

Some time after this date John furnished another firebrand for the market of gossip. Their eldest child had left her body, — a girl of about a dozen summers, — and, as the family were sick, John employed the sexton to take the body to the grave-yard and bury it, without a priest or funeral, or even followers to the grave. The enraged Christians were almost ready to dig it up and hang him, and bury both decently, as they called it. But John only laughed at their rage, and did as he had a mind to do.

March 12, '55. — The team lands him in Pittsfield, twenty years, lacking a few days, since he left. The voters had been called to the town-hall to hear a speech from Mr. Clark, of Manchester, an acquaintance of the Lone One. He was to follow in a speech to the Republican voters ; and next day was to be election-day in the state. Only one citizen knew the Lone One was present ; and as Mr. Clark was compelled to leave at the close of his speech, he was requested to announce a stranger to follow in a speech, but not to name him, for he was now nameless; probably not twenty people in the town knew he was living, and only the one knew he was present. It was a surpris*ed* party, as he made his way to the stand through the anxious crowd, and, mounting the rostrum, deliberately releasing himself from his extra coat, he soon called to their minds the last election in which **he took an active** part with some of them, when many others now **active** among them were playing around their cradle-beds or mothers' laps. Then he told them of his travels in the West and **the** South, — in the border free states, and in the **border** slave states, — and explained the contrast, and many of his observations and experiences. All persons of all parties were chained by the thread of his discourse and the story, and looked sorry when **he** closed, which was compelled by the *late*. Then followed a scene such as we cannot describe. A hundred persons rushed to greet him, each eager to clasp **his hand, and** many to be recognized in person or in family; but none, save two little boys, of the name or family with whom he had lived out his boyhood. The lawyer and the eldest brother had removed from the town; the father and the one with whom he had served his time had removed over Jordan, and left only the two little boys at the old homestead. They were born after he left, of a second wife. After much entreaty, and many apologies to fractional relatives and others, he finally went home with the Drake family, several of whom, now men and women, were little children when he left, but in and of a family of dear friends much visited by him for several years, and near Brackett's homestead. **Half** an hour's visit to his old home was all he could spare, and many short calls among them — one on a cousin and her happy home. One whose mother was a sister of Simon, and who married into the name, and, dropping this one daughter on earth, went home to heaven, leaving the husband to marry again, but not to crowd the lovely daughter out of sole heirship. Therefore, she brought her husband to the fine old home on the hill, and there still lingered the almost octogenarian parent, with two wives in heaven, and none on earth. Sophronia was overjoyed to meet him, for she had loved him as a cousin in his youth, and to her he was still a relative, and ever had been. Four days, and all the visits were closed, **and** the one lecture in the church on the Western States had awakened the interest, and sufficed to let them know he had outgrown the boyhood, and their scorn and contempt for his birth and youth.

March 16. — Returned to Concord ; 17th, to Boston ; 18th. **lectured twice in** Chelsea, and quartered at the excellent and happy home of Capt. Williams, and found the quiet and happy parents of Mrs. W. and Mrs. Alvin Adams (Mr. and Mrs. Bridge), on whose souls the sunshine of the next life was shining brightly, enabling them to see and feel the life to come while yet lingering here in feeble bodies. Met and visited old and new friends at many homes, in Boston and vicinity. Lectured almost constantly.

March 23. — Stood on the Winnesimmet ferry-boat, with uncommonly large number of passengers, when a large ship, launched from the stocks, came directly toward it. So doubtful were the chances of " fore or aft " passage, that the engineer stopped the wheels, and in one minute all the frightened and screaming crowd would have been under the mighty ship's prow, and under water, but for a mighty yell of some person, given with power enough to induce the engineer to put on the motion at full force, by which the flat ferry, with its load of passengers, mostly ladies, was pushed forward, and the monster grazed the stern as she passed the frightened crowd. " Narrow escape ! " they cried, and some thanked God, and some the engineer, and some the man that yelled. The Lone One looked coolly on, calm, and prepared for either sphere of life and action. Half an hour after, he was on a train of cars that ran against a team just returning from a funeral, and narrowly escaped an upset and destruction of property, and preparation of material for more funerals ; but narrow escapes are frequent on the cars.

March 26. — Farewell to Boston. Stop over in Springfie'd

and hold up at the Palace Home, in Hartford. Excellent circle, and visit with best of friends.

March 29. — Met with the Associationists in New York city, and made speech for theory, and recounted unhappy experience. Went home with the old reformer, Tappan Townsend, **of** Brooklyn.

March 30. — In eve at conference of spiritualists, but found more wrangling than harmony, and few harmonized spirits in attendance. Could not find out their object.

Sunday, April 1. — Lectures in Stuyvesant Institute in day, and in Dodsworth's in eve, to crowded hall ; at the close of which many applications were made for him, but his time was limited, and he could not engage. Overheard a judge say that was the best lecture they had heard in the hall ; but the press said very little about it, of course, for he was the World's Child, not of distinguished parentage, but born in its lower circle, and slowly wending his way to its outer spiritual sphere.

April 2. — A highly intellectual treat, in a visit with Ernestine L. Rose ; and then on the cars bound to Cleveland, with short stop at Cuba ; found Hattie watching by the side of her soon-to-be-released father. Cora, whose father had been called through the cholera-gate to the other life, was on her mission elsewhere, but her Lovisa-mother was aiding Hattie. Only themselves can tell how glad they all were to meet again one so nearly allied to them in the dispensation of the new gospel.

April 6. — Once more in Cleveland, and meet the Mary F., whose soul was now freed from its legal earthly bondage, by her effort, and now she could say to Mr. L., marry now, if you wish, the girl you love, for the court has freed you from me by my request. No friend of hers could be more rejoiced at her freedom than the Lone One, except it might be the one with whom her existence soon after blended, and with which it still remains blended. Sunday he lectured twice, and Mary once, in the Melodeon ; but, for want of proper notice, to small audiences. Hers was a noble effort, and a beautiful lecture, and she felt her freedom as her soul bounded with its outstretched wing once more in the world of mankind, — a woman, free, though despised by many of those in bondage. Her free heart went to its true mate soon after, and found its home where no law of man could *make* or *mar* the union.

April 15. — One of the happiest and best visits of his life at Akron and Middlebury, with lectures, and his artist-friend and her mother and several others, all of whom endeavored to contribute to his happiness, and whose kindnesses he never will forget in this **world or** the world to come. Coasted and lectured along the way westward, at Elyria and other places.

April 23. — Brought up at L. Martin's, in Adrian, Michigan, one of the neatest little homes that the spirits could find on earth. No pet but the cat soils the carpet, and even the talking is mostly done by the visitors; but this was always one of the best homes for the Lone One, and where he ever found a hearty welcome, and efforts and notices for lectures, which to him were now almost his meat and drink. Next in Detroit to meet an esteemed friend, with the soul of an angel in earthly form, whose mate had been snatched from her arms by the cholera, leaving her to guide and train up the boys alone. This elegant and highly-refined lady was ever a fast friend of the Lone One, in sunshine and storm ; for she knew his life and labors were above the vile dregs of society, that ever slandered and abused him. She believed in eternal life, and that she should again meet her husband in a new home, and of course this heresy rendered her unpopular ; but she was free, and the angels administered unto her.

April 29. — Three very good audiences in Detroit, in Fireman's Hall, listened to his voice. Some excellent friends at Jackson made his short visit highly pleasant ; and at Albion the hall was full of listeners, for the cause had made much progress there through the labors of Mrs. C. Sprague, afterwards Mrs. Tuttle, one **of the ablest and** best of medium-speakers in the field " to this day."

Sunday, May 6. — The hall at Battle Creek was well filled, to listen to the well-known voice of the Lone One ; and the Bedford

school and the Cornell home received its accustomed visit. Waded
through Chicago, but no call for news from the other life there.
They were mostly engaged in speculating with corner-lots, and
stocks, &c.   In Milwaukie, the 9th, and met audiences in the hall
at each appointed hour; very good interest.   Closed his course on
Sunday, the 13th, and parted with Dr. Greves and many excellent
friends; and on the 15th reached his Ceresco home and the bosom
of an anxious family, who had watched each approach as **the**
weekly letter reported it, after an absence of little over ten months.
Eager friends came gathering round, and wondering enemies
sneaked out of sight, ashamed and conscience-smitten for their
abuse and slander.   Rum and religion had doubled teams in Ripon
and Ceresco, and sent a mob after some new settlers or visitors in
the place, who, it was said, had lived, or were living, together as
man and wife without permission of a priest; and one deacon, of hard
history and bad repute, entered a complaint against the new comers,
although he had never been in a house when they were in it, **nor**
ever spoken to them; but his oath to what he knew nothing of, was
sufficient, with the prejudice, to arrest and bind over the two
strangers who had been guilty of living in the place for a few weeks,
— married or unmarried, no one knew, save what they said themselves, and they denied the right of a priest to marry them.   They
were strangers to the Lone One, and all others in Ceresco, and the
man subsequently proved himself unworthy the martyrdom; but **they**
found bail for appearance at county court, and that **was the** end
of the matter, for **the influence** of the little Ripon pettifogger did
not reach to the county seat, and the district attorney knew better
than to tax the county with his ridiculous nonsense.   In the midst
of all this **the Lone One** had good audiences on Sunday, the 20th.
Even many of the rowdies came to hear him, and listened quietly,
and as usual found the pious enemies had lied about him, and taken
advantage of his absence to spread the lies.

During his last absence six families, four of them old citizens
of irreproachable character, and two new settlers, united themselves, as they called it, into what was called the Ceresco Union,

and issued a circular, which was published in several papers, setting forth their unobjectionable views, and inviting friends who agreed with them in sentiment to come and join them, and settle in Ceresco. No noise, objection, or prejudice, was raised about or against the Union, until a Dr. Newbury, from New York, came there, and gave a course of lectures in which he defended the freedom of the sexes, and opposed all marriage and restraint of law on the rights of women, &c.; the mob spirit arose, set on by religious bigotry, and an attempt to mob him called out the families who composed the Union, and they defended him until his lectures ended, and he left to return no more. But they had brought down the curse of the rabble and the busy pettifogger, who, about this time, got control of a little squib sheet that advertised the goods of Ripon for the country market, and in this he puffed himself, and let off his venom on the Ceresco Union, with great applause from the enemies of Ceresco. At a distance, the whole scheme was charged to the Lone One, and Newbury was said to have been sent there by him, although he never saw this Newbury, "to this day," nor heard of him except in Ceresco; and, although he never belonged to the Union, nor heard of it till its circular was published, and **neither** condemned nor endorsed its **sentiments.** But **he** was ever ready to maintain the freedom of speech, and the right of every person to teach whatever sentiments he or she pleases, as those who do not wish to hear could certainly stay away. **More than** five hundred newspapers in the nation copied slanderous imputations about the Lone One started by **the** little sheet at Ripon, and by a worse and more reckless, *Courier,* **at** Oshkosh, which procured its vile lies from the pettifogger, who was personally under obligations to the Lone One, from which he released himself by such abuse; but he had a reason, previously **given in** these pages. An acquaintance and personal friendship was all the connection the Lone One ever had with this or any other union, except the old Phalanx, which died in '50, and ever after which, he intended to fight on his own hook, and be the expo**nent** of his own views, as he is, boldly and openly. But his home

was in Ceresco, and he was a spiritualist; and if " Free Love " or
any other subject could be used to prejudice the people, it would
be charged to him.

May 25. — Started again, and lectured in Fond-du-lac in eve,
and next day reached Sheboygan Falls, and Sunday, 27th, lectured
in new church to good audience, and on 28th in court-house at
Sheboygan. Tuesday, his eldest son arrived, and they took boat
for Chicago, and the son went on to Battle Creek and to the Bedford
school and Cornell home, where he found a welcome, and better
friends than he ever found out of his own home. The father
stopped in Chicago, and whistled off to Rockford to sleep at the
happy home of his friend Dr. Rudd. Dr. Haskell had the circles,
and his paper, going forth to spread the truth, but was not satisfied
to have the work go on so slowly. Three lectures were well attended on Sunday. In Dixon, June 6, one lecture; made a
good impression. Next Peoria, the handsomest of handsome
cities in Illinois, took down a course of lectures well got up by
two of the Higgins brothers. By the 11th was again in Rockford, and on the 12th met once more the three sisters at Rockton.
The mother had now escaped from her body of pain, and the home
was broken up.

June 13 *and* 14. — Lectured in Beloit, Wisconsin, but not to
large audiences; 15th, in Belvidere, and on Sunday, 17th, in
Waukegan. A good spiritual atmosphere ever surrounded this
place, for its best citizens were converted to harmonial religion.
Via the cities to Beaverdam, where he met his old friends, once of
Rockford, Mr. and Mrs. Archer, and had a pleasant visit and good
audience in the evening, and on the 22d was again at his home in
Ceresco. This short trip had been made that the wife might get
ready to accompany him East on a visit to her paternal home,
with the younger son. The elder son was now at the Spiritualists' Home in Bedford, Michigan; the daughter had taken, and
was teaching, a school in an adjoining town; the house was partly
rented, the goods were packed up, and preparations soon made to
leave the slanders to a free circulation, and they had a glorious

run after he and the family were gone. All was soon ready, and on the 28th of June the friends collected and parted with the three, and they started, not sure of a return, even if prospered, for he had long since resolved to change his home, or rather hers, for one more congenial to their views and feelings.

Sunday, July 1. — Lectured at Sheboygan Falls, and recruited for the journey ; her health was better than for years before, but still feeble. The Harmonial Philosophy had wrought in her great physical, **spiritual,** and mental changes, which had changed life from a burden to a pleasure, and now she too had to share the **abuse and** slanders of his enemies. No sooner were they out of town than lies, of the most absurd and ridiculous character, were reported about them ; and frequently, while on the journey, where he was known and she was not known, were remarks made about the woman he had travelling with him, and persons heard to say they did not believe it was his wife. By this journey, the only one in which he had been accompanied by a female, he was long reported as travelling with strange women all over the country. Never, until he began to talk and write about the abuse of the marriage contract, and advocate changes that would release only **the** sufferers, **was there a** word of slander against his moral or social character ; but since he had made that a theme, every time he was seen with a female he was suspected of illicit intentions. Both were now free and happy, and these slanders did not reach their souls, but usually fell, like scalding water, on those who reported them. Speedily they journeyed, by boat, to Chicago, and, after a short stop in that whirlpool of civilization, by rail to Battle Creek, where his many friends were soon her friends also, and, meeting the son at his new home with the Cornells, they soon learned of his attachment to the place and people.

While here the Lone One bargained for an acre of land, and resolved to put up a small house soon as he could do so. Soon after this purchase, the proprietors surveyed the village plats of Harmonia, and his proved to be a corner-lot, opposite the school-house, and in the town of Battle Creek, with the road between

it and the school-house, a town-line road dividing it from Bedford. The plat is on a beautiful plain of light, rich soil, and each
lot has one acre or more. The Michigan Central Railroad passes
one mile north of the school, and the Kalamazoo River beyond,
but near, the track. Battle Creek station and village, one of the
most active, enterprising, thriving, and liberal towns in the **state**,
is five miles south-east of the school, and the mail, and other
business of the school and settlers, is still done there; for,
although the place had been long settled, and was not new, yet
it was, and is, only the home and the school of a few reformers.
The soul-and-body devoted H. Cornell had, of course, been abused,
like other reformers who attempt to teach without permission
from, and submission to, the clergy. But he was not a man to
faint, or fail, but was one of the few true souls with whom the
Lone One felt united in a life-struggle for reform; and he now
resolved to be interested in the school and its progress. Although
he had no dollars to invest, and no religion to endorse it to the
pious, yet he had friends not a few, and a wide and extensive
acquaintance with reformers, and as much hatred and enmity in
the bosoms of the wicked and superstitious as almost any man in
the nation; and both of these were necessary and useful to him
and the school. Leaving this new home, — for such it now
became, — and the many friends in Battle Creek, they visited
Jackson, and the elegant home of Mr. and Mrs. Isman, and that
best of families and ladies, in the cottage of J. G. Wood;
roamed through state-prison, full of pity for the convicts, which
bore the wife's heart down into its depths of sorrow, for she was
a woman of deep sympathy, and a soul that was ever touched by
suffering in its tenderest chord. " I will never visit another such
place," said she, as they left the gate and entered the carriage
with the happy Mrs. Isman and her very intellectual mother.
That kindest of friends, N. Stone, was in the dépôt at Detroit,
waiting for the family when the cars drove in; and soon the little
boy, full of life, health, and animation, was coasting about the
hotel-home of this excellent family, and the wife found such

friends as she can never forget in Mrs. S. and daughters. "How much they seem like *our* folks!" she said, as they retired.

Sunday, July 15. — The three lectures were well attended, and next day the cars were whistling down the Canada Railway with the father, mother, and boy, two of them the same that fed on salt and potatoes, and more recently on slander and falsehood; and the father the same that had committed one great crime, for which he had suffered all his life, namely, that of being born of an unmarried mother; and the same who had slept with the cows on the beds made warm by their bodies, had been sold into sixteen years' bondage because he was motherless and never had a father on earth.

July 18. — Roam about Niagara Falls and Suspension Bridge, a happy little group, enjoying the rich scenery and magnificent mechanism as freely as if they were rich and popular, in fortune and fashion. The rainbow hoop, the Maid in the Mist, the stairs, the waterfall, and the Indians, have all been described till no further changes can be rung on them; and we will pass along down Lake Ontario on a fine boat, and smooth water, and in the morning through the Thousand Islands, with their rocky peaks, skirted by a rich green shrubbery, to Ogdensburgh. There again take to the whistling horse, and be put "over the road." What a country, in contrast with the West, meets the eye on the North ern road, till you near Champlain, when, of a sudden, you seem in the very heart of the smooth, rich farms of the West; but the line is short, and, ere you are aware of your location, among the mountains of New York and New England, Rouse's Point is the cry, and Champlain smiles in your face — for she never frowns.

July 19, 1855, 5½ P. M. — Cars stop at Milton, Vt., and horse drinks, snorts, and starts. Three seats from the forward end of the first passenger-car sit four persons facing each other; the Lone One and wife, and a Methodist man and wife from Chelsea, Mass. Much they had talked of religion and spiritualism, and many other topics, in the long journey by boat and car. Their window was up, and they were enjoying the fresh air after a severe shower, and admiring the lake and mountain scenery, a little boy was watching the happy faces of his parents from the other side of the car, when a sudden and terrible explosion, a crash, and convulsed trembling commotion, with hideous yells, all burst upon them. "Don't stir!" exclaimed the Lone One, putting out his hands to catch his wife, who was pitched forward on to him. Only an instant, and the car full of living beings was at rest and right side up; but without was horror. The engine and tender were half buried in mud and water at the foot of the bank, the baggage-car had disengaged itself at the couplings, and the top gone down one side and wheels the other; and the two passenger-cars, both well filled, occupied the bank, but not track, alone. Directly under the seats of the four was a car-wheel, and under the wheel the mangled body of Mr. Bush, a conductor of the Burlington train, which was awaiting him ten miles below. The engineer was under his machinery, deep, dead; and the fireman lay mangled on the bank, in a condition from which death soon released him. The little boy and pious woman were frightened almost to a loss of reason. One look and word from the father brought the boy to a state of calmness; but the woman was not as easily calmed. In vain the two spiritualists, both calm as if nothing had happened, tried to pacify her; but the mangled bodies would almost convulse her with agony. "Why," said the Lone One, "have you such fear of going to heaven? Christians ought never to fear death, as it is their only gate to heaven, and a sure escape from further risk of hell. You had better change your religion for ours; then you will not fear death any more, for, with us, he is conquered."

"Well, it is strange," she replied, "how you can be so calm and cheerful."

Another train soon came to their relief, and, the baggage being collected, with the passengers, the scene of the boiler explosion was soon out of sight, and the three, well in body and mind, were sleeping in their seats as they wound around the mountains on the crooked path of the Vermont Central Road, in a dark night, and brought up at White River Junction at three A. M., when they bedded down at the Junction House, and the frightened Christians got more calm by morning. Next day, by cars to Claremont, and stage to Newport, they reached the pious and once happy home of her brother. The girls were glad ; all were glad to see the brother and uncle, whom they had never met before. They liked him much ; but, when he came to speak in the Universalist church, and with effect, then the priest was aroused, and religion in danger. Soon these relatives were supplied with the slanders of the clergy, one of whom, a man who said he had been to Ripon and preached there, going so far as to tell this brother — who, of course, believed it, because a priest told it — that a warrant was already in the hands of the sheriff of his county awaiting his return, and, no doubt, would soon lodge him in jail or prison ; when, in truth, no process, civil or criminal, had ever been issued against him, and never a complaint made against him, except by slanderers. A few months after, when he returned to Ceresco and wrote his wife from there, while she, still visiting her relatives in **New** Hampshire, asked the pious brother what he thought had become of the warrant and officer, etc., " O," said he, " I suppose he has settled it." But this was as true as any of the stories circulated by his religious enemies about him, which answered their end here and in some other places, namely, to prevent his influence and sentiments reaching those pious ones who could be influenced by them. It was not so at the mountain-home where the family were reared. There was a happy home, and a welcome from the souls of all ever greeted them both. Their religion partook of nature and humanity ; and they loved God *in man*, and showed, by doing good to their fellow-beings, that they were relying on works, not words, for salvation. A few days he roamed over the rocks, feasting on wild berries and pure air, and the atmosphere of kindred, new to him ; then moved along his way, and, July 29, lectured three times in Lawrence, and found a hearty welcome among the many friends in that place, and at the happy home of his cousin. Next day, in Boston, many familiar faces greeted him; but short calls were the order now. Aug. 1, he landed in Portland, where several days were spent most pleasantly, one on an uninhabited island in Casco Bay with a picnic party — a romance. All strangers to him in the morning, and none by evening.

Sunday, Aug. 5. — Three lectures in City Hall used up the day. Here he met his old friend from Rockford, Ill., Dr. Haskell, and they journeyed together up the road to Gorham, and to the top of the White Mountains ; the seven last and up-hill miles on foot to the Tip-Top House, where they dined on the 8th of August, and, in a beautiful day, stretched their vision in all directions, trying to see more, when every look was a feast. The clouds floated in beautiful richness around the summit of the great rock-heap, called Mt. Washington. When the lungs had feasted, and the eye was tired, he took leave of his friend, who was intending to return to the Glen House and Gorham, and pranced nine miles on foot down the west path to the Notch House, where, late and weary, he arrived, and found the best of fare for the best of pay. Registered for the stage at four next morning, and when the porter came to call him it was raining, blowing, thundering, **and** lightning, as if the gods of wind and weather were mad with fury. "Call me to-morrow morning, and let the stage go," said the voice within. — "Ay, ay, sir !" and the storm beat on undisturbed by the stage. When the morning came, he walked around the Glen, but he could not see the **top**. To him it was delightful to see the storm beat itself to pieces against the everlasting rocks and *profile* cliffs of that romantic spot. With evening came the sunshine ; the dancing rills came sparkling and tumbling down the cliffs in rattling joy and sportive frolics, that made him wish everybody could see them, and learn with him to worship Nature, and enjoy her heaven.

August 10. — Left the Notch, and at night slept in Concord, at the quiet home of his spiritual brother Aldrich, and on Sunday, **12th,** lectured three times in the Universalist church of Manches ter, to very large and highly-delighted audiences. But here, as everywhere, as soon as he began to exert an influence, falsehoods were immediately peddled to counteract it, successfully with some, although never injuring him, nor marring his happiness, only as he saw others deterred from examining the, to them and him, most important of all subjects. Here he met many friends, and had one of the best of visits; then whistled along, calling on friends in Boston, where they had more speakers than meetings, in hot weather. 17th, at Plymouth, sailing about the bay, on new vessel, with one hundred and fifty invited guests, mostly ladies. The captain and owner being a spiritualist, of course the Lone One and the ladies had an invitation to a ride, and it was delightful in the fine breeze. 18th, visited Plymouth Rock and Pilgrim Hall, and examined the relics of the colony and his ancestors, and the grave-yard on the hill-top, with its Puritanic epitaphs, and rock head-stones for the saints and the rich ; the graves of the poor he could not find, except the new or recently-made ones. 19th, Sunday, lectured twice in a hall to fine audiences, at this Old Colony home, where once the Puritans had all the religion and control of the station; but intelligence had now almost crowded it under ground, with the dead bodies of those who once defended it with law and force.

August 20. — Return to Boston, and met A. J. Davis and his happy mate at the Fountain House. "Ah, Mary," said he " thy hands are stayed up now, even to reach the home of angels."— " Yes, I am happy, but I feel as if I must not fold my arms to rest, but work for the great cause of emancipation, elevation, purification, and development, for my sex and the race." — " Yes, and may God bless and speed you both in the holy mission of reform in an ungrateful and scornful world."— " Yes," says Jackson, " but the sun shines on those who reach the mountain-top both earlier and later than on those in the valley, and by that means we have begun our heaven here." — " Somehow," says the Lone One, " the sun of the spiritual harmonial home shines in thy soul all the time, lighting and warming it in its inner temple, where the nettle-shaft of slander cannot reach."

August 21. — Resting in the beautiful home of the author of the " Hen Fever," in Wyoming, where hangs the full-length portrait-present of Queen Victoria, and many other ornaments, but, best of all, the happy faces of wife and daughter. The slanders, started so long before at Ripon, and based entirely on the stolen letter and its progeny, had now assumed a shape for newspapers, and were bandied, with his name, about the city papers of Boston and New York, as if they were items of news. Well, many people knew that his reputation must be impaired, or the cause of spiritualism would increase in every place he visited, and such places were not likely to be few. Even the *New York Tribune* soiled its columns with an article from a dirty sheet at Oskosh, Wisconsin, which could not possibly say worse things about him than it did about Greely and his candidates and measures, and with the editor of which they would have been ashamed to be seen in the street, and the columns of which would be **no** authority with the *Tribune* on any subject but against spiritualism. A note from the Lone One inquired of Greely the reason of this slander, and required a correction ; which was readily made, with the **excuse** that it was floating through the press unrefuted. So it ever would have been, in all papers opposed to reform ; **but** the *Tribune*, the *news*paper of so many reformers, ought to have, at least, the slightest evidence before it slandered a person whose whole life, and means, and energies, had been devoted **to reforms ; but** it, on being notified of its position, took back **all it** could, without defending spiritualism, against which one **of its** editors had a religious spite and spleen to **vent.** They ought **to have** known better than to be caught in this trap, **when** they were themselves connected in this same slander **by** a more conservative portion **of** the press. Other papers he did not notice, for he knew many of them were **not** read to find truth, and that few believed what they saw in such secular and sectarian sheets as circulated base **false**hoods, both personal and general, about spiritualists.

22*

August 25. — His wife meets him at Manchester, and they visit the quiet home of Dr. Hanson, where Susan makes every good visitor happy, when she is there. Sunday, 26th, lectured three times in Granite Hall to good audiences, but not as large as in church. 28th, they visit Lowell, and meet A. J. and M. F. Davis, and the four have one of the little social circles, where harmony and happiness flows like a river, from celestial fountains. " Now," said the Lone One to his mate, " I have fulfilled one promise, to introduce you to the happiest man I ever saw, and one of the happiest couples." A. J. D. lectured in the eve, and thus for the first time she heard him speak before an audience. Next they visit his cousin in Lawrence, where she found another happy home and couple.

September 1. — The harmonial four met again in Boston, at the Fountain House. Sunday, 2d, he returns to Lowell, and lectures three times to full hall. Next they visit Salem, and the widow Endicott's neat and happy home; then down to Lynn, and into Dungeon Rock, where the man who has faith in spirits like " a grain of mustard-seed " is trying to remove a mountain of rock off the bodies and treasures of the dead pirates, which legends and spirits say are buried in the cave under the rock. His faith is better than his prospect. Climb the High Rock, and visit the Hutchinsons in their home, and she looks from the tower where he had often been, over the bay and islands and Nahant, &c.; visited Nahant, and heard of the sea-serpent from brother Buffum. 9th, lecture in Lynn, to small audiences, in hot days. Next they visit Chelsea, and Capt. Williams; and Boston, and Alvin Adams; and thus the mate found many of his temporary elegant and happy homes, and best of friends. Walked down Cornhill, and in office, and he introduced her to W. L. Garrison, and thus fulfilled another promise, to introduce her to the most Christ-like man in the nation. She acknowledged both, and enjoyed much these visits and acquaintances. They found also those full-blown souls, J. S. Adams and Hattie. She was soon tired of sights and sounds in Boston; when they retired to the elegant home of his friend in

Wyoming, where she could rest, while he met his appointments to lecture in Stoneham and other places. There, too, they found the excellent and beautiful family of Mr. Mendum, of the *Boston Investigator*, and she had some pleasure in recounting the many years this had been their family paper, and ever esteemed and respected.

Sunday, September 16. — Lecture in Reading to good, but not large audiences. 17th, she returns to Newport, and he spent the week in Boston, Lawrence, and other places, and Sunday at Lowell, — lectured three times. Found some of the Norris family, one of the nephews of Brackett, and Moses, a lawyer of some note in the city, and a Dr. Hook, with whom he schooled in old Gilmanton; but how few were these old acquaintances in New England! 25th, he reached Newport, and was again at the old homestead on the mountain. Visited some friends, and on Sunday, 30th, lectured again in the church, and Miss A. W. Sprague, trance-medium, and an excellent speaker, spoke in evening; had good meetings.

October 3. — He bade adieu to the rocks, and homes, and wife, and boy, in Newport, and leaned westward, toward the son and daughter. But stopped to lecture in Claremont one eve; then to Woodstock, and met the two Randalls, both of whom were now doctors, — once husband and wife *by law*, now free by decree. She of Philadelphia, and he at the old homestead, settled, divided the property, and divorced; but did not quarrel about it.

Sunday, October 7. — Lectured in church at South Woodstock, to very intelligent audience. Next day rode in stage with very intelligent lady, Mrs. Hutchens, a teacher of penmanship, to Barnard, where he met some good friends. Soon passed on to Bethel station, and backed down to Lebanon, New Hampshire, where he had appointments to lecture, and where he found one of his best, pleasantest and happiest homes, at the fine residence of A. Pushe and E. J. Durand, and their wives, all of one family, and one heart; and the happy face of Minnie, the lovely little daughter of Mr. and Mrs. Durand, ever after welcomed him, as one of her friends, to their home full of music. He sang:

> " No roving foot shall crush thee here,
>   No busy hand provoke a tear."

From the beautiful village of Lebanon, and his first but not last visit, he moved to Montpelier, a small, but very aristocratic capital of Vermont, where, on Sunday, Oct. 14, his three audiences were mostly composed of members of the legislature, which gave him three of the most intelligent audiences of the season, to which many words were freely spoken and a fine impression made. Here, for the first time, he met the medium-poetess and teacher, Mrs. Frances O. Hyzer, and her sister Carrie, the seer of beautiful visions. The little huddle of neat cottages, crowded closely on the scanty pattern for a village and capital, fairly stuck into the hillside, and the high hills ready on either side to come down and bury up the place, steeples, aristocracy, and all, when the scriptures shall be fulfilled by the levelling operation, make Montpeliar a romantic and interesting place. Burlington, Vergennes, and Middlebury, each gave or received a call; and East Middlebury took several lectures, while he visited his old friends at the home of L. C. Hyde. The college was firm as a granite rock, and had about as much life and progress as that geological specimen of crystallization. It ought, and, for the good of the race, it might as well, be put away in the cabinet of curiosities, as a fossil of theology, crystallized by science. 19th, had an excellent audience in Vergennes, and much interest; and Sunday, 21st, gave three lectures in Burlington to intelligent and respectable audiences. But the college faculty stood aloof in great dignity, despising the new truths; and Bishop Hopkins, driven on to the romantic point of land-in-the-lake, quaked and shuddered with horror at the near approach of the Devil to so many mediums; and John G. Saxe said funny words in poetry about modern spirits and mediums, but affected great reverence for similar persons and events of Bible times. Poor soul! he will sing more truthfully when the shell breaks, and he, hatched out, can sing and fly at the same time.

The grove-church, in the beautiful and romantic Burlington of Champlain, **was** already leaning toward spiritualism, and the old fogies were running with props and rests to stay its unstable form, and prevent it from going over; but in vain — it had started never **to stop,** and the spirits still **are** watching **and aiding it in the** change. Middlebury took two **lectures,** and a few **of the** wild **students called to hear about** the Devil's doings, or see them, **and** soon found the Devil was in their theology and the professors, **not** in this lecturer. Rutland, **24th,** he met his old friend from **Barnard, with his** daughter, a sister of Belle, bound for Iowa, to teach **and find a new** home with old friends. Parted with her father with **tears, and** he returned to **his home, and soon** after removed to his **new home** over the valley **of** death, while she was far away in Iowa. In the care of the **Lone One, she took** her first ride in the cars from Rutland, Vt., to **Burlington, Iowa,** *via* Troy, N. **Y.,** to the Falls and Wire Bridge, **where her wild** and happy Green **Mountain** heart bounded with joy and admiration of nature's magnificent scenery, **and the** rivalry of **art** in her bridge-contrast. Satisfied with gazing, they mixed **in** the crowd at the dépôt, and were soon passing Canada towns, and over the ferry at Windsor, and at his home with friend Stone **in** Detroit, where they rested over the Holy **Sabbath** for him **to preach, and hear** S. J. Finney, who was then in the city, doing a great work in probing theology.

Monday, 29. — They whistled along, and when Battle Creek sounded from the platform he stepped **off,** and left **the lonely** girl among strangers, far from home, ticketed **from** Vermont to Iowa. "Write me how you get through." — "Certainly;" and the letter came, saying she wept at the thought **of** being alone among strangers **so far from home. A** kind face saw her weep, and came to inquire the **cause, and, on learning it, replied,** "Why, we are going almost **to** Burlington, and came from New England also; **my** son will see to thy trunks, and thee will have no trouble with them;" and thus grief brought relief and good friends, as it often does, even in the cars. Next morning she was in the stage, and **at** noon, at Kossuth, landed **at** the door of her friends, where **a** hearty welcome and a ready school greeted and employed the Vermont girl. The pious guardians of public morals at Ripon and Ceresco probably never heard of this journey and company, or it would have furnished **the best load of** fuel they ever collected for their fires, except **the** stolen letter; yet **he** never saw **the girl** except once at her home and on this journey, but she and all **the** family are eternally **his** friends, as are **all** true **and pure** spirits, who know him **as he is,** a defender everywhere of honesty, **purity,** poverty, and virtue. The glad face of the son soon met **him at the school, and assured** him of **content and** satisfaction with **the new home;** and they renewed arrangements **for a** little cottage in **the old garden-acre of what was once a** part of David Brown's farm, now of Harmonia, and **the home of reformers.** The daughter had closed **her school with entire satisfaction, and returned to their** Ceresco home, where she was mistress of her part **of the** house, and guardian of the effects of the family, but quite lonesome, and not happy in a place where **her** ears **were constantly** greeted with **slander** and gossip about the beings to whom **her soul was** devoted, and bound in stronger ties of filial affection **than ever** existed in the hearts of bigots or the slanderers; for **never was there** a stronger attachment existed between a father and daughter than between these. **At** this time, and ever after, **he** left the standing offer to his enemies, that he would cease preaching spiritualism whenever they would produce **one** family of **five persons,** like his own, in father, mother, **and three** children, three **or more** of whom belonged to an **evangelical church, in which the whole** family were as happy, harmonious, and as much attached **to** each other, as his were; and, as this was the only way they could **reasonably expect** to silence him, some thought they ought **to try,** but those who **knew the** condition and relation of his family knew **it would be a** vain **effort,** for such religion **was** itself a barrier to the happiness they **had attained.** At Jackson and Albion he had a visit with his excellent friend from Detroit, whose soul was in **the** sunlight of Divine truth; his lectures were well attended, especially at Albion, where Mrs. Tuttle **had** done so much work for the angels. At the Michigan Ceresco he met some old friends, and especially one true and tried one of long standing, a citizen of the Wisconsin Ceresco, in A. D. Wright, and also his father's family.

Nov. 9. — Fitted out his son for teaching during winter, and left him to seek a school in Indiana, and moved on his mission to Union City, thence to Coldwater, and met Grace Greenwood, and her mother Clark, and others; then to Adrian, where, Nov. 18th, he gave three lectures, and found his old homes and tried friends, Martins and Chandlers, with ever-open doors, and ready efforts to collect audiences. All his receipts were divided between the mother, and son, and daughter, according to their needs; and he moved steadily on, with the same economy that he had exhibited through life.

Nov. 20. — In Port Huron he began a course of lectures, sent for and sustained by a devoted soul in Dr. Noble; and, on the 28th, returned to Detroit, made a short and ineffectual effort the second time at Pontiac, but it was dark yet in that place. Finney was cultivating Detroit, and he moved on to Ypsilanti, and thence to Ann Arbor. In each found a few good friends, some false ones, and many enemies, and became more satisfied than ever that selfish persons could not become true spiritualists, at least in soul; found a noble soul in his old infidel friend, H. De Garmo, and others in E. Sampson and J. Volland, etc.

Dec. 16, *Sunday.* — Three lectures were well attended in Ann Arbor; many students of the university were in attendance, betraying a liberality not to be found at many colleges. Incidents which occurred in visits and circles might be more interesting than these notices, but this was the public labor of the Lone One, and is given more to show the contrast with his early life and condition than for its interest to the reader.

Sunday, 23. — Lecture three times in Adrian; well received by many and increasing friends. Next stay was in Perrysburgh, Ohio, a beautiful town on the Maumee, above the Toledo of sin and sickness, money and rum, business and confusion. At Perrys-

burgh he found one of the best of homes at Hon. A. Smith's,
and there, while giving a course of lectures, the year died at the
close of Dec. 31st, leaving him in this home not the orphaned and
friendless boy, but the popular and successful lecturer; not the
victim slain by slander and falsehood, but the soul triumphant
over misfortune and persecution, by energy, **and** a clear conscience,
and unvarying toil.   Now he knew that

> " Love is to the human heart
>   What sunshine is to flowers ;
> And friendship is the fairest thing
>   In this cold world of ours."

And

> " When thy struggling **soul hath** conquered,
>   When the path lies fair and clear,
> When thou art prepared for heaven,
>   Thou wilt find that heaven is here."

Section IV.

1856. — COSMOPOLITE. — ITINERATING.

TO THE UNSATISFIED.

Why thus longing, why forever sighing
    For the far-off, unattained, and dim,
While the **beautiful,** all around thee lying,
    Offers up its low **perpetual hymn?**

Wouldst thou listen **to its** gentle teaching,
    All thy restless yearnings it **would** still :
Leaf, and flower, and laden bee, are preaching,
    Thine own sphere, though humble, first to fill

Poor indeed thou must be, if around thee
    Thou **no ray** of light and joy canst throw ;
If no silken cord of love hath bound thee
    To some little world, through weal and **woe** ;

If no dear eye thy fond love can brighten,
    No fond voices answer to thine own ;

> If no brother's sorrow thou canst lighten
>   By daily sympathy and gentle tone.
>
> Not by deeds that win the world's applauses —
>   Not by works that give thee world renown —
> Not by martyrdom, or vaunted crosses,
>   Canst thou win and wear the immortal crown.
>
> Daily struggling, though unloved and lonely,
>   Every day a rich reward will give ;
> Thou wilt find by hearty striving only,
>   **And truly** loving, thou canst truly live.

Jan. 1, 1856. — The Lone One in Ohio, lecturing; the wife
and boy in Newport, N. H., visiting. The eldest son in Indiana,
teaching; the daughter in Ceresco, Wis., in school, at their home,
boarding with Dr. Fletcher, then occupying the house of the Lone
One, but who has since moved to the kingdom of heaven, where
he has not yet begun to keep house, because his wife has not
crossed over yet. Thus one of the best-united families, each
reading letters every week from all the others, began the year far
apart; but we shall call the roll before the year is out, at the
new home. New Year's morning in Perrysburgh; evening in Elyria, where a course of lectures were given to intelligent hearers.

Jan. 8. — Cleveland, and met Cora and Hattie Scott, from Buffalo; Cora had now become one of the finest and best trance-me-
diums of the **nation**, and astonished even believers, often, with her
angelic ministrations. Met the Koons, not from the tree-tops, but
from Athens, and saw the mediumship which brought forth such
wonders at the celebrated " Koons' rooms; " met his devoted
friend, L. E. Barnard, who published for him two thousand copies
of a pamphlet, containing three lectures, which were soon sold,
and a demand for more sent forth; but it could not be answered,
for it was not stereotyped. Met H. F. M. B., still struggling in
bondage, and waiting for freedom impatiently, which she soon after
found, with nothing else but the greater scorn of the deeper stained.

Sunday, 13. — Lecture in church in Ravenna; next, Akron,
and the excellent friends on the hill had a visit; large audiences

attended the call in both villages; next in Cleveland, — small audiences in the evenings; and on Sunday, 27th, in Litchfield, — a full house three times listened to his version of the gospel. Glad faces always meet him in that town with a welcome. Constant calls and lectures, nearly every evening, now occupied his time on the Western Reserve, where the new philosophy was and is as prevalent and well understood as in any part of the nation. The people of that region will ever bear testimony to his success and ability, for there he is well known both as a man and speaker.

At Wellington, February 24th, an impulse was given to the cause that has not been lost, nor is it likely to be; and, on the 25th, he gave the closing lecture of a season course, for a society in Mansfield, which had mostly Christian officers. It was a bitter pill for them, but delightful to the audience, many of whom joined in a call for him to come soon after and give a course; but other engagements prevented then and ever since, but may not always. In Cleveland, March 4th, message from a spirit which escaped by apoplexy from the beautiful form, a young lady, whose body he watched while the spirit was formed and met its parent over the corpse; a stranger to him till the scene occurred, but not after.

February 5. — Met with William Denton and others in convention, at Dayton, and here found some of the best and truest friends he ever found. Gave a course of lectures, and found a course of friends to himself and the angels. We shall not name them here, but *he* will not soon cease to name them. This city, already one of the strongholds, became one of his most important stations, and soon the home of William Denton, one of the ablest and most logical and lucid public defenders of the Harmonial Philosophy. Next visit was at Harveysburg, Warren Co., Ohio. Here he met the poor old man, who, when young, learned to preach, and followed it until he found the doctrine was not true; and they fed him and his family for his labor; and when his honesty compelled him to cease preaching, they turned him off to starve. But he was able to keep souls and bodies together, in his family, by un-wearying toil for scanty pay. At his (Alfred Carders') home he found more love and more poverty than in any home he visited in the West. A lovely daughter, of twenty-two years, was wasting and almost gone with consumption, and to her he bent his steps and words every day; cheered, comforted, consoled, and loved her as **if** she were his own daughter; magnetized her both in body and spirit, and, when he went away, sent a comforter to her from the spirit-friends that visited him from the other sphere, who told her to be of good cheer, and she should soon be with them in heaven. And she was soon with them, and often came to him to thank and bless him for the cheering words in her last days of earth, and to urge him to console and comfort her dear parents. Martha's name often came to him from stranger lips, and often does she visit him when alone, and awaken him from sleep to whisper peace, and joy, and love, from her happy home, where the love she cherished and cultivated here, where she had little else, has made her rich indeed, while many are poor about her who had much else, and little or no love, while here. The happy and excellent home of Valentine Nicholson cannot be forgotten either by this or other visitors who have found its pleasant atmosphere and breathed it.

March 15. — The journal says, Lecture in the dark pit; but it must be a mistake; although no doubt he will, if the orthodox enemies succeed in sending him there. It was in Waynesville he lectured, and that is not very near the pit, although they have been using brimstone in their pulpits many years, and it is dark as Egypt theologically and metaphysically, and will ever be so while it depends on brimstone light from pulpits. Gave a course of lectures in Marion, in a church, to large audiences, and planted the cause permanently there. Next course was given in a Methodist church in Geneva, Ohio, to good audiences of intelligent hearers. Found excellent homes and best of friends in Jefferson, at the homes of Hon. B. F. Wade and Joshua R. Giddings, whose liberality and intelligence had led them early to investigate this philosophy and embrace it. At Andover, Ohio, a full course of lectures, in a church, met the demand, and supplied it well. Here the priests came to hear and talk, but they soon found they had the hot end of the stick, and quickly let it go and set their devil on, while they ran off shouting "Free-Love," because that was the best subject to arouse the mob-guardians of public morals. But there is not enough liquor used in Ashtabula Co., Ohio, to enable the haters of reform to get up a mob. The most quiet and orderly audiences ever attend lectures in this county; for it has a **most intelligent and liberal** population, equalled by very few counties in the nation. Visited several old stations, and lectured successfully everywhere. The demand ever increased for his services. Made new points continually, and among the important and permanent ones was Milan, one of the most beautiful villages in the state, and with a very intelligent population, and hence well fitted for the new philosophy. Here he found several families of the best friends he met in the state, and ever after loved to visit the place. Honest, earnest, devoted, and unswerving in the cause, **were some of** the friends here, and hence the work went steadily **on.**

Sunday, May 4. — Lectured in church at Clyde, and stationed with an excellent brother, the Universalist preacher (Mr. **Brown**). Found him a true man, and a real philanthropist in deed, rather than in word. Made a point at Frémont, with a firm and true friend in Judge **Justice.**

May 8. — Landed at his Adrian home, at the foot of the hill, where a neat house, and open door, and cordial greeting, were ever ready. Here he met his son, whose schools had closed, and with him visited the university at Ann Arbor; and on the 12th they reached their new home, and laid out the plans and work of building **the** house, etc. Hardened his hands to labor, and rested the brain for a time, but lectured Sundays, and occasionally evenings. Visited Allegan and Otsego, and gave lectures in each.

June 6. — Deliver address at commencement. Had a fine day, and excellent time and exercises, and many friends from a distance in attendance ; among them his excellent and much-esteemed medium-friend from Detroit, whose soul dwelt still in the sunshine of the spheres.

On the 7th he was in Chicago, at the home of his Higgins brother ; and Sunday, the 8th, lectured twice in Harmony Hall ; and on the 10th reached his Ceresco home, and anxious and loving daughter, whose overjoyed heart bounded with unspeakable **joy**. As she sprang to embrace him when he alighted from the stage, the driver held up to let the passengers see the expression, then remarked to them,

"That 's the Free-Love home ! They are free lovers ! "

A laugh on the passing winds swept by. But he took no notice of the remark ; for he had learned Sir Walter Scott's rule of conversation, which many others ought to learn. Thus :

> " Conversation is but carving :
> Give to each guest just enough ;
> Let him neither starve nor stuff ;
> Give him always of the prime,
> And but a little at a time."

The family to whom he had leased his house had moved out of it, and out of the state ; and his agent had rented a part of the tenement to two widowed sisters, a few weeks before his return. This furnished ample material for the Christians and loafers to make up the report, and circulate it, that he had taken his wife to her friends and abandoned her, and returned to live with these two widows, because they too were spiritualists, and of his acquaintances. The story took well with the Christian endorsement, but soon died, like all the others, none of which had a better foundation; but it lasted a few weeks, with a modification that charged him with giving them the rent, and staying with them nights while there ; which, although his daughter was there all the time, was negatived by the facts that they paid the rent in full to the agent, and he did not stay in the house a single night, nor more than one evening till ten o'clock, during his stay in the place, which was shortened to the least time necessary to pack up and dispose of his goods and business, for a move. But it was of no consequence about the facts. Like the wolf and lamb, in the fable, when the wolf accused the lamb of contaminating the water which the wolf was about to drink, " Ah !" said the lamb, " but it runs from you to me!" — " No matter ; your ancestors were guilty, and you must pay the penalty by death." So of him ; no matter whether true or not, he is a spiritualist, and must be slandered. How could he prove he had not taken his wife to her friends and left her, and now come to sell his goods and move away? Of course he had broken up housekeeping, and his family was destroyed, showing one more of the terrible effects of spiritualism. But on Sunday, June 15, many of his old friends collected to hear him lecture, and grieved at his moving away from the valley. One more incident at this time furnished also material for abuse and falsehood, most of which, in this case, came from the side of those who chanced to be " Free Lovers ; " for he received as heavy shots from that side as from the other. A fine, intelligent girl of fourteen, a schoolmate of his daughter, whose father was in the spirit-world, and mother a cripple, on charity, was struggling day and night to keep her place in school, by taking washing, or any honorable work. A temporary citizen, who came to sojourn with a fine-looking and intelligent lady-companion, both strangers to the Lone One, had been coaxing and teasing this girl to leave her school and go with him, as an " affinity," to the new home in prospect in Kansas. She had not consented, but her destitute situation, and want of sympathy and love, had some influence in his favor, and she communicated the facts to her friend, the daughter of the Lone One, who implored her father to try to save and aid her ; which he at once did successfully, bringing from her the expression, in tears, " You are the first man that ever talked to me like a father since mine died !" and this she often after remarked to others. She broke the magnetic chord of the stranger, who was very angry at the one who caused it, impugning his motives, and charging him with the same object himself had in view. This made a good story, and ran wide and well, and all the better because it came from an enemy of marriage. But he saved the girl, and had and still has her blessings, and those of her spirit-father and earthly mother; and, what was more to him, the deeper devotion of his daughter, who ever esteemed and loved the girl as a sister. He directed her to go to her friends and stay till he could find means and a place for her in his family and **the** school, where she could complete her education; and, although he did not see her again for more than a year, yet, by correspondence and the little aid he could afford her, she kept steadily the course he advised, ever feeling towards him the affection of a child.* This was one of the basest acts of his life in the eyes of his enemies, and one that afforded him much joy and satisfaction, and brought him the approbation of angels; **as did** many others that brought curses and slander on earth.

On the 19th he and his daughter bade adieu to the valley, and its scenes, and citizens, and with a load of movable effects reached the cars at Waupen, and via Iron Ridge soon reached Milwaukie. Thence by boat to Chicago, where the goods were sent forward to the reach of the son at Harmonia, while the father and daughter stayed in Chicago, for him to give a course of lectures to small but intelligent audiences. Here the daughter also found a home, and the best of friends, with the Judson and Mary Higgins.

June 30. — The daughter and father reached the new home, and met the happy son. She was pleased, and many who met her loved her, as her friends do everywhere; for she had much of the ardent, enthusiastic, and affectionate spirit of her father, and was ever said to be like him. She ever was his pet, fond and playful as a child with him, even to womanhood. She was soon in the new garden, harvesting the **ripe fruit,** happy and highly pleased with the prospect of a new home, where she hoped the slanders of the Ripon loafers would not reach her ears; for she was still sensitive, although she saw that they had no effect on her father, and that he was the happiest man whom she ever saw.

* She is now in his family, with his daughter.

Once more the Lone One took up the laboring oar, and doubled teams with his son, to urge on the work on the new house (a small cottage, sufficient to answer until he could sell the Wisconsin home). Early and late he toiled, and hardened to labor, until July 11th, when again, with the daughter, he journeyed onward to Adrian. Of all the good friends who urged him to leave the daughter with them, while he went East for the mother, he selected the one at the neat little home at the foot of the hill, in Adrian, where the demand for children was greater than the supply, — a reverse of the usual condition in marriage, — and where the age **had** long since put an end to all expectation of little ones. Here he left her with a real aunt and uncle, whose kindness never will be forgotten by father or daughter, while memory allows such acts to last.

Sunday, July 13. — Lectured in Adrian to good audiences, and on Monday returned to his son and the new home, where he toiled on till July 23d. Thence over the way to Burlington, Vt., where **he met** the old friends, and on Sunday, the 27th, lectured in that fine town to a small audience. Met the warmest and best reception he ever met in the place, and on the 29th he reached his wife and boy, at the mountain home in Newport, happy as happy could be, at the expected meeting. The relatives glad and happy to see him, all except the brother, whose religious zeal was bordering on **frenzy, and had almost** destroyed his naturally kind heart and good humor.

Sunday, Aug. 3. — Lectured in the chapel in the village, where more pride and ignorance than knowledge and wisdom prevented many from attending. But the few did hear, and understand, and **the** good seed was sown. The ball set in motion, the car moved on.

Sunday, Aug. 10. — Three lectures in Unitarian church in Athol, Mass., to large, intelligent, and attentive audiences, and left with many blessings, and requests to return soon as possible. Boston, Chelsea, Mt. Auburn, &c., had his time and attention for a **few days,** with excellent friends and best of fare, till the 14th, when a grove was his canopy, a picnic party his audience, from Lowell and Lawrence — happy day, soon lost from all but memory.

Sunday, Aug. 17. — A large hall in Lawrence was well filled three times, to listen to his words on the life to come after this. Lowell was next the resting-place, at the home of J. **F. Evans,** where we left him when we finished this narrative, in September, 1857.

On Sunday, 24th, three audiences collected, the last in Huntington Hall, where more then eighteen hundred people assembled to listen to the voice of the Lone One, the same poor, despised orphan of the mountains. But this was not the largest, for he had several times addressed over two thousand people, and felt appreciated by his audiences. Made many new friends at Lowell, at this visit, and then left them for Manchester, where he mingled with the great political crowd for a day ; then moved to Concord, to meet his wife and boy, and go on to Lebanon, to the happy home before referred to, and to meet there several evening appointments.

Aug. 29, 30, 31. — Quartered with the preacher at South Royalton, Vt., where they attended, and he took active part in the state convention of spiritualists and mediums ; and to them, and many others, it was the happiest meeting of their life. Fifteen hundred people with every chord of their beings beating in harmony and happiness is not a scene often met with in this turbulent world ; but it could be seen on Sunday at this convention. It was a tearful parting to some, but not consequently unhappy. They went to their homes better, and happier, for this glorious time of spiritual feasting. Many speakers and mediums were in attendance, and none more happy, and gladly received, than the Lone One. O, what a contrast in his life, and what still greater contrast between the feelings of these appreciating friends and the slandering enemies of him ! The angels were ever with him, and approving his life and actions, and most those acts which the enemies most vilified. Next they spent a week in a visit at the beautiful Eden home of his friend in Essex, while he lectured in Williston,

Essex, and Burlington; and she rested, for the long level of track and water, over which they made rapid speed, and pleasant trip, to Detroit, to meet again that best of friends, the Landlord-spiritualist.

Sept. 11. — The three were in Battle Creek, all safe; and soon the fourth, the eldest son, was with his mother and brother — a joyous group, with the daughter still out, but near, and soon to come into the renewed family circle in the new home. The house was not yet in readiness, and again his hands were in the work, pressing **it to** completion, aiding the son and workmen. All covered with rags and mortar, one day, while plastering his house (for this he did himself), he was called by the professor to go over to his room, and meet a stranger who had called to see him. Without a change he walked to the room, and met a professor of a medical college, who had heard him lecture, and admired him, and called to see him. It was a fine joke, and enjoyed by both then, and at a subsequent meeting, when he was again on duty.

"Now," said the professor, "I see why you are the favorite with the masses. You do not despise toil, and cannot be ashamed of any man, however low his place or calling." — "That is so," he replied, "and I must tell you how I sometimes talk to people. I called on a friend in the East not long ago, who was a hard-working man, with near a dozen children, and large farm well stocked. His first wife had been worn out by hard work and raising babies, — mostly by the latter, — and I asked him what he lived *for*." — "You tell," said he. — "Well," said I, "if you make me tell, I must judge by appearances; and I should say to work, to eat, to sleep, to raise children, to get rich, then die and rot and be forgotten, except by the children, half of whom will curse you for bringing them into existence (for they will lay it to you, and not to God), with diseased bodies, to drag out a miserable existence here, and then die also, and be forgotten, except by perhaps other poor diseased children." — "Well, what's the remedy?" said he. — "Why, stop raising children, when you have more than enough already, and teach them, and yourselves, what to eat, and

live on half the expense, by throwing out of the catalogue tobacco
tea, coffee, pork, pepper, and most other condiments and meats,
and live temperate, sober, and godly lives, and not work half as
hard, and feel twice as well." — "That is it," said the professor.
" I wish you would talk thus to all who need such lessons."
— " But they will not hear it ; for either lust and sensualism, or
religion, are in the way, and few can give up the foods and drinks
that keep up the fires of lust and passion, and such do not know
the joy of pure lives." — " True, true ; but what a work we have
to do ! " — " Yes, but you see I am a mason, but not a *free* one,
to-day, and now my worship is work." — " Yes, and I will not
detain you longer ; so good-day, and success."

Crowding forward the house by day ; lecturing in evenings to
students, and others, mainly on diet and regimen, etc.

October 4, 5. — Attends the yearly meeting of Friends of
Human Progress at Battle Creek. Much pleased ; took active
part and much interest ; spiritualism a ruling element in the
meeting, and H. C. Wright a prominent actor ; much pleased
with him — liked him more and more as he became better acquainted with him and his motives. He took very little part in
the great national campaign excitement now agitating the people,
yet felt an interest in the issue, but did not expect the results to be
such as the opposing parties contended for ; for well he knew that,
other causes being much deeper than political excitement, were
already working out results and changes for the future of the
nation ; and well he knew that measures were proceeding in the
spirit-world to effect a complete disintegration of parties and societies in this, both political and religious, to result in a complete
individualization and sovereignty, preparatory to a higher order
of life and harmony on earth, in connection with the spirit-spheres.

October 14. — Reached home with the daughter, and the happy
family were all together at the *real* Harmonia home of Mr. Cornell, where they were ever cared for as his own family, until the
new house was ready to receive them. Each Sabbath he met an
appointment at some town, and during the week toiled early and

late on his house, till October 27, when it was dedicated as the cottage home, and warmed by the happy faces of the young friends, and soon after became one of the happiest homes in the nation , for it was and is the home of true spiritualists, to which each reader of this narrative is cordially invited to " come and see."

November 4. — The great national struggle came to a crisis, and broke. He dropped his vote into the crowd, where it fell still as a snow-flake, and counted one, and then pursued his labor in a snow-storm, with the son, collecting and setting apple-trees presented to him by an excellent friend, which he found in H. Willis.

November 7. — Lodged in Chicago, and Sunday, 9th, lectured three times in the commercial whirlpool, to small audiences — no excitement. At Elgin, Dagget's home and a good church were open to him, and he used them. Found hearts and hands ready and willing to aid the onward march of the car of progress in that beautiful and thriving town on the Fox River.

November 16. — Met H. C. Wright at Rockford, and had a pleasant and happy visit ; but Henry did the talking, according to appointment.

November 23. — Closed a course of lectures in Mendota, to good audiences, and warm friends of him and the cause. Found it an excellent point for the new gospel, and a poor one for the old. Backed up to Waukegan next, and had a fine visit and audiences. Spent the snow-storm days in Milwaukie, and met Emma F. Jay, with her last name almost changed. Also met that executive pioneer, Joel Tiffany, the sunny face of Ex-Gov. Tallmadge, and, happiest of all, Dr. Greves, and many old friends of his, who were also, of course, friends of the angels. Lectured but once, and returned to Waukegan, and met his old and true friend Dr. Haskell ; then to Chicago, and in circle at the magnificent home of Dan Richmond, the man who was able and willing to make spiritualism popular and respectable in that city, if wealth and business talent could give it that position. Via Michigan city to La Fayette, Ia., and at the new home of those bold defenders of reform, Dr. Stockham, and Alice B. Stockham, the wife, and also the M. D., whose ambition and enterprise had induced her to study through the Medical College at Cincinnati, **closely** after Carrie. She and her husband had taken **up** the loose ends of reform in **this** town, and were already making **progress**, and removing obstacles from the way of lecturers. He also found the quiet home of John O. Wattles a few miles **distant, and** the fine old homestead of Dr. Welsh at Weau station, **and soon** found good and true hearts were not scarce in the land **of the** Hoosiers. **Next at Dr. Shaw's, in Indianapolis**; but this was the capital **of the fine** state, and of course fashion, and pride, and ignorance, used bigotry for knowledge, to rule **by,** and turned up its noses at reforms or reformers, -- especially reforms in religion, -- **for they had** Abraham for **their** father, **and** Moses for their law-giver, and wanted no better. All else was heresy, and of course he could not make a point of importance here yet. One lecture and **a few hearers was all.**

December 21. -- Closed course of lectures and fine long visit at Dayton, Ohio, where old and new friends were, as ever, glad to **meet** him. Next at Richmond, **where the** straight-line Quakers were already committeeing **out** their members from society for believing in a spirit-world, and that it was at hand, as Jesus said it was in his day on earth.

Sunday, **28.** -- Two lectures to large audiences, in Cincinnati, closed the visit and business, to back up to Richmond, and lecture **once** more to the Quaker stock of that neat little city of plain **style** and excellent people; then to the capital again, and by extra efforts of Dr. Shaw and the spirits be saved from a typhoid fever, with which he was threatened. **But they** succeeded in two days in turning it off, and barely saved him while the old year died and was gathered to its fathers, leaving the Lone One, on the night of December 31st, in the chamber of Dr. Shaw, alive, but restless with pain and fever. Then it bade its friend, the Lone One, farewell. " Farewell ! " came the answer.

" Soon my task will be completed,
Soon your footsteps I shall follow

To the islands of the blessed,
To the kingdom of Ponemah,
To the land of the hereafter ! ''

BY THE GREEN MOUNTAIN BARD.

There have been noble men, whose highest, holiest thoughts
Were born in solitude.
Alone in some vast wilderness they wandered forth,
And there communed with nature, until
Its inspiration roused the slumbering soul,
And from its depths brought forth some glorious vision,
Fairer than earth's creation, which in a higher world
Shall yet be realized.   For what the soul creates
To the soul's realm belongs, and never can be more
Than dimly shadowed forth on earth, where
Skilful hands are ever ready to embody in external things
Its high imaginings.   And such are they
For whom the earth hath no companionship.
They mingle with the world, but are not of it.   With hearts
All formed for sympathy and filled with highest love,
They stand alone.   Alone ! because inflexible in truth and virtue.
Alone ! because the inward voice can never yield
Its sense of right to the great world's applause.
Alone ! because the clamorous multitude will never grant
The meed of praise to virtues not their own.
And yet not all alone.   For ever to the heart thus throned
In solitude kind spirits minister, outpouring high
And glorious thoughts, and kindling sweet emotions in the soul,
Until it revels in the light of heaven, and slakes its thirst
In its undying founts, whose crystal waters back reflect the light of trut
  and wisdom.

Section V.

1857. — FRACTIONAL YEAR, AND RETURN OF WANDERER TO THE HAPPY HOME. — A VOICE FROM HOME.

" Thou art not here ! 't is spoken still
 Within the forest shade ;
'T is murmured by the babbling rill,
 'T is whispered through the glade ;

At even's calm, when twilight broods,
  And silence fills the air,
The gloomy shadows of the woods
  Tell **me** thou art not here !

" And ever as I **trace the way**
  By woodland or **by stream,** —
The haunts of many a happy day,
  Of many **a** happy dream, —
As, lingering by the rustic seat,
  Or antique bridge so near,
My heart doth quicker, wilder beat,
  I feel thou art not here !

" Yet wood, and brake, and running stream,
  Are green, and fair, and bright ;
The sun smiles forth a welcome beam,
  And glad scenes meet my sight.
The birds, the winds, commingling song,
  Steal on my anxious ear ;
But even music's charm hath gone —
  Alas ! thou art not here ! "

Echo from the south :

" Alas ! alas ! doth hope deceive us?
  Shall friendship, love — shall all those ties
That bind a moment, and then leave us,
  Be found again where nothing dies ?
O, if no other boon were given,
  To keep our hearts from wrong and stain,
Who would not try to win a heaven,
  Where all we love shall live again ! "

Jan. 1, 1857. — The sick year died, and the sick man recovered, and closed the visit at the capital with the kind family, and whistled out to Knightstown and lectured twice on Sunday ; then to that handsomest town in Indiana, Terre Haute, where the fine home of **T. A.** Madison received him cordially, and the church door opened for him, and the people came in good numbers to listen to the gospel of the Lone One, surrounded by angels, and cheered on by a "great cloud of witnesses, unseen, though near."

January 9. — Crossed the river and entered St. Louis; coasted about the city; called on many friends, and among them one family of long and lasting friendship, with whom he had boarded at the capital of Wisconsin several winters. **Spent** some pleasant hours with these, N. and M., both of whom were among his most devoted friends. Lectured on Sunday to large audiences, and several evenings to less numbers. Closed the course, and gave one on temperance on Sunday, the 18th, and, on the 20th, recrossed the river through crowded ice, and in freezing cold, and whistled along the path where cold is no obstruction, to Cairo, and at **night** bedded in a state-room on the steamboat Illinois, bound for **Memphis.** One hundred and fifty passengers, or more, nearly as many cattle below, and heaps of flour, made up the loading of the noble boat; and she started and paddled slowly her way through the floating ice till within thirty or forty miles of Memphis, when **the ice** had the track, and would not switch off for her to pass; there she laid up till the passage to Memphis, usually of twenty-**four hours, was lengthened to** thirteen days. Once only the heart **of the Lone One** quaked for a moment. It was night, — near morn, — dark as the darkest; the passengers and crew were in the world of sleep, all save the watch and the Lone One; he was on the guard of the boat, early risen, to observe and listen to the breaking and crashing of the ice, which was giving way to the rain and current. The boat was out in the stream, fastened only by **ice. Nearer** and nearer the crashing and breaking appeared. No object could be seen beyond the lights, which were dim and nearly tapered into morning. The boat started, and with terrific crashing, and cracking, and creaking, she moved rapidly down the current. The officers were soon out, but nothing could be done for her but to let her drift with the ice and current, in total darkness. Every moment she seemed going to pieces to him who was not accustomed to the battles with ice and stream. But short was the time. She was soon fast, hard aground, with bow high up on heaps of ice at the shore, and the torch-lights soon showed them they could step on shore from the boat. Few of the passengers knew of the peril till all was over. But the orphan, who had not intended to bed his body in the drifts of the Mississippi, was on the alert, not in terror, but calmly watching passing events in which he felt deeply interested. They had plenty of time to get her off before the ice opened in the river below to let her through. On this and other boats he found greater varieties of people than he had ever before met. The Southern planter was there, generous, open, frank, free, intelligent. The Yankee, from away down East; the Western banker and trader, full of brag and tricks. The gambler, open and generous, and ready to fight or to treat you. The cattle-trader, cool, sober, calculating on his profits and losses. The boat's officers, gentlemanly and pleasant to passengers of all kinds, but terrible and savage to the hands under pay, swearing oaths that would start all but the ice. Ladies of as great a variety; wives, sisters, daughters, mothers, and even the concert-singers, the Riley Family, in glee and song, were there, full of music, with a comic addition from New Hampshire in the genius of Connor. "Is your name ———?" said a voice from the corn-crib below, one day, as he was wandering among the machinery of the boat. — "It is." — "I thought I knew you; father and I boarded with you up in the woods at the old saw-mill, in South-port, and do you remember me?" — "Yes, and your father, **too**; but what are you doing here?" — "Feeding these cattle. I get fifty dollars and my fare to feed them down, and fare back, — have a farm in Iowa, and this is the way I am improving it. Come down and tell me your history, and let us talk over old times." So they did lead out some of their histories. When the days had numbered the baker's dozen, the ice softened, and the Illinois broke her path through, followed by four other anxious and waiting boats, and hailed from below by the officers and passengers of sixteen boats all waiting to get up river. Some with guns, and some with shouts, expressed their joy; but the Illinois passed quietly on to Memphis, and soon further down even to the crescent city; but the Lone

One went on shore at Memphis, and soon found new friends and a hearty welcome as a lecturer. Homed with the celebrated Dr Gilbert, of cancer-cure notoriety, where wealth and kindness both met the Lone One. Gave a short course of lectures; was well paid.

February 9. — Took passage for New Orleans on S. B. Moses, McLelland, with pleasant officers and passengers from Ohio River, mostly from Indiana ; moved majestically down the mighty river, along the banks of which he viewed the splendid palaces and rows of slave shanties. The magnificence of the feudal castles of the middle ages, with the hovels of worse than serfdom in contrast. The towns and cities much like those of the North, leaving the great contrast between North and South mainly in the rural districts. It was an interesting sight and subject, and made its picture on the memory of the Lone One indelibly, from which it may some day be taken off on paper, but not here.

February 13. — The boat up to the wharf, and the passengers were soon in the omnibus-city of New Orleans, where friends, not a few, were ready to greet, and expecting, him. A score of letters awaited him at the post-office, and magnificent homes were opened for his stay. Sunny as a summer-time were the days and faces around him ; fine audiences assembled in a neat hall to hear his words, and pressing invitations urged him from place to place, but all in temperate, moral, and consistent company, and exhibitions. No theatre or gaming-house was visited by him during his stay ; but all the interesting places of business and art had a passing notice. Found several old friends in the city, and **one who** had shared with him in the Phalanx struggles, then a young man, now a citizen with wife and babies, living happily and temperately in New Orleans. The city was full of life, and business, and strangers, and the gardens rich with flowers, as the parlors, and sometimes the streets, were with silks and doeskins, beavers and bonnets. Near a dozen lectures; more homes, and still more visits ; much pleasant conversation ; many friends, and pressing entreaties to return, and ample pay for the journey, were all realized; and on the second of March he ticketed over the back track to Memphis, loaded with bouquets of elegant flowers, took the steamboat Virginia, to breast the current northward; and sailed with fine weather, but had one terrible squall, with rain and hail like shot from a loaded gun, from which they escaped damage and danger by tieing up to a tree, on the lee bank, just in time to escape a capsizing or a complete destruction. No other important event occurred on the upward course. The Lone One watched the gamblers till he was tolerably well acquainted with their "poker" game, and saw how the sober and shrewd ones caught the green and dissipated ones; but he had never bet, and never would his principles allow him to take part in games for money. An old black man, nearly blind, was one day put on the boat to change places; with solemn and sorry countenance he sat on a stool near a stove-pipe on the guard of the boat. Early in the morning the Lone One observed his sorry face, and thought of his own early life. When no one was in sight he passed him, and placed a half-dollar in his hand without a word, when the sorry face, stammering, accosted him : " Massa, — massa, — don't you want — buy — somebody ? " — " I am a poor man," was the only reply, as he passed, and suppressed the tear by turning to other scenes. He never read Uncle Tom's Cabin, and probably never will. He made, on the boat, the acquaintance of a cotton-planter of Tennessee, whose generous heart, and beautiful and intelligent daughter, urged him to visit their home at Nashville. His cotton-farm was on the river below Memphis, where he said he worked about three hundred negroes, and where they earned him, on an average, three hundred and fifty dollars each, per year; but he said he was ever careful to have a kind overseer, to have them well fed and clad, and all their wants cared for, and they seemed as happy as the cotton-spinners of New England, but not so intelligent. Still, he thought Tennessee as a state might have her interests advanced by abandoning slavery. So many think in Kentucky, and Virginia, and Missouri, but few in Louisiana or Mississippi, &c.

Lectured on the steamboat President; chatted with the preachers,

&c. ; and passed Cairo, and reached the floating-ice, and at length St. Louis, on the 12th. Soon he was again with old friends.

Sunday, 15. — The hall was well filled, and his discourse well received as ever. He was ever appreciated in St. Louis. Took the snaky path of the iron horse, and stopped over at Alton, Terre Haute, La Fayette, and Richmond. Lecturing three times in the court-house at La Fayette, March 22d, and evenings in the other places, and three times in Cincinnati, on Sunday, 29th ; then rested over one week at Dayton, Ohio. Met William Denton, and many other true friends and true reformers, and closed his lectures on the 5th of April, and soon was at another excellent **home in** Milan, where another week was used up in the best of company, with lectures to fine and attentive audiences. Next in Cleveland, with two lectures on Sunday, April 19th, to large audiences; then at Grafton, Liverpool, and on Sunday, 26th, in Wellington, where he met large audiences. Everywhere the cause seemed to be on the increase, and fast gaining with, and in, the best of minds and families. During his winter sojourn in Ohio, in 1856, he delivered one hundred and eighteen lectures in one hundred and thirty-two consecutive days ; but in this last visit he had travelled much more, **and** lectured less frequently, losing much time on the river, and South, where people are not so much in a hurry for religion, and **where they never take the** kingdom of heaven by storm, if they do anything **else.** Closed his visit in Ohio with April, and on May-day reached Adrian, and found the ever-welcoming hearts of friends ready to meet him.

May 3. — Lectured in Adrian, and stopping on the way at Raisin, **to** magnetize **a** sick patient for two days, on the 6th reached his cottage home, where the glad hearts gathered around **him to** listen to his words of love and wisdom, for he had both to distribute.

Here we shall tie up this line, although he only remained a few weeks, and left again for the East, on a tour of lecturing, and, for aught we **know, is** wandering still, turning a corner at home two or three times **a year.** " If you were **my** husband, ' said a woman, "I would get a divorce, if you would not stay at home with me."—"Perhaps not, madam. If I am as bad as my enemies say I am, it must be a great blessing to my wife to have me always absent from home." — "Well, then, I would certainly have a divorce." — "That would be right, **madam; but it** is lucky that I am not your husband : **you are saved that** trouble."

"Where is he now?" said a voice, the first of June, '57. — **At** the quiet, happy, **and** beautiful **home of** E. Rulon, at Raisin, Michigan, **writing in a** book. "**Where is** he now?" said a voice on the Fourth of July.— "In Buffalo, amusing himself with the folly of those who are showing off the **monkey-tricks of a** military parade." — "Where next will he rest?" said an inquirer, deep down in July. — "At the Garden-of-Eden home, in Essex, **Vt.**"—"Then he will see A. J. **Davis** and Mary." **So he** did, at Burlington. Do not think he was idle all this time; for he is never idle, as his enemies well know.

Aug. 20. — "Where is he now?" said a pleasant voice at the West. — In the little bed-room at the old homestead of his wife, where she spent so many happy hours in her days of girlhood, writing in a book. "Let him go; he is a strange man."—"But why don't he stay at home like other folks, and work for a **liv**ing?"— Let him answer; I cannot. **But you may** write for him what the angel did :

> "Abou Ben Adhem (may his tribe increase !)
>   Awoke one night from a deep dream of peace,
>   And saw within the moonlight in his room,
>   Making it rich, and like the lily in bloom,
>   An angel writing in a book of gold ;
>   Exceeding peace had made Ben Adhem bold
>   And to the presence in the room he said,
>   'What writest thou?' The vision raised his head,
>   And, with a look made of all sweet accord,
>   Answered, 'The names of those who love the Lord.'
>   'And is mine one?' said Abou. 'Nay, not so,'
>   Replied the angel. Abou spoke more low,

But cheerily still, and said, ' I pray thee, then,
Write me as one that loves his fellow-men.'
The angel wrote and vanished.   The next night
He came again, with a great waking light,
And showed the names whom love of God had blest,
When, lo ! Ben Adhem's name led all the rest ! "

Life's journey now is well begun,
And will not close with setting sun,
But through the future swiftly run.

Section VI.

SUPPLEMENTAL AND CONCLUSIVE.

IF I WERE A VOICE.

If I were a voice, a persuasive voice,
    That could travel the wide world through,
I would fly on the beams of the morning light,
And speak to men with a gentle might,
    And tell them to be true.
I would fly, I would fly over land and sea,
Wherever a human heart might be,
Telling a tale or singing a song
In praise of the right, in blame of the wrong.

If I were a voice, a consoling voice,
    I 'd fly on the wings of air ;
The homes of sorrow and guilt I 'd seek,
And calm and truthful words I 'd speak,
    To save them from despair.
I would fly, I would fly o'er the crowded town,
And drop like the happy sunlight down
Into the hearts of suffering men,
And teach them to look up again.

If I were a voice, a convincing voice,
    I 'd travel with the wind ;
And wherever I saw a nation torn
By warfare, jealousy, spite, or scorn,
    Or hatred of their kind,

LIFE-LINE OF THE LONE ONE.

I would fly, I would fly on the thunder-crash,
And into their blinded bosoms flash ;
Then, with their evil thoughts subdued,
I 'd teach them Christian Brotherhood.

If I were a voice, an immortal voice,
  I would fly the earth around,
And wherever man to idols bowed
I 'd publish in notes both long and loud
  The Gospel's joyful sound.
I would fly, I would fly on the wings of day,
 Proclaiming peace on my world-wide way,
Bidding the saddened earth rejoice —
If I were a voice — an immortal voice !

THE WORLD WOULD BE THE BETTER FOR IT.

If men cared less for wealth and fame,
  And less for battle-fields and glory ;
If writ in human hearts a name
  Seemed better than in song and story ;
If men, instead of nursing pride,
  Would learn to hate it, and abhor it —
      If more relied
      On Love to guide,
  The world would be **the better for it.**

If men dealt less in stocks and lands,
  And more in bonds and deeds fraternal ;
If Love's work had more willing hands
  To link **this world to** the supernal ;
If men stored **up Love's oil and wine,**
  And on bruised **human** hearts **would pour it**
      If " yours " and " mine "
      Would once combine,
  The world would be the better for it.

If more would ACT the play of Life,
  And fewer spoil it in rehearsal ;
If Bigotry would sheath its knife
  Till Good became more universal ;

> If Custom, gray with ages grown,
> Had fewer blind men to adore it —
>> If talent shone
>> In Truth alone,
> The world would be the better for it.
>
> If men were wise in little things,
> Affecting less in all their dealings ;
> If hearts had fewer rusted strings
> To isolate their kindly feelings ;
> If men, when Wrong beats down the Right,
> Would strike together and restore it —
>> If Right made Might
>> In every fight,
> The world would be the better for it.

We never did inquire into the causes or circumstances which gave rise to the birth of the Lone One, nor did we accept any dream-interpretation of its mysterious origin. There is little doubt that, like most unwelcome births, both in and out of legal wedlock, it had its origin in the condition of body produced by the use of tobacco, liquors, coffee, tea, and animal food ; for it has been fully established by physiology that, without these, men and women cannot long be improperly addicted to that passional indulgence which leads to such unpleasant, and often painful, results ; and these are also ascertained to be the causes, together with out-door exercise, of the wide difference in the passional and lustful condition of males and females, giving a great preponderance to the former. Beginning this line at the obscure end, we have seen the appropriateness of the lines of J. G. Saxe :

> " Of all the notable things on earth,
> The queerest one is the pride of birth,
>> Among our ' fierce Democracy ! '
> A bridge across a hundred years,
> Without a prop to save it from sneers,
> Not even a couple of rotten Peers.
> A thing for laughter, fleers, and jeers,
>> Is American aristocracy.

" Depend upon it, my snobbish friend,
Your family thread you can't ascend,
Without good reason to apprehend
You may find it waxed at the further end
  By some plebeian vocation !
Or, worse than that, your boasted line
May end in a loop of stronger twine
  That plagued some worthy relation !

" Because you flourish in worldly affairs,
Don't be haughty and put on airs,
  With insolent pride of station !
Don't be proud, and turn up your nose
At poorer people with plainer clothes,
But learn, **for the sake of your mind's repose,**
That wealth 's a bauble that comes and goes,
And that proud flesh, wherever it grows,
  Is subject to irritation.''

And, approaching the other end, we **have** found **the Harmonized**
and happy soul and family in the true spiritualist ; and we **have**
found that spiritualism, **or the** Harmonial Philosophy, is the
cause. Spiritualism **as a** belief, or knowledge of facts, may be a
philosophy ; but spiritualism **as** a religion, **as a** practical thing
of life, **and** manifestation, **is a reform in** life, and exhibits itself
in a reformation **of body and actions.** Every true spiritualist will
strive to regulate his or her life by the true science of **life and**
health, and, not following any visionary fanatic into any extremes,
will consult science, and rely on her and the **general** experience
of the race. **Such** will not take isolated cases of experience ; for
by such it could be easily **proved that a man** should drink a quart
of rum each day to be healthy, or that each should use a pound
of tobacco per week. But they will take the aggregate testimony
of the living **and** the dead, and, if corroborated by science, will
make use of such to reform in life and condition this and succeeding
generations. Then, as both philosophy and experience prove that
the correspondence of tobacco is profanity, nervous irritation,
poisonous and polluting effects and influence, and science proves

its effects ever evil, and only evil, on a human system, therefore the true spiritualist will refrain from its use, and discourage it in all others, by every mild and gentle effort, and kindly persuade all, as far as possible, to turn it out, with its undignified and ungentlemanly counterpart — profanity. As both science and experience establish the fact that intoxicating drinks are injurious, evil, pernicious, and tend greatly to subvert and destroy human happiness by expressing their correspondence in strife, wrangling, quarrelling, fighting, both public and private, reaching its extreme in wars and murders; therefore they should, and will, be abandoned by spiritualists, and all reasonable effort made, in kindness, mildness, and candor, to discountenance and discourage their use. As science and experience both prove that swine's flesh is invariably impregnated with pus and scrofulous matter, which is carried into the human body with it when used for food, and that human bodies are mainly composed of the material assimilated from the food; and that thus " man grows like what he feeds on," and that we would not like to have our bodies, and the bodies of those we love, like swine's flesh, and with the mental expression in correspondence, of low, vulgar, bawdy and lustful stories, actions, and language; therefore, all true spiritualists will avoid making swine's flesh an article of food, as far, and as fast, as convenient, especially for the young and tender forms of children, whose bodies and minds are being developed and matured for life, and whose happiness depends on purity, harmony, and health.

As both science and experience prove that tea and coffee, steeped and drank in decoctions as a beverage, and especially hot, are extremely injurious to the nervous systems, especially of the young, and are very expensive to large families, and almost invariably destroy the teeth by being used as many families use them, — therefore, as a matter of economy and health, spiritualists will discourage and discontinue the use of these beverages, especially for the young, as far, and as fast, as convenient and practicable. As both science and experience teach that the human body, to enjoy health and happiness, does not require irritants or stimu-

lants as condiments in food, and seldom requires stimulating food,
— therefore spiritualists *to be reformers*, and, to be healthy and
happy, will be temperate and prudent **in the use** of foods and
drinks, and learn to live soberly, temperately, naturally, and economically, **and by** this means more easily accomplish **the more**
important mental and spiritual reform which must **bring the race**
into harmony.   As science and experience both prove that **anger,**
hatred, scorn, contempt, **ridicule, jealousy,** envy, malice, with
their train **of** swearing, lying, gossipping, backbiting, &c., all tend
to make society and persons unhappy, and those most so who use
them most, — therefore **all spiritualists, to be reformers,** must
dismiss all these enemies **of peace and harmony** from their own
minds, **and forever** keep **them out of the bill of fare served** up to
others ; for by these reforms only can the race be reformed — in the
reform of the individuals, singly **and severally.**   As **both science**
and experience prove that **the fragrant flower sheds most fragrance**
around its parent stem, and in the bush where it grew, so spiritualists, whose lives are reformed, and whose souls are full of **love,**
will express most love and harmony about their homes, and to
those with whom they are most associated, and draw to them most
love in return **from those** with whom they deal most ; and thus
spiritualists will become harmonized and reformed individuals, —
harmonized and happy families, — harmonized and happy husbands
and wives (whether in both legal and spiritual affinity, **or not),**
— harmonized and happy parents, brothers, sisters, children,
friends, members of society, and citizens ; and thus, when spiritualism shall reach, and do, for all people what it has **done** for the
Lone One and his family, the world will **be** full of happy people,
and the kingdom of heaven will be on earth, in the hearts of the
people ; and all will thank God for life and existence, and love
one another, — most the kindred, beginning with the nearest ;
next, the friends ; next, the strangers ; and last and least, the
enemies (if there be any) ; and thus love all, and hate none.
Then all will feel this world is but a " stepping-stone to brighter
worlds above."   Then sweetly and beautifully will each one ap-

proach and pass that time and event when he or she will be " free,
free from the shell."

> " The ivy in a dungeon grew,
> Unfed by rain, uncheered by **dew** ;
> Its pallid leaflets only drank
> Cave-moistures foul and odors dank.

> " But through the dungeon-grating high
> There **fell a** sunbeam from the sky ;
> It slept **upon** the grateful floor,
> In silent gladness, evermore.

> " **The ivy felt a tremor shoot**
> Through all its fibres to the root ;
> It felt the light, it saw the ray,
> It strove **to** blossom into day.

> " It grew, it crept, it pushed, it clomb ;
> Long had the darkness been its home ;
> But well it knew, though veiled in night,
> The goodness and the joy of light.

> " Its clinging roots grew deep and strong ;
> **Its stem expanded firm and long** ;
> And in the currents of the air
> **Its** tender branches flourished fair.

> " It reached the beam, it thrilled, it curled,
> It blessed the warmth that cheers the world ;
> It rose toward the dungeon-bars ;
> It looked upon the sun and stars.

> " It felt the life of bursting spring,
> It heard the happy sky-lark sing ;
> It caught the breath of morns and eves,
> And wooed the swallow to its leaves.

> " By rains and dews and sunshine fed,
> Over the outer walls it spread ;
> And, in the day-beam waving free,
> It grew into a steadfast tree.

" Upon that solitary place
  Its verdure threw adorning grace ;
  The mating birds became its guests,
  And sang its praises from their nests.

" Wouldst know the moral of the rhyme ? —
  Behold the Heavenly Light, and climb !
  To every dungeon comes a ray
  Of God's determinable day."
        25*

CHARACTER OF THE LONE ONE,

PSYCHOMETRICALLY DELINEATED BY ANNE DENTON CRIDGE, OF DAYTON, OHIO, 1857.

FROM A LETTER PRESENTED BY A FRIEND.

LARGE language; expresses himself readily and with ease. Composition well developed and active; in connection with language, can express his thoughts in writing as well as verbally. Lower perceptives full, upper perceptives average. Reflective faculties large and active. Has a healthy brain, but it looks as if the frontal lobe had been of late somewhat overtaxed. Has a comprehensive mind; reasons and argues not from a small circle of facts, but from a large and varied collection. He is always more anxious for the truth than to make out a case. He does not build up a theory in his mind, and then look around to see what arguments he can find to sustain it; but builds upon facts, and gathers from the whole of nature. Has a good faculty for analysis, correspondence, collecting and applying, &c. Rather large benevolence; a strong nerve-aura current passes from it to the intellect, and follows where the intellect approves and directs. From the posterior portion of benevolence, I perceive another current flowing through spirituality to concentrativeness; a current from firmness unites with it; these united currents flow to the reflective faculties, and these organs act together in some way, but I do not exactly understand how; I should think that, as it passes through spirituality, he is philanthropic in a spiritual and reformatory direction. Veneration about average. Firmness large. Combativeness rather large. Destructiveness small; but acts vigorously with the frontal lobe. Acquisitiveness full; would like to make money **and** do well, but wants to make it in connection with progressive and reformatory labors. Warm and well-developed backhead. Philoprogenitiveness quite active, but the organ not prominent; is fond of children, and pleasant and mirthful among them. Concentrativeness large; it acts vigorously in connection with the frontal lobe. Self-esteem full. Attachment to home, to place, strong. Conjugality rather large; it aches somewhat; there is a feeling of sadness in connection therewith. Amativeness quite full; it is pure, and acts through conjugality and the intellect. Is **a great** admirer of intellectual women, and would be likely to express **it.**

RELIGION, like all, or nearly all, of nature's exhibitions, has a trinitarian development, and expresses usually, in the individual and the race, three distinct phases, or planes. The first and lowest form is Idolatry, or the introduction of a God to the mind. This embraces all forms of worship in which devotion is paid to an *object*, a *thing*, a *person*, or a *being*, which the worshipper calls **God**. It does not change the nature or character of the devotion to change the substance of which the God is composed. Whether it be of clay, or stone, or wood, or gold, or flesh, or spirit, or the most refined element of which a form can be constituted, the object is still an Idol. The character, quality, and composition, of the thing, or being, only determines the degree of taste and refinement in the worshipper. It is still idolatry, so long, and so far, as it conveys or attaches devotion to an object as God. *A* God, or *the* God, always denotes an object, and expresses Idolatry. These expressions always point to an object, and every object can be comprehended by the mind, or surrounded, which is to comprehend, in the sense we use the term. Every being, person, or thing, has diameter and circumference, and by these we can measure every object, whether we call it God or any other name. It does not remove the worshipper from Idolatry to place the being out of the reach of the person worshipping. It is truly a low form of Paganism to carry a God about one's person, but not so far removed from the practice of carrying the revealed will in a book about the person, as some human beings do, as some might suppose. It is as really Idol-worship to send the veneration to the sun or stars, as to a car of Juggernaut, or a statue of Diana, to a Temple, Church, or Throne of Grace. Philosophically speaking, it is the same phase of devotion to worship a Christ, or a spiritual being set up in the ideal world beyond the external **sight and** senses, as to worship a stone or wooden God. The composition and quality of the object **can never alter or** change the nature of the devotion, nor can the place where you set up your object or image change, in the least degree, the character of the worship. A degree of progress in the individual or worshipper is all that is manifested by these conditions. It is an evidence of our advanced idolatry to place the God in the ideal sphere, and compose his body of a rare and highly etherealized element. Nor does it change the nature of the devotion from idolatry to increase the real or supposed power and attributes of the God. Every man clothes his God with such attributes **as** his capacity can furnish, nor can do more. There are men now living on the earth whose power and capacity exceeds that of many Gods which, or who, have received the devotion of mortals; and there are, no doubt, millions of beings whose conditions are vastly superior to any idea now entertained by a mortal of a personal God. The man who carries his God in his pocket, or tied up in his hair, clothes him from his own mind with all the attributes, and qualifies, with all the good adjectives his storehouse can supply, and a Chapin, or Beecher, or a Parker, if they have a God, can do no more. They have placed their God, or Gods, (for I am not sure they all worship the same one) a little further from us or from their hearers; made him, or them, of a little finer material, and ideally clothed them with more **and** higher attributes, each and all in accordance with their refinement, mental development, and the age and country in which they live and preach. There is no reason or philosophy which can terminate Idolatry with the composition, position, or attributes, of the object worshipped ; and no reasoning mind will ever attempt to define where Idolatry ends, and leaves an object and centralized devotion, on a being, or thing, or individual.

Let no one accuse me of treating his form of worship as a sin, or even as an evil. It is not more a sin to be an Idolater than it is to be a child. It is the childhood of Religion, and as natural and legitimate as our physical childhood; and as naturally pre. cedes our higher religious expressions as the physical wants precede the mental and **spiritual,** or as the demands of our physical nature precede those of our intellectual. All men are by nature religious, and first Idolaters. A human being without veneration would be what nature cannot furnish. It is an essential part of **all** and every human being. Persons in one plane do not always perceive it in those of another plane, and hence term them Atheists; but in a true, an absolute, and a philosophical sense, there never was, and never can be, an Atheist. The honest and sincere devotion given to the highest object we can conceive of, is true religion, or *true* devotion; and is all that can be required of any person.

More than nine tenths of the human race on earth at this time are in the plane of Idolatry; and a vast and almost innumerable host of those who have left the earth are also in this plane; for a change of body does not always change the religion of the mind. All forms of sectarian Christianity are Idolatry in a refined form, and far advanced from some of the Pagan forms of worship, and perhaps below some of the wild Red men; for the Indians of our continent actually had a great Spirit-God; ideally superior to the Incarnate God of most Christians. All persons and the race will as legitimately grow out of these forms of Idolatry as they grow out of child-stature, or child-clothes; and they would be very much like the boy in his father's boots, coat, and **hat,** to get on a higher form before they had outgrown this. When we become men and women mentally, we shall put away childish things. The doll-pet of the little girl, and the top-toys of the boy, are laid aside, for real children, and real dogs, horses, &c. So will your little Idol-God be laid aside and neglected for a real conception of God, — not *a* God, or *the* God, but *God !* Idolatry, too, has its three-fold expression. Its sensual or material phase, in which its devotion is paid in sacrifices or offer**ings of** beasts, **or grain, or** gold and valuables, as an atonement, to obtain thereby a forgiveness. And, second, in prayers and ceremonies, personal sufferings, pilgrimages, penance, vows, deeds of charity, flattery, and personal sacrifices. And, third, belief in creeds, doctrines, dogmas, Christ's atonement, the love of God, and the forgiveness of sins for Christ's sake. There is really no less Idolatry in one than the other, but only a different degree of Idolatrous devotion. It is not less an Idolatry to worship a Holy Ghost than to worship the Ghost of Hamlet, or Banquo, of Moses, or Swedenborg, or Cobbett. It is only in degree ; **for it is** ghosts, and only ghosts, whether you apply the term Holy, or any other term, so long as it is a being, or person, or thing, even though placed in the spiritual, or elemental, or ideal life. **Again,** I repeat, that in classing Christianity with, or rather in, Idolatry, I am not condemning it as sinful, or wicked, or bad ; but, on the other hand, I esteem it as a virtue to be a sincere Christian, and to express the honest devotion of the soul in that higher or highest phase of the religion of childhood. God, angels, spirits, could expect no more than the honest devotion of the heart up to its maximum capacity ; and he that gives this does all his religious duty, and fulfils the requirements of his devotional nature ; when, and as, the capacity changes, the quality, not always the *quantity*, of devotion will change, and new ideas, perceptions, appreciations, and capacities, will change the expression of our devotion, always growing and refining with our knowledge. Many modern Christians, honest in their devotions, and rising to their highest capacities and appreciations, suppose they have attained the perfect and ultimate system of devotion, and thus all the world must come to their standard ; but this is also the case with many planes below them. The Mormon, and Mahometan, and Pagan, each expect the same for their religion, and with equal propriety, except that the best phases of sectarian Christianity are in advance, and one or two sects are on the very verge of the next phase ; as, for instance, Unitarianism, running through Theodore Parker and Ralph Waldo Emerson, grows into the next phase, or Pantheism.

It is of no consequence that those who are blind cannot see religion in these advanced phases, or in Pantheism.   Emerson is not less religious than Bishop Hughes, or Dr. Dewey; nor is any full-blown Pantheist less a man of devotion than the veriest Pagan Idolater.   He worships in another phase of devotion and development.   The lowest forms of Idolatry require a visible and tangible God.   The worshipper must see and *feel* his God.   A little further along, and he can dispense with the feeling, or tangibility, **but** must see the God-Sun, or Moon, Ark, or Holy object; **then** a little further, and he can give up the sight to the seer, or prophet, or priest, and send and receive messages through these mediums; then a little further, and he can dispense with all sight, and lodge his God in the ideal realm, far away from sight and sense, and then send all his devotion and bestow it on the Idol-God in the ideal realm; then loses *it* or *the* God entirely, and becomes a Pantheist, or a creature of growth and natural development; leaving off the small-clothes, and little and big idols, **he** becomes a man in religion.

All belief in special incarnations, special providences, interpositions, and Divine Providences, miraculous manifestations, and supernatural powers, actions, and exhibitions, belongs to Idolatry, and its personal God, in some of its forms.   The Pantheist discards all these, as the developed mind does the phantoms and goblins of the boy and the dark.   Idolatry is the religion of ignorance and innocence, which pertain to childhood, in the individual or the race.   It is made up of especialities.   The God is an especiality, and especially endowed, and makes especial manifestations, and has especial favorites and pets in this life, and the next, if there be a next; for all idolaters do not believe in a next life.   God is personal, and of course tangible to some of the senses, physical or mental; for all who believe in *a* God must have one with form, and of course possessed of diameter and circumference, and thus be comprehensible by the mind.   A chosen God can have a chosen people, a band of chosen servants, and he will of course bestow favors on his pets and favorites.   There is really very little difference between the children playing with their pets and the God playing with the devotees in the phase of Idolatry, or the devotee treating of his God and his attributes, and laws and dealings with man. Both are good enough, and proper in their places, but are poorly adapted to manhood. One more century, with the ratio of progress of **the last** ten years, in our country, will be sufficient to carry the Idolatry from our nation to the museum, where it may be preserved as a relic of the early time, and as precious as the bones of saints in the cathedrals **of** the Mother Church. The dim Bible-light will be superseded by a bright sun-light, and the Idol-God will make way for other and higher worship. The swaddling-bands will be laid aside, the "leading-strings" cut asunder, and men will walk out of these Idol-creeds in freedom of thought and expansion of mind, and will no longer need a God to carry in the pocket, or to sit in the temple, or to reign on a throne of ivory or gold in the ideal realm. Pocket-idols and pocket-revelations will lose their especial sacredness, and man will no longer bow in prayer to Gods of wood or stone, or sun or stars, or beast or man, or spirit, or ghost, or king, or being, here, or anywhere; but he will not have less devotion or veneration than now, nor be less religious and virtuous, but far more, and have and express a far higher and better devotion than in this phase of Idolatry. I am aware this seems terrible infidelity to an Idolater, but it must come.

The second phase of Religious devotion, or Pantheism, is the religion of intellect. Some persons, and indeed most persons, in the plane of Idolatry, suppose there is no devotion or religion in Pantheism; but this is only because they cannot see in this intellectual religion the devotion of their own phase. The real Pantheist is as much and as really a man of religion and devotion as the Idolater. Some persons are born with organizations adapted to, and which carry them into this phase as soon as the brain is ripened, even without any action or reading on the subject, save what is presented in nature. These persons are often very much blamed by devotees at the shrine of Idolatry, and are often called reprobates in religion. But the majority of persons reach this phase by the exercise of the intellect. Most of the distinguished scientific and metaphysical minds who have lived during the last two hundred years have been in this plane of religion, because their reasoning powers were too much unfolded to remain in the plane of Idolatry. Idolatry reasons **little.** Pantheism reasons much. Some leading minds in the churches have **also** reached this phase, but expediency and the condition of the minds of the great body of the devotees have usually prevented **them** from expressing their real belief. Indeed, one declaration or admission of many religious writers and speakers leads directly to Pantheism, viz., the immateriality of God, of mind, and of the spirit-world; for this is equivalent in science to a denial of their existence, except as admitted by the Pantheist as connected **with** and expressed in the material and tangible substance of **earth,** and other bodies like it in substance. The Pantheist has no personal God, no individualized or special incarnation, and, in fact, no incarnation at all; for to him mind or its exhibition is a phenomenon of matter, and, like the shadow, disappears when the substance is removed which presented it. To **the** developed Pantheist, or the worshipper in the first plane of this phase, the earth and all appurtenances thereunto belonging **is God; all the God** there is, he says, because this is all **that he can recognize as real** existence. But the more **expanded mind takes in the** stellar region, and some of the elemental substances **which fill the** apparent space between these bodies. To these **substances they** attribute **as** causes all motion, life, sensation, and **intelligence, because** they only find them expressed in and **through this kind and** condition of existence. They **deny the absolute** existence of mind, because they could not find it with the scalpel or in the crucible of the chemist. They found **no more difficulty** in accounting for the magnificent motions and **exact order of** the solar and other **systems, as** resulting from the orbs themselves, **than** they found **in** accounting for the exhibitions of mind in man, or instinct in animals and plants; and they could **no** more find God **by** dissecting the systems of worlds, than they could find mind by dissecting the **man; and** hence they worshipped the negative side of the universe, because *it* only was tangible to their faculties, and could thus be reached. *All* they could get evidence of, as an existence, was to them God, and they let their devotions flow to the material or negative side of creation as God. They took the Pagan's Idol and melted it, to show him there was no God about it, more than about any other lump of clay, or stone, or gold. They pointed the sun-worshipper to other suns, to show him his was not God, or, if so, only one of many. They pointed the worshipper of Christ to his defects, — submission to material law, and to the precepts and examples of other good men, — to show he was no more God, or a God, than other men; and while they refused to worship him, they esteemed him according to his merits, as they understood them. They denied and entirely repudiated the Divine revelation of the Christians, by producing positive proof from science of its errors, absurdities, and falsehoods. They melted down and dissolved all forms of Idolatry by reason, as the sun does a frost in a clear morning. Pantheism in good hands was always invincible to Idolatry, and in every contest left its victim floored, or skulked away behind the superstition and ignorance of the age. All miracles and especial providences were declared to be either natural occurrences, or not to have occurred at all. Under this phase of religion, superstition and Idolatry seemed to be fading fast, and Pantheism seemed destined to triumph as the religion of manhood and age for the earth. It did not necessarily deny a spiritual or elemental life, but usually denied it because it had not sufficient tangible evidence to sustain and defend it. A few Pantheists were, however, believers in a spirit-life as succeeding this, but had no conception of its duration, or of the conditions of its existence. The principles of philosophy, the laws of nature, the demonstrations of science, the facts of experience, the conclusions of reason, were the creeds, the liturgy, the belief, the prayer-book, of the Pantheist; and with these he could and does overthrow all structures of Idolatry and superstitious devotion to a personal and Idol God, and especial revelations and providences. The distinguished men and women of Europe and America, who have stood out on the face of society in bold relief during the last two hundred years, have been mostly Pantheists in religion; and they have not been wanting in devotion, but have only been wanting in Idolatry. Pantheism has at last met a foeman "worthy of its steel," and one before which it falls as Idolatry does before its potent **weapons — a** phase and system of religion holding to *it* the same relation it holds to Idolatry, and that is termed Spiritualism, or more appropriately Harmonialism. Idolatry fears, cringes, prays — never reasons. Pantheism **reasons, respects, admires.** Spiritualism reasons, admires, loves, venerates, sees, and feels. Pantheism made God of all material substance, and mind **a** manifestation. Spiritualism incarnates God in all and every form and substance of matter, and receives and believes God the motive-power of all manifestations.

This third phase, to which I have now so legitimately arrived, has its correspondence in wisdom, in the judicial power, in the conjugal relation of the sexes, in religion. It is the ultimate and truly harmonial condition and age of man in the individual or the race, and in its religious devotion gives the superior expression to this high and natural desire of our nature. Spiritualism supplies to the material **universe** the other **side and** half of itself, and gives us the true form and condition of ourselves and the world. To use a figure, Idolatry was the Garden of Eden and its pair of especial pets; Pantheism **was the** flat earth and the tribes and nations, and spiritualism is the globe and **its** races, with distinct and numerous origins. Spiritualism supplies to the universe the real, substantial, and material condition of mind, and its action on, and, **in** the negative substance, called, for convenience' sake, matter, and exhibits forms aggregating, sublimating, and segregating, continually and eternally, without diminution or increase of either mind or matter, and forever producing in this contact and action motion, life, sensation, intelligence, and development; and thus a new phase of devotion is presented, another side to man individu- **ally and** collectively, and **to** all tangible existence a positive is supplied to its negative, and the harmony of the universe is at last discovered. Spiritualism admits all the principles and demonstrations of Pantheism, and supplies to it what it always lacked and felt the need of, — an active and motive power, with intelligence to account for intelligence in objects ; for Pantheism could never show how intelligence could come from a source entirely devoid of it ; and while it could easily show the fallacy and defects in Idolatry, it often became entangled in its own reasonings, and found a web of its own construction holding it in meshes too strong for its power.

The Spiritual or Harmonial philosophy did not supply a personal God to worship, but it did supply Divine Mind to the Infinite universe, and it was like letting in the sunlight upon the darkened earth. It also found and established the existence of a human mind **to** each human form, and of course, according to fixed principles of philosophy and Pantheism, proved it could never be annihilated, or cease to exist. It also found why and how the exhibitions of intelligence could legitimately find expression in the universe and in man. Spiritualism carried the devotion of those who had reached it to Divine Mind, and found God, or mind, everywhere, in every form of which the senses or the reason could take cognizance, forever revealing law and order, facts and truths, to each, and through each, individual form. It had no difficulty in proving immortality for man, for it found in him a mind, and a unit, or entity, and forever indissoluble ; and while he acted on, and in, a negative form of matter as a body, — an aggregation only temporarily, — he had in himself eternal duration, and might safely say he was possessed of all power in heaven and in earth ; for he was positive to all conditions of matter below himself, and could use each form and leave it without being himself lost or destroyed by the separation of the parts which composed his body ; and, deprived of one form, he could aggregate and organize another of similar or dissimilar matter, and again enjoy for a season, in it, a sunshine of existence, as Divine Mind does in worlds.

The true infinity was now introduced to the mind and comprehension of man by spiritualism, or, what would be more proper, if an *ism* must be used, *mentalism*. Many persons call themselves spiritualists who are only Idolaters, and some who are Pantheists; but the true Harmonial man, **or real** spiritualist, has outgrown all these child-clothes, and has no Idol in book or image, but has God or Mind in everything and everywhere, and ever worships the Infinite and the everywhere-God, — not the **throne-**God, or the God of Moses and the Jews, nor the Jesus of the Christians, nor the earth, or earths, of the Pantheist, — but his God is, and was, and will be, when all these forms change or dissolve and reünite in other forms. The never-changing mind of the Universe, ever changing matter and acting on it in forms, becomes God, and draws out the devotion of the true spiritualist, and it can be expressed anywhere, and any time; for Divine Mind is really omnipresent and omnipervading. No century-rule used to measure time can determine the age, nor any league-rule find and determine the diameter. I use the masculine sometimes, because mind is masculine or positive, and not because Idolaters usually have a man-God, or God-man, to worship. Mind is always masculine, matter always feminine, and cohesion is the sexual expression of a certain condition and combination of mind and matter. So is life, and sensation, and intelligence, each in its respective plane; but of **these** I shall speak more properly in another lecture.

I have now laid out these three phases, and every human being is paying his or her devotion in one of the three; and each may register and station, or examine and report himself or herself, where and as, he or she pleases, at leisure. All are on the line, and all have devotion, and all do express it. All persons do pray, for prayer is only wish, or desire, and no person **can** exist without it, nor can any person express devotionally this prayer to a thing, or power, or existence, which he or she believes to be inferior or only equal **to** self. The answer or response to prayer may be expected through or from an equal, or even inferior; but some power is

recognized as superior, and acting on and through the instrument.
Fear is the peculiar attribute of Idolatry. It ceases in Pantheism,
and in independence and manhood. *Try*, and *do*, reason and learn,
are the peculiar attributes of Pantheism. Love, deep, sincere, fear-
less, ardent, and overflowing, is the peculiar attribute of the spiritual religion.   All fear ceases in the mind of the true spiritualist.
Death, hell, and the grave, lose all their terrors, and man has only
love in the place of fear, and looks to each change which nature
provides and presents to him as a step leading higher, and to a still
better condition for enjoyment.   He fears no terrors of the law,
and expects no particular day of judgment; but every day is his
day of judgment.   He has no tyrant, with iron rod and shining
crown of diamonds, to appease ; but an ever-present mind, smiling through immutable laws, which are ever working out happiness
for each being who is in harmony with them. He depends on condition for happiness, not on belief or faith, and ever tries to put
himself in true relations with **the laws** of nature and God.   **To**
the Idolater the spiritualist is like the Pantheist, Infidel, because
he has no personal God; and is to such person what the Christian
with his spirit-God, **or** Holy Ghost, **is** to the Pagan with his visible Idol — the latter cannot see or touch the Christian's God, and
hence concludes he has none.   So the Christian cannot comprehend or mentally recognize, measure, and surround, the Infinite
Divine Mind, and hence concludes spiritualists have **no God**, and
little or no devotion ; but **manhood** will dissipate **these** toy-Gods,
for the individual and the race, and spiritualism will introduce
God to the Pantheist.   Every person with a body weighing two
hundred pounds, and measuring **six** feet in length, is not a man or
woman; for many such **are only** children, even after they have
been to college, and come **out** with a parchment and honors ; and
indeed these colleges are, to use again a figure, places where a
band of unyielding metal is often put around the head to hold
from expansion the intellect, and expand the perceptions in dig-
ging *roots* of Greek and Latin ; or to send up, like a sugar-loaf,
the veneration in Idolatrous devotion, instead of cultivating, in a

natural way, the true growth of brain, and thus the **real and true** religion of manhood. Spiritualism must and will renovate and change entirely our system of education, and bring **our** colleges **up to,** and into, the teaching of the religion of manhood, or spiritualism. Every person **is an Idolater, a** Pantheist, or Spiritualist. Reader, which art thou ? If either of the two first, **there is** work before thee, and the tools are ready at thy hand, and thy power is ample to use them ; and in thy lower plane of devotion thou canst **not know the beauty** and joy of the higher and more unfolded life and religion of **the** third phase until thou hast tasted it. **Learn,** grow, develop, unfold thy powers **and** faculties, and become a **spiritualist in its** true and real sense, **and come to the knowledge of the truth as it** is in the Harmonial Philosophy !

AN ANGEL'S VISIT.

BY HATTIE.

An Angel came to me, **one night,**
  In glorious beauty clothed,
And with sweet words of hope and joy
  My way-worn spirit **soothed.**

He fanned my cheek and **burning brow,**
  And cooled my fevered brain,
And with his own deep music-voice
  Sang many a loving strain.

He bade me ask for any gift
  Within his power to give :
For death's cold arms to bear me hence,
  Or countless years to live ;

For riches, honors, and domains,
  A sceptre, crown, and throne ;
For friends with loving hearts to twine
  Around my happy home.

" Not these, dear Angel bright," I cried :
  " From each and all I 'll part,
If thou 'lt bestow that richer gift,
  A pure and spotless heart."

The Angel smiled (with such a smile
  As only angels have);
Then, sighing low, a diamond glass
  Into my hand he gave.

" O, mine is not the power," he said,
  " To fit thy heart for heaven ;
The gift to purify thy soul
  Unto thyself is given.

" But look within the faithful glass
   That I have given thee,
And there within thy outer self
   Thy inner self thou 'lt see.''

I looked — 't was strange, but there I saw
   Two beings joined in one ;
For clearly through the outer shell
   A radiant spirit shone.

Long, long I gazed, and years on years
   Seemed there to pass away,
But still I saw that spirit bright
   Grow brighter, day by day.

At last 't was free — free from the shell
   That dimmed its brilliant glow,
And upward flew on angel-wings,
   And left the shell below

www.ingramcontent.com/pod-product-compliance
Lightning Source LLC
Chambersburg PA
CBHW031033120726
47905CB00007B/2172